The
Frontiersman's
Daughter

The Frontiersman's Daughter

A NOVEL

LAURA FRANTZ

Revell

a division of Baker Publishing Group
Grand Rapids, Michigan

© 2009 by Laura Frantz

Published by Revell
a division of Baker Publishing Group
P.O. Box 6287, Grand Rapids, MI 49516-6287
www.revellbooks.com

Printed in the United States of America

Library of Congress Cataloging-in-Publication Data
Frantz, Laura.
   The frontiersman's daughter : a novel / Laura Frantz.
      p.   cm.
   ISBN 978-0-8007-3339-1 (pbk.)
   1. Frontier and pioneer life—Kentucky—Fiction. I. Title.
PS3606.R4226F76 2009
813'.6—dc22   2009007483

Scripture is taken from the New American Standard Bible®, Copyright © 1960, 1962, 1963, 1968, 1971, 1972, 1973, 1975, 1977, 1995 by The Lockman Foundation. Used by permission.

11   12   13   14   15   9   8   7   6   5

For my granny Lena Blanton.
I miss you more than words can say.

1

Kentucke, Indian Territory, 1777

In the fading lavender twilight, at the edge of a clearing, stood half a dozen Shawnee warriors. They looked to the small log cabin nestled in the bosom of the greening ridge, as earthy and unassuming as the ground it sat upon. If not for the cabin's breathtaking view of the river and rolling hills, arguably the finest in the territory, most passersby would easily dismiss such a place, provided they found it at all. The Indians regarded it with studied intent, taking in the sagging front porch, the willow baskets and butter churn to one side, and the vacant rocking chair still astir from the hurry of a moment before. Six brown bodies gleamed with bear grease, each perfectly still, their only movement that of sharp, dark eyes.

Inside the cabin, Ezekial Click handed a rifle to his son, Ransom, before opening the door and stepping onto the porch. His wife, Sara, took up a second gun just inside. A sudden breath of wind sent the spent blossoms of a lone dogwood tree scurrying across the clearing. From the porch, Click began speaking in the Shawnee tongue. Slowly. Respectfully. A smattering of Shawnee followed—forceful yet oddly, even hauntingly, melodic.

Sara and Ransom darted a glance out the door, troubled by every word, yet the unintelligible banter continued. At last, silence came. And then, in plain English, one brave shouted, "Click, show us your pretty daughter!"

Within the cabin, all eyes fastened on the girl hovering on the loft steps. At thirteen, Lael Click was just a slip of a thing, but her oval face showed a woman's composure. Her pale green eyes fastened on her father's back just beyond the yawning door frame.

She put one cautious foot to the floor, then tread the worn pine boards until she stood in her father's shadow. She dared not look at her mother. Without further prompting she stepped forward into a dying shaft of sunlight. A sudden breeze caught the hem of her thin indigo shift and it ballooned, exposing two bare brown feet.

The same brave shouted, "Let down your hair!"

She hesitated, hearing her mother's sharp intake of breath. With trembling hands she reached for the horn combs that held back the weight of fair hair. Her mane tumbled nearly to her feet, as tangled and luxuriant as wild honeysuckle vine.

Woven in with the evening shadows was a chorus of tree frogs and katydids and the scent of soil and spring, but Lael noticed none of these things. Beside her, her father stood stoically and she fought to do the same, remembering his oft-repeated words of warning: *Never give way to fear in an Indian's sight.*

Softly she expelled a ragged breath, watching as each warrior turned away. Only the tallest tarried, his eyes lingering on her as she swept up her hair with unsteady hands and subdued it with the combs.

At last they were gone, slipping away into the wall of woods. Invisible but ever present. Silent. Perhaps deadly.

Evening was a somber affair, as if the Shawnee themselves had stayed for supper. To Lael, the cold cornbread and buttermilk that filled their wooden bowls seemed as tasteless as the cabin's chinking. Somehow she managed a sip of cider and a half-hearted bite now and then. Across from her, her mother managed neither. Only her younger brother Ransom ate, taking his portion and her own, as if oblivious to all the trouble.

Looking up, she saw a hint of a smile on her father's face. Was he trying to put her at ease? Not possible. He sat facing the cabin door, his loaded rifle lounging against the table like an uninvited guest. Despite his defensive stance, he seemed not at all anxious like her ma but so calm she could almost believe the Indians had simply paid them a social call and they could go on about their business as if nothing had happened.

He took out his hunting knife, sliced a second sliver of corn-bread, then stood. Lael watched his long shadow fall across the table and caught his quick wink as he turned away. Swallowing a smile, she concentrated on the cabin's rafters and the ropes strung like spider webs above their heads. The sight of her favorite coverlet brought some comfort, its pattern made bright with dogwood blossoms and running vines. Here and there hung linsey dresses, a pair of winter boots, some woolen leggins, strings of dried apples and leather-britches beans, bunches of tobacco, and other sundry articles. Opposite was the loft where she and Ransom slept.

The cabin door creaked then closed as Pa disappeared onto the porch, leaving her to gather up the dirty dishes while her mother made mountain tea. Lael watched her add sassafras roots to the kettle, her bony hands shaking.

"Ma, I don't care for any tea tonight," she said.

"Very well. Cover the coals, then."

Lael took a small shovel and buried the red embers with a small mountain of ash to better start a fire come morning. When she turned around, her ma had disappeared behind the tattered quilt that divided the main cabin from their corner bedroom. Ransom soon followed suit, climbing the loft ladder to play quietly with a small army of wooden soldiers garrisoned under the trundle bed.

Left alone, she couldn't stay still, so taut in mind and body she felt she might snap. Soon every last dish and remaining crumb were cleaned up and put away. With Ma looking as though she might fall to pieces, Lael's resolve to stay grounded only strengthened. Yet she found herself doing foolish things like snuffing out the candles before their time and pouring the dirty dishwater through a crack in the floor rather than risk setting foot outside.

The clock on the mantle sounded overloud in the strained silence, reminding her the day was done. Soon she'd have to settle in for the night. But where was Pa? She took in the open door, dangerously ajar, and the fireflies dancing in the mounting gloom. She sighed, pushed back a wisp of hair, and took a timid step toward the porch.

How far could an Indian arrow fly?

Peering around the door frame she found Pa sitting in the same place she'd found him years ago that raw November morning after his escape from the Shawnee. They had long thought him dead, and indeed all remnants of his life as a white man seemed to have been stamped out of him. His caped hunting shirt was smeared with bear grease, his deerskin leggins soiled beyond redemption. Except for an eagle-feathered scalp lock, his head was plucked completely clean of the hair that had been as fair as her own. Savage as he was, she'd hardly recognized him. Only his eyes reminded her of the man she once knew, their depths a wild, unsurrendered blue.

Tonight he was watching the woods, his gun across his knees, and his demeanor told her he shouldn't be disturbed. Without a word she turned and climbed to the loft where she found Ransom asleep. There, in the lonesome light of a tallow candle, she shook her hair free of the horn combs a second time.

The shears she'd kept hidden since the Shawnee departed seemed cold and heavy in her hand, but her unbound hair was warm and soft as melted butter. She brought the two together, then hesitated. Looking down, she imagined the strands lying like discarded ribbon at her feet.

A sudden noise below made her jerk the scissors out of sight. Pa had come in to collect his pipe. Her sudden movement seemed to catch his eye.

"You'd best be abed, Daughter," he called over his shoulder, his tone a trifle scolding.

She sank down on the corn-husk tick, losing the last of her resolve, and tucked the scissors away. If she changed her mind come morning, they'd be near. Catlike, she climbed over the slumbering body in the trundle bed beneath her, surprised that a seven-year-old boy could snore so loud.

The night was black as the inside of an iron skillet and nearly as hot. She lay atop the rustling tick, eyes open, craving sleep. The night sounds outside the loft window were reassuringly familiar, as was her brother's rhythmic breathing. All was the same as it had ever been but different. The coming of the Indians had changed everything.

In just a few moments' time the Shawnee had thrown open the door to Pa's past, and now there would be no shutting it.

She, for one, didn't like looking back.

2

Lael leaned over her mother's shoulder, thinking how small and dark she was, her hair black as a crow's wing yet tipped white at the temples. Standing behind her so fair and tall, they hardly seemed related. Lael supposed she was her father's daughter from head to foot. Sometimes it seemed she'd received nothing from her ma except the privilege of being born.

Lately Lael wondered if she might better understand her ma if she tried to be more like her. As it was, she couldn't quite grasp her mother's longing for a civilized life and her hatred of all things savage, nor her stubborn refusal to stoop to settlement speech, never uttering so much as an *aye* or a *nay*. Around her Lael took care to never utter so much as an *ain't*.

She watched as Ma fumbled with a bolt of cloth, nearly sending it off the table. Lael caught the fabric with a steady hand, struck by sudden sympathy. Her ma hadn't stopped shaking since the Shawnee appeared. Had it been only yesterday? Since then she'd waited for Pa to announce he was moving them to the fort like he'd done in the past when Indian sign was prevalent. Keeping them at home, especially in light of her mother's nerves, seemed tantamount to sitting on a keg of gunpowder. But Pa was not given to flinching at shadows, even if his wife was.

"I never thought to see such fine fabric on the frontier," Lael finally said, helping to smooth out the soft folds.

Just last winter they'd paid for the costly silk with three bundles of feathers and a bearskin. A pack wagon had come to the fort just before Christmas with a wealth of eastern cloth, and they'd liked this best. In the candlelight the green fabric looked like a polished apple. An extravagance of milk white ribbon lay alongside it, garnered with a bushel of salt.

"Time you had a new dress, and some petticoats beside," Ma said. "Susanna weds the first of June. We've nary a week to finish this gown if you're to stand up with her."

So soon, Lael thought, but given the trouble, would they go to the wedding? She felt like holding her breath in anticipation. Settlement frolics were few and far between, and she so loved to dance. She'd been pleased but not surprised when Susanna had picked her as a bridesmaid. Ever since settlement school they'd been fast friends, unsullied by the trouble swirling around them. Although Pa disliked the quarrelsome Hayes clan, he had a soft spot for Susanna. He wouldn't attend the wedding himself but said she could. Now she prayed he'd not change his mind.

"I'll help sew," Lael offered, though she hated to. Handwork had always eluded her. She was ashamed to admit her uneven stitches were pronounced "crooked as a dog's hind leg" by every seamstress in the settlement.

"I'll manage," Ma said with a sigh, straightening to look her over. "But I do wish you'd stop growing. You're a whole head taller than me already. And look at those feet! Why, they're as big as your pa's!"

Lael said nothing to this. There was simply no pleasing her mother. She nearly winced as Ma passed to the back of her and clucked her tongue ominously. With a start, Lael touched her heavy braid and remembered the scissors.

"You'll not take a hand to her hair, Sara Jane." From the shadows her father forbade any further talk. He sat by the rock hearth in a ladder-back chair, his rifle against one knee, a small worn copy of *Gulliver's Travels* in his hands. He'd read it countless times, both aloud and silently, and could quote long passages by heart. Somehow it had survived his Indian captivity, returning as intact as he himself.

As Lael studied him he looked up at her, the light of affection in his eyes. Once again she found herself wishing she could sift his secret thoughts. It was too quiet in the cabin. Every ear seemed tuned to trouble. She glanced toward a half-shuttered window, her thoughts in a worried tangle. Surely the Shawnee wouldn't come a second twilight eve.

Ma rose from the table in search of something, while Ransom lounged near the barred door with Nip and Tuck. The old hounds weren't often allowed inside. Their presence was another reminder of how everything had changed. Nip was asleep, but Tuck's heavy head was raised as if listening. Lael felt unease steal over her at his intensity. Animals always sensed trouble first, whether it was hens refusing to lay or cows balking at being led to pasture.

"I never misplace my scissors," Ma was saying, rummaging through her sewing chest in a corner of the cabin. Her strident tone cut through Lael's reverie and sent her scurrying up the loft ladder where she groped about in the darkness beneath the trundle bed. The cool metal was a potent reminder of what she'd almost done, and she breathed a silent prayer to the Almighty who'd spared her so foolish an act.

How could she possibly have lopped off her hair then stood before the whole settlement, shorn like a sheep? But it wasn't the settlement she cared about, truly. Only one man mattered, and merely thinking about him sent her down the ladder with a pink sheen to her cheeks.

Furtively she placed the scissors next to the fine fabric, saying nothing but feeling her father's eyes still on her. Tonight his close attention was especially unnerving. Since yesterday he seemed to regard her in a new way—fiercely, even a bit desperately—as if she might disappear and he wanted to be sure he remembered every nuance of her form and face.

Despite the heat of the closed cabin, she shivered. Her father was a man of deep feeling and few words, and tonight his eyes told her a host of things she'd rather not know. She sat down on the bench beside the trestle table, hardly hearing her ma's exclamations of pleasure at the reappearance of the shears.

A hard knot of alarm formed in Lael's throat as she toyed with the frayed hem of her cambric apron. If only Pa would explain some things, help her make sense of the Shawnee's sudden appearance. Her nerves were rubbed raw when it came to the tallest warrior, the one who'd called her out of the cabin. He had so startled her by speaking English that her eyes had lingered on him a bit too long, and now her memory refused to give him up.

But it was more than this, truly. The bewildering way Pa had spoken to him—to them all—only added to her confusion. As the strange Shawnee words spilled from his lips like music, every syllable undergirded with familiarity and affection, she'd known without the slightest doubt that these six warriors were no strangers.

"Lael, are you listening? We'll have to make half a dozen jam cakes for the wedding supper," Ma was saying, her hand slicing through the green fabric with the newly sharpened shears. "That calls for thirty-six eggs, so be sure you don't drop a one." Her warning gaze touched Ransom then took in Lael. "You'll need a new pair of shoes if you're to stand up before the whole settlement. I'll not have you barefoot, or worse, in moccasins."

Lael shifted uneasily in her seat, amazed at her mother's sudden shift in mood. How could she possibly talk trivialities at such a tense time?

"I suppose my old slippers might fit you, though they're liable to rub you raw with all the dancing. I'll never forget when Will Blanton wore those too-tight boots to his own wedding years ago. One made a sore on his heel and he lost a leg." Laying the scissors aside, Ma crossed to a large trunk and opened the heavy lid, sorting through a host of nearly forgotten things, finally holding the shoes aloft. Long and elegant with small, square heels, they were the color of butter and spoke of a different life—a civilized life—lived long ago. Their appearance seemed to unlock a storehouse of memories, and Lael saw a sudden wistfulness touch her mother's face.

The shoes fit, but barely. Lael stood unsteadily, accustomed to being flat-footed. It was sheer work to keep from wincing. A few sets of Roger de Coverley in these and she might lose a leg too. Still, she'd manage if it would please her ma.

From the door, Ransom looked hard at her, then ran a grubby hand through hair as black as Ma's own. "Do we have to stay for all the dancin'?"

Ma gave a slight shrug and resumed her cutting. "You'd best speak to your sister about that. I believe she's as intent on the dancing as you are on the wedding supper."

His eyes sparked and he looked at Lael. "Reckon you'll get married next?"

She nearly smiled, but the sweet thought was snatched away when she looked at her mother.

Ma's eyebrows arched. "Married? Well, I can't imagine whom to."

"I can," he replied with a wide grin. "Everybody in the whole settlement knows she's sweet on—"

"You'd best keep your tongue between your teeth, Son." Pa's chair, tipped back till now, came down with a decisive thud.

The rebuke settled harshly in the still cabin, and Lael watched as Ransom scampered up the loft ladder out of sight.

Looking after him, Ma's voice wilted to a whisper. "I've been meaning to talk to you about Simon, Lael."

Simon. They could never speak of Simon civilly, if at all. He was a Hayes and belonged to that segment of the settlement Pa had blacklisted long ago. She was glad the dim light hid her face. Glancing toward the hearth, she found Pa had resumed his reading. Privacy in a cramped cabin was hard to come by.

The snip of the scissors seemed to underscore Ma's words. Her bent head nearly touched Lael's own. "I don't mind if you dance with him a time or two, but any more than that gives rise to gossip. The way he . . ." The cutting ceased as she groped for the right words. "The way he corners you for every single set is unseemly."

Lael took a deep breath. "It means little, Ma, truly. Simon taught me the steps when I lived with them years ago. We've been dancin' together since I was Ransom's age."

Ma's mouth set in a firm line. "There's no need to remind me of all that. Best leave the past alone."

At once Lael realized her error. "But I didn't mean—"

Ma began folding up the cut-up cloth, signaling an end to the conversation. Just as suddenly, Pa got up and unbarred the door, Nip and Tuck in tow. Lael fought the urge to follow him, to find some solace lest she spend another sleepless night. But he seemed in no more mood for conversation than her ma.

Reluctantly, Lael climbed the loft ladder to where the shadows hid her as she shed her dress. Too weary to free her hair from its tight braid, she lay down atop the worn coverlet and let her gaze linger on the fitful form of her brother. He rolled this way and that in the trundle bed, as if trying to escape a bad dream.

Bending low, she touched his dark hair, the ends curled with sweat. Tomorrow she'd teach him to make a fan from the old newspaper she'd seen spill out of the trunk when Ma was searching for the slippers. Perhaps they could sit on the porch come morning and fan themselves for a spell since Pa was allowing them to do little else. Being confined to the stifling cabin a second day couldn't be borne.

She'd sooner face the Shawnee.

3

The next morning Lael sat imprisoned on the porch behind the screen of roses. Done with churning, she collected the ball of butter and salted it, setting it in a covered crock to carry to the springhouse. Pale yellow light framed the eastern forest, and the woods were a symphony of sound. She looked up as a joree bird called from a laurel bush. The sound was so pure it seemed to pierce her with its sweetness. She waited a few seconds before she gave the answering call, smiling as it echoed back to her. She liked daybreak best, unsullied as it was.

Every morning of her life she'd come out onto this porch to find things the way they'd been the day before. She loved the solid beauty of the barn and the skeleton of a fence that ran to the river and hemmed in the horses. The woods surrounding the cabin were ever changing with the seasons yet somehow stayed the same. Even the old door stone beneath her feet was as much a part of her as the roses that hid the lazy slant of the porch while attempting to climb into the cabin.

She could hear Ma moving about with a kind of restless energy, not yet at work with her spinning wheel. Ransom was still abed and out of mischief, but Pa had been gone long before daylight. She caught sight of him now emerging from the trees, his rifle nestled in the crook of one hard arm. He wore the garb of the woods, buckskin breeches and long linen hunting shirt, heavily fringed to wick away water. She could see him scan the clearing, weighing every nuance and shifting shadow.

He moved the quietest of any man she knew. Even his dogs had been trained to walk softly behind him, noses to the ground, nearly tripping over their cumbersome ears. Nip and Tuck had been yearlings when Pa led his first party of settlers over the Gap the Indians called Ouisita. No man had lived in Kentucke then, either Indian or white, though the Shawnee and Cherokee claimed it as a sacred hunting ground. She reckoned they still did, leaving plenty of sign in the settlement and taking what they pleased.

Pa paused briefly to look east, and she did the same, her gaze lingering on the far mountains framed with yellow light. Was he remembering his roots or missing the land from which he came? She doubted it. He rarely spoke of his Quaker heritage, though Ma talked freely of her own family, English weavers who'd come to the colonies fifty years before.

She always listened quietly as Ma shared memories of her loved ones, but to Lael they were simply names without faces, all of them. She'd never known anything but Kentucke, never been beyond the wilderness, nor wanted to. Ma's talk of cobbled roads and church steeples and hordes of people pressed together in one place left her cold.

Pa paused at the far end of the porch to drink deeply from a gourd dipper hanging above a piggin of water, his eyes on the woods all the while. For a man not yet fifty he looked older. Hardened, careworn. His tobacco-brown face was as lined as the marks on a surveyor's map, but his frame was as lean and well muscled as that of a far younger man.

Lael stood up slowly, the crock of butter at her feet. The half hour she'd spent churning had given her sufficient time to gather the courage to confront him. She simply had to know about the Shawnee—what they wanted and why he hadn't moved them to the fort.

"Any fresh sign, Pa?" Her voice shook a bit and belied her skittishness.

He turned earnest eyes on her and took his time answering. "Aye. One Shawnee in particular."

One. The tall one? Somehow she sensed it was, and looked down at her apron, a flush creeping into her face. He was studying her again in that absorbing way that made her feel he knew her every thought—or worse, that she was somehow the cause of all the worry.

"Any trouble elsewhere?" she asked.

"None that I know of," he replied, a wry twist to his mouth. "Just hereabouts with a gabby yellow-haired gal in an indigo dress."

Giving him a halfhearted smile, she fingered her heavy braid. "Ma keeps threatenin' to shear me."

He shifted his gun to his other arm and returned his attention to the woods. "Reckon she thinks she'll save the Shawnee the trouble."

At this she sobered, searching for a speck of teasing in his sober features. Suddenly the almost romantic notion of letting down her hair for all those dark warriors turned terrifying. "Pa, you don't think . . ."

He lifted linen-clad shoulders in a shrug. "With the British paying bounties for settlement scalps, it might prove a formidable temptation."

"But I thought—" She paused, pushing into uncharted territory with her next words. "I thought since you . . . knew them, lived with them . . ."

A flash of something inexplicable crossed his face, and she sensed she'd gone too far. Never had they spoken of the past or the Shawnee, and doing so now seemed to bring about a wall that shut her out. Stung, she sought for words to soothe the strained silence, but her mind emptied of anything but a simple "sorry."

Her lips parted, but before she could utter another sound, he said, "Stay close to the cabin."

With a warning look he was gone, leaving her alone with all her anxiety. She sat down hard in her churning chair, near tears, forgetting the crock of butter. *Oh Pa, I'm sorry, truly sorry. But there are so many things I long to know.* She watched him disappear into the woods leading to the river, fighting the urge to run after him. Reaching into her pocket, she removed the aged newspaper she'd meant to make into a fan for Ransom. Just this morning she'd remembered it, wedged as it was between the trunk and a wall, forgotten. Before she'd pocketed it she caught sight of three arresting words: *The White Indian.* Beneath this, in bold print, was her father's name.

Now, unfolding the paper, her own hands seemed to tremble. The *Virginia Gazette* was widely circulated in the settlement, Kentucke being thought of as an extension of that state. Sometimes Pa left copies of it about the cabin. But never before had she seen this. Dropping her head, she read quickly, hungrily, not wanting to be discovered, vowing to return it to the trunk when she was through. The entire front page was devoted to her father with a detailed sketch that was remarkably his likeness. Was this why Ma had kept it?

The headlines presented the story of his captivity with startling simplicity. Though it had been well over six years since he'd disappeared, she knew the facts by heart. The day their world was upended, her father had been on a salt-making expedition for the settlement. This was tiresome, sweaty work, the steam of the huge kettles competing with the suffocating heat. But salt was survival, necessary for preserving meat and curing hides, and the salt-rich Licking River provided plenty.

It had been summer and twilight, her father's favorite time of day. She knew just how the river had looked then—a beguiling blue before giving way to silvery white to match the moon. Without so much as the rustle of a bush for warning, the Indians had surrounded them. Her father had been the first to lay down his rifle. Rather than fight, he'd *surrendered.*

The very word seemed at odds with everything Pa was, yet that's what he'd done. She fought the urge to ball the paper into her fist. What choice did he have when faced with ninety-three Shawnee? He'd been but one of twenty men from the settlement. Her father was no fool. She read further without wanting to, a hard knot forming in her throat.

He soon learned the Indians were planning to attack Fort Click. With most of the settlement men away making salt, the stockade was easy prey. Certain all within would be killed or captured, her father had struck a bargain. He assured the Shawnee the fort was at its strongest and the planned siege would be a costly mistake. If the Indians would take him and his men prisoner instead, and assure them fair treatment, they could be ransomed to the British in the north for bounty.

She stopped suddenly, the words a blur of black ink. All she remembered of her father's absence was the hollowness of hunger and a loneliness she couldn't name. The fort's corn crop soon ran out and there were too few men to supply meat for all the women and children within. Babies died. An old man shot himself in the blockhouse. With the first snow came much sickness. And while they suffered, her father turned Shawnee.

Unable to read further, she folded the paper and tucked it away, but the memory seemed to dog her as she did her chores. On her hands and knees, scrubbing the puncheon floor with sand and a bristle bush, she tried to forget about the past. At the same time, she made sure the paper was safe in her pocket. When she was alone again she'd read the rest.

Toward noon, Nip and Tuck's barking brought her back onto the porch. Tied up in the side yard, they were a welcome alarm and she relaxed at their halfhearted warning. In moments a familiar figure crossed the clearing on a big bay horse, copper hair bright as a candle flame. Lael flew off the steps, skirted the dogwood tree, and felt the cool breath of the stone springhouse as she passed.

She could hear her mother's frantic calling, but she kept on, scattering chickens and kicking up dust devils as she ran. Seeing Susanna turned Lael's thoughts at once to Simon. Same astonishing hair. Eyes like chicory coffee. The familiar mouth and noble nose. But whereas Susanna was small, her brother was easily the tallest man in the settlement.

As Susanna slipped to the ground, Lael hugged her wordlessly. Susanna studied her with a half smile, smoothing her wrinkled linsey skirts. "It's been too long, Lael Click. How you keepin'?"

"Right smart," she said, her smile snatched away by the sight of Susanna's father emerging from the woods behind them on a matching bay.

Lael studied him, a bit breathless. Since when did Harrison Hayes set foot on Click land? The hard lines of his face were like limestone, and not a nod of acknowledgment did he give her, though she stood directly in his path. Spotting her pa along a rail fence in the pasture, he made straight for him, leaving the two girls alone.

Susanna took the opportunity to pass Lael a piece of paper, folded tight. "From Simon," she whispered.

Startled, Lael slipped it in her pocket, tamping down the urge to open it in plain sight.

"Pa's here to settle a land dispute, if you're wonderin'," Susanna told her. "I asked to come along—begged, nearly. I've been afraid you'll not come to the weddin'."

"Ma's already at work on my dress," Lael reassured her, turning to watch the two men.

"I'm glad to hear it," Susanna said, standing beside her. "Isn't it a wonder? I don't think they've spoken since the court-martial. But Pa's desperate to settle this tetchy business with the Canes."

Lael nearly smiled at the irony. The Canes and Hayes, clearly the most contentious clans in the settlement, had brought about

23

the court-martial against her father years before. Now Harrison Hayes had come begging. With Pa appointed as magistrate, what choice did he have? His only recourse was to ride clear to Virginia and seek counsel. Watching, she felt a tad uneasy . . . yet jubilant.

Lael turned back to Susanna. "Only a few more days and you'll be wed. You look wonderful—like a bride should."

"I'll be glad to get the deed done and move on over to Cozy Creek. Will's finally finished the cabin. He's not built the barn yet, but your pa said he'd help."

"We'll be glad to get you as neighbors," Lael told her. "Pa's always had a fondness for Will."

Will, but not Simon. If only he thought so well of Susanna's brother. The court-martial had taken care of that, though it had been father, not son, who'd started it. A tiny flicker of hope rose in her heart. Perhaps now, with Hayes here, matters would mend.

Susanna untied her bonnet and began to fan herself. "I'll be glad to get shed of the fort, though Ma's sad to be losin' both of us at once. I guess you heard Simon left home in the spring. He has four hundred acres of his own now, surveyed by your pa and registered with the Transylvania Land Company."

Lael looked at her and the quiet fell between them like a curtain.

"You didn't hear, did you?" Susanna surmised. "Well, it's true. Simon's got a fine piece of property near your Uncle Neddy."

Lael's surprise deepened. She'd not seen Simon for months, or Neddy for years.

"I know there's still bad blood between your pa and his brother," Susanna said softly. "But Simon's got a good neighbor in Neddy." She paused as if weighing each word, her eyes on Lael's. "Neddy asked Simon about you—said he'd like to see you."

Lael felt her color rise. "Seems like he'd rather see Ransom than me."

"A man ought to be able to see his own son." Susanna's voice was soft but filled with conviction, mirroring Lael's own deep feelings, though she didn't say so.

"Ransom doesn't know about Neddy," Lael told her. *Not yet.* But everyone else in the settlement knew who sired Sara Click's son.

Susanna touched her arm. "I know you don't like to talk about the past, so we'll just talk about the future." Her tone turned a trifle teasing, the light in her eyes inviting. "I've been thinkin'— since Simon's standin' up with Will at the weddin', and you with me, why not make it a double match? You're nearly fourteen."

Fourteen to Simon's twenty. Lael put her hand in her pocket absently, feeling for the note. Ma had been fifteen when she married Pa. *And thirty-two when she ran off with Neddy.* That memory wouldn't budge, no matter what. She could still recall the precise shade of her mother's dress the night she disappeared. An unforgiveable forget-me-not blue. Only six, Lael had been left at the fort and the Hayes clan had taken her in. Like a stray cat, some said.

"I'd rather have you for a sister-in-law than anyone in the settlement," Susanna went on with a winsome smile, filling the silence.

"Seems like Simon should be the one askin' me, not you," Lael chided softly.

"Maybe he is," she replied, pointing to Lael's pocket. With a smug smile she turned and climbed back up on her horse, the copper coil of her braid touching the bay's broad back.

Lael looked over her shoulder and found the two men still deep in conversation. Standing so far from the cabin left her feeling slightly skittish, though she knew Pa's surveillance never ceased. She dried her damp face with the hem of her apron, looking askance at the noon sun.

As if sensing her mood, Susanna glanced toward the woods. "What's this I hear about the Shawnee comin' to your cabin?"

Lael turned back to her, wondering just how much she knew. "I don't think they meant any harm. I wouldn't be here if they did." Even as she said it the remembrance brought heat to her face.

"You'd best be careful," Susanna cautioned. "I've heard what happens once they get hold of us womenfolk."

Lael wrapped her arms around herself, amazed that she could shiver and sweat all at once. "What do you mean?"

"Well," Susanna said, voice low. "Old Jemima Talbot was taken by the Cherokee as a girl in North Carolina. On the trail to the Indian towns . . . *she had to pick their hair for nits."*

Lael waited for more, then smiled with relief. "Is that all?"

"Is that all? No, that ain't all. *Then they picked hers."*

Lael laughed and touched her own clean braid. "Jemima's lucky she kept her scalp. I aim to do the same. And I promise to be right beside you come the sixth of June."

With a cursory glance at the woods Susanna chuckled and waited for her father to join her. As they rode away she looked back once, mouthing the words Lael had been hearing all her life. *Take care, Lael Click, or the yellow jackets'll sting you.*

The old settlement saying squared sourly with the near breathless elation she felt when her fingers touched her pocket. The Shawnee might sting, but they couldn't steal her joy. Her hands almost seemed to dance as she held open the note. There, upon the scrap of paper, as big and bold as Simon Hayes himself, was a heavy scrawl that seemed more command than invitation.

Lael Catherine Click, save every dance for me. Simon Henry Hayes.

26

4

The next morning Lael felt an unusual lightness in spirit. Thoughts of the frolic to come, of fiddling and feasting and dancing, filled her with gladness. Even her chores seemed less like work and more a means of drawing her closer to the coveted event. Pa had eased his tether a bit, letting her go to the barn and springhouse but no farther. With Simon's note in her pocket she felt she'd turned a new page and taken a step toward the future.

With a wary glance at the woods she entered the barn, thankful for the stillness of the bright May morning. Settled beside the docile Tillie, she filled her bucket and squirted a stream of milk at a passing barn cat before rising from her stool and journeying to the springhouse. The heavy door creaked and the shadows within smelled of dirt and dampness and pickled beans. Wrinkling her nose, she lifted her heavy bucket and poured the warm milk into a cold crock, then toted a piggin of old cream to the cabin.

She paused for a moment to admire the roses wending their way along the porch rail. The buds were open and a warm wind spread their scent hither and yon. All was still save the rooster crowing around the side of the barn. 'Twas early still, though Pa had gone hunting hours ago. She considered his leaving a good sign, as he'd kept so close to the cabin lately.

Her bare feet tread the worn porch planks when she noticed her churning chair was slightly askew. The strangeness of it slowed her. On edge again, she set the bucket down hard and hesitated.

At the far end of the porch, coiled like a copperhead, lay a necklace.

Her gaze ricocheted to the woods, then back. She heard Ma moving about the cabin, busy at the hearth most likely, judging from the sizzle and snap of a frying pan. A dozen different emotions sliced through her, but fear cut the deepest.

She bent and grabbed the necklace, gathering the beads into her balled fist. Oddly, they were warm and she longed to look at them.

"Lael, aren't you done yet?" Ma called.

Done? She swallowed, feeling a bit ill. Why, she'd hardly begun. She sank into the chair, heart hammering. How in heaven could she sit and churn when the gift giver likely watched her from the woods?

She cast a glance at the dirt yard. Pa could ferret out a moccasin print at fifty paces. She saw none, nor wanted to. Just then Ma appeared, wiping her hands on her apron. Lael tried hard to smile but still looked stricken. Her hand closed tight around the beads as if squeezing harder would make them disappear.

Ma stopped just shy of the door, dark eyes intense. "Lael, are you ailing?"

"Just a mite woozy, is all," she managed. Truly, she didn't lie.

"I reckon I've been workin' you overmuch. A body's liable to melt in this heat." Ma took the lid off the churn and emptied the cream in.

The smell of it nearly curdled Lael's stomach. Desperate, she grabbed the dasher with her empty hand. "I'll be fine, Ma, really I will."

Now that was a lie.

That afternoon, Lael dampened the rows with a gourd dipper, the tension inside her ratcheting up alongside the rising heat. The garden, framed by a paling fence, was within a stone's throw of the cabin. There Lael never left her mother's watchful eye.

Had it been only this morning that she'd found the Indian

beads? Since then time seemed to have ceased and flown, causing dread to tick inside her like a clock, drawing her ever nearer to some unspoken calamity. Despite Pa's presence, she felt nearly frozen with fear. Through the screen of roses she could see the glint of his gun barrel as he sat on the porch.

His voice was deep and untroubled as he spoke of mustering the settlement militia at Fort Click. Several settlement scouts had brought word that the Shawnee leader, Blackfish, was ailing and there was to be a new chief. In the meantime bands of young braves were coming across the Ohio, making mischief, and reports of horse stealing abounded. Some of the more contentious settlers were threatening to take matters into their own hands and shoot at whatever provoked them. But this was hardly the time for a wilderness war, not with all the trouble between the Redcoats and colonists in the east.

Leaning on her hoe, Lael stood, sweat trickling down her face and neck. Through the trees the river beckoned with a blue finger, making her feel feverish with longing to jump in, dress and all. The memory of how she once did with near abandon seemed to cut her. Now the Shawnee were out there, somewhere. Waiting. Watching. Biding their time till they caught her unawares at the river. Or calling the cow home from the woods. Or digging herbs in some lonesome hollow.

Had she become something of a prize to them, being Ezekial Click's only daughter?

Her fingers went to her pocket, now nearly bulging with newsprint, Simon's note, and the blue beads. Like a string of speckled robin's eggs, their glassy brilliance took her breath. She'd seen the beads the traders used in their dealings with the tribes. Pa kept a glass bottle of them under the bed, a veritable rainbow of bewitching colors blended with silver ornaments and tinkling brass cones. Some had clear cores the Indians called white eyes. But never before had she seen beads of such a startling blue.

Packed away in her pocket, she longed to look at them but

knew she mustn't. They would stay a secret to her dying day. What a ruckus she'd raise if she pulled them out to parade them! Her forehead furrowed as she thought of where she might hide them lest they spill out of her pocket and expose her. Perhaps in the woods, if she could get to them.

The Click cabin was beginning to feel overfull of secrets. Her mother's. Pa's from his Shawnee past. Even Ransom's, though he didn't know he had any.

And now her own.

Sometime in the night Ma had finished the apple-green dress. Lael awoke to find it dangling from a peg opposite her bed, two days ahead of the nuptials, leaving time for the fine fabric to hang and work out the wrinkles. The finery lent a touch of civility to the rough wall she'd been looking at her whole life. She spied two new muslin petticoats as well and the slippers sitting underneath in expectation. With the stifling June heat she'd need no stockings or garters. When Ma wasn't looking she planned to shed her shoes for the dancing, hiding her bare feet beneath the generous hem of her gown.

Rolling over, she ran a hand underneath her pillow, netting the blue beads and Simon's note in one sweep. The necklace provoked her, while the note continued to please no matter how many times she read it. The dilemma she now faced was how to appease both Ma and Simon. Her mother would be watching to see how many sets she danced, and Simon would simply keep asking.

Pushing aside the thin sheet, she swung her feet to the floor, crossing to the cracked glass to take a long look at herself. *Pale as frost.* She'd finally slept from sheer exhaustion, but the worry she felt seemed to tell on her face. Would Simon notice—or care? She'd not seen him since winter when they'd last spent time at the fort and he'd been spelling his father at the smithy.

Although he was supposed to be intent on shoeing their new gelding, the way he'd looked at her as she waited with Pa turned her to jelly. Each time she saw Simon he seemed to have changed ever so slightly. Taller, broader of shoulder, with a hint more swagger to his step. Sometimes he seemed almost Goliath-like. Willowy as she was, she barely reached his chin.

"Lael, you'd best come down and eat your breakfast." Ma's voice seemed shrill in the stillness, and Lael hastened into her linsey shift, forehead furrowed.

Their close confinement of late was clearly taking a toll on her mother. Lael could hear her muttering as she moved about the cabin and hoped Ransom was well out of her way, as it was he who got the brunt of Ma's broom and ill temper. She sighed as she pocketed both the note and beads. What would Ma do if she knew the Shawnee had come calling not once but twice?

Click, show us your pretty daughter.

The memory made a deep ache inside her. She looked askance at the length of her hair. Like a bolt of yellow cloth, it seemed to have no end. Hastily she braided it, wondering whether to wear it up or down for the wedding, only to hear Ma call a second time.

"Comin', Ma," she shot back, tying off the end with a piece of whang leather. She'd save her ribbons for the wedding. Today was wash day—a hot, smelly business if there ever was one. Descending the loft ladder, she spied the hipbath by the hearth and caught the tail end of her father's stride as he went out the door.

He'd brought the tub in on account of the festivities, she gathered. Its rotund belly held twenty-two buckets of water from the spring that bubbled in back of the house, a rare treat when heated and scented with the soft soap they made. Ma added a handful of lavender to sweeten each batch, and the smell lingered long about the cabin. But the tub was out of place in summer. Its appearance spelled trouble, or at least caution. Until now, the river had sufficed in warm weather, its cool blueness as refreshing as it was deep.

"I've already milked," Ma said over her shoulder, frying bacon in a heavy skillet. "You've been acting so poorly, I thought I'd better let you sleep."

Lael sank onto the bench, suddenly wearier than when she'd gone to bed. Did Ma somehow suspect the beads hidden away in her pocket? She tried to smile as Ma passed her a bowl of mush laced with long-sweetening and a strip of bacon. Across from her Ransom finished his helping and eyed hers. When Ma turned her back, Lael slid her bowl toward him, and with a grin he gave up his.

"Well, at least your appetite's some better," Ma said, coming back around and eyeing her empty bowl. "Now go on and see to the garden. Something's after my melons."

A bit lightheaded, Lael went out, her need to see her father nearly overwhelming. The clearing and outbuildings stood golden in the rising sun, empty of his reassuring presence. She hesitated before stepping off the porch, hoping he'd appear. Her attention was drawn to the smoke pluming in back of the cabin, making the place appear like it was on fire.

Ma had hung a huge kettle to boil, and the smell of lye was overwhelming. Mouth wry, Lael watched Ransom wander out and cavort about the flames, as naked as decency allowed. Stripped to his skivvies, he set to work chopping brush with his small hatchet and feeding the fire while she rounded the cabin to tend the garden.

Though still early, sweat darkened her hairline and trickled into her eyes, stinging them as she walked. If this was but June, July would be all ablaze. Folks were already talking about the queer weather. Winter seemed to have jumped right into summer, bypassing spring altogether.

At the garden gate, her fingers fumbled with the latch on the paling fence but touched fabric, not wood. She drew back as if bitten.

There, draped over the gate, was a blanket.

An Indian blanket.

The familiarity of it stunned her. Hadn't she seen the very same hanging from the tall Indian's shoulder when the Shawnee came calling? The square of white wool bore a solid blue stripe. Backing up, she tried to take a breath, but it caught in her throat. This time there was no ignoring the footprints. Mingled with those made by her own moccasins, they stretched solitarily to the woods.

"Lael, I want you to water the beans a mite heavy this morning and then—" Ma came around the corner, seeing her daughter standing in front of the blanket she couldn't hide. For a moment her expression was empty, then understanding dawned and she gave a startled cry.

With a ferocious jerk, Ma pulled the blanket from the pickets and rushed to the back of the cabin. Lael ran after her, aghast as her mother threw the gift into the fire. Billows of gray smoke poured forth as the heavy wool smothered the flames beneath the kettle.

"Nay!" Lael cried.

Pushing past her, she grabbed a corner of the blanket and pulled it free. Would her mother's impetuous act bring death down upon them? Shawnee were watching from the woods—whether two or twenty did not matter. Frantic, she scanned the clearing.

Oh Pa, where are you?

Holding the blanket tight, she stamped out the fire from it with one moccasin, sickened as she did so. Did her actions encourage her Shawnee suitor? In saving the blanket did she somehow seal his ardor? If she'd been in doubt about the beads, the blanket confirmed her fears. One look at her mother's face and she knew Ma surmised the same. The Shawnee had come calling again, and his intent was now clear.

The blue beads seemed to burn a hole in her pocket.

5

By sunset the air inside the shut-up cabin was stifling and still, and they could hear the cow bawling to be milked beyond the barred door. Lael peered through a crack in the shuttered window, searching for any sign of the Shawnee. A footfall on the porch made her breathless. When she heard the reassuring voice of her father calling her name, she fumbled with the latchstring and let him in.

Even before he set eyes on the fire-blackened blanket in the cabin corner, her tense expression told him what she couldn't say. Setting his rifle and powder horn atop the trestle table, he listened as she poured forth her story. Unable to hide them any longer, she produced the blue beads. "I found these on the porch yesterday morning."

Ma's sharp intake of breath jarred her. She hadn't meant to deceive, just mollify her ma. Why had she thought hiding them would be a simple matter? A lie always came to light. Pa had taught her to be truthful even if it hurt.

Her mother's hand came down hard and swept the necklace off the table. The beads clattered to the floor but didn't break. The leather string that bound them was too strong. Next she turned on Lael and smacked her hard, then ran weeping from the room.

Like a flustered squirrel, Ransom looked out from under the table where he'd been hiding and scampered up the loft ladder. The cheek that bore the stinging handprint led to a queer emptiness in Lael's breast.

"Pack your things," Pa told her. "We're headed to Pigeon Ridge."

Pigeon Ridge was miles away and already the twilight was falling fast. Seated behind Pa on a dun-colored mare, Lael watched as the dying sun pulled a purple curtain over the mountains and seeded the sky with a million stars. She knew they'd soon be benighted in the woods. *Better that*, she thought, *than a cabin crammed with ill will*. Evidently her father felt the same.

As they rode, she finally gave in to the question she'd longed to ask ever since the Shawnee first appeared in the cabin clearing. "Pa, I've been wonderin' . . ." She swallowed hard, the words seeming to stick in her throat. "Are you afraid the Shawnee mean me harm?"

"I'm not fearful, just cautious," he said evenly. "They're somewhat chancy. Best stay one step ahead of 'em."

"But I don't want to cause trouble for Ma Horn," she said quietly. "Seems like the Shawnee'll be able to find me up on high same as at home."

"Not likely. They're a mite afraid of her."

"What?" She leaned into his shoulder, breathing in sweat and damp linen.

"Every time she meets up with an Indian in the woods, she acts crazy or spouts Scripture at 'em so they leave her be. You're safer with her than you would be locked up at the fort."

Truly? A tickled smile pulled at her solemn face, and she nearly laughed outright. She let the strangeness of the words seep over her and settle her. Now that he'd spoken, it seemed he'd left the door open for her to ask him a dozen other things, things no one had dared ask him, not even Ma. Quietly she rehearsed them in her heart. *Pa, did you like living with the Shawnee? Do you ever miss those days? Did they come by the cabin just to see you? What exactly did they say?*

Taking a deep breath, she gathered her courage about her, then felt it dwindle. Last time she'd probed, he'd called her a gabby, yellow-haired gal and shut her out. Maybe she had no right to ask about his past. But it seemed that his past was now intruding on her present in a bewildering way.

As they brushed by a sorrel tree she stripped off one narrow leaf, chewing it to quiet her thirst. If only she had something to still her heart. She fished in her pocket, empty of the beads now, and found Simon's note alongside the old newspaper. This would have to do.

When the darkness hemmed them in and they could go no farther, they made a cold camp in a small clearing. Crickets hollered all around them and sang them to sleep as they lay on hard ground with nary a blanket. Before dawn they rose, dew covered and slightly stiff, and journeyed on.

After being tethered to the cabin for days on end, Lael felt a queer elation with every step, her spirits rising like the swell of mountains they traversed. At noon they crested a steep divide and looked down upon the river bottoms from which they'd come. Far below, the Kentucke River lay at low ebb, a startling sapphire blue.

Lael took off her bonnet, the fabric limp and lifeless in her hand, the dye long since washed out. Though the sun couldn't touch them through the thick stands of timber, the woods were nearly suffocating. Even the mare turned mulish. Stopping at every creek and branch, they chewed on ginseng root to revive themselves.

Toward nightfall they found themselves high atop a rocky ridge where the air was thin and pure and the sound of pigeons punctuated the growing gloom. Weary, Lael studied the one-room cabin in their path, mountain laurel hugging its walls as if hiding it from passersby. She doubted there were many. A rail fence zigzagged across the yard, penning in poppies and hollyhocks, bellflowers and foxglove, reminding her of her mother's own.

"I misdoubt even the Indians could find us way up here even if they wanted to," she said as they drew nearer.

A woman, lean and brown as a strip of jerky, stood in the doorway as if expecting them. There was no porch, but a fine rock chimney climbed one wall, puffing smoke. As she dismounted Lael lost her bearings and swayed, then felt her father's hard hand steady her. She'd not make a fool of herself and faint, she determined. She reckoned she'd caused enough trouble for one day.

After a long night on hard ground and nothing to eat, they were welcomed with a water bucket and gourd dipper. Lael drank thirstily, standing apart from her father and the only granny she'd ever known. They spoke in low tones and she could only guess what it was they said, struck by her pa's sudden talkativeness. The woman who listened was no stranger, and Lael felt relieved at the very sight of her.

A great aunt in the Click clan, Ma Horn was a spinster whom some said had a horde of shillings stashed away beneath the thatch of pea vine and clover around her cabin. But no one truly knew, for Ma Horn was more interested in the ailments of others than telling secrets about herself. She'd come to Kentucke on Pa's second foray years before, the only woman among eighteen men. Together they'd built the cabin in the tiny clearing, a place few had seldom seen. Ma Horn was often on the move, dispensing tonics and herb bundles, and usually came to them.

"Come in the cabin, Lael, and rest a spell," she finally said, wiping gnarled hands on a worn apron.

Lael. Lay-elle. The genteel pronunciation of her name was

not lost on Lael. Of all the Click clan, Ma Horn was the only one who could pronounce her name properly. Not hard and fast like Ma spoke it, often in a fit of temper, nor the neglectful way Pa had of just calling her "Daughter," but soft and dreamy as a song. After all, she'd been named after Ma Horn's own mother.

She watched as her father turned and rode off down the mountain without so much as a backward glance. The slight stung far more than Ma's smack, and she bit her lip before turning and following the old woman into the tiny cabin. Once inside the gloom made her pause. Only one window, a stingy square above a trestle table, let in light. In the corner was a feather bed, the once fine coverlet white as a cloud. A single chair sat to one side of the fireplace. Everything was as clean and spare as could be.

Without a word Ma Horn removed the lid from a black kettle and forked a potato onto a wooden plate. A slice of hoecake and some bacon followed. Without being told, Lael took a seat at the table and ate everything without a word, aware of being watched. Afterward she fell back on the feather tick and went to sleep.

When she opened her eyes she spied what seemed to be a hundred sundry baskets suspended from the cabin ceiling. Without stirring, she watched Ma Horn move about, using a long-handled wooden hook to fetch this one or that. Remembering what day it was, Lael nearly groaned as she turned over and buried her face in the feather tick. Images of Susanna in her heirloom wedding dress, of trestle tables mounded with roast meats and ripe vegetables and stack cakes, of old Amos's fine bow hand as he pulled out his fiddle, threatened to undo her.

She shut away the thought of Susanna's dismay but had less luck with Simon. What would he think in her absence? Pondering it all, her disappointment was bitter and complete. By supper she was nearly sinking. Even nature seemed unkind, the day dawning bright as a bride, then fading to fill the sky with a full moon. *A lover's moon.*

If Ma Horn noticed her distress, she made no mention of it. As she packed her clay pipe full of dried tobacco crumbles, Lael reached into the hearth embers with a little shovel and retrieved a live coal with which to light it.

From outside the open door came the plaintive sound of doves cooing. Listening, Lael felt almost at home. She loved the mountain silences, so different from the river bottoms below. In times past this place had eased her heartache; perhaps now it might even dull the sting of Ma's slap and Pa's forgetfulness in saying good-bye.

At her feet lay a tangle of honeysuckle vine, soaked and set for weaving into baskets. Ma Horn had taught her the art years before when she'd toddled behind her in the woods. She was glad to be occupied, her hands deftly working the handles first, then the baskets themselves, finally joining the two.

Across from her, Ma Horn puffed contentedly on her pipe, watching her weaving. Tendrils of tobacco smoke encircled them, oddly fragrant. She was so often quiet, like Pa himself, and Lael felt a little start when she finally said, "So Captain Jack's come a-courtin.'"

Her hands stilled on the basket. "Who?"

"The tall Shawnee who come by your cabin."

The tall one. Lael felt a small surge of triumph at learning his name. *Captain Jack.* Oddly, she felt no embarrassment. Lifting her shoulders in a slight shrug, she continued pulling the vines into a tight circle. "He come by, but I don't know why."

"Best take a long look in the mirror, then."

Lael's eyes roamed the dark walls. Ma Horn didn't own one.

"Beads and a blanket, was it?"

She nodded and looked back down. "I still can't figure out why some Shawnee would pay any mind to a white girl like me."

Ma Horn chuckled, her face alight in the dimness. "Why, Captain Jack's as white as you are."

"What?" she blurted, eyes wide as a child's.

Ma Horn's smile turned sober. "He's no Indian, Shawnee or otherwise, so your pa says. He was took as a child from somewheres in North Carolina. All he can remember of his past life is his white name—Jack." She paused as if weighing what she knew. "You could say he and your pa are right well acquainted. He was one of the warriors who captured him and his men and carried them to the Falls of the Ohio."

Listening, Lael looked back. Her recollection of the young warrior standing outside their cabin was as fresh as yesterday. Silver arm bands. Buckskin breech-clout. She'd counted three eagle feathers fluttering from his dark hair. The telltale trade blanket had been draped over one broad shoulder, and his skin was baked the color of dried blood. Captain Jack looked Shawnee to the core.

She suppressed a sigh. "Ma nearly had a fit, finding six Indians at her door."

Ma Horn drew deeply on her pipe. "And you didn't?"

"I . . ." Lael left off, unable to sort out the tangle of emotions she'd felt at their coming. Fear. Curiosity. Fascination. Shame. "It's been hardest on Ma," she lamented, looking down at her basket.

Ma Horn nodded sagely. "I reckon she don't like the reminder."

So that was it. Ma's black mood hinged on being confronted with a past better left alone. Lael looked hard at Ma Horn, free to ponder it all for the very first time. She felt a sudden stab of sympathy for her moody mother. Was she now reliving the ugly day of Pa's capture? Her own disgrace? Could she ever forget the shock of his homecoming or the ensuing silence that shut them out and seemed to overlook two lost years? When they thought the worst was over, the Canes and Hayes clans had brought about a court-martial branding him a traitor. Had that returned to haunt her too?

"Some family skeletons are best left buried," Ma Horn said, interrupting her reverie.

Lael sighed and set down the basket. "Seems like the Clicks have more than their share."

The old woman's face creased like a dried apple when she smiled. "We ain't a boresome bunch, are we?"

Lael shot her a wounded look. "Am I supposed to be proud of that?"

"Beats cryin', don't it?"

Lael swallowed down another sigh and looked at the finished baskets at her feet. Tomorrow they'd fill every one. The long days offered plenty of daylight to wander the woods, and a huge harvest still waited. As if pondering the work ahead, Ma Horn rose from her rocking chair and bade Lael good night, taking a small pallet in the corner and leaving Lael the prized feather tick. Though she'd protested, Ma Horn wouldn't hear otherwise.

Left alone, she moved the tallow candle closer and took Simon's note from her pocket. Smoothing the crumpled paper, she wondered if Ma Horn watched her from the shadows. The bold words still seemed to leap off the page. That he'd remembered her middle name and signed off with his own was almost intimate somehow. But it was what he didn't write that held her. Simon Henry Hayes was in need of a wife and he meant to have her.

She expelled a rush of air, suddenly sleepy, wondering when her father would come back to fetch her. How had he and Ma explained her absence at the wedding? Likely, they hadn't. Her disappearance would simply be another secret whispered of in the settlement. Just one in a long line of secrets.

Truly, she thought wearily, *the Click clan is rife with them.*

41

6

Lael and Ma Horn traipsed from hollow to cove, then ridge and river bottom and back, baskets adorning their arms like jewelry. Every morning they would go gathering once the dew was dried, with nary a thought for the heat. Though her feet felt scalded, Lael refused to complain, knowing she'd toughen in time.

"Take care to find four of the same plant before you take the one, lest they won't grow back," Ma Horn cautioned her, standing knee deep in a patch of boneset.

Lael helped strip the tiny white flowers and leaves from the stalks, listening as Ma Horn talked.

"Boneset tea will nearly always break a fever, but it'll make you sick if you take it hot. Now, look at this Jack-in-the-pulpit. Take this here hoe and dig some roots. Nothin' better for snake-bite."

Up so high, Lael seemed to shed her burdens. Thoughts of Captain Jack were fleeting, if at all. She had less luck with Simon. The note remained in her pocket, perused in solitary moments when she relieved herself behind a bush or tree. With Ma Horn busy stuffing her head full of herbal lore, Lael felt she was back in settlement school again, only the learning was different and altogether more pleasurable.

Unexpected riches bloomed around every bend. Golden ginseng. Velvety sumac. Indian peaches and pale red serviceberries. Lael would bend down a limb and stand and eat her fill before filling her basket. Once back at the cabin, they dried herbs and berries on strips of chestnut bark in the sun. A butter churn was filled to the brim with blackberry wine. Lael looked about in wonder as every barrel, bucket, piggin, and washtub seemed overflowing with nature's offerings.

Ma Horn never stopped until nightfall when she'd crack the cabin door and sit and smoke her pipe. Her rifle was ever near, a reminder of troubled times. Lael wondered if she used it for much other than meat. She didn't know what one old woman and an older gun could do against even one Indian but held her tongue.

Each evening Ma Horn would make a tonic, one for herself and one for Lael, and Lael would try to guess which herbs she'd used by the way they scented the room.

"Take this basswood blossom tea," Ma Horn urged. "It's good for female troubles. I'll settle for some clover. It'll help me to sleep."

"But I don't have any female troubles," Lael said. "Leastways, not bodily."

"Well, fine and dandy, just drink it down anyway. It does a body good."

June melted into July. The woods were kiln hot, flowers and berries bursting forth before their time. Lael felt feverish and wondered how her mother's garden fared. Up so high, Ma Horn had no garden to speak of. Most everything she ate she ate wild from the woods. Meat and meal were traded for her herbs, but when her larder ran low, she simply prayed and it was provided.

"The Almighty knows what I need before I ask Him," she'd say, "but I ask just the same."

Lael wondered if the Almighty knew she needed to stay atop Pigeon Ridge, out of sight and trouble. She missed home, but not Ma's fractious temper. Once Pa came and left a sack of salt, but they didn't see him, busy as they were gathering wads of wild grapes and Indian peaches to dry. Although he wasn't there, she sensed he was often with her. Comforted, she clung to this whenever she felt afraid, when the shadows of twilight fell and she imagined she heard Indian drums in the distant darkness.

As the days melted together they worked feverishly to harvest all they could, for it would keep them—and the settlers—in good health through the coming winter. When the gathering was done, they simply filled the hours a different way, distributing tonics and herb bundles all over the settlement. Once, Lael awoke to find Ma Horn gone, but by dusk she'd returned with a fresh ham to hang and a mess of beans as payment for a birth. Twins, she said.

"Ain't you ever fretful, Ma Horn?" Lael asked, staring pensively at the dark woods.

But Ma Horn just chuckled, revealing tobacco-stained teeth. "If them Indians want my old hide, they can have it."

Lael found it hard not to laugh at the sight of her on old Soot, her black-clad legs thin as broom handles, one stiff petticoat rising above boots bearing silver buckles. With her black bonnet on her head, she looked dark and pensive. Like a crow, Lael thought.

"I believe your pa's fixin' to come get you," she said in early August. "I'll sure be lonesome when you go. But before you do, there's one last call we need to make."

The intensity of her tone made Lael wary. "Where to?"

Ma Horn looked straight at her. "Your Uncle Neddy."

She felt her mouth go slack, then she recovered and looked around for the mule. She'd not thought of Neddy since Susanna had mentioned him in early summer and revealed that his land bordered Simon's own. What would Pa think? Ma? Neddy's face came to mind, more shadow than substance. She'd spent years trying to put his memory down only to have it resurrected twice now.

Ever perceptive, Ma Horn studied her and said, "You still sore about it all?"

Lael shrugged, her face as stoic as her father's. The youngest of the Click clan, Neddy looked enough like Pa to be his twin, and some said this was the reason Ma ran off with him. But to Lael they were as different as sugar and salt. While Ezekial Click was taciturn and callous, Neddy was like his name, affable and dreamy, tending his crops by day and reading poetry by night.

Ma Horn's voice was gentle yet firm. "Your ma thought your pa was dead, understand."

But he wasn't. She bit back the retort and stared straight ahead. If not for the Hayes clan, who would have taken her in when she'd been left at the fort? Though Ma had come to her senses in just a few days, the damage was done.

"I remember how excited you was when it was your mother's time," Ma Horn said quietly, getting back on the trail. "I thought for sure the way she was carryin' spelled a girl."

Lael smiled wryly. Ransom Dunbar Click was hardly the girl she'd been hankering for. Even Pa had seemed surprised, as if he thought such dallying was sure to produce a female. Recently escaped from the Shawnee, he'd come in and held the infant up to the light. The tiny boy grimaced and opened wide blue eyes. Looking on, Lael thought he was the handsomest baby she'd ever seen, no matter who'd fathered him.

"One Click's as good as another," Pa had said with a shrug, handing him back to Ma.

And so it was that Uncle Neddy, a bachelor recluse, fathered his first and only son. Pa's revenge was to keep him.

"I haven't seen hide nor hair of Uncle Neddy since Ma ran off with him," Lael told her.

"Well, time's a-wastin'," she said.

The trip to Uncle Neddy was not a simple social call. As they neared his home place, Lael remembered he'd never married and rarely went to the fort named after his brother, even in times of Indian trouble. Though he'd once been a beloved uncle, Lael felt he was dead to them. His name was never mentioned, at least not in their own cabin.

But now, riding nearer, the past was fast unfolding and curiosity overcame her with every step. "What's ailin' Uncle Neddy?"

"Settlement fever."

Lael shuddered. The malady was generous with its misery, sapping the life from many a settler, fooling them into a period of wellness only to take them down at a later date. "You see him often?"

"Often enough. He's in need of an herb bundle now and again."

"What do you suppose he'll do when he catches sight of me?"

Beneath the black bonnet came a chortle. "What'll you do when you catch sight of him?"

Lael fell silent, unable to say.

Ma Horn continued, her voice a bit hushed, as if sharing some family secret. "Neddy's changed a mite. I give him a Bible sometime back, after all the trouble. He was always one for readin', if you remember. Before long I began to see a change in him. Turns out he can quote whole passages by heart. All that bitterness toward your pa—his lonesomeness for your ma— just left him. I reckon if you spend enough time in the Word it changes you, just like Scripture says."

Lael thought of their Bible at home, rarely removed from its wooden box. Only in times of stress did Ma reach for it. And Pa, never.

In the distance, Neddy's cabin was nearly as small as Ma Horn's, hemmed in by corn on all sides. Lael flicked a yellow jacket off her sleeve and tried to swallow, but her throat was so dry she felt strangled. The sun was directly ahead and heat shimmered all around them, the land giving off its rich, ripe scent. They dismounted and from somewhere—the fields?—Neddy appeared. Lael took off her bonnet and flipped her heavy braid back over one shoulder, her feet in a firm stance that belied her skittish feelings.

He was walking slowly toward them, scarecrow thin, his fair hair tied back with whang leather. When he saw her, he stopped. She took a shy step toward him and did the same.

Try as she might, she couldn't master her swirling emotions. Something lonesome and long dead pulled at her as she looked at him and remembered a great many things at once. Neddy reading to her in the firelight. Neddy teaching her to spell her name. Neddy bringing her a sugar lump from the fort store. Tears mingled with her salty sweat and stung her flushed face.

Without a moment's hesitation Neddy did what Pa would never do. Reaching out a long arm, he pulled her into a snug embrace and let her cry.

"Lael girl, you look the same as you did when you were six years old, only handsomer." His voice was deep and warm; he smelled of smoke and dirt and toil. His thin face seemed almost to shine.

"Well, now," Ma Horn huffed, looking as if she might crow at any minute. "Let's go in and have us a little visit."

7

In the dog days of August, Lael was called home on account of a letter. As it passed from her mother's hand to her own, Lael was doubly struck with the indigo wax seal and the elegant hand that had penned the ivory envelope. Though the edges were crimped and the ink slightly blurred from days spent in a saddlebag, it was nevertheless a wonder. Suddenly the queer, formal handwriting took a familiar turn. *Miss Mayella!*

Had it been only three years since Miss Mayella had left the settlement school and returned home to Virginia? Since then no genteel teacher had dared venture to the frontier, with the British giving guns to the Indians and the colonies at war.

With Ma looking over her shoulder, Lael devoured the shocking contents. A teacher was needed in the settlement. Who else, given her high marks and her father's reputation, could it be but Lael? If she would accept the position, a small stipend would be paid by the Virginia Society of Education.

Lael let the letter fall to the porch planks where Ma snatched it up. Home less than a day, she couldn't seem to get her bearings and now was befuddled with this unpleasant proposal.

"We'll have to tell your pa the good news," Ma said, a tad triumphant.

Lael sat down hard in the churning chair, all the breath knocked out of her. Was Ma so anxious to be rid of her? Ma's wide, satisfied smile belied her need to restore the Click name to its former glory, before all the trouble had tarnished it. Lael could decipher her thoughts simply by studying her.

Unable to endure it, Lael looked away. Surely she could count on Pa to see reason. Why, she was no more a teacher than he was a preacher. Ma simply hadn't pondered it properly. She was needed here, truly. All the chores of autumn were yet undone, as evidenced by the burgeoning garden and field of corn.

And her favorite task by far—digging ginseng for profit—was about to begin. Ma Horn had told her all the best places to find the rich roots, even drawing a crude map of sorts, marking coveted spots known to few in the settlement. Lael liked the thought of earning money this way, exchanging it for some trinket for her mother and Ransom or perhaps a beaver-felt hat for Pa.

Weary from the long trip down the mountain, Lael was glad to see the day dwindle to an end so she could escape to the loft. After being gone for so long the loft seemed strange to her—smaller and more crowded. Or perhaps it was Ransom who had changed. He seemed all knees and elbows now, nearly filling the rectangular trundle bed. She could see so much of Neddy in him, and the likeness touched her.

Tonight he seemed as restless as she, the heat lying like a wool blanket over the top of them, suffocatingly close.

"I can't sleep," he said softly, reaching up to touch her hand as it dangled over the side of the bed.

"Lie still and I'll tell you a story," she whispered into the darkness.

"About Pa?"

"Aye, about Pa," she said, thinking of Neddy. Her voice was soft as she began, mindful of Ma and Pa just below. "Back before you were born—long before there were any forts or settlers here—Pa came into Kentucke."

"By hisself?"

"Aye, by himself. He'd had a friend who'd gone before him, crossing over the Cumberlands, but he'd never come back."

At this Ransom rolled closer, and she wondered if the story was too stirring, true as it was. Lowering her head, she made her voice as soothing as could be. "Pa thought he might find his friend and see what the land was like besides. Once he crossed the gap he felt like he'd entered a new world, full of animals he'd never before seen—and trees and rolling rivers he couldn't name. He became so lost in the wonder of it all that he forgot to be careful. It wasn't long till he sensed he wasn't alone."

"Shawnee?"

"Cherokee," she answered. "They tracked him to some limestone bluffs not far from here, where the river bends toward the first falls. He stood with his horse and his gun overlooking the water far below, and he did the only thing he could to save himself."

"He . . . *jumped.*" Ransom's breathless whisper seemed suspended in the hot air.

"Sure enough. He jumped straight into the arms of a sugar maple, just filled out with spring leaves. A big branch broke his fall and he landed on his feet. He still had his rifle but had to leave his horse behind."

"Did he ever find his friend?"

Lael fell silent. *One week later he came across his friend's body in the hollow of a sycamore tree, an arrow protruding from his back.* "I'll save that story for another time. Now go to sleep."

He obliged, his breathing soon even and restful, making her feel less lonesome. Lying atop the faded quilt, she could see the outline of the apple-green dress in the dimness, but its beauty failed to move her. She supposed Ma had forgotten to store it away, rarely coming to the loft except to hang strings of beans and apples to dry. Not a word had she spoken about the wedding, except to say they'd gone and bid a blessing to the happy couple.

She lay a long time, trying not to think of Simon. Strangely, Lael felt homesick, her mind returning to Pigeon Ridge and Ma Horn's tiny, shady cabin. Up so high, the mountain air was blessedly cool in the evenings while the river valleys here below seemed gripped with fever.

Rolling over, she wiped her brow with the edge of a sheet and groped for her brush on the small shelf above. The mother-of-pearl handle conformed to her hand, a present from Pa from some trading post in Pennsylvania following one of his long hunts. The stiff bristles slid easily from her sunburned scalp to the silky ends, freshly washed and smelling of soft soap and lavender. Counting out her customary hundred strokes, she set the brush aside and began braiding the long length.

Let down your hair.

Would the memory of the Shawnee calling to her ever dim? Now that she was home, would they return? Were they watching her window even now? The moon, blessedly bright, cast gentle light on the cracked window frame. Her hands stilled on her half-finished braid, and she got up and edged closer to the opening. But it wasn't what she heard or saw that touched her with an icy finger of alarm.

It was what she sensed that scared her.

In two days' time, Pa came home with the finest horse Lael had ever seen. Black as night, the stallion high-stepped its way into the clearing and up to the cabin steps as if demanding introductions.

Ransom gaped from the cabin stoop, his grin wide and empty, having just eaten an apple that stole his two front teeth. "Where'd you get that fine animal?"

"Fort Harrod," Pa said, examining the horse's teeth.

"How much you trade for 'im?"

"I didn't trade. I paid," he replied, going along with the boy's attempt at manly banter.

"Who's he for?"

"The new teacher."

Ransom swung around to look at Lael where she sat paring apples on the porch. Pushing her displeasure down, she took a bite of apple and looked the other way.

"You mean you get to be my teacher," Ransom called to her, "and sass me all day long?"

Reluctant, she got up and fed an apple to the animal, admiring him despite herself. She needed a means to carry her to the settlement school, but a mule would have been sufficient. Looking on, she sensed this horse was high-spirited and intelligent and hard to handle.

"What's his name?" Ransom asked.

Pa shrugged and looked at Lael.

"His name is Pride," she stated matter-of-factly as if she'd been waiting to name him all her life. Beside her, Ma seemed to swell, already sitting on her high horse.

Aye, Pride, Lael mused, trying not to cry.

Pride goeth before a fall.

8

Fort Click stood staunch in the Indian summer sun, its outlying cornfields erect and baked a burnt brown from the waning heat. Above its massive gates her father's name had been carved for all to see, the letters as bold and roughhewn as the man himself. Despite this, Fort Click was more stranger than friend. Only in times of Indian attack did they grace its gates and live within its walls. The mischief the Shawnee had made coming to their cabin wasn't enough to send them there.

As she rode beside her father, Lael could see women carrying buckets to the spring between the fort's south wall and the river two hundred yards distant. The fort's massive gates, front and back, were open wide, the sentries at their posts. Inside the stockade, a dusty common divided rows of cramped cabins and at the far corners immense blockhouses loomed, their projecting second stories rife with gun holes. It was the southeast corner she knew best, having once lived there with the Hayes clan.

"Ezekial!" From every corner of the fort came greetings as folks hurried out to meet them. Lael was used to the fuss, even found it amusing, if maddening. Sometimes a simple errand kept them overnight as he was called upon to settle a dispute or discuss the war, sign some document or meet with settlement scouts.

She smiled, thinking it was good to be back among people, at least the ones who respected her father. But she herself soon drew a small crowd on account of her fine horse. The attention the stallion garnered stained her face an unflattering crimson, and she tried to hide behind the brim of her bonnet. She was none too comfortable in her dress, either.

Ma had insisted she look the part of the schoolteacher, even if she didn't feel like one. The moss-green fabric was overly warm and itchy against her skin, the kerchief at her neck so starched it could stand by itself. The dread in her heart deepened when she caught sight of the schoolhouse centered in the common. Rarely used of late except to store corn, it looked more like a coop with the chickens scratching about in the dirt yard before the door.

She could hear Harrison Hayes at work in the blacksmith's shop, and the sound buoyed her a bit. With a nod, Pa veered off toward its rough walls, taking Pride with him. She started toward the schoolhouse on foot, hoping to see Simon. He was frequently at the fort, Susanna told her, when he wasn't at work on his four hundred acres. It was this, and Ma's insistence that she take the position, that had finally swayed her.

Throwing open the schoolhouse door, she entered, only to be stung by the stifling heat. There were no windows to speak of, just a few log loopholes covered over with oiled paper, letting in precious little air and light. Despite the benches and one crude desk and chair, it was austere as could be. Some kind soul had cleaned it up in advance of her coming, but the smell of corn and hay still lingered.

This was the place she'd come as a little girl soon after Pa's capture. Susanna had been here—and Simon. A host of memories had been made within these walls, most of them bittersweet. Miss Mayella had been here, with her fancy dresses and her blue-veined hands. The smell of her perfume had been near to divine, and Lael remembered that she'd never raised her voice, not once.

A small noise startled her. She spun, her skirts grazing the dusty floor. Simon? *Nay.* The sight of an almost forgotten figure made her heart hammer a bit harder. Piper Cane. Piper had been here too, but she hadn't been a friend then . . . or now.

"Hello, Piper." The words seemed a bit strained, too forced to be friendly.

The young woman said nothing in reply, just pushed her small sisters toward the empty benches at the back of the room. They came forward, heads down, taking a seat. Try as she might, Lael couldn't recall their names. The Cane clan lived just beyond the fort's gates to the west, and the Clicks gave them a wide berth.

"I could hardly believe it when I heard. But here you are . . . the new teacher." Piper's voice was the same as it had been. A trifle high, still girlish. She'd simply grown taller, her once flat figure bewitchingly buxom, the peculiar shade of chestnut hair that marked all the Canes stacked like a beehive atop her head.

She looked past Lael as if remembering days gone by, her features pinched with displeasure. Lael swallowed down a bitter reply. Piper was likely carrying the Cane grudge against the Clicks to the grave. But Lael hardly blamed her. Piper had lost a beloved brother at the salt licks when Pa surrendered. And he'd never come back.

She stayed silent, relieved when other children started coming in, noisy as a flock of geese. She'd not even had to ring the bell. Piper soon slipped away and Lael went to the door, her hands full of a slate and stylus to count attendance. She smiled in remembrance as every girl dropped a curtsy and every boy bowed as they entered. Miss Mayella had once insisted on this, and though Lael had not thought to enforce it, the genteel custom lingered.

Fifteen pupils, most of them small. She turned and recounted primers, woefully short. When she swung back around, all were seated, dinner baskets tucked beneath the crude benches. Inside the small windowless room, she eyed the log loopholes and felt nearly suffocated. It was only nine o'clock. As the children spelled and read in unison, then chorused Scripture verses by teams just like she remembered from Miss Mayella's time, her mind wandered.

Each time she took her eyes off the boys at the back of the room there was a ruckus. She'd been warned about the Cane boys being lively, but on this first day she figured she'd have no trouble. They were too big for school, truly, and she'd turn them out if she had to. Ever since the salt licks the Canes had made trouble for the Clicks with their talk. Had their rancor followed her to the schoolhouse as well? Catching Hezekiah Cane's eye, she stared him down. He quieted and she continued the lesson.

At day's end, she drank deeply from the water dipper, unmindful of the dead rat at the bottom of the piggin. One obliging boy carried it out by its tail, just as he did the snake atop her desk the next day. She froze, mindful that the whole class looked on. Who was to blame for this piece of work? The only ones she could ascertain were guiltless were the smallest children on the front bench, the wee girls as fetching as a row of flowers.

Color high, her patience was fraying fast as thread. Her only salvation lay in knowing Ransom wasn't here to tell Ma and Pa about the trouble. Just that morning he'd come down with a toothache and Ma wrapped his swollen jaw with an onion poultice, insisting he stay behind.

Coe Cane snickered from the back row. The minutes dragged on, dwindling to the spelldown at day's end. She went to the door and studied the sky. The sun foretold one o'clock. If she dismissed school too soon, would anyone care? She reckoned there was no hurry. She wouldn't return home till week's end. She'd be staying with Widow Douglas, an arrangement Ma had made without telling her until just this morning. She'd simply handed her a knapsack of her belongings and said she'd see her in a few days' time, then hastily kissed her cheek. Though Ma never said so, Lael knew she was fearful of the Shawnees' return and thought sending Lael to the fort would remove the danger. But the brisk send-off hurt just the same.

She turned and surveyed her students, most of which were scratching at their slates . . . save two. Going to the back of the room, she rang the bell. On a slate atop her desk, misspelled but full of meanness, were scrawled two telling words.

Injun lover.

9

Lael plunged Pride into the dense woods east of Hackberry Ridge, putting as much distance between her and the fort as possible. Instead of being nearly befuddled by the beauty of late fall, the colorful maples and oaks she so loved left her cold. They shed their brilliant leaves despite her indifference, goaded by a bitter wind, and her simple cape was soon splashed with crimson and gold.

A storm was coming—she could smell the dampness—but she didn't dare start home. The musky, spicy shadows of the woods drew her in and she gave Pride his head, feeling she'd lost her own. For hours she wandered, so lost in thought that she paid no mind to the lengthening shadows and the sun's cold tilt to the west. All was quiet until a twig snapped a brittle warning.

At the sound she leaped off Pride and slipped behind the rotting top of a sycamore snag. Its bulk hid her well but the stallion followed, his shrill whinny exposing her. Breathless, she peered through the dead branches and her stomach seemed to drop away. An Indian pony? Its rider was yet obscured by brush, but the sudden sight of boots and breeches assured her this was no Shawnee. She got up from her hiding place and onto Pride's broad back in a rush, praying the rider would veer the other way, but he'd already heard her and was now headed straight for her. *Simon?* Of all the places she'd longed to meet him, here and now hadn't been among them.

Simon Hayes looked as smug as Lael had ever seen him.

Astride a horse nearly as fine as her own, he refused to let her pass on the narrow mountain path. The surprise she felt at meeting up with him and the pain of her present predicament nearly left her speechless.

"Kindly remove your hat," she said at last.

He paid her no mind. The dun-colored felt remained firmly in place. He leaned forward in the saddle, looking like he owned time and would take all he pleased. Dusk was falling fast, casting velvety shadows in all the nooks and crannies of the woods.

His grin was telling, even conspiratorial. "What's the buzzel?"

She stared at him, impatience etched across her every feature, and hated that her voice wavered. "What do you mean, what's the buzzel?"

He grinned. "The buzzel is Lael Click ousted the Cane boys from her schoolroom just yesterday after grabbing the two mongrels by the scruff of the neck and knocking their heads together, at which time she quit herself."

"Those Canes are copperheads!" she confessed, fighting tears. "I was plumb worn to a frazzle by their everlasting abuse. Besides, I'm a poor hand at teaching."

"How many days was it? Two? I could've told you that you don't belong in any schoolroom."

Stung, she stammered, "Wh-where do I belong?"

He removed his hat and placed it over his heart, though his eyes remained faintly mocking. "Up on my four hundred, Lael Click. Where else?"

Flushing to the soles of her moccasins, she averted her eyes, wondering if she could get around him and home. *Soon.* She reckoned he was even bolder now that he was alone with her. Rarely had she seen him looking so handsome. His powerful height was apparent even as he sat on his horse. And his eyes, a deep coffee brown, seemed almost to caress her. Though he fascinated her, he also frightened. She'd never before been alone with him, and she knew Pa wouldn't approve.

He replaced his hat. "I could have taken care of those Cane boys iffen you'd just asked me. Better me than you—and without all the tongue waggin' either."

She sighed. "So the news is all over the settlement."

His nod was curt. "You Clicks create all manner of tattle."

Pride snorted and took a skittish step back. Lael ached to leave. "I'd best get. I've yet to tell Pa."

The thought of the coming confrontation made her squirm. That she'd dallied a full day wandering hither and yon, only postponing their meeting, made it worse. What if Ma had heard the news already?

"I suppose now is a terrible time to propose," he told her, suddenly rueful.

She looked at him in wonder. Truly, he had no shame, wooing her as he did when he could see she was in a dither. It took all her nerve to return his flirtatious banter and say, "Your timin' needs work, Simon. But elopin' might sit better than my quittin'."

He grimaced. "I doubt it. I'd hate to stare down your pa's gun barrel once we jumped the broom. Besides, I can't marry someone I ain't never courted or even kissed."

She flushed and looked to the shadows. They'd both be benighted in the woods if they weren't careful, thereby heaping scandal upon scandal. She'd never before been kissed, and his talk of it turned her to mush.

"Reckon I'd best see you home," he said at last. "It wouldn't do to leave you out here alone. Some Indian'll steal that fine horse out from under you, or you atop it."

She shivered as a cool wind whipped up and he turned his horse around. Even in the shadows, Simon's hair was the russet of an autumn leaf. *'Twould make a fine scalp dangling from a painted scalp hoop and sold to the British for bounty*, she thought.

Their eyes darted to and fro as they rode single file. 'Twas a dangerous time to be about. At the edge of the cabin clearing they dismounted and he tried to kiss her. Butterfly-like, she eluded him, drawn to the lights of home.

"You'd best stay for supper," she called, her voice soft, tremulous.

But the shake of his head was adamant. "I'd sooner face a Shawnee war party than your pa tonight."

Behind them, Pa had come out onto the porch. Lael turned, feeling like she'd just set foot in a snare. Surely he could see the possessive way Simon held her arm . . . the late hour . . . Pride's lathered state.

A single command brought Ransom running. Without a word he reached for the reins and led Pride into the barn. Without so much as a backward glance, Simon rode away and left Lael to face her father alone.

Ma's heaviness of soul was reflected in her face. "You mean to tell me you up and quit teachin' here yesterday without so much as a word to me? And I've gone and spent your stipend from Virginia!"

Lael stood in the door frame, wilted by her mother's words. "I'll pay back the money, Ma, I promise."

"Your pa paid a small fortune for that fine horse you have. What about that? You fancy you'll pay that back too? And what of the gossip goin' round? I'll likely hear of my own daughter from that tittle-tattle Mercy Cane. And who on earth will take your place as teacher? Miss Mayella—"

"Enough, Sara," Pa said.

Worse than her ma's scolding was her pa's silence. As Ma spun away behind the hanging quilt wall that marked their bedroom, he stood by the cold hearth, arms crossed, face set like flint. He seemed to stare a hole right through her and her legs felt weak as wax.

"No doubt the Cane boys had it comin'," he finally said. "I never figured you for a teacher. My quarrel with you is your wanderin' in the woods. Don't think Captain Jack has forsaken his suit where you're concerned, Daughter. I've heard otherwise."

The warning sent a chill clean through her. Eyes wide and wet, her hand shot out and clutched the heavy fringe of his hunting shirt. "Pa, promise. Promise you'll come after me if—if he—"

He waited for her to finish, but she couldn't.

He simply said, "'Twould not be a bad life, Daughter."

At this, all the air went out of her.

He continued, so calm and quiet she thought she'd misheard. "Truth be told, I'd sooner see you with Captain Jack as Simon Hayes."

The hurtful words stilled her heart. Her hand fell away from the worn linen, but their eyes locked and held, hers full of unasked questions, his an unfathomable blue.

"Oh Pa . . . you don't mean . . ."

There was steel in his gaze and unmistakable warning. "Aye, Daughter, I do."

10

Lael wandered the river bottom like a broken compass, walking every which way but home. She knew Pa shadowed her, but she couldn't see him. Bonnetless and barefoot despite the first frost, she bore her ginseng bundle on her back with nary a thought for the money it would bring. Money enough to settle the stipend with Ma. Money enough to tuck away for a rainy day when a bit of frippery was called for.

But it wasn't these things she thought of. Her heart had been cut to pieces by Pa's strong words, his indictment of Simon Hayes. *'Twould not be a bad life, Daughter.* His whispered words followed her, stinging like a bee.

She hardly blinked when the ginseng she'd dug brought a king's price. Riding hard all the way home alongside her father, she soon deposited a kerchief of shillings in front of a surprised Ma. Without waiting for her to count the coins, Lael climbed the loft ladder and stuffed some of her belongings in a knapsack. When she came back down, her ma sat in her rocker, the money filling her apron.

'Twas a good time to go see Ma Horn, Lael decided. She hadn't mentioned her plan, but now, with all the chores of autumn done, perhaps she could rest a spell. Strings of dried apples and leather-britches beans hung from the rafters, crocks of crabapple jelly and cider cooled in the springhouse. The corn was cribbed and a new ash hopper stood in back of the cabin. Surely Ma couldn't think of another thing to hold her.

She passed onto the porch, stooping to kiss Ransom. The roses seemed to bid her good-bye. A bit faded, the canes all a-tangle, the blossoms drooped and spilled spent petals onto the worn porch planks. As she looked around, exasperation stabbed her. Where was Pa? She was ready to go, yet she hadn't asked his permission. Dare she simply go? Right now? By herself, if need be? After all, he couldn't remain her lifelong shadow.

"I'll be leavin' now, Ma. Tell Pa I'll be back shortly."

Ma said not a word.

A brilliant moon, round and white as a biscuit, dogged her as she walked high atop the ridge. She'd left Pride behind as a horse made altogether too much noise. She much preferred her own mended moccasins. Did her father follow on foot as well? Twice she whirled about, sure she heard him. But the woods would not give him up and remained silent and shadowed. She dared not think of Captain Jack.

All around her expansive outcroppings of rock wooed her to the very edges of eternity. Winded, she paused atop dizzying drops and gathered her breath. Far below, an occasional curl of smoke revealed a hidden cabin. Farther still, the Kentucke River was but a sliver of silver thread.

Strange how well one's eyes adjusted to the growing gloom, she mused, continuing long after dark. Nature seemed to be tucking itself in for the night, dwindling down as if sleepy. As she walked along the familiar trail she seemed to shed her burdens. Beneath the great cathedral of trees, the quiet seemed holy, not haunting. She found the place she and Pa had camped and bedded down beneath a sheltering sycamore before resuming her climb the next morning. Toward dusk the next day she found Ma Horn dragging a hemp sack and gathering pine knots off the forest floor.

"I've come to stay a spell," Lael told her.

She straightened, gleeful as a girl. "I've been wonderin' when you'd come back."

This time the door to the tiny cabin stayed shut against the coming cold. As Lael ate her supper of stale cornbread and cider, Ma Horn tossed two pine knots into the fireplace and lit up the whole room.

"I had to get away," Lael confessed between bites. "But I didn't tell where I was goin'."

Ma Horn chuckled. "That don't mean your pa didn't foller you up here."

Lael flushed, gullibility gone, and watched as Ma Horn unfolded her thin frame to pluck her pipe from the mantle overhead. Tobacco smoke soon perfumed the air, mingling with the earthy smell of roots and herbs. There was comfort in this old cabin, sparse and solitary though it was, and an absence of secrets, so unlike her own. Here truth lived in every corner. Ma Horn had no skeletons to speak of. She'd been right to come here, Lael thought, heartsore as she was.

Giving her a sidelong glance, Ma Horn ventured slowly, "Your ma still tetchy?"

Lael sighed and pushed her empty bowl away. "Tetchy as the day is long."

The old woman took a long draw on her pipe, her mouth pinched at the corners. "Sara's never been one for the wilderness."

The fire popped and called for another pine knot. Lael pitched one in but said nothing. Truly, her ma needed to return to the Carolinas, to be among civilized people, far removed from the savage. Lately her hot temper had mellowed to something far more troubling—a joyless resignation. It cast a pall over the cabin, wounding everyone within reach. Somehow it seemed to have even followed her here.

Ma Horn winked at her, lightening the mood. "I hear your ma keeps threatenin' to cut your hair but your pa won't let her."

"Ma fears it would make a fine scalp," she said wryly, touching her heavy braid. Slowly she wound the length of it around her wrists, imprisoning herself as she sat.

Ma Horn's thin face grew thoughtful as she crumbled more tobacco. "I don't think scalpin' is what Captain Jack has in mind."

Lael looked up. "We've seen no sign of him or any of them since the beads and the blanket."

"Oh, you ain't seen 'em, but they've been by all right. Your pa says Shawnee sign crisscrosses your place like a buffalo trace."

This almost made her smile, though the thought of being watched made her feel queer through and through. Like the beads and the blanket, the Indians were still there, just hidden. Come winter, what would Captain Jack do? He'd not linger long, she wagered, in woods that had shed their leaves and no longer sheltered him.

She took a deep breath and her green eyes reflected her disquiet. "Sometimes I think he'll not go away . . . till we meet."

Ma Horn merely nodded, no mirth left in her face. "Say the two of you was to come face to face, what would you do?"

Lael looked toward the fire, pensive. She'd pondered this very thing again and again without answer. The prospect was so terrifying it took her breath. *Never give way to fear in an Indian's sight.* She'd stood tall the first time, on the porch with Pa. But once she was alone . . . what then? Her fearless father had a very timid daughter. Shame spilled over her and she nearly flinched under Ma Horn's heavy gaze.

"I reckon I'd fall to the ground in a cowardly heap," she confessed.

Ma Horn shook her head slowly, her wrinkled face dark with warning. "Your pa would be dead if he done that. You got to stand, girl. No matter whether they kill you or capture you, you stay standin'."

Stay standing.

Lael pitched the last pine knot into the fire, the simple words echoing in her head and deepening the dread in her heart. As she readied for bed she thought she heard the haunting call of a mockingbird beyond the shuttered window. The sound sent a chill clean through her.

Hadn't Ma Horn once said a mockingbird's night song was a death token in disguise?

11

With autumn waning, Ma Horn moved to the fort for the winter and Pa brought Lael home. She stood in the cabin door, a linsey shawl about her shoulders but still barefoot as if to protest the coming cold. Wordlessly, she watched her father prepare to leave on a long hunt, stung by his calm deliberation. Somehow she'd thought he wouldn't go with the threat of the Shawnee still about them, yet she reckoned even she couldn't come between him and his love of the woods.

Since she was small and he'd taken to the woods for months on end, it was she who helped him pack what he needed for the long weeks away. She'd always hated leave-takings, and this day was proving especially difficult. Hanging her shawl on a peg by the door, she bit her lip to keep her composure and reached for his weapons.

Her fingers traced the familiar initials scrawled across his powder horn before she hung it from the strip just above his shot pouch. Fashioned by her own hands when she was ten, the leather was worn but sturdy enough to hold a chunk of lead for bullets, a brass mold for casting them, and flint and steel to start a fire.

Before her on the table, laid out like a surgeon's tools, were the items she now took stock of. A bit of jerky. A twist of tobacco and ginseng root. Mittens. Patch leather and an awl for mending moccasins. A tomahawk, his father's before him, shone sharp and smooth beside a sheathed hunting knife.

Quickly she caught up the new linsey-woolsey shirt, which Ma had woven and she herself had washed, and pressed it to her nose. The smell of linen, earthy yet so clean it smelled sweet, made her eyes water. Rolling it up, she reached for a wad of unspun tow with which to clean his rifle.

Done, she decided, wiping a hand across her eyes. Partings were painful as lancing a boil, and she was simply no good at them. Was it any wonder Ma and Ransom were nowhere to be seen? If she'd been a boy, she'd be packing up a tote of her own things beside his.

Passing onto the porch, she studied him as he readied his packhorses by the barn. When he returned come spring, the two animals would be heavily laden with furs and he himself nearly unrecognizable with a full beard, his long hair crying for a comb and a cutting. Once, when she was but five, he'd returned after half a year away and she'd hid in Ma's skirts to escape his strangeness. But the familiar smell of him, and his voice, deep as a well, eventually brought her around.

Always he brought her something back. A lace handkerchief. A biscuit mold. Flower seeds. A two-tined fork and jelly spoon. A painted paper fan. A metal tea caddie with a tiny lock. This time what would it be?

What if he never came back?

He stepped up onto the porch. What did one say upon parting, she wondered, perhaps once and for all?

Pa, watch your back.

Stay warm and dry.

Don't dally.

Already he looked strange to her, dressed as he was for the woods. Turning, she led him to the table and watched as he examined his weapons. The danger of his task, not understood by her before, now seemed fathomless. Yet his demeanor befuddled her; he might have been going on a simple Sunday stroll. She swallowed down her fears and went back out onto the porch.

In time he followed. Though he said not a word, he took her hand and pressed something into her palm, then folded her fingers tight around it. When he'd gone she opened her hand and saw a blur of blue beads.

With Pa away, they moved to the fort. In years past they'd simply stayed put at their own cabin and awaited his return, wrapped in a cocoon of snow. But this time, with no explanation given and none needed, he'd ordered them within Fort Click's picketed walls. There, Lael felt safe but strangled by the smallness of life.

Here, their cabin door did not need stout bars, and the leather latchstring could be left out in welcome. There was little to do but stand by the shuttered window and peer out on the wide common that separated the rows of cabins, always a hive of activity even in the cold. Grizzled trappers came and left, as did new settlers seeking shelter. Ma's dark mood eased noticeably as she sat and spun the hours away while Ransom wrestled with the boys and dogs outside. Copies of the *Virginia Gazette* were passed around as freely as gossip, reminding Lael of the paper no longer in her pocket. Its absence chafed at her a bit. She'd either misplaced it or lost it, perhaps in the mountains on the way to Ma Horn's.

The southeast blockhouse, home to the Hayes clan, was missing the two family members most important to her. With Susanna married and living over at Cozy Creek, and Simon up on his four hundred, Lael's memories of times shared were all she had. Curiously, there were no other girls near her age save Piper Cane. Now ensconced as the new teacher, Piper was often seen about the busy common. Each morning after breakfast, she strolled to the schoolhouse and rang the morning bell. Ransom went unwillingly, returning home to regale them with the day's events.

"Today Noah got switched twice and Louise cried in the corner again," he said between mouthfuls of biscuit. "Three more kids come in from Virginia, and Teacher said the fort's gettin' so crowded you can't cuss a cat without gettin' fur in your mouth."

Ma snorted, but Lael was not interested in schoolhouse antics. Though she escaped to Ma Horn's cabin at the fort as often as she dared, time hung heavy on her hands. She sought solace in the fort's store, which smelled of coffee beans and leather and snuff. She'd roam the dimly lit interior, her fingers never far from Simon's note, always alert for the sight or sound of him.

Soon the weather turned as nettlesome as her mood. Heavy sheets of rain kept her confined to the cabin, where she stitched on a sampler beneath Ma's watchful eye. Always she wondered how her father fared and when he'd return to take them home.

If he returned.

In the cramped loft by the light of a grease lamp, Lael penned a letter to Miss Mayella. The day before she'd mashed and boiled the hulls of walnuts, adding vinegar and salt until the mixture set and became brown ink. Now, taking up a crow quill, she dipped the tip into a small stone well and wrote in a clear hand:

Dear Miss Mayella,

It pleasured me greatly to receive your letter, though teaching did not turn out as I had hoped. I am well. There has been no Indian trouble for some time now . . .

She paused, blowing lightly at the ink. What reason could she give for quitting her post as teacher? She lay the quill aside and hugged her knees to her chest, shivering. Next to her Ransom lay lost in sleep, his breathing quiet and deep.

71

She took up the quill again, but the lamp smoked and went out. Leaving the unfinished letter on the floor, she climbed atop the corn-husk tick, wrinkling her nose at its rustling and hissing. She wondered if Simon had a fine feather one up on his four hundred, then quickly shut the thought away.

What had Widow Watson told her just yesterday? That Simon Hayes was sparking Piper Cane? He'd begun courting her at Susanna's wedding, the very one she'd missed. She felt bruised by this new knowledge—and betrayed. Though she'd kept her face carefully composed at the revelation, her heart had twisted with hurt. If true, she was doubly stung by his choice. Why Piper? Overripe as an Indian peach, she'd be more than willing to let him woo her.

When no one was looking, Lael had taken Simon's note and pitched it into the fire. The orange flames quickly reduced it to ashes, somehow solacing her. But her pocket, and her heart, felt strangely empty . . . but for the blue beads.

12

Restlessness clawed at Lael like a cat. With her chores done she was free to roam, though her allowable range was woefully short. The fort's front gates were ajar and the sentries a bit lackadaisical at their posts. The Shawnee weren't known to be winter raiders, and with Pa away, discipline among the militia was a bit lax. Still, they straightened when they saw her, as if something of his indomitable spirit shone through her and stood them at attention.

She and Ransom ventured out along the river, snug in heavy socks and scarves. It had rained the day before then turned bitter, and the world had frozen to crystal. Surely there was no sweeter sight than the river and grass and trees looking as hard and shiny as candy. They'd come out to cut branches of mountain laurel whose waxy leaves stayed green in winter. Though Ma had shaken her head at such high-minded notions, Lael was intent on trimming their tiny cabin from mantle to windowsill with greenery for the holiday.

They'd not wandered far from the fort, but they had tarried and their faces and hands grew pinched by the cold. The leaden sky seemed close enough to touch as they crested Hackberry Ridge. At their backs, the militia was drilling again, a jarring sound that spoke of coming conflict, at odds with Christmas peace.

When they returned half frozen to the cabin, Lael draped the laurel around the mantle's wide wooden shoulders then set about making tea. Still shivering, she ladled water into an iron kettle and hooked the handle onto the iron crane before swinging it back over the flame. The hearth was soon redolent with sassafras, the roots brewing up strong and pink. She set out three wooden mugs, then remembered Ma was next door at Ma Horn's winter cabin and Ransom had ventured outside once more to scrape with some boys. She hardly heard the knock on the door but felt it open, letting in a *whoosh* of bitter wind.

The bulky figure that filled the entryway made her turn her back at once. Unbidden, Widow Watson's words stiffened her spine and made the heat creep into her cheeks. Where was Ma when she needed her?

"I ain't seen you for two months and your backside is all the greetin' I get?"

The harsh words made her spin around, and her own pointed reply shot like small arrows through the cold cabin. "Truth be told, I'd as soon fill your hide with lead as look at you, Simon Hayes."

His mouth twisted wryly. "'Tis too cold for fightin' words, Lael. I'm comin' in, like it or not."

She could hardly stop him, nor could she keep herself from looking at him. His hair was freshly washed—she could tell by the way it curled and shone—and his buffalo coat was clean and new. He was staring at her, reminding her that she looked less than comely in her simple linsey shift and loose braid.

He shut the door with a decisive thud, watching as she took the kettle of tea off the fire and set it on the table. Good manners waged a silent war within her, but she couldn't bring herself to ask if he wanted a cup. Not with the new knowledge that festered in her heart.

Her voice, when it came again, was calm but pointed. "Been courtin'?"

He studied her for a long moment and said tersely, "She was handy, is all."

"Handy," she echoed. For a fleeting moment Lael felt sorry for Piper Cane. How was it to be handy to a man, like a second-best set of moccasins or an old mule?

"There ain't been nobody but you, if that's what you're wonderin'," he told her unflinchingly, eyes on her all the while.

"I was wonderin'."

"I merely danced with her a time or two. I never kissed her."

"That ain't sayin' much. You never kissed me . . ." Her voice trailed off in shame, and she couldn't look at him. Only a hussy would say such a thing. It seemed Ma crouched in a corner, watching her misspeak. He tossed his heavy robe onto a rocking chair and took a quick look about the cabin. When he strode up to her, she felt herself go limp.

She shivered again as he brushed back the wisps of hair around her face before placing his cold mouth on her warm one. But it was hardly the kiss she'd been hankering for.

"I ain't your sister, Simon," she chided, stepping back. Turning, she poured herself a cup of tea, surprised at her steady hand.

His silence delighted her. Speechless, he was. The remembrance of their meeting in the woods when *she'd* been the one at loose ends and he'd taunted her unmercifully was somehow set right.

"I'll be back tomorrow night, Lael Click, and you'd best be ready," he said, voice stern. "If you're not, I know somebody who is."

Turning her head slowly, she gave him a half smile. Her anger was thawing now, fast as a frozen puddle in spring.

At twilight the next day Simon came. Her back to the door, Ma sat spinning, seemingly unaware of his intentions. Lael hadn't told her he'd been by or that he had promised to come again.

He didn't enter, just motioned for her to follow. She slipped out quietly into the deepening dusk, oblivious to the cold. She'd not taken pains with her appearance lest she alert both Ma and Ransom, but her hair was freshly brushed and plaited and she'd sprinkled a bit of rosewater on her dress and wool cloak.

There were chaperones everywhere within the fort's walls—a melee of dogs and children, three women grinding corn, a group of militia men smoking and arguing politics near the smithy. All this was precisely what Simon meant to avoid, she guessed. Holding firmly to her hand, he hurried along the south wall until they'd slipped beyond to the back gate. She nearly balked at his boldness. What would Pa say?

Determination dogged his every stride. If his courting of her was to begin in earnest, his gait seemed to say, it would be well away from the eyes and ears of the fort.

At the river they slowed, not yet speaking, and when she saw the waiting canoe, a clump of bittersweet at its bow, she felt torn in two.

"Simon, I—" Her eyes fell on the bittersweet's burnt-orange beauty and then darted to the far shore. "What if there's trouble—"

He shook his head. "There'll be no trouble with the militia about, Lael."

Indeed, it seemed so. But more than Indians, it was her father that fretted her. Wouldn't it be just like him to watch her from the woods? And wouldn't the Indians warm to a challenge, making mischief in clear sight of the fort?

She watched as he untied the hemp rope that secured the boat to shore. Seated, the bittersweet in her lap, she studied him in the deepening darkness. A half moon peered over his left shoulder, turning the river silver white. Lael felt caught up in a dream of danger and delight.

She could not—would not—speak. The gentle slap and slice

of the paddles through the water propelled them quickly upriver, the moon following them all the while.

"Cat got your tongue?" he chided.

She bit her lip. "My pa will tan your hide—and mine—if there's trouble."

He grinned. "Assumin' there's any hide left to tan."

She shivered and turned her attention to the far bank, noting he wisely kept to the safe shore. Soon the river's shoals and bends grew unfamiliar to her, though apparently not to him. He rowed with a purpose, his eyes never leaving her face.

Have minutes passed—or hours?

All at once he stilled his paddling. "Look up yonder, Lael."

He gestured to something behind her, and she turned slightly so as not to rock the canoe. "Yonder where?"

"High on that ridge, above the mist."

She looked and understanding dawned. This was his ridge, his four hundred. Beyond the mist and moonlight she nearly expected to see a castle crowning the bluff, so great was her excitement. She sighed and her breath made a cloud in the cold air.

"I've got a cabin site staked out, but I aim to know how you want it set up."

"Set up?" she echoed.

"One room or two. A dogtrot or no."

A little thrill shot through her. She could feel his eyes on her though hers remained on the ridge. "Two big rooms," she said in a near whisper. "With a dogtrot betwixt them."

"Two hearths, then?"

"Aye, and a puncheon floor."

"Pine or white oak?"

"Pine," she said, a smile in her voice.

"How many windows?"

"Three each."

"A south porch?"

She turned back to him. "Aye, and a climbing rose all across it."

"Done."

Laying aside the paddles, he caught her hands in his and pulled her to him. Her knees came down on the bottom of the boat and she was wedged against him, bittersweet and all. Through the layers of her clothing and cloak—even through his own buffalo robe—she fancied she felt his heartbeat. Her own seemed stilled, as if what was about to happen was too much for her fledgling senses. A flurry of fancy words followed by fancy kisses.

And kiss her he did. She marveled at the smoky, musky scent of him and how his whiskers chafed her cheeks. These were no sisterly kisses, truly. She felt she would drown in their sweetness and lifted her face for more. When at last he drew away, she felt bereft.

"Run away with me—tonight."

Above them the brilliant moon beckoned, promising to light their way.

Her voice sounded queer and far off, weak with longing and despair. "No runnin' off like Ma done, Simon."

He looked at her for a long moment and she at him. *So be it*, his expression seemed to say. The pull of the paddles drew them back toward the fort against their will. A bevy of stars had come out, some as big as the beads in her pocket.

Did she look like she'd been kissed? Would Ma know just from the sight of her? The fort common was nearly empty now. Simon walked her to the cabin door but didn't touch her again. She slipped inside and found Ransom peering down at her from the loft, his eyes bright as a coon's. Ma was sound asleep in her chair.

Simon would be back for Christmas, he'd said, to court her and to kiss her yet again. Then, come spring, with the cabin nearly done, he would face her father.

78

13

To be sure, Lael thought, these were the finest pair of stockings she'd ever made. She finished them and lay them over her lap, glancing up as Ma placed two mince pies to cool on the cabin windowsill. Five pewter plates shone on the small table at the heart of the cabin, the centerpiece a jar of brandied peaches.

Lael looked about the room, wanting to fix the scene in her mind for always. A tumult of waxy green mountain laurel cascaded over the mantle. A right terrible waste, Ma had said, but it did look festive with Simon's bittersweet interspersed with it. The sight brought a blush to Lael's face even now as she recalled every detail of their row on the river together just two nights past.

With Pa away, Ma asked Simon to take Christmas dinner with them. Lael was glad yet wondered if he'd miss the merriment of the large Hayes clan. Pa didn't hold to such bedevilment as the Hayes clan was given to. His own Quaker boyhood nearly prevented him from celebrating Christmas altogether, for true Quakers dismissed the day as any other. But Ma insisted it be observed, if quietly, with Bible reading and singing hymns. Though it was just midday, fires were being lit on the common in advance of the fiddling. Earlier that day Rab Calloway had driven in a load of cider from his farm for the frolic, and old Amos, the fort fiddler, had sampled a barrel, eyes agleam.

Simon ate heartily of the turkey Ma Horn had roasted on a spit. There was corn pudding and potatoes, turnips and fried apples and a rectangle of johnnycake on a large wooden platter. Simon's mother had sent a flask of blackberry wine, and each of them, save Ransom, sampled its tart sweetness. By meal's end Lael felt a tad giddy, what with the overly warm cabin and Simon's hand on hers beneath the table.

His beloved nearness nearly made her rue her refusal to run away with him, especially since he'd just whispered that a preacher was within fort walls. A Christmas wedding seemed a fine thing but for Pa's warning words echoing in her ears. The thought of him returning home to find Simon as his son-in-law made her wince. Still, she wondered if he wouldn't get used to it given time.

Night was falling fast. Ransom got up to feed the turkey carcass to the pack of dogs outside. Beyond the cracked door, a keening wind blew. Simon leaned over and murmured something in her ear. His warm words smelled of blackberry wine but were lost in the commotion outside.

Ma was the first to the door. Ma Horn followed, her smoking pipe abandoned at the hearth. Absently, Lael remembered she'd not yet given Simon the socks she'd made. Now he was pushing away from the table at the queer noise made by the fort's dogs. Their mournful baying, at first distant, grew hellish.

Lael was the last one out of the cabin. A press of people were at the fort's gates, now rapidly swinging shut. Sensing trouble, Lael sought out Ransom. But it was too late. He'd already seen the sickening sight.

Lael stood nearly witless on the frozen ground. Coming at her was a woman—nay, a girl—her dress dark with dirt and blood. Even her chestnut hair was matted, partly covering her face in filthy strands. She was supported on both sides by members of the militia who righted her when she stumbled.

"It's a haint!" Ransom cried, darting behind Lael.

But this was no ghost. This, Lael realized with keen horror, was Piper Cane.

Ma Horn's cabin was suddenly a beehive of activity. The more capable women, Ma included, came in to tend the stricken girl, whereas a party of men, led by Colonel Corey, rode out of the fort. The bonfires were lit after all, but this was no celebration. Militia lined the pickets, peering through the gun holes, but no fiddle music was heard.

Dazed, Lael stood outside without her cloak, unmindful of anything but the wretched sight of the girl she'd never liked. Simon found her and set his own coat about her shoulders.

"The Canes were burned out—all killed but Piper," he told her. "Shawnee."

Stunned, she could only look at him. All killed but Piper. Mathias and Mercy Cane. The brothers Coe and Hezekiah. Two small sisters. And a baby—hadn't there been a baby?

"Poor Piper," she murmured.

"Lucky Piper. Out chasin' cows when death struck."

Ma called to Lael from the cabin door. Reluctantly she left him and turned to do Ma's bidding.

Inside, the women were bathing Piper, laboring to remove all physical traces of the hideous scene. The girl shivered as water and soft soap cascaded over her while she sat stiff as a corpse in an oaken tub. Her shaking didn't end when she was clothed in Lael's spare dress and moved to the fire, where Jane McFee combed out her hair. Dear Jane, who'd lost two husbands in the Indian wars, and whose old, usually steady hands now seemed to tremble.

Lael went to throw out the wash water, ashamed of her revulsion. No doubt the Shawnee had taken out their scalping knives before setting fire to the place. Was this what she'd come home and found? Lael blinked back hot tears. While there was no love lost between her and the Canes, seven people had perished. And one girl left destitute.

Colonel Corey and his party of scouts returned on the fifth day, having warned the nearby settlements. They'd tracked the winter raiders along the ancient Warrior's Trace to the Falls of the Ohio and no farther.

In Ma Horn's tiny cabin Piper Cane said not a word, just sat in the hickory rocker by the fire. A pall had been cast over any notion of courting. Lael was left to simply dream about her canoe ride with Simon and speak with him in snatches.

On New Year's Day, Piper Cane left Ma Horn's and saw the light of day. The dark-haired girl walked as slowly and unsteadily as an old woman across the common to the large blockhouse that was the Hayes' home, Simon's mother supporting her. For in the end it was the Hayes clan that took her in.

14

The snow came, transforming all that it touched, as if even nature wished to erase the bloody events at the Cane cabin. The massacre had cast a funereal pall over all, even as the snow in all its bright and silent beauty encased the pickets in ice and turned the river to silver.

Lael longed for Pa's return, her angst tinged with boredom and disbelief at what had befallen the settlement. With the Canes killed, the schoolhouse closed and all manner of people crowded into the fort, some families living two to a cabin, lest their fate be the same.

With so many people present, Ma Horn was never idle. Though her abode was even smaller than her cabin atop Pigeon Ridge, she crammed each corner and crevice with healing herbs. As winter set in, the grippe seemed to visit every family, and even Lael herself took to bed with a fever, burning up and shivering by turns beneath a Star of Bethlehem quilt. Ma Horn poured all manner of tea and tincture down her, and on the fourth day she arose, ready to resume her chores.

As she stood over a log trough full of rainwater under the cabin's eave, stirring in wood ashes to make washing suds, there came a commotion at the front gate.

Two men hobbled past the sentry and stood just within the fort's walls. Within minutes a crowd began to gather and frightful weeping could be heard. Lael hung back even as Ma pressed forward. Though hardly recognizable after more than six years away, two more men taken captive with her father at the salt licks had finally come home.

⟨⟩⟨⟩⟨⟩

Strange, Lael thought, how the Click clan could never seem to get shed of the past and all its secrets. Standing at the back of the crowd, she saw nothing familiar about the half-starved, barely clothed men before her, their bare feet scalded from walking the many miles from the British stronghold of Detroit.

Because the men's families had long since given them up for dead and returned east, they were now without kin or cabin. It was Ma Horn who took them in, burning their louse-ridden clothes and cutting their long hair before doing so. Once they'd shaved and bathed, Ma brought a tray of stew, bread, and cider to their door. But the men demanded whiskey and a meeting with Pa and the fort's leaders, most of whom were away scouting and hunting.

Ma Horn plied the men's frazzled forms with moonshine and tinctures and kept them to their beds, allowing them but one or two visitors at a time. Weak and sickly though they were, Hugh McClary and John Watson were a huge curiosity, drawing every last man to the tiny cabin to rehash the events of the last six years.

"Let them talk. 'Tis a tonic in itself," the old woman said.

But Lael sensed trouble. Within days of their return, as Ezekial's name grew more muddied, there was renewed talk of renaming the fort. Hugh McClary spoke out most strongly in favor of the notion.

Ma snorted when she heard the news. "I suppose he's callin' it Fort McClary already," she retorted bitterly before returning to her spinning.

Now, years after the fact, Pa's name was again being tied to treason. Long forgotten was his court-martial and subsequent exoneration. Yet McClary refused to let the past rest. No one truly knew what happened at the salt licks all those years before, he argued. Who was to say even now that the absent Click wasn't out working with the Indians and British to bring about their doom?

Lael could hear him loud and clear in the evenings as they shared an end wall with Ma Horn's cabin. When others came to visit the two recuperating captives, raised voices could be heard through the log wall. Though Ma said nothing, Lael could not stand the idle chatter. Yet where could she go except to stand out in the snow?

The fort seemed to churn and foment in Pa's absence. Though McClary and Watson made plans to return to their families in Pennsylvania, they were far from well and could not travel. As long as McClary remained, his ill will permeated and poisoned the fort. Lael had long watched her father outwit the smartest men and smooth all manner of ruffled feathers. Their present predicament begged for a cool head and restraining hand.

Oh Pa, come home, wherever you are.

Lael knocked then pushed open the door of Ma Horn's, careful not to upset the heavy tray she carried. With Ma abed with the grippe, it fell to Lael to fix supper for the invalid men and serve it, and tonight Ma Horn was nowhere to be seen.

From the shadows Hugh McClary stared at her, his emaciated face more skeleton than whiskers. John Watson nodded her way in friendly fashion, then looked away as if embarrassed to be seen in his bed clothes.

"Ain't you Zeke Click's daughter?" McClary said. "You look some like him."

"Leave her be," Watson warned from his bed.

The smell of sickness and herbs hung about the room. Lael remembered someone saying McClary had lung fever and the French pox. Ma had blushed scarlet at this, though Lael didn't know what it meant. Maybe the sickness made him mean. Carefully, she approached the table and set down the tray. The aroma of hot hominy and pork gravy made her mouth water.

"I ain't eatin' nothin' from the hand o' no traitor," McClary continued, thrashing on his pallet.

"She ain't no traitor, you idiot! Her pa saved your hide at the salt licks," Watson said, struggling to sit up.

"That Injun lover! He saved hisself, turnin' Shawnee while we sat rottin' in some British prison six years. I'm surprised he come back here after fallin' in with Chief Blackfish. All that talk about bein' adopted turns my stomach."

"The talk's true," Watson said, breaking into a sweat from the sheer exertion of sitting up.

"I'll tell you what's true . . ."

Lael began backing up toward the door. *Where was Ma Horn?*

"The truth is there's more than one blue-eyed Injun brat beyond the Falls of the Ohio where Zeke Click's concerned."

Lael turned and fled the cabin, leaving the door wide open in her wake. The cold night air assaulted her senses as she ran through crusty snow, stopping just inside the stockade where she hid in a dark corner. Sliding down against the frozen pickets, she buried her face in her apron, but no tears came. Truly, she was beyond tears. Her small world, made up primarily of her pa and unsettled as it was, seemed to unravel fast as twine.

She knew what McClary meant. Just lately she'd begun to wonder herself. While Ma dallied with Uncle Neddy, did Pa not do the same in the Indian villages? Had Chief Blackfish not only adopted him as a son but presented him with an Indian bride? Two years was a long time to be away. Had he fathered other children besides her? "Blue-eyed brats," McClary had called them. If so, how did he know, imprisoned as he'd been in Detroit?

'Twould not be a bad life, Daughter.

Suddenly Pa's words took on new meaning. Perhaps he'd found the Indian life very good indeed.

15

The snow continued, turning the fort to ice. Even Ransom grew restless, tired of playing on the cold common.

"Ain't Pa ever gonna come back?" he asked.

"Soon," Lael reassured him, beginning to wonder herself. She had a fierce hankering to see Susanna in her new home and hear if the rumors about her expecting a baby were true. Mostly she longed to escape fort walls, for her run-in with Hugh McClary dogged her like a black shadow.

Even Ma seemed to sense her restlessness. "Now's as good a time as any to teach you how to spin flax," she said, "since you're done knitting those socks for Simon and your pa."

"I'm no good at spinning, Ma," she lamented. She took up another hank of yarn and remembered what Ransom had overheard hanging around the blacksmith's shop. Simon was up on his four hundred again, and she'd heard that with the help of Neddy, his nearest neighbor, he was at work building a cabin.

Their cabin.

Come spring, would she be there? Come spring, what would he say to Pa?

But spring seemed years away. With the Canes buried but two weeks and Piper in seclusion in the Hayes' blockhouse, time seemed to stand still, frozen into place by snow and the sameness of fort life. Even McClary's unending chatter seemed ground down by fatigue. Not so many men came by Ma Horn's cabin these days.

"I'd be obliged if you'd help me make some shoepacs," Lael told her ma once she'd stopped her spinning.

Using strips of sturdy whang leather, they sewed high tops onto her moccasins and lined them with otter fur, creating snug shoepacs. Next she knitted herself stockings, and Ma made her a large linsey shawl, which she folded into a triangle and draped around her shoulders for warmth. A shapeless fur hat made from beaver pelts replaced her limp summer bonnet. At last, in a heavy dress dyed butternut brown, she could face the cold as often as she pleased.

But there was nowhere to go beyond the fort's four walls. Fear kept them all inside, the fate of the Canes an ugly reminder of what likely awaited any who wandered.

Was this how Pa felt within the crowded, fetid fort that bore his name? There seemed no greater punishment, Lael reckoned, than to be confined to the company of a passel of people crammed together in close quarters. As each day dawned and ebbed, she longed for wide open spaces where she could draw an easy breath, but fear kept the fort gates locked tight.

Standing along a high wall, peering out a gun hole toward the frozen river, its surface a gunmetal gray, she pondered the fear that had shadowed her for fourteen years, just as it had most who'd ventured over the Cumberland into Kentucke. She wondered if it would dog her all her days. If Pa wrestled with fear, she never knew it. Perhaps that was why his name was chiseled above the front gates. Even the Indians made no secret of their admiration for him. Indeed, their respect ran so deep it extended to her, a cowardly, would-be woman.

Pa would not trade freedom for fear, so why should she? Her father's blood ran in her veins. Might hers not contain a bit of boldness besides? Would she one day look back and regret a life of stepping carefully? Was it not a form of slavery?

Aye, she would rather die than sit here another day.

Quietly, so furtively as to be almost Indian-like, she unhobbled Pride and led him to the fort's back gates. The sentry on watch simply stared at her.

"Please open the gate, sir. I wish to pass."

She didn't know his name, but he knew hers. Behind his brushy beard his brogue was thick with Ireland. "Miss Click, what would your father be sayin' to that?"

She nearly smiled. "I think he'd ask what took me so long."

For a fleeting moment she thought he would deny her. Then turning a wary eye past his post, he unbarred the massive gates and cracked them just enough to let her pass. Thanking him, she got up on Pride's bare back, her fingers embedded in his thick mane, and rode out.

When the gates thudded shut behind her and the bolt slid into place, she had but one fleeting moment of terror. Dawn painted the sky with sepia light. She wanted no onlookers on this, her first foray into newfound freedom.

Heading east, she followed the sun. Pride seemed as exhilarated as she, kicking up snow and snorting wildly. Once she lost her shawl and went back for it, knotting it so that it would stay put about her shoulders. Strangely, she wasn't cold. Beneath her fur hat, one plump straw-colored plait hung down her back to the horse's belly.

Soon she stood in a clearing. A blackened cabin and a once proud cornfield had been reduced to soot and stubble, as if a great unruly beast had stomped the cabin and crushed it, then gobbled up the corn with a fiery breath. Only the chimney of gray river rock remained. All around her the grass was still scorched save for a gentle rise to the west where a stately maple shaded seven mounds of earth and rock. Gravesites. This was the work of the Shawnee.

At Cozy Creek she took some parched corn from her pocket, her fingers pausing to caress the blue beads. As she ate, she moved out of the dark woods into a clearing where the sun worked to thaw the winter ground. A joree bird wintering in the valley called to her. *To-wee . . . to-wee.* She whistled back, a shrill sound in the stillness.

As she róde she scarcely passed a single cabin belching smoke. Their own sat silent and shivering against the snowy ridge, giving her a twinge of homesickness. Some folks, like Uncle Neddy, stayed put in times of trouble, but most fled to the fort. She crested Hackberry Ridge and reluctantly rode down to the fort in time to help with supper.

"Mush again?" Ransom whined.

She served him anyway, weary of the sight herself. When would Pa return with fresh meat? Their store of salt was dwindling and she feared she was about to go stockade-crazy.

Swallowing a sigh, she removed the kettle from the fire and poured two cups of black bohea. Poking around in the cupboard produced no long-sweetening, and so they were left to choke down the bitter brew plain. The cabin was all too still. Ma had been quiet all evening and had not resumed her spinning, and Lael missed the familiar whirr of the wheel. She was prepared for some protest about her wandering beyond fort walls, and so it didn't surprise her when her mother started in.

"I wondered how long it would be before you went the way of your father." There was weary resignation in her words and a kind of bewilderment in her eyes. "Nothing on earth could tempt me beyond these walls, yet you seem drawn to it. I can't stop your wanderin', but I wonder what I'll tell your pa when you don't come back."

"Tell him you just can't pin a Click down," Lael answered matter-of-factly, though she felt sudden sympathy for her mother sitting there hunkered down, so small and weary and worn. Was this what fear did?

As for herself, she felt alive, renewed, about to leap out of her chair. Tomorrow beckoned, promising untold pleasures and wonders.

Where would she go?

Oh, but it was a fine thing to be free. Standing atop Moccasin Knob, where eagles soared, the world was at her feet. Throwing her arms wide, Lael twirled around atop the knob like a toy top, spinning and whirling until dizziness slowed her. The snow had melted and the sun, as if emboldened by her antics, shone forth in a cloudless sky.

Heading west, she traversed Log Lick Trace, soon walking on unfamiliar ground, the going a muddy mess what with the sudden thaw. She could make more than twenty miles in a day on rough ground but knew Pa could go farther. She imagined meeting up with him and fancied seeing surprise and admiration in his keen blue eyes. But never anger.

The clear day beckoned her on, made her bold. At last she came to Muddy Creek, a place she'd been warned away from her whole life. Indian sign was nearly always to be found there. A crude cross on a low rise marked the site, a silent reminder of the massacre three years past that befell a party of settlers who had pushed too far into Indian territory.

Pausing with the sun at her back, she studied the scene and said a quick prayer for peace. Not six steps later she came across the first Indian sign. Instead of fleeing, she followed it clear to the mouth of the Red River where the footprints ended.

Retreating, she fairly ran back to the fort, dusk at her heels.

No longer did the sentries look long after her and shake their heads. She smiled at the stir she'd created. Wasn't it a wonderment, some said, how Lael Click could wander unmolested in the very woods where they themselves would likely be hacked to pieces? Aye, the legend of her father seemed even to follow her.

16

Common sense told Lael it was time she began carrying a gun on her forays. Gathering the ginseng money she'd saved, she went to the fort sutler and exchanged her shillings for a flintlock rifle and a good supply of powder and shot. Ransom looked on with awe, as the rifle was taller than he.

For once Lael was glad the good Lord had made her a tall woman. The rifle was lighter than Pa's own, the stock made of hard maple and blackened with soot. Best yet, she could ready it for immediate use, though learning to load it in good time proved a challenge. She'd watched Pa countless times measure a charge from his powder horn into the muzzle, then ramrod the bullet to the bottom of the bore. She recollected how easily he primed the lock with a little powder before closing the pan cover and cocking the lock, readying it in under a minute. He was the only man she knew who could reload on the run.

"I bet you can't shoot that thing," Ransom said sleepily, watching her from the loft.

The cabin was quiet save the two of them. Ma had gone visiting and now, left to themselves, they could say what they pleased.

"Pa showed me how when I turned twelve," she said. "But I've hardly fired one."

"I heard tell Jane McFee can stand up to a gun hole good as any man."

"You heard right." Truly, Jane McFee, now approaching sixty, had a man's hand with a gun. Lael longed to be like her, though she didn't know if she could shoot to kill.

"I reckon you could pick off a painter pretty quick." Ransom scratched his head as if thinking. "Maybe a bear too."

She took up a rag and began polishing the stock. An animal was the least of her concerns, but she didn't say so.

Ransom rambled on. "You see Simon? He come in just today, but you was gone. He disbelieved me when I told him you were on one of your rambles."

Simon? Here? Getting up, she stepped to the shutter and looked across the common to the Hayes' blockhouse where a window was etched in yellow light. How did Simon and Piper Cane fare in the same cabin? she wondered. Piper hadn't yet come out of seclusion. Ma Horn said she sat silent in a chair with nary a word to anyone. Lael pitied her plight. Would Simon amuse her, make her laugh? No matter. Simon was safe within fort walls, and she'd no doubt see him come morning.

At dawn the militia drilled then took a brief rest before again picking up their guns. A line of men snaked across the cold common, each bearing a rifle. At the end of the line stood Lael, at first merely curious about their marksmanship. She noted the various men, their different weapons and how each was handled. Simon, ahead of her, seemed oblivious to her presence.

Several men hooted when old Amos, the fort fiddler, rolled out a charred keg of whiskey. So this was the coveted prize, she surmised. Colonel Corey set up a target just outside the fort's gates, facing the river. Here the riflemen could be heard and seen by any enemy. Yet at the first sign of trouble, the men could easily slip back into the fort.

"Now, watch this, little miss," said the grizzled woodsman ahead of Lael. "Colonel Corey can put nineteen bullets out of twenty within an inch of a nail. Not a man can best 'im but your pa."

Indeed, in addition to Colonel Corey's fine manners, he was good with a gun. He hit the nail on the head nearly every time, finishing and taking his place behind her in line. When he saw her, his eyes registered surprised pleasure, and he swept off his hat, taking her cold, callused hand and bringing it lightly to his lips. She smiled a rare smile, revealing even white teeth, then placed her hand back into her pocket beside the blue beads.

"To what do we owe the pleasure of your company, Miss Click?"

"To your fine marksmanship, Colonel," she said simply, untried at the art of flirtation.

"The noise of the guns does not annoy you?"

"Nay, I'm afraid I've been hearing them my whole life."

His eyes fell on her rifle. "Would you care to try your weapon? I can assist you."

"Aye, thank you kindly."

His eyes lingered on her face—a tad overlong, she thought. Behind them now, Simon stewed, his face a study of anger and disbelief. Anger at the colonel's attentions? Surprise at her presence?

The men no longer kept to single file. When it was her turn, they fanned out about her, clearly intrigued by her presence. Standing beside her, Colonel Corey made several suggestions. Listening carefully, her range about sixty yards, she cocked the lock, then fired. Her aim was a bit high.

"Try again," said the colonel kindly. "My own men get three attempts."

And so, feet splayed to steady herself, she reloaded and fired again. A hush fell over the men upon the discharge. The post shook as she hit the target dead center. Even Colonel Corey, schooled in deadpan, looked astonished. A cheer went up from the men, all save Simon. She flushed, aware of the recoil's hearty kick and the ensuing smoke.

"Excellent. Now again," the colonel encouraged.

She obliged, reloading in less than a minute. Drawing a steadying breath, she fired a final time. Again, she hit the target's center.

When the applause had died down, Colonel Corey said, "You seem to have your father's unerring eye and arm. Please, join us for a drink."

And so she did, but only a sip. The potent brew, relished by the men, burned her throat and befuddled her senses. Thanking the colonel, she soon departed to her own cabin, aware that many of the fort's women were watching her. Even Piper Cane—could it be?—stood looking at her from an open blockhouse window.

"Ma says you're gettin' too big for your britches," Ransom told her in the empty cabin.

"They may be big, but they ain't bored."

"Is it true you hit them targets dead on two out of three times? I reckon even Pa would be proud of that."

"Eat your mush and hush."

Already she was planning her next foray, this time with her rifle. The security of it would let her roam a bit farther, perhaps overnight somewhere. She had a notion to head toward Bullitt's Lick but dared not give voice to this piece of rashness. Farther west, this isolated post led to the Falls of the Ohio and rarely passed a peaceful day. But with Pride and her rifle she would attempt it.

Still, Ma's words rang a warning in her ears: *I wonder what I'll tell your pa when you don't come back.*

A knock, hard and loud, sounded at the door. Ransom opened it to reveal Simon, his head bent to get in the door frame. As if sensing a coming conflict, Ransom scampered squirrel-like past Simon's legs out the door. Lael stood, her supper unfinished. In the stuffy air of the cabin she smelled liquor, so strong it seemed Simon had been pickled in it.

"I've come courtin'," he announced, kicking the door shut with his boot.

She eyed him warily, thinking how Colonel Corey's fine manners jarred sourly with this show of brutishness. "Well, you can leave your whiskey behind next time," she chided.

Stepping deeper into the dimly lit room, he tripped over the leg of a rocking chair then clumsily righted himself.

Stifling a laugh, Lael put one hand over her mouth. "You shouldn't be here, Simon. At least leave the door open. Folks'll talk."

His head came up. "Tongues are already waggin' about your wild ways. Openin' the door won't stop 'em." He sat down abruptly and ran a hand over the stubble of a two-day beard. "I ride in yesterday and all I hear is 'Lael Click done this' and 'Lael Click done that.' Your pa better come back soon and rein you in since your ma can't. My pa says Colonel Corey is so besotted with you he commands his men to open the gates for you day and night."

Lael moved to put more wood on the fire and opened the door nonetheless. Arms crossed, she said a trifle testily, "You're just sore because I'm the better shot."

His scowl intensified. "Beginner's luck, is all."

She poked at the fire with an iron rod. "How's the cabin comin'?"

"Slow, what with the snow and all, but it'll be done come spring. I ain't changed my mind where you're concerned, Lael Click. You're raisin' such a ruckus, I figure your pa'll just plain give you to me to get shed of you himself."

She laughed outright at this then sobered. "See any fresh Indian sign up your way?"

"Some horses were stole from Pogue's place."

"How's Piper?"

"Poorly."

Clearly, he was in no mood for sober conversation. Lael turned and there in the open doorway stood Ma Horn. From the look on her face as she surveyed Simon, Lael gathered she felt the same about him as did Pa. Without acknowledging him, she came into the room. Simon stood unsteadily and left with nary a word. Perhaps their dislike was mutual then.

"This here herb bundle's for Neddy. I have a feelin' he's poorly," she said, shutting the door. "Will you take it to him on your next ramble?"

"Aye, in the morning." Gladness washed over her. Obviously, Ma Horn didn't mind her going.

Her aged face creased with a knowing smile and she said, "Whenever I see you set out, I just say a little prayer. Just remember, won't nothin' ever befall you that the good Lord don't allow."

High up on Neddy's homestead, Lael didn't return to the fort until suppertime the second day. When she entered the cabin, both Ransom and Ma nearly fell on her, their relief was so great.

"I was about to call out the militia," said Ma in scolding fashion.

"No need," Lael said, depositing her saddlebags and rifle by the door. "I've just been to see Uncle Neddy."

Her mother's mouth dropped open.

She sashayed past, removing her heavy cloak and hat. "He's just fine, in case you're wonderin'."

Truly, Uncle Neddy had seemed pleased as punch to see her, weak as he was. They'd broken bread together and then, as evening set in, the fever took him, and Lael stayed to nurse him through the night. The boneset tea she'd brought seemed to help, and by noon the next day he was up and around again. When she left, he insisted she take a crock of long-sweetening for her trouble, which, she replied, had been no trouble at all.

She deposited the crock on the table in front of a stunned Ma. Neddy's name had not been mentioned between them for years, and Lael, for one, was glad to break the silence. Without another word, she washed up and wearily climbed the loft ladder to bed.

17

Surely Pa would be home soon.

Lael pushed farther into forbidden territory. Drowning Creek. Log Lick Trace. The Little Muddy River. On a day edged with frost, she came upon a hackberry tree that bore his initials deep within its bark. *EEC. February 22, 1778.* Just two days past. At the sight, she knew her wandering days were almost over.

Homesick for him, her cold fingers traced the familiar lettering in the rough trunk. For just a moment she forgot where she was, deep in the heart of the dangerous Warrior's Trace.

The movement that stirred the stand of mountain laurel at her back failed to warn, and the Shawnee surrounded her in a sudden ghostly circle. Pa's words of warning echoed thunderously in her ears. *Never give way to fear in an Indian's sight.* Her head came up, but her rifle was leaden in her arms, primed and cocked but useless. All six Shawnee had tomahawks in hand. By the time she could draw a bead, her head would be split open wider than a watermelon.

The warriors circled her, their expressions sober, head feathers a-dance in the winter wind. Six sets of eyes held unmistakable warning. Already she felt shackled, though they hadn't laid a hand on her. The fear that they might made her bold.

She made straight for the smallest brave, the butt end of her rifle pointed like a battering ram at his belly. The impact nearly toppled her, but she got past him. Dropping her gun, a wildness seemed to possess her and she ran like fire across the forest floor, leaping over bushes and around trees, her dress hardly slowing her.

At her heels came a tall warrior, playing a fast and furious game. He'd dropped his buffalo robe the same instant she'd dropped her rifle, the thrill of pursuit in his every step. His terrifying footfall seemed to shake the very treetops. He was only toying with her, she knew, and would soon overtake her. Her lungs were near bursting—she vowed she would die before she let him touch her—but if she kept on going she'd run right into the ground.

Stay standing.

Another leap over a half-frozen creek and she swung around, chest heaving. Graceful as a bull elk, he slowed, his moccasins digging deep into the wintry ground. When he faced her, she saw that he was hardly winded. Now close enough to touch her, he did just that. His rough fingers skimmed her trembling jaw. No malice marred his striking features. His startling eyes, green as her own, told her it was him.

Captain Jack.

She felt woozy with fear and fascination.

"Click's daughter," he said easily, then pointed to her pocket.

What? How did he know she kept the beads near at hand? Startled, she reached down, her eyes never leaving his face, and pulled out her treasure. They nested like a bounty of robin's eggs in her open, trembling hand. At the sight of them a satisfied smile softened his intensity.

Taking the beads, he returned them to her pocket. Hungrily, his eyes roamed her vulnerable face, lingering on her unkempt hair and parted mouth as if measuring every ragged breath she took. He reached for her hand ever so slowly, as if she might take wing and fly away from him.

She would not, could not, look away from him. The pressure of his palm against hers . . . the raw strength of him . . . the unclouded invitation in his eyes . . .

A guffaw, rude and loud, broke the spell. As the other warriors reached them, Lael moved to stand in Captain Jack's shadow. Still, he didn't release her hand. Warily, her eyes swept the circle of Shawnee, then stopped cold at a familiar figure.

Pa!

Her shock was so apparent, the Indians erupted in laughter. Suddenly it all came clear. He'd been with them from the first. And he meant to teach her a lesson. Was this his punishment for her wandering ways?

Yelping, Nip and Tuck came forward to sniff her skirts. Sheepish, she eyed the Indian she'd nearly gutted and saw he held her rifle.

"Howdy-do, Daughter," Pa called.

At this, the Indians laughed harder, all but Captain Jack. Letting go of her, he took her father aside. His impassioned words were in Shawnee, but his intent was clear. The tall warrior was arguing to have her. The strangeness of this struck her. She and her pa were outnumbered six to two and could easily be overtaken if the Indians so desired.

She stood staring at her pa, so bearded he was almost unrecognizable. Captain Jack gestured to her, his movements graceful and pleasing. She longed with a deep gnawing to know what it was they said, but she made herself look away and down at her moccasins, one of which had torn and was unraveling.

Standing in the midst of these hardy, tawny men, she felt a smidgen of what her father seemed to feel for them. Admiration. Envy. Awe. Her own reserve began thawing as Captain Jack took her to a little clearing, well away from the others, and they worked together to make a fire. Still, she felt a tremor of unease. This was a white man, she reminded herself, despite his buckskin and feathers and thorough Shawnee manner.

"You were not much afraid when I went after you," he said with a little smile.

"Oh, I was afraid," she confessed, picking up some pine knots. "But then I saw that it was you . . ."

"I see your father in your face, and that is good," he told her. "You have his courage. We were glad to find him hunting today."

A flicker of alarm lit her eyes. "You mean him no harm?"

He straightened to his full height and looked down at her. "He means us no harm, so we are at peace. Among our people he is *nenothtu oukimah*, a great chief."

"But I've heard—"

"You have heard that the Shawnee kill escaped captives once they are found?" His eyes held hers steadfastly. "Lesser men, yes. But not your father."

Considering his words, she held her cold hands toward the curling orange flames, finding it hard to look away from him. Here was one of the men who had taken Pa from her years ago, yet her heart twisted with empathy when she thought of how he too had been torn from another life.

"I have so many questions," she said quietly, eyes on the fire. "About you." *About the past*, she thought, looking over her shoulder to where her father stood speaking with the other Shawnee.

Captain Jack nodded as if he understood, and patiently coaxed the fire into a golden glow of warmth and light. His response shot such hope into her heart that she had to turn away lest he see the tears shining in her eyes. A bit of her nervousness eased, and she began to enjoy this strange and wondrous twilight, thrilled with Pa's sudden return.

The cold deepened and a light snow began to fall. The Shawnee began studying the sky, talking among themselves. While they made camp, Pa left to hunt. She watched him go, her high spirits suddenly sinking like stone. What if he returned and they'd taken her away? But he soon came back with a deer, which she helped skin and dress then roast over a generous fire.

'Twas a strange supper, sitting like the guests of honor, while the Shawnee passed the choicest pieces of meat to her father and herself. Her cold fingers took the venison hungrily, and she was careful not to let the juices run down her chin. Not a scrap of meat remained after their feast and then the dogs gnawed on the bones.

Afterward, in the firelight, she mended her moccasin with an awl and sinew, aware of Captain Jack's eyes on her. He was, she decided, as smitten with her as Simon was. She found the attention more pleasing than provoking and was drawn to his quiet confidence and easy manner.

"Not this . . . *this.*" Captain Jack took the shoe from her, his voice low and gentle.

How old could he be, truly? Thirty or better, she guessed. As he worked, she let her eyes linger on the fine lines of his face. Not a trace of the white man remained. With patient hands, he showed her how to double loop and tie the string to better bind the worn leather. As she watched, one brave called out something in jest and Captain Jack hurled her moccasin at him across the fire.

They were teasing him for all his attention to her, she knew. Smiling, she glanced at Pa, but he was relating some story in Shawnee to the man beside him. Her ears warmed to the talk and laughter all around. The camaraderie thickened as the night deepened. 'Twas harder and harder to hold her eyes open. Twice her head tilted and hit Captain Jack's hard shoulder, but he didn't seem to mind, nor did she.

Bedtime found her rolled in a blanket, feet to the fire. A hundred unasked and unanswered questions lodged in her breast, seeming to multiply by the minute. Never in her life had she felt so queer, wedged between Captain Jack and her father in a tight circle of Shawnee. Her last thought before she surrendered to sleep pinked her cheeks.

What would her mother say to see her so? Or Simon?

When she awoke, the Indians were gone. Had she only dreamt it? Nay, the ground where they had bedded down told her it was true. Only she and Pa remained. A fierce longing to have them back swept through her, at odds with her relief at finding them gone.

She said aloud, "That was the queerest night I ever spent, wonderin' if I'd wake up captive or free."

Pa looked up from reloading his rifle. "Best be gone before they change their minds about you—or the both of us."

She looked around in surprise. "Where are your pack-horses?"

"At Logan's Station. When I got wind of Captain Jack's huntin' party, I cached them there. No sense in spoilin' their hunt by handin' them all my furs. I done that a time or two before."

Lael remembered all too well—mostly Ma's temper at losing half a year's wages. Unsteadily, she stood. Her very bones seemed as frozen as the hard ground, and her skirts were speckled with blood from butchering the deer. But her stomach was still full, content with the choice venison. She figured the Shawnee could be gentlemanly when they pleased. Even her mended moccasin felt like new.

"Come along, Daughter," Pa said, whistling for Nip and Tuck. He passed a hand over his scraggly beard and studied her, his blue eyes warm. "You've grown prettier since I last saw you. Only your hair's a mite shorter."

Her cold fingers flew to her braid. Land sakes, but he gave her such a fright! "I'm surprised it ain't plumb gray after yesterday!"

she shot back at him, examining the heavy plait. He hesitated, then laughed outright as she gasped and held the missing end aloft. Although still bound with her favorite ribbon, it had been cut square across and now resembled a straw broom.

"Captain Jack said he'd take some of you if he couldn't have all of you," he said, the mirth in his eyes making light of her ire.

"And you let him?"

"Seems a small price to pay to keep you."

"When? How?" she sputtered.

"Near dawn, with his scalping knife."

"While I slept?" She swallowed hard, for she was sounding like Ma now, all growl and bite.

With a wink, he turned toward the trail, toward the fort, leaving her to fall in step behind him. She reached into her pocket and fingered the blue beads, wondering if Captain Jack would keep her hair close as well. Sighing, she took a reluctant step away from the dying campfire.

Time spent with the Shawnee only deepened their mystery instead of unraveling it. Was this Pa's feeling too? Having lived among them, did he feel the same irresistible, if dangerous, pull to be with them? Was this how the Indians felt about him? Though she didn't ask and he didn't answer, she knew.

She wondered if she'd ever see the Shawnee, or Captain Jack, again.

18

Lael stood with her father in the center of the fort common, his packhorses burdened with all manner of furs, a passel of people there to welcome him. Snow was falling, but no one seemed to care. Colonel Corey and the militia had welcomed him in with a volley of gunfire. Her ma and Ransom could hardly get to him for the press of folks hungry for news of any kind, all anxious to hear if he thought it safe for them to return to their homesteads beyond fort walls. Out of the corner of her eye, Lael noticed Hugh McClary coming out of Ma Horn's cabin, but she thought little of it.

In time, the welcoming throng began to disperse and the family faced the bearded, muddy, trail-worn figure they hardly recognized. Even Nip and Tuck looked pinched and weary, ready to drop.

Looking hard at Lael, Pa turned to open one of his saddlebags. She clasped her hands together, expectant. Had he brought her something then?

Behind them, someone shouted hoarsely from the door of a cabin. A warning? Thunderous gunfire ripped through the common, scattering stock and settlers. Pa was turning around, holding something in his hand, when he fell. Blood spattered onto Lael's butternut dress. The gift—a small box—dropped to her feet, and then she followed, falling hard to the ground after him.

At first glance it seemed two had fallen from Hugh McClary's bullet, but Lael had only fainted. Colonel Corey carried her to the Click cabin while others moved her father. The trail of blood on the ground marked an inglorious homecoming. A scuffle ensued as McClary's rifle was wrested away despite his screaming epithets and obscenities in a whiskey-soaked voice. He would soon be locked up and flogged, then forcibly evicted from fort walls. This was lenient punishment, the colonel said, as he doubted even the Shawnee would want him. And all this after one of the Click clan's own had nursed him through the weary winter.

Lael rose up to find him lying on a bed surrounded by a press of people. Colonel Corey tried to shield her but she pushed forward, chilled by the sight of so much blood. After some minutes Ma Horn determined the wound was in Pa's right thigh. His face faded to the color of gray linen as a fellow trapper worked to extract the ball while she attempted to stay the bleeding.

She looked up suddenly at Lael. "Fetch some comfrey and snakeroot from my cabin."

Lael ran next door, her hands far calmer than her twisted insides. With some help, she concocted a poultice. When at last the ball had come out, they cleaned the wound with corn liquor and applied the snakeroot while Ma Horn tore linen into rags for bandages.

For a sudden, dizzying moment, Lael felt the stuffy room sway and suffocate her. She put one hand out and covered Pa's still, cool wrist. Beneath her fingers she could feel the rhythm of his pulse, and it steadied her. Still, the bandages turned scarlet as soon as they were applied, and they were pulled free for fresh ones. Ma Horn began binding the wounded leg so tight the entire thigh was soon encased in a cocoon of cloth.

Lael sponged Pa's face with a damp rag, but he didn't so much as twitch. What if this small gesture was to be the last given to him? What if they were to next wash his body for burial? She'd be left with nothing but the hoard of unasked riddles and questions that had dogged her since childhood. She swallowed hard, feeling small and scared again, just as she had years ago when learning of his capture. She glanced toward Ransom, his still, bent body crumpled in the door frame. No one in the cabin spoke. A vigil had begun that would not end until he awoke or passed on. The heavy bleeding and threat of blood poisoning still loomed.

With a heavy sigh, the trapper retreated to the warm hearth to finish off the rest of the corn liquor. Colonel Corey stood at the door, barring entry to those who waited outside.

After a while they heard cries of "String up McClary!"

The trapper swore, setting down his jug. "McClary's the cause of all this blood and trouble, him with a temper that would curdle milk."

Inwardly, Lael flinched. His words bore the makings of a deadly feud. But she knew the trouble had begun long ago at the salt licks when her father had been faced with an impossible choice. Truly, he had saved the settlement. Hadn't both judge and jury said that it was so at the court-martial? But Hugh McClary believed none of it.

"He'll live, but he'll limp to his dying day," Ma Horn pronounced when the danger seemed past.

Lael fell to her knees in the cold loft and said a prayer of thanksgiving to the Lord for sparing him. With McClary not seen since the flogging and no fresh Shawnee sign about, it seemed they could finally go home to the cabin and abide in peace, at least for a time.

Before she blew out the candle and slipped under the coverlet, Lael took out the gift from Pa and held it in one cold hand. Aside from the blue beads, she'd never owned a piece of jewelry, at least not a civilized one such as this. The pale pink and ivory cameo fit in her palm, a profile of a pretty girl etched upon its shell surface, her flowing tresses entwined with leaves and flowers and berries like some woodland fairy. She reckoned she would never wear it, as it was too fine to be pinned to a homespun dress. But she would keep it with her always, in her pocket, alongside the blue beads.

19

Before spring, Simon came.

From the yard one crisp morning, Lael heard Ransom shout, "Rider comin'!" She was inside the cabin with her mother, salting venison and layering it in a tub. At Ransom's call, Ma passed to the window and peered beyond the shutter, a slight frown creasing her face.

"'Tis Simon Hayes," was all she said.

The words set Lael's face afire. She'd not seen him since he'd come drunk to their cabin at the fort and put her down for her wandering ways.

Hastily, she wiped salty hands on her apron and looked down at her soiled dress. Too late to fuss, she decided. Barefoot, she passed onto the porch and walked to the end where the wild roses stood waiting for winter's spell to release them to blossom. Still, the bare, thick canes formed a screen of privacy. She sat down in the cane chair and waited.

Horse and rider came to a stop by the springhouse. Ransom greeted Simon and they exchanged a few words before Simon went into the barn, leaving his horse to the boy. Lael knew then he'd come to see Pa about her.

She sat still as stone, her eyes fixed on the barn door while her heart thrummed a bit wildly in her chest. Her hands were red and chapped from the salt, and a cut on her palm where the knife had slipped stung unmercifully. She smiled wryly and tucked her bare feet underneath the hem of her dress against the chill. If Simon had come courting, he would court her shoeless and bonnetless or not at all.

The minutes grew long, and her eyes never left the barn door. She tucked a strand of hair behind one ear and willed him to appear. From the yard Ransom resumed splitting burly ash logs into kindling. The *chop-chop-chop* jarred her nerves till she could stand it no longer. Peering through the screen of rose canes, she hissed, "Ransom, git!"

He paused in mid-swing and grinned at her before laying aside the ax. She watched his back as he retreated to the springhouse, likely to snitch a cup of buttermilk, and she breathed a grateful sigh.

When Simon finally appeared, he did not so much as glance at the cabin. Out the barn door he blew with a purposeful stride and, in one quick motion, untethered and mounted the horse Ransom had tied to the rail fence. Before she could step off the porch and call his name he was gone, into the woods and lost from sight. Her spirits, which had soared at the mere sight of him, now plummeted to her toes.

She walked straight to the barn. The door was ajar and Pa's back was to her. He was repairing a harness and seemed to take no notice of her entrance. She had made it a practice never to disturb him if she could help it, but today the self-made rule was cast aside. The sight of his bad leg, still bandaged, pained her, but her anger welled up within her in a hot rising flood and made her breathless. She stood just within the barn, breathing in the scent of leather and hay and livestock, a hundred questions hot on her tongue.

Without turning around, he said, "Daughter, I cannot let you wed young Hayes."

The statement struck her hard as no hand could ever do. She could only gape at him, certain he'd change his mind when Simon told him of the cabin he'd built, the stock he'd secured, and the cotton and tobacco, all for their future.

Turning, he looked straight at her, his blue eyes like deep water. "No good can come from such a union."

She swallowed a tart reply. "You sent him away."

"He never spoke with you?"

The ache in her chest was so strong she almost couldn't answer. Unable to look at him, she looked at her feet. "I reckon he thought better of it since you two had words."

His voice turned gentler. "Daughter, do you love him?"

"I—I don't know," she stammered, afraid saying more would set her to bawling.

"You'd know if you did," came his grave reply. "I misdoubt he cares for you like you hope. Word is he's tied to Piper Cane. And the jug."

Word is . . . rumors, all! Her face deepened to scarlet. To hear such from her pa was shameful indeed. In a fit of fury she flung the lovely cameo from her pocket. It came to rest in a pile of hay near his feet. He eyed it with characteristic calm, revealing nothing, before looking at her again.

"Simon Hayes is all show and no stay," he warned. "No daughter of mine is going to be tied to a trotter."

A trotter. Next to a coward this was the worst possible brand. Suddenly she didn't know whom she was most angry with— Simon or Pa. Her heart felt like a kettle left too long at the fire, boiled dry, about to explode. Balling her hands into fists, she sought words but none came.

Laying the leather aside, he faced her once again. "You'd best put all thoughts of marryin' aside. Come spring, you'll be leavin' the settlement."

20

As long as memory served, the image of Pa, made years younger in broadcloth the rich brown of chestnut, his face clean-shaven beneath a beaver felt hat, would never leave Lael. Sitting across from him in a lurching coach, the likes of which she'd never seen, she thought how strange he looked out of buckskin—not a woodsman at all, but a judge or a preacher or something other than who he was. His sandy hair, the color of her own, had been twice washed and swept back from his face in waves as soft as a woman's, then tied at the nape of his neck.

Since leaving the settlement it seemed she'd shed a trail of tears. There had been time enough to bid good-bye to Susanna, Simon, and Ma Horn, but their sorrow had only made matters worse, not better. As soon as Pa's leg enabled him to travel, they'd departed, riding back over the gap through which he'd come all those years before. This was her first foray out of the wilderness. She felt suddenly bewildered, thrust into a strange, new world like an infant from its mother's womb.

By the time they reached the Clinch River in Virginia, they were beyond the frontier, past fear and Shawnee and stock-ades and uncertainty. Her old life was extinguished as fast as a candle flame as they sped east toward civilization and crowds and comforts.

As they set out, she'd asked, "Pa, where are we headed?"

"Briar Hill," he answered simply. Where Miss Mayella lived. What she should have asked was *Why?* and *How long?*

In time she would regret her reticence. Briar Hill was some four hundred miles away, days upon days of hard travel.

Eventually she became too tired to talk. The sights before her snatched speech. Wide roads. Bells ringing from clusters of brick buildings. Churches with white steeples. Coaches and chaises and contraptions too smart to believe. Queer trees such as cypresses and pitch pines. And more people pressed together in one place than she had ever thought possible.

Was this her punishment for wandering? Or her reward? Did Pa feel he could no longer protect her from the Shawnee, limping as he did with an injured leg? Or was he afraid she'd run off with Simon?

Everywhere they went, be it inn or coach or tavern, there was talk of the war with England. Her soul seemed to shrink from such news and from the restless crowds. To maintain her bearings, to remember who she was, she recollected the eternal stillness of the frontier forest . . . the flash of fireflies at dusk . . . the feel of the milk churn in her hand and the moment she knew the butter had come . . . the bubbling of the branch . . . the way the dogwoods, blossoming now, danced in the wind. Except for her memories, all she had left of her old life were the blue beads in her pocket.

When she felt she could go no farther, the coach rumbled to a stop before a white-columned building shaded by a cluster of enormous oaks. Their rustling was like a balm to her nervous spirits. She had forever loved the wind and here it was to welcome her, whispering a greeting through the new spring leaves.

Emerging from the coach, Lael saw that they stood on a hill that sloped gently to a rose garden and, beyond that, the sea. She gaped at the sight of all that spangled, shimmering blueness, looking like the sky turned upside down. As if prompted by some unseen clock, the door of the brick building opened and Miss Mayella herself came forward, embracing Lael and erasing all the years that had come between them.

Her former teacher looked much the same—all silk and lace and milky skin—and Lael's eyes fastened on her smile, feeling it was the only thing that propped her up. "Welcome to Briar Hill. You must be weary from your travels. No doubt, Miss Lael, you'll become célèbre here, being from the frontier and having so famous a father."

Miss Lael. Never in her life had she been called Miss Lael. Never in her life had she seen Negroes dressed like gentlefolk in black trousers and pristine shirts and shoes with shiny buckles. Never before had she seen the grace with which a cluster of girls in indigo moved across the expansive lawn toward the sea, hardly walking at all but gliding, lace-edged parasols in hand. Never before had she been in rooms that echoed and smelled of books and leather and lemon oil.

She felt suddenly small and awkward and homespun. Even clothed in her best apple-green dress, she sensed she was out of place, a spectacle. Suddenly it all came clear. Pa was going to leave her here with these people to winnow the wilderness out of her.

The spring breeze turned wintry then, and she felt the same strange desolation she'd felt as a girl upon hearing of his capture. And then, as if he sensed her misgivings, he suddenly took his leave. Doffing his beaver hat, he failed to kiss her cheek. If he had, she would have clung to him, weeping. Instead, in silent agony, she remained by Miss Mayella, staring down the long emerald drive after him.

She stood as she would so often in the days to come, looking westward. Just stood and looked, not speaking or even weeping, just waiting.

"I'll be back to bring you home," Pa said as he left.

It was a promise she wondered if he would keep.

21

Lael felt fettered, shackled to books and clocks and finishing school rules. Within a week, she'd written each rebuke she'd earned from her teachers in a journal Miss Mayella provided.

You must be a lady before you can act a lady.
No more ayes and nays, only yes and no.
A lady's skin must be milk white, not tobacco brown.
Always be in a good humor.
Never look a gentleman directly in the eye.

Stuffed into whalebone stays that poked and prodded like the most ardent suitor, she walked about in an indigo dress as if encased in armor, her white collar and cuffs irreproachable. Even the ribbons in her hair had been ironed, just like those of her twenty-six schoolmates. The only difference, she reckoned, were the blue beads in her dress pocket and the rising homesickness in her heart.

"Briar Hill grows on you in time," Lydia Darrah assured her. The oldest girls were paired with the youngest, and Lydia had been assigned to Lael. They shared an attic room with four other girls, their slim beds laid out like garden rows and covered with cabbage-rose coverlets.

"Our time isn't always taken up with French and music and writing. Those with the highest marks may attend the opera and theater. I doubt that will change even with the war on. Aren't we lucky the British are still fighting in the east and haven't yet moved south?"

Lucky? Lael wished they would so she could go home. Keeping abreast of the war became her mission as she smuggled copies of the *Virginia Gazette* into her room, defying the headmistress's latest rebuke: *A true lady does not pursue politics, particularly matters of war.*

Perhaps she could simply run away, straight back into Simon's arms. Or Captain Jack's. As the days passed, she no longer looked for Pa's return but Simon. By now, Simon would have planned to come after her. She was not so far away, and the Hayes clan had kin in Virginia.

As summer waned, her hopes flickered like a spent candle. Might he write her a letter? A letter was a simple matter, to be savored and tucked in one's bodice and read again and again.

But no one wrote. Not Ma, not Pa, not Susanna. Not even Ma Horn. Lydia Darrah felt so sorry for Lael she shared her own letters. Soon it became a game in their attic room, the six of them circulating mail and discussing the lives of family and friends. Lydia. Sophie. Euphemia. Molly. Esther Ann. Lael fed them tidbits about her frontier life to make up for her lack of letters.

"You should write a book," Lydia told her. "You make up quite the best stories I've ever heard."

Molly lit a candle, defying their bedtime curfew. "Tell us again about Captain Jack. Did you say he has green eyes? How queer that he's lived as an Indian for so long but can still speak English!"

"Show me the blue beads," Esther Ann begged. "Do you think you'll ever see him again?"

Somehow, sharing her past kept it as near and dear as the beads in her pocket. Yet spilling her secrets seemed also to tarnish them and make them less sacred. As the days passed she grew quieter. Practicing her penmanship, she composed copious letters to Susanna that were never mailed, detailing her melancholy. When she partnered with her dancing master, she pretended he was Simon. Playing pall mall on Briar Hill's expansive lawn, she purposefully hit her ball through the wickets far into the park of trees, just so she could pretend she was in the woods again, with Captain Jack at her heels.

Despite her daydreaming, she excelled in every subject except the art of fancy needlework. While the other girls embroidered and tatted lace, Lael sewed shirts for the Continental Army and kept abreast of the war. General Washington had just established West Point as his official headquarters, and the long-awaited French fleet was now lying at anchor off Sandy Hook in Delaware. But she read that Washington was already growing weary of French officers who acted in a condescending manner toward him and his men.

Despite the war, a late-summer dance was to be held at Briar Hill. Lael marveled at the gowns the girls had brought with them for just such an occasion. Her apple-green dress, now too short and too snug, was sorely lacking.

"Lael, you must wear one of my gowns," Lydia told her, throwing open one of her trunks to reveal a rainbow of fine fabric and lace. But Miss Mayella had other ideas, and a seamstress was called in from nearby Williamsburg.

"Your father has generously provided funds for a new gown," Miss Mayella explained with a smile. "A girl's first ball is an extraordinary event. You do want to attend, don't you?"

Lael looked pained. "I—no." Would *no* forever nettle her tongue? A simple, settlement *nay* was what she longed to say. "I have no heart for it."

Miss Mayella gestured for Lael to sit down with her in a deep window seat that overlooked the sea. "You have been here four months, Lael. What would you rather I tell your father? That you are learning and growing and making him proud, or so homesick he will have to come and get you? I must give him honest answers."

117

Lael sighed. "Pa was wrong to bring me here."

Miss Mayella's mouth set in a soft line. "I don't think so, Lael. There is a purpose in everything, so Scripture says. 'A time to be born, a time to die. A time to laugh, a time to mourn.' Even, I think, a time to be a lady."

Her face turned entreating. "How long will it take? To make me a lady, I mean?"

Miss Mayella looked like she might laugh. "That, my dear, is entirely up to you."

Lael looked down at her hands, her long fingers no longer tanned by the sun, her callused palms softening. All the wilderness was slowly seeping out of her. If she hurried the process, might Pa not fetch her sooner? If she dallied, he might let her linger.

She decided a Briar Hill ball might be at least as interesting as a fiddle on the fort common, and when the day came, she no longer felt like a crow among cardinals, smothered as she was from head to toe in rose silk. Standing beneath crystal chandeliers, the heat of a hundred candles turned her face the color of her gown.

"Why, Lael!" Miss Mayella had exclaimed. "You look positively regal."

Regal. Another word for too tall, she reckoned. Yards of silk, the color of the cabin's roses, framed her bare shoulders and cinched her waist before flowing to the floor in a cascade of white lace. Delicate ruffled sleeves left off where snug, white gloves began. *A lady with ill-fitting gloves cannot be well dressed.*

Aside from her too-tight shoes, a painted fan finished her toilette and had a language all its own. Turning her eyes on the Twin Oaks gentleman in evening dress across the crowded ballroom, Lael slowly twirled her fan in her right hand, meaning *I love another.* Next she brought the fan to rest over her left ear. *I wish to be rid of you.* Finally she pressed it to her left cheek.

No, thank you. Would the men understand this unspoken communication? Around her, Lydia and Esther Ann fluttered their fans as well, but flirtatiously.

'Twas a good night to run off, she decided. She wouldn't be missed in the press of people. A full moon beckoned off the ballroom's veranda. Just beyond, the sea was a bewitching silver. She slipped outside. The great oaks and elms on Briar Hill's lawn were as dark and forbidding as the frontier forest but smelled more of the ocean than the wilderness.

"Would you care to dance?"

She spun, startled, and faced a boy—a man?—nearly as tall as Simon, though his hair was as fair as her own. Her silk skirts settled, and she raised her fan to touch her left cheek in refusal. He waited, the perfect gentleman, as she fought a furious battle, all her wilderness ways rebelling against the lady she was fast becoming.

His outstretched hand seemed a bridge to her new life at Briar Hill. Once crossed, she would turn her back on her beloved wilderness, on her girlhood and all she held most dear. No longer would she be simply Lael Catherine Click of Kentucke, but Miss Lael of Briar Hill.

Truly, what choice did she have?

Reluctantly, she placed her gloved hand in his and felt his fingers tighten around hers, leading her back into the crowded, candlelit ballroom.

Help me, Lord. Help me get home.

It was the first prayer she'd prayed in a long time, for she felt the Almighty had failed to hear her thus far. Perhaps, she decided, God would rather listen to the prayers of a lady. He didn't seem to hear the ones of a homesick settlement girl torn between the savage and the civilized.

"Lael? Where are you?" Lydia Darrah's voice seemed to echo off the stone portico, her tone a trifle exasperated. "It's your birthday—what are you doing out here alone?"

"Enjoying turning seventeen," Lael replied, the stone bench beneath her warm and inviting. Hemmed in by a flurry of blossoming lilacs, she was nearly concealed in her painted silk gown, for it was the same shade as the heady, fragrant flowers. She nearly laughed as Lydia—dear, near-sighted Lydia—crisscrossed the lawn looking for her.

"I've brought you a surprise," she said, ducking into the lilac bower to sit beside her. "But you'll have to read it aloud to me, as I've forgotten my spectacles."

Sitting shoulder to shoulder with Lael in the spring sun, Lydia passed Lael the latest issue of the *Virginia Gazette*. Looking down, Lael scanned the front page, eyes lighting on a boldly printed column bearing a beloved name. For a moment her smile nearly slipped, but she kept it in place for Lydia's sake. Still, it hurt her to hear about Pa this way, secondhand, seemingly a continent away.

"Well, go on," Lydia urged.

Lael scanned the newsprint. "My father is surveying near the Falls of the Ohio with George Rogers Clark, so this says. And settling disputes over land claims." She couldn't say more for the lump in her throat, relieved when Lydia took back the paper.

"Rather dry reading this time," Lydia said. "I much prefer reports of his exploits in Missouri territory or treating with Indians."

Lael turned thoughtful eyes on the trimmed lawn that rolled in gentle Virginia fashion to a fringe of sand that seemed to hold back a wealth of blue water. Today—her birthday—the Atlantic curled and foamed just as it had every spring, with an awesome familiarity that nearly eclipsed the memory of Kentucke altogether.

She'd come out here today to hide among the lilacs, shutting her eyes against all the refinement and elegance and ease surrounding her, willing every hazy detail of her home place to come back to her. Three years she'd been here, and the hollow feeling in her heart told her she'd likely be here three years hence.

"Any letters lately?" Lydia asked, tucking the newspaper out of sight.

"None from Kentucke," Lael answered. "Just a note from Esther Ann in Philadelphia."

"Announcing her debut, I suppose."

"Aye—yes. She's become a bonafide colonial belle."

Lydia leaned over the bench and took in Lael's slim bare feet. "You might be a belle too if you'd wear some shoes!"

They laughed, and Lael tucked her toes out of sight. "'Tis my last holdout against civilized life. Look at the rest of me. I fairly shine with refinement. My bare feet simply remind me of who I really am."

Lydia's smile turned pensive, and she tucked a strand of russet hair into her carefully pinned chignon. "What's to become of us, Lael? Now that Euphemia has returned to England and Molly and Sophie have married, we're the oldest ones here. And Miss Mayella has turned us into student teachers, like it or not."

"*Not*," Lael said, smoothing her shiny skirts. "But at least we're out of indigo and those awful pressed collars and cuffs."

"Sometimes I think we'll always be here, till we turn gray . . . hobbling about these old halls with canes—"

"Nay!" The forbidden word burst forth with such unladylike force that Lydia drew back. Lael was instantly sorry and gave Lydia's arm a reassuring squeeze. "The war won't last forever, you know, and your father will finish fighting and take you home."

"*If* we Americans win the war, you mean. You forget what will happen if England triumphs. My father and every other Continental officer will be tried for treason."

Lael shook her head, thinking of all the recent reports she'd heard and read. "Our side seems to be winning."

"This week, anyway," Lydia mused, reaching out to pluck a lilac. Bringing it to her nose, she said, "Enough melancholy talk. There's to be a ball tomorrow night. What will you wear?"

"My royal purple sacque dress," Lael said with a winsome smile. "And my two bare feet."

"That seems rather dangerous given all your partners."

"Thankfully they're not all toe steppers, though they do tend to be shorter than I am. And it's not me they're interested in but my father's exploits, same as you." She bit her lip and said quietly, "I'll take a long-legged frontiersman any day."

Lydia studied her thoughtfully, as if all too aware of the heartache beneath her simple words. "Sadly, you'll not find any frontiersmen around here."

And that, Lael lamented, was her principal complaint about Briar Hill.

The tea room on Lee Alley was just beyond the gates of Briar Hill, and Lael fled to it as often as she could. Sometimes she would sit alone at a tiny linen-draped table, a wide window before her, admiring the fine thistle pattern on the exquisite English china, if not the owner's Tory leanings. Occasionally Lydia would join her, and they'd talk of anything but lessons and pupils and finishing-school rules.

Today, as autumn transformed the world outside the shop window with a windblown assortment of scarlet and gold leaves, they huddled over their steaming cups, breathing in the scent of Egyptian chamomile and oranges and a host of other exotic things.

"I've heard the 'queen' is about to issue a new edict," Lydia told her in hushed tones.

A wry smile pulled at Lael's face. "Banning us from Tory tea shops? I'd heard the same."

"She's a hard headmistress. I've often thought how well she fits her name."

Lael toyed with a silver sugar spoon absently. Truly, Alexandra Ice presided over Briar Hill with the cold formality of a queen. And it was this that had finally goaded Lael into action. She gave Lydia an apologetic look, feeling the need to tell her first. "Perhaps now's a good time to reveal I'm planning to leave this place."

A flash of concern darkened Lydia's face and nearly made Lael wish she'd not said the words. "Has your father sent word he's coming for you?"

"Nay. I sometimes think he never will, so I'm taking matters into my own hands."

"When?"

"Not now. Next spring."

"I'm glad of that. But Kentucke? You're hardly the sturdy frontier girl who came here four years ago. You've grown soft, as you've said yourself."

"Aye, and I'll grow even softer if I stay." Lael leaned back in her chair, knowing her news wasn't welcome and wanting to take away the sudden sadness in her friend's eyes. "With the war nearly won, you'll be leaving too."

But instead of bubbling over with enthusiasm at what lay ahead, Lydia reached up and rubbed her temples with gloved hands. The unusual gesture pinched Lael with alarm, and she noticed Lydia's high color. "Lydia, are you unwell?"

Lydia looked down at her unfinished tea, her shoulders lifting in a little shrug beneath her scarlet cape. "Just a headache."

"I'll ask Mrs. Moss for some thyme tea then." Rising, Lael started to turn away, but Lydia caught her arm. "Just help me back to Briar Hill. Perhaps if I lie down . . ."

The odor of camphor and the oil from cupping lamps reached Lael as she stood in the hall outside the room she shared with Lydia. As she watched the doctors—dark, dour men suffused with their own self-importance—hover over her friend as she lay on her bed, she felt a terrible disquiet.

Could Miss Mayella sense her agitation? Surely so, for she reached out and squeezed her arm as they waited, saying, "Dr. Clary will bleed her to restore the body's balance, and all should be well."

At this, a cold hand seemed to clutch Lael's heart. "But Lydia's afraid of bloodletting—"

"Lael, please." The pale, composed lines of Miss Mayella's face tensed. "She's passed into unconsciousness. Besides, the doctors know how to best treat such a fever."

Did they? Lael's eyes fastened on the lancet Dr. Clary held. Why were his hands shaking? Was he addicted to drink like the last physician who'd come? The assortment of brass scarificators and bronze cups gleamed harshly in the lamplight, and she turned her back in silent protest.

Unbidden, the hazy image of Ma Horn sprang to mind. Bloodletting was against nature, she'd often said with vigor. Such a practice caused more misery than it relieved, and Lael had shared this with Lydia. Besides, Lydia had a terrible fear of worms and spiders and snakes.

Oh Lord, please don't let her come awake.

The bloodsucking leeches were applied nearly round the clock, but blessedly, Lydia remained lost in the fever's delirium. Lael sensed that she was more ill than they'd let on, and the following hours only confirmed this as her fever climbed higher.

Looking on, Lael wondered what cruel twist of fate kept her friend's father on some far battlefield while his only daughter lay dying.

At last, Lydia's next of kin, an aunt in Williamsburg, was sent for.

When she wasn't teaching, Lael stood by helplessly in the hall, wanting to shout at the doctors to take their cupping sets and get out. What Lydia needed most was a healer like Ma Horn, who'd break the fever with boneset and cold cloths and kind words. The thought brought about such a crushing wave of homesickness that Lael rushed to the window of her empty classroom in a near panic and considered leaving before winter set in.

Leaning her forehead against the chill glass, she weighed what she would need to travel four hundred miles through still-hostile wilderness. A horse. A gun and powder and lead. Flint and steel to start a fire. Enough warm clothes and provisions to take her there. She'd be fighting the elements all the way now that winter neared. And Lydia—she couldn't leave Lydia till she got well or . . .

In a week's time, Lydia was whisked away to convalesce with her Williamsburg relatives, who announced she would not be returning to school. Her teaching responsibilities were given to Lael, who felt the weight of them settle over her and shackle her to Briar Hill in new ways. As the autumn days grew darker, the panic that had settled over Lael upon Lydia's leaving returned with chilling regularity.

Oh Pa, where are you? Will I ever see you or Kentucke again?

22

Briar Hill, Virginia, 1783

The high-ceilinged room was filled with the cold light of early spring, not unlike that spring five years past when Lael and her father first set foot on Briar Hill. Alexandra Ice presided over the small gathering in a black satin gown with pearls draped like rope about her wrinkled neck. She looked, Lael thought again, like a queen. Dark and dour, she'd said little thus far, but her eyes, needle sharp, roamed the room as if ferreting out the slightest infraction.

Miss Mayella was present, as were all Lael's instructors. Each wore the characteristic dark silk and lace except Lael. She was dressed in a traveling suit of fine black cloth with fifty faux-pearl buttons from collar to hem. In her hands she held a straw hat, the only hint of color allowed her. Its lavender feather fluttered softly in a draft as she set it atop her lap.

"First, I want to offer my condolences regarding your great loss," the headmistress began. "You have been an exceptional student and assistant teacher. Your father would have been proud."

The letter bearing the black wax seal, with its news of Pa's fate, lay in her pocket alongside the blue beads. Lael sat very still, her eyes on the wide oaks just beyond the narrow windows, their vivid greenness heralding spring despite the sudden cold. *Dogwood winter*, she mused for a moment, her concentration slipping. The dogwoods were blooming now from cabin to river, and if she hurried she might just see the last of their showy splendor . . .

"I think I speak for all of us when I ask you to reconsider your rather rash decision to leave us. We are in need of another instructor at Briar Hill."

"I hope to return to Kentucke right away—after I see my mother and brother in Bardstown." She colored slightly as she spoke, wondering if they knew her mother had already remarried and, with Ransom, had left the settlement. She had told only Miss Mayella, stumbling with embarrassment over the news that had come at the end of Ma's grievous letter.

"Women are so few on the frontier, Lael. You must not judge your mother too harshly," Miss Mayella had told her.

But Lael felt fresh resentment flare within her as she sat stoically before her instructors. Ma's mourning hadn't lasted two months, and her haste to marry again seemed a blatant show of disrespect to Pa's memory.

The headmistress said, "I suppose you plan to teach at the Kentucke settlement school."

"No, I . . . I have no desire to teach at all."

"Then what do you plan to do—you, a young woman, alone?"

Lael hesitated.

"There are still wild savages about, mademoiselle," her French instructor warned.

At this Lael nearly smiled. "Not so many as when I was a girl, I should think."

Another of her teachers pressed, "But how shall you support yourself if you do not teach?"

Put in some corn. Dig ginseng in the woods. Ride up and down the hollers and balds. Just . . . be. She said nothing, knowing how foolish this would sound to them. All but Miss Mayella.

The lines of displeasure in the headmistress's face deepened. Her thoughts were plain. *All the years of study wasted!*

"I shall take my books with me," she said quietly. "They are like old friends and shall be put to good use."

"All right then. But if you should ever change your mind," came the terse reply, "you can always return to Briar Hill." *When your plans fail and you realize how utterly futile—and dangerous—it is for a woman alone on the frontier, you may fall back on our beneficence,* her tone implied.

But Lael was finished with Briar Hill forever. Dutifully, she would write to let them know she was well and settled. But for five long years her soul had chafed at a life lived by unbending rules, when every thundering strike of the grandfather clock in the great hall signaled prayers to be said, lessons learned, niceties uttered, and meals taken.

Alexandra Ice lifted upturned palms in a gesture that signified resignation. "I should be quite apprehensive in regards to your future, Lael Click, but for one thing: You are your father's daughter."

In the long years between leaving Kentucke and finally escaping Virginia, Lael had hoarded every single shilling Pa had sent her in hopes that they would someday see her home again. Now with sufficient funds needed to travel, she set out, though she was unprepared for the unceasing spring rains and the nearly impassable roads awash with mud on the first leg of her journey.

Traveling by coach, she took lodging in respectable inns and taverns, eating little and sleeping less, always looking out for trouble. Her twin trunks would follow later, bearing her books and dresses. By the time she reached the Virginia border and secured a horse and food and shunned a guide, it was as if her sheltered, cosseted life at Briar Hill had never been.

She'd thought to meet up with other travelers. The newspapers had reported them pouring through Cumberland Gap on the trail Pa had first blazed, spurred on by the war's imminent end, or coming down the Ohio River on flatboats to start new settlements. But not a soul was to be seen. The edges of the wilderness wooed her, still and lush, an eternal green. She fancied Pa's spirit lingered on in these woods. Heading west, she'd not made many missteps. Somehow it seemed he was with her, careful to keep her on the right path.

On the sixth day, before darkness fell and the moon rose, when the deer gathered at the watering places, she came upon a bonnet. It lay limp and lifeless along a creek bed and had no color at all, the dye long since washed out and bleached by the sun. Reaching up, she touched the wide brim of her own straw hat, recalling how she hated wearing a bonnet. Unable to see beyond the wide brim, she always felt boxed in, her head hot beneath the cloth. Had she not felt the same at Briar Hill and even Fort Click when the wild woods beckoned? Was Pa's wanderlust not her own?

As she rode on she heard rather than saw the hot springs, clear and warm as fresh milk. Above the springs was a cave, breathing a cold sigh into the tepid night air. Fireflies winged all about her, and it was here that she made a cold camp.

Piling her traveling clothes atop a rock, she slipped into the steaming water and gasped with glee. The water swirled and bubbled, smelling of sulfur, assuaging the weariness out of her. Unpinning her hair, she ducked under the surface, then sat where the warm water was up to her neck. Looking up, past the towering elms and oaks, the sky called to mind the Star of Bethlehem quilt, white with stars.

When she had pulled free of the spring, her long hair covering her nakedness, she combed through the sandy tangles before making a braid. There was no more need of a fancy traveling suit, black as it was for mourning. She traded it for a light linen dress, rolling up into a blanket near where her horse was hobbled, wanting a fire but too tired to make one. And too careful.

In the morning she worked at igniting a small amount of powder with a spark from a flint, feeding the small flame with dry leaves and twigs. She mixed water with meal and a pinch of salt and set some small cakes on a flat rock in the heat of the fire for her breakfast. Out of another leather pouch she took a bit of dried meat and chewed on this while waiting for the cakes to bake. Once finished, she was careful to put out the fire, raking the coals flat and dampening the ground with water, then covering it over with dirt and leaves. She wanted to be certain she left no trail. From this day forward she would keep to the waterways when she could to hide her tracks, just as an Indian would. She recalled Pa had done the same.

How many days had she traveled? Nothing seemed familiar to her, and yet she kept in a westerly direction, certain she would eventually come to the Louisa, or Kentucke River. She recollected the Shawnee called it the Chenoa, the telling landmark she looked for.

Time and distance worked to dull her excitement at leaving Briar Hill but did nothing to unburden her. Cold, hard grief now seeped in, her shock at learning of Pa's fate now giving way to a fearful hurt. She was heading home, but what awaited her? Several years had been lost to her. Letters from the settlement had been few and far between. Ma had written but twice, and only Pa had visited her at Briar Hill, returning once that first spring, but it proved so painful he never came back.

When she saw him, she'd been certain he meant to take her home. "Oh Pa, I was a-feared you'd forgot all about me," she gushed, gladness spilling out of her. "I've got to get shed of this place. I always believed you'd come get me in—"

"This place grieves you, Daughter?"

130

"Oh, it's tolerable. But I never liked it. I reckon I'll like it a heap better when it's behind me."

His usual stoicism turned to sadness, as if any hope he had of her happiness had been struck down. What girl, taken from the wild woods and tucked into the cocooned, comfortable world of Briar Hill, could want for anything at all? Was that what he thought?

"Your teachers tell me you're doin' fine."

Fine? She didn't feel fine, she felt sick with a hunger for home that never ebbed, only flowed. And she didn't look fine, what with the ladies being so shy of the sun and the elements and covering up every chance they got. She was pale as frost herself and longed to be barefoot and brown as dirt.

"Your ma sent you some crabapple jelly," he told her. "And this here's from Ransom."

At the sight of a linen hankie full of dried flowers, she burst into tears. And she did what she vowed she would never do— she clung to him until he had to pry her arms loose to leave, his face so filled with angst it nearly broke her heart in two . . . even now. Recalling this last encounter with Pa, she couldn't see the trail for her tears, but she kept on, bowing to the wind as it began moaning through the treetops. A thunderclap nearly unseated her, and her horse reared then veered off the trail. Another gust snatched away her straw hat, and it went flying birdlike behind her, ribbons fluttering. Lightning lit the woods and the wind twisted the trees into grotesque shapes, keening and crying in mournful melody.

For the first time in years she felt fear. The mare sensed it and grew more skittish, plunging into a briar patch and tearing her skirt. Sliding off, she grabbed hold of the bridle and with all her strength, pulled the animal beneath a rock overhang just as the heavens opened and poured forth a cold, pounding rain. Nay, she could go no farther this day.

23

That night she dreamt she was on the river again. Only this time Susanna was with her, both of them dangling cane-cut feet in the cold water. She was paddling, but the oars were as willful as twin mules, going every which way but the way she wanted. The canoe was like a leaf caught in the current, the wind shoving them toward the opposite shore—the Shawnee shore.

Susanna screamed, but Lael was speechless. There, crouching low behind a tangle of mountain laurel, was Captain Jack, just as she'd known he would be. All at once she was drenched with river water. He was dragging her and gesturing to the scalping knife at his waist. Behind her, Susanna screamed and screamed and would not stop.

She came awake at once, throwing back the thin blanket that seemed to hold a weight of water. The only sound was the drip of the rain outside the rock shelter. For a few lonesome moments she sat, heart a-gallop, not drenched in river water but her own salty sweat. She shut her eyes tight as if to block the dream.

What had Ma Horn once told her? *Stay standing . . . won't nothing ever befall you that the Lord don't allow.* If this was true, she reckoned the Lord had allowed Pa to die. Yet couldn't He have reached a hand down from heaven and helped her father at the last? Couldn't He have soothed the swollen river long enough to let him pass?

She broke camp and continued on her way. She knew she must still be mourning for the blooming dogwood and wild plum in her path only cut her with their beauty. Still, nothing looked familiar. Sometimes it seemed she was just circling, crisscrossing her own tracks, completely befuddled.

Lost, the still woods seemed to whisper. *Lael Click . . . lost.*

Had Pa ever been lost? Nay, not lost, she remembered him saying, but he confessed he'd once been bewildered for three days. Right then and there she got off her horse and knelt down in the cool, damp clover. She could ill afford to be befuddled three days, so she bowed her head and prayed to be set on the right path.

Soon after, she came to a wide trace, rutted and worn away by the trek of buffalo. The trace gleamed hard and white in the spring sun. Something within her, some remembrance long buried, broke free.

She was almost to the river.

The Louisa. The Shawnee Chenoa. The Kentucke.

The name mattered little. She was coming home.

She'd long dreamed of returning in spring when the dogwoods and wild plums were white as fine linen against the greening woods. In the meadows the rye grass and clover tickled the bottoms of her feet for she'd long since abandoned her boots. They hung from the saddle by their laces, forgotten.

The sun had come out as if in welcome, raising her spirits. She took a deep breath as she caught sight of the Kentucke River, winsome and curvaceous, a timeless blue. Beyond its spring-swollen banks on the opposite shore were the huge oaks and elms she'd known from childhood that now hid the Click cabin from view.

She'd come this way to avoid the settlement. She wanted to look again upon the place from which Pa had made his timely escape from a party of Cherokee when first coming into Kentucke all those years before, leaping off his horse and jumping off the rocky bluff into the waiting arms of the maple below. There it stood, solid and newly green and far taller than she remembered.

Unafraid, she urged the mare forward into the river. As if sensing her ease, the horse swam effortlessly into the cold current to the bank beyond. She could see her old homeplace now, chimney and all, and the sight made her oblivious to her dripping dress and saddlebags.

From a distance the cabin looked unchanged, hugging the tangled hillside, the grassy yard dotted with stumps and framed all around by the dark woods. But never in her remembering had the cabin sat so lonely and desolate, inhabited by pigeons, the chinking crumbling, the porch sagging beneath the weight of time and roses.

Nearly noon now, she climbed the hill and tethered the mare to a rail fence fashioned by Pa's own hands. The sun-warmed wood was soothing against her fingers, and along its length twined blackberry vine. Slipping off her heavy dress, she draped it over the fence to dry and retrieved another from the saddlebag.

How small the cabin looked! Her eyes ran over its hand-hewn details as she approached. The substantial chimney of river rock and mud. The tiny loft window. The old worn door stone. The sagging porch now bereft of Ma's rocking chair. She would need a rocker. Pa always said mountain ash couldn't be beat for furniture. A porch without a rocker looked naked and unsightly. And the rose canes—pretty though they were—would have to be cut back lest they grow right through the cabin door.

She kicked at a pile of dry leaves on the porch with a bare toe and watched them crumble to dust. Her whole being longed to straighten up and polish and set things right. This was home . . . *her home!* She felt like crying with her gladness.

At the door she paused, suddenly chilled, as the sun passed behind a cloud. Who had last passed through this door? Pa? Her mother? The day she'd left the settlement still hung heavy in her heart. She'd been but a girl then, heartsore and homesick. Now she was a woman, much the same.

She pushed against the heavy door, and it groaned in resistance. The room was dark and musty, and she went to the windows and threw open the shutters. Cobwebs caught in her hair, but the light was a welcome sight, dispelling every shadow. She made a face at the mess, as the chinking between the logs had begun to crumble and now littered the floor. The cabin had sat empty for a long time—after she'd gone to Virginia, her family had moved farther west to the Falls of the Ohio, where Pa built another cabin and surveyed land.

But truly, little had changed within. The long trestle table and benches were in the middle of the room, whitened with dust. The rope bedstead occupied one corner but was bare of a tick. On the mantle rested two wooden bowls and some gourds. Ma had taken little, she realized. But then, she'd had no need of such homely things, living in town and married to a man of means.

Next she inspected the barn and was surprised to find the old plow there along with a broom and some old tools. Taking the bucket, she drew water from the spring, thinking how fine the cabin looked with door and shutters wide open in welcome. It was dusk when she finished scrubbing the worn floor with sand and water and an old petticoat.

Chilled, she longed for the comfort of a fire. Taking the flint from a saddlebag, she coaxed a flame at the hearth, feeding it twigs and dry moss before adding old wood from the barn. The fire crackled and smoked gratifyingly, and she leaned back on her heels, cast back to another time when Ma had done the same each morning. The iron spider sat in back of the fire, blackened from years of use. Ma always said her chimney drew the best in the country.

But there would be no supper since she'd run out of provisions. By the light of a candle she took out a scrap of paper and quill and ink and began thinking of all that she needed. Salt. Cornmeal. Potatoes. Coffee. Sugar. Hunger made a long list, she mused. She had some money left and needed to go to Fort Click soon or starve.

But . . . what if Fort Click was not Fort Click at all but had been renamed? Five years away was not a coon's age, surely, but long enough to have wrought change in the settlement. Could it be true that numerous cabins now surrounded the stockade? What if Ma Horn had passed on?

She blew out the candle abruptly and retreated to her makeshift bed of old hay and quilts before the flickering fire. For a time she tossed about uncomfortably, finding the hard floor even less hospitable than the spring ground. She'd grown soft, she thought ruefully. Hadn't Pa preferred the forest floor in and out of season to a corn-husk or feather tick? She could hear his voice now as clearly as if he called from the corner.

Settle yourself, Daughter. There's worse things than a hard bed.

She listened to the faraway scuttle of a mouse in the loft and fell into an exhausted slumber.

24

Early the next morning she took the path to Pigeon Ridge. The familiar trail was overgrown, which Lael took as a troubling sign. But at every turn was a lovely gift—a clump of dewy violets, some tender shoots of salat, a fine mist that hung like a bridal veil from the treetops.

She knew at first sight that the cabin had been empty for some time. Tears of disappointment stung her eyes as she opened the door and stepped inside. There was no rocker by the fire or honeysuckle baskets overflowing with herbs and roots. Empty and cold as a tomb, not a stitch of furniture remained.

Ma Horn had not passed on, surely. Someone would have sent word from the settlement to Briar Hill. Theodora Humboldt Horn had no Kentucke kin but Neddy, yet someone would have taken her in if she were ill or infirm.

Lael could not rest until she knew where Ma Horn was. With Ma Horn gone, Susanna and Will were her closest neighbors. She had no choice but to take the mare, for the Bliss cabin at Cozy Creek was miles away. She missed so much by riding, failing to see all the little details spring had wrought. The morning was the warmest yet, and a faint wind stirred the newly leafed trees all around her, creating lacy patterns of light on the forest floor.

Halfway there, she stopped to drink at a spring and stared at her reflection in the whispering water. Suppose Susanna didn't recognize her—or was sore over her lack of a farewell long ago? As she rode, she prepared herself for their reunion. Maybe Will had moved them west to Missouri or some other distant place. With her heart beating so furiously it seemed a bird had been loosed in her ribcage, she took a deep breath.

As she drew near Will's old place, three children played beneath a pine, unaware of her approach. There was a curious absence of barking dogs. She remembered that Will had a penchant for dogs—not just any dogs, but tried and true bluetick hounds from Virginia.

She tied the mare to a fence and stood watching the children. She could see Susanna and Will in their small faces. The youngest, a girl, toddled about on fat legs and pulled at a cat's tail. The older two, both boys with dirty faces, were making stick drawings in the dirt.

Not wanting to startle them, she whistled softly. The girl looked up and, seeing her, bawled, "Ma-Maw!"

Susanna came running. Across the yard the children scrambled, hiding in her skirts and pointing toward Lael.

No light of recognition lit Susanna's face. For a moment Lael felt foolish—and speechless. Had she changed so much? As in days past she was bonnetless and barefoot. Her hair hung down her back in a long braid with little wisps about her face and she wore a simple linen dress with little trim.

Suddenly, Susanna threw up her arms. "Lael! Lael Click! Is that you?"

Lael smiled and held out her hands. "Here I am."

Susanna started across the yard, stumbling over her children in her gladness. The women embraced long and hard, then pulled apart in laughter.

"Why, I never!" Susanna exclaimed, looking her over. "You're supposed to be at some fancy school, fillin' your head with facts and figures—or so the settlement gossip goes."

"I've come home, to stay."

"To stay? Where?"

"Pa deeded me the land—all four hundred acres," Lael told her proudly. "I aim to live there."

"Alone?"

"Nay, not alone. There's my mare—and I'll have some chickens and a milk cow as soon as I'm able."

"Oh, Lael, it is you! Only you could talk so! But what about your ma and pa—and Ransom?"

Lael sobered then. "Pa's gone, Susanna. Last December, on the way to map the Missouri River country . . ." She nearly stumbled over the words as she said them, recalling anew the day she'd received Ma's letter.

Susanna, slack-jawed with shock, looked at the ground. Her children hung on her apron but were silent. "We never heard it here. We been cooped up in the cove all winter; not once have we been to the fort since fall."

"Better you hear it from me than some settlement ninny," Lael said. "Pa drowned crossing the Missouri on a cold, rainy day. The river was swollen from the winter thaw . . . the current was too strong. The Spanish government had granted him land in Missouri, and he was going to claim it."

Susanna looked bewildered. "You sure? That sets queer with me."

Lael could do nothing but nod, the threat of tears too near.

Wet-eyed herself, Susanna pressed on. "And your ma?"

"Ma's remarried and lives in Bardstown. Ransom's with her." For a fleeting moment Lael felt guilty she'd not stopped and seen them. But her heart was yet too sore, her resentment too fresh about Ma's remarrying. She'd simply wanted to come home as fast as she could with no detours along the way, though she did miss her brother.

"Ransom. He was just a little feller when you set out. I misdoubt I'd know him on sight."

They fell silent for a moment, then Susanna hooked her arm

through Lael's, calling to her oldest boy, "Henry, go water and hay that mare. Then we'll all go in the house for some pie and coffee."

They said little once inside. Susanna bustled about the cabin, fetching dishes and cups from a corner cupboard—not the daily wooden ones, but the chipped blue china her mother had brought over the gap from North Carolina. She set the kettle over the fire while the children vied for the biggest piece of pie and the closest seat to Lael.

"My oldest is Henry," Susanna called over her shoulder as she made coffee. "Then there's Ben. And my baby—well, she had such fair hair and green eyes I couldn't call her nothin' but Lael."

"Lay-elle," the little girl echoed shyly.

Lael smiled and reached out to touch a wisp of the fine baby hair. "I'm honored, Susanna. Did Will put up too much of a fuss?"

Susanna smiled and poured the coffee. "He wanted to call her Matilda Jane after his mother, but I stood my ground. I said she'd never know the difference, her being grave-bound and all. He called her Matilda for a week then gave up." She sat down and sampled a piece of pie, then looked at Lael long and hard. "You don't have the look of a lady, all huffy and high-minded. I was a-feared you would be. Now your voice, it's some different."

"Oh?"

"I have a notion you could talk a blue streak and I wouldn't know a word you'd be saying. But that dress of yours is as homely as mine."

Lael looked down and smoothed a crease. "It's a simple one. I was afraid you wouldn't know me if I wore anything else."

Susanna looked dashed. "I hope you have some fancy dresses. It would tickle me to see somethin' other than homespun."

Lael smiled, thinking how she had once felt the same, in awe of satins and velvets and pretty painted silks. "Henry, fetch my pack, if you please."

140

From the pack Lael pulled out a small straw hat encircled with silk pansies and a pair of kid gloves. Susanna drew in her breath, and six childish eyes rounded in delight. "I've no pretty dresses with me today. Just these—for you." Lael set the hat atop Susanna's head, and little Lael clapped in delight. "A sight better than an old poke bonnet!"

Susanna laughed. "And these gloves are soft as butter. They'll do fine to cover up these knotty hands of mine." She removed the hat and set it in her lap. "There's big changes in the settlement, Lael. Last spring the men built a church just beyond the fort's west wall. There's no preacher yet so it's sat empty over the winter, but sometimes a circuit rider comes round. You should hear the singin' on Sundays. Like a choir of angels."

Listening, Lael forgot her pie and coffee, a tangle of bittersweet feelings in her breast.

"There's been lots of changes, mostly good. But the old timers are passing on," Susanna went on.

Lael swallowed and the words formed an ache in her throat as she asked, "And Ma Horn? Is she . . . well?"

"Ma Horn moved to the fort two years back, being blind in one eye and all. She can't get around like she used to, and there's been a sight of sickness in the settlement. She ain't been up here since she birthed Henry."

"But that was years ago!" Lael exclaimed.

"I birthed the last two myself, with Will's help," Susanna said with a touch of pride. "But I do miss Ma Horn. No one else knows where the best ginseng grows and all them healin' herbs."

Susanna poured more coffee and Lael looked around, sensing her friend's contentment. "This is all so good . . . the pie . . . you . . . the children. Are you happy, Susanna?"

Susanna shooed the children back outside but left the door open. When she sat back down her eyes were alight. "I done right by marryin' Will, Lael. He's a good man."

"Where is he?"

"Took to the woods with his dogs this morning. Say you'll stay for supper, Lael, and spend the night. Say you'll stay till we get our visit out."

Lael smiled. "Then I don't expect I'll ever leave."

When Will returned after noon, he carried a wild turkey, his pack of tired dogs close behind. His eyes twinkled when he spotted Lael. "So the good Lord has brought you back to us."

Lael smiled. "I don't know if it's the Lord's doing or my own."

"Either way, we're mighty glad to have you," he replied, handing her his catch. "Now let's see how a fine Virginia lady handles an old bird. Or are you still your father's daughter?"

The rest of the day was spent in many of the domestic duties Lael had nearly forgotten. Scalding and plucking the bird. Digging for potatoes stored in straw in the springhouse. Grinding corn into meal for bread. Setting the table and filling the salt gourd.

The interior of the cabin held all the touches of a man's hand that warmed a woman's heart. A sturdy pine cupboard with a leaf pattern whittled in the doors. A cradle big enough to hold two babies. A spinning wheel under one shuttered window.

After the supper dishes had been cleared away, and Will and the children were in bed, Lael found herself alone with Susanna before the fire. Outside, the katydids chorused in the calm of the warm night, and far beyond the shuttered windows a wolf howled. Lael felt a little thrill that she could hardly recall the civilized sounds of Virginia—bells tolling, carriages clip-clopping, the incessant hum of voices day and night. Her mind seemed clear and spacious and settled for the first time in years.

"There's been no Injun trouble for some time now," Susanna

said in a hushed voice. "The worst of it came before you left, when the Canes were killed and burnt out. Since then there's been some horse stealin' and random killin' but no attacks on the fort."

She got up and moved about the room, checking the latches on the shutters and the heavy bar across the door before taking her seat with a sigh. Watching her, Lael sensed there was more than Indian trouble on her mind, and she braced herself to hear whatever Susanna held back.

All day long they had skirted the subject of Simon, at times coming dangerously close when Susanna spoke of her kin or the goings-on in the settlement. All day the suspense had been building around the omission of his name until here at day's end they could hide from it no longer.

Susanna gave a push to the rocker that was across from Lael's own. "I never thought to see you again, Lael. None of us did. The day your pa pulled out, Ma Horn said we'd not see hide nor hair of you again, and everyone believed it. But it's queer, ain't it, how you come to be here right now, like you knowed . . ." She broke off and looked into the fire, fingers twining and untwining in her lap. "It's queer how you come back, just in time."

Lael sat utterly still. An uncomfortable silence fell between them like a chasm neither was willing to cross. Lael studied her old friend, her thoughts wild with speculation, her heart like a stone in her chest. Susanna would not look at her. Lael's voice was soft. "Say it, Susanna."

Susanna looked up, her eyes reflecting resignation. "Simon is to wed Piper Cane on Sunday next."

Lael let the words flower fully in her mind with all their unwanted implications. "Sunday next," she echoed.

"Aye, at noon, alongside the river by the fort."

Lael swallowed, her mouth dry. After all this time the sting of betrayal still hurt. Years before she and Piper and Simon had been linked in a strange and twisted love knot—and were still. She said dully, "I should have expected it long before now."

Susanna reached across and clasped her hand. "But you've come back! There's still time! Once he knows you're here—"

"Nay!" Lael exclaimed. "He mustn't know."

Susanna looked incredulous. "But he must! Why would he dally with the likes of Piper Cane these past five years? She's badgered him into marrying her, is all. He was heartbroke when you left. All he ever wanted was you, ever since you forted up with us when you were just a young 'un."

Lael shook her head. "There's much that you don't know, Susanna. The past is the past. Let's leave it be."

"Tell me you don't love him, and then I'll leave it be. Tell me that."

This time Lael looked away. "I loved a boy once. I hardly know the man."

Simon Hayes is all show and no stay.

"Simon's the same as he ever was, only handsomer," Susanna said softly.

Lael's heart twisted painfully. She longed to ask, *How handsome? How tall? How deep is his voice? Does he ever speak of me?*

Susanna continued in a rush, "You should see his homeplace! He got an extra thousand acres from the land commission, and he's put in the first crop of tobacco in this country. Everything he touches turns to gold, and I ain't just sayin' so 'cause he's my brother." Her mouth turned grim. "But he's makin' a mistake come Sunday. You remember how Piper Cane had no kin after that Shawnee raid so Ma took her in. Ma always was one for strays and orphans and the like. I never wanted it to happen, but Piper Cane, with her bewitchin' ways, stayed on long after, and I saw her work quite a spell on Simon."

Lael shut her mind against the thought of Simon and Piper

living and loving beneath the same roof. "He's made his choice," she said flatly, beginning to let go of the dream she had carried in her heart for so long.

Abruptly she got up and opened a shutter and leaned out onto the sill, letting the night breeze brush her face and wanting to clear her head of all she'd just heard. Behind her, Susanna came and placed a gentle hand on her shoulder. "I always wanted you for a sister, Lael, and it ain't too late."

For a long time Lael stood alone by the window until her legs grew numb beneath her, the still night like a balm to her unsettled spirits. She was glad she'd come, but all the joy had gone out of the visit. She retired to the corner bed Will and Susanna had graciously given over to her. The corn shucks rustled beneath her weight and felt strangely comfortable. But sleep did not come.

In the morning, after some half-hearted bites of cornmeal mush laced with sorghum and cream, she prepared to leave, smiling wryly as Susanna supplied her with a generous supply of meal and other necessities. She hadn't had to say a thing about her need, but somehow Susanna knew. Around her the children ate cheerfully, anxious to meet the day. She teased and talked with them and envied them their innocence.

Her last words to Susanna were soft but stern: "Not a word to anyone, you hear?"

Susanna shook her head in consternation, but there were tears in her eyes. "You're a hard one, Lael Click. Suppose somebody sees you?"

Lael turned the mare toward home. "Nobody will."

25

In the days to come Lael was careful to keep to the cabin. No longer did she make a fire in the hearth lest someone see the smoke from the chimney. Blessedly, the days were warm. She took her meals cold but hardly ate at all. Susanna had given her an ample supply of bear bacon, hominy, salt, a pouch of dried apples, and a sack of dried beans to tide her over till she could go to the fort.

She avoided the river, though once, under the cover of twilight, she walked down the long, sloping bank to bathe. With great effort, she shunned all thoughts of Simon. But like the memory of Pa he was everywhere, enduringly linked to the river and the woods and hills around her.

Perhaps I was wrong to come back. But in her heart she knew it was the only place to be. Here it was a wonder to shake off time and be free of its pressures and restraints. She recalled the silver pocket watch given to her by Miss Mayella when she'd finished her first year. It was perfectly round with a dainty chain and a filigree of leaves on its face, but she'd been unable to truly appreciate its beauty. She'd sold it before leaving Virginia, and the extra funds had helped her come home.

And so she spent her first days rediscovering her homeplace. She trimmed back the rose canes, newly leafed and already heavy with tiny buds, inspected the harnesses and bridles hanging in the barn, sorted through Pa's tools, sharpened the ax head, and added to her list of needed supplies.

On a whim one day she climbed to the loft and there, beneath a pile of straw, long buried, lay her rifle and the Indian blanket with the blue stripe, one corner still fire-blackened. She took up the gun but let the blanket lay for now, awash with memories. What had become of Captain Jack? The haze of years had come between them, severing her infatuation with him, if not her lingering fascination. She was slowly letting go of Simon. Time to do the same with the Shawnee.

For two days she labored at replacing the chinking that had crumbled all over the plank floor. She trod a worn path to and from the river, gathering mud to press between the logs. Her shoulders and arms ached from heaving the buckets, but her reward was a deep, dreamless sleep each night.

She plotted out a corn patch small enough for a woman alone to turn her hand to yet ample enough to see her through the winter. Looking out over the vast meadow that had once been a sea of corn, she felt a tiny prick of alarm. How would she, a girl gone soft, ever turn over the sod? The field was overgrown with rye grass and clover and blackberry vines thick as rope. It had once taken all Pa's strength, and her ma with him, to wrestle the land into submission.

Still mulling the corn, she repaired the paling fence that once framed the garden spot to the left of the cabin, then began to turn over the soil with a shovel for a vegetable patch. In her hands the dirt was black and loamy and smelled richly of spring, promising potatoes and beans, squash and turnips. Susanna had said that watermelons were now being grown at the fort!

As the day approached when Simon would wed, Lael's spirits began to sag, though it signaled an end to her self-imposed exile, and once again she could ride into the settlement, head held high and free, an independent woman.

The wedding day dawned bright and glorious. The sun's first rays crept onto the cabin porch and peered at her through the shuttered windows. She rolled over on her makeshift bed and thought wistfully, *This is the day I might have wed Simon Hayes.*

By noon she'd climbed to the knob. Up high, she felt stronger and more settled. She watched the sweeping arm of the sun change the valleys below from green to gold and noted that the swallows flew low to the ground, a sure sign of rain.

That evening it did rain, falling hard and clean on the cabin roof. 'Twas a fine night for wedded bliss, she mused. As a girl, she'd often dreamed of being a bride, but maybe it was time to put that wish away. She'd been unlucky in love even at Briar Hill. No man had ever turned her head, trapped as she was in the past. Those fine city dandies hadn't the appeal of the stalwart woodsmen and Indians she'd been raised with.

Maybe I'm meant to be alone like this. No husband, no babies in a cradle, no rocking chair in which to nurse them and kiss them and croon to them. Just me, and only me. For always.

Chilled, she finally lit a fire and looked back just once, recollecting how she and Simon had rowed the river in a boat with bittersweet at its bow and he'd begged her to run away with him.

The Sabbath passed quietly, but on Monday she steeled herself for the coming confrontation. Lael chose a plain indigo dress and put her hair up with a multitude of pins, topping it off with the straw hat she favored. For once she regretted she had no bonnet to hide behind.

She could have found her way blindfolded to Fort Click. She crested Hackberry Ridge with a queer feeling in her whole being. The sun was in her eyes, but the settlement was plain before her. She felt like a girl again, come to fort up in times of trouble or simply fetch supplies with Pa. For a fleeting moment she drew the mare to a halt, unable to go on.

The fort had two new blockhouses and its gates were open wide, a sign of peaceful times. The outlying cornfields looked newly turned, pale green stalks thrusting through the rich soil. The new church stood apart, its logs green and shiny. And then there was the river with paths worn to and fro, and the twin springs shaded by the age-old tree Ma called the divine elm.

Recognized or not, she knew she would create a stir simply because she was a woman and she rode alone. At the gate a group of men looked up as she passed. She lowered her head and eyed the row of cabins. Susanna hadn't told her which was Ma Horn's. She looked about in bewilderment, passing children and dogs at play on the common, her ears assaulted by the high-pitched ring of the blacksmith's anvil. But it was not Simon's father who hammered hard at the smithy, for the Hayes clan had moved farther west.

She tethered her horse to a nearby post and knocked on the cabin door she remembered. Her spirits fell when there was no response. She knocked again, so loudly this time she felt she was calling all the fort's inhabitants out of their cabins and announcing her presence. And then she remembered: Ma Horn was half blind and a bit deaf, Susanna said. With a push at the door, she entered, standing on the sill long enough for her eyes to adjust to the gloom.

From the shadows came a beloved, quivery voice. "I've been prayin' for your return, child. Five long years. And now the good Lord has seen fit to answer my prayers."

Ma Horn was much changed. Lael knelt by the old woman's rocker and laid her head in the apron-covered lap and cried, tears of gladness and of mourning. Ma Horn's arthritic fingers stroked her bent head and the years fell away and she was a child again, loved and understood and at rest.

"Did they try to take all the wilderness out of you at that fancy school?"

Lael assured her they had not, pointing to her bare feet as proof.

"Law, but you're a sight for sore eyes. You look the same, only you've growed taller. You always did have the prettiest head of hair in the country."

They drank steaming cups of sassafras tea, and Lael felt a bittersweet sadness. Everything felt strange, a bit rusty, as if she herself had changed so much she couldn't quite get comfortable again. Several times the old woman reached out to pat Lael's hand or head as if to convince herself she'd truly come home.

"So your ma's took another husband. It's to be expected, her being a woman who can't do without a man and pinin' for your pa."

"Mr. Ashcroft is a barrister," Lael told her. "They met when he settled Pa's estate. It was through him that Pa deeded me the land."

"Your pa did right to leave you the land. I reckon you'll be stayin' on then."

"Aye, it's my home. I never should have left it."

But Ma Horn shook her head. "It ain't fittin' for you to be livin' alone, child."

Lael squeezed her bony, work-hardened hand. "Come home with me. Let me take you out of this place. Let me be your eyes and ears from here on."

But Ma Horn only smiled. "This here's my home now and I don't often pass a lonely day. Folks come as far as Castle Rock to get my remedies and to sit a spell."

Lael looked up, wondering how she possibly went herbing. Overhead were the same baskets she helped fill when they went a-gathering in the old days. The pungent scent of herbs—a touch medicinal and somewhat spicy—pervaded the gloom. Just this morning Lael had come across a patch of ginseng along the creek bottom and the sight nearly unseated her from her horse.

"I aim to dig some ginseng for profit. I'll bring you some if you need it," she promised.

"Bring some coltsfoot and a peck of salat too. There ain't nothin' like salat to strengthen the blood come spring."

Before Lael finished her tea, Ma Horn was dozing in her chair. She was loath to leave, yet she had other business to attend to. The long list in her pocket would take time to settle. She moved to the door noiselessly, but before she could open it Ma Horn came awake.

"Are you pinin' for Simon, child?"

Lael tied the ribbons of her straw hat under her chin with deft fingers and forced steadiness into her voice. "Some. But I don't aim to pine long for a married man."

The sutler said there was no wagon to be had, just a two-wheeled cart. Lael decided it would suit her, perusing the store's dimly lit interior and peeking into kegs and barrels as she went. The walls were thick with merchandise, from hand tools to sundry spices. She marveled at the improved selection and wondered where the old storekeeper had gone. What Ma would have given for some nutmeg! A wood-and-tin nutmeg grater proved irresistible, and a small collection of bottled mustards and vinegars was purchased as much for sentiment as practicality. Pa had always been fond of such. She had trouble keeping to her list the longer she tarried.

As the storekeeper weighed salt and cut deer hide for moccasins, she felt him cast sly glances toward her, her pale profile half hidden beneath the straw hat. She finished counting out her money while he gathered up the heaviest goods and followed her into the blinding sunlight.

They worked together to hitch the cart to the mare, failing to notice the small crowd gathering. When the cart was finally loaded and tied down and she turned to mount her horse, she looked up.

"Well, I'll be switched if it ain't Lael Click!"

On the other side of the mare stood old Amos, the fort fiddler, nearly toothless and with a grin so wide it seemed about to swallow his face. She grinned back at him, then just as abruptly he sobered. "I was real sorry to hear about your pa."

The sorrow in his eyes touched her, and she looked around as other faces came into focus. Old timers, all of them. There was Jane McFee and Silas Minor who had first come over the gap with Pa. And then there was John Logan, a surveyor and hunting partner of Pa's as well.

She greeted them, and the crowd pressed closer and began to pepper her with questions. Five years was a lot of territory to cover, she thought, but she answered them as best she could. Not one of them cautioned or rebuked her for living alone, but she could read the concern in their faces.

"I got a good rooster and some hens I can spare you," Jane offered kindly. "Some rags too, if you'll be needin' rugs to pretty up your place."

"If you need some seed, I got some extry to give," Silas said.

She knew better than to refuse them, and so, with a promise to return on the morrow, she got up on the mare and bid them good-bye. She had much yet to do this day and, with a renewed sense of purpose in her heart, she waved farewell and set out toward home.

26

Woven with the evening shadows was a chorus of tree frogs and katydids. Lael washed up the dishes she'd bought at the fort, hanging her dishrag to dry on a stump and carrying the rinse water to the garden. It was so lovely and cool for a June evening that she brought her journal and ink onto the porch. With a steady flowing hand she dated her next entry.

June 4, 1783. The weather is dry and fair . . .

She looked up at the fading skyline, with its wisps of gauzy clouds. Mare's tails, Pa called them. She lay down her quill, remembering her own mare. At her call, only the sigh of the wind was her answer. It had become an evening ritual to take her to the outlying meadow, but tonight she'd forgotten. She stepped off the porch, looking to the wall of woods to the west. Behind her, the cabin sat in shadows. Though belled, the mare was nowhere to be found, and the darkness was deepening.

Perhaps a painter was about and the mare had spooked. Horses feared painters like people feared haints. Slowly, she retraced her steps. As she rounded the cabin she heard a deep, distressed whinny. To her dismay, the mare had trampled Ma's bed of black-eyed Susans hugging the chimney wall. The proud flowers lay crushed and askew, their petals scattered. Before Lael could take one more step, the mare bolted and ran off toward the river.

And then she knew. Dogs gone queer. Hens refusing to lay. Cows milling about, refusing to go to pasture . . .

With a small cry she ran inside the cabin. Her thoughts were flighty and vacuous. With furious haste she moved about. She became her mother again, slamming the shutters closed and barring the door, laying the rifle upon the table with powder and lead, finally banking the fire. She stopped short of climbing to the loft and drawing the ladder up after her.

Soon the sound of hoofbeats thundered, but in her befuddled state she couldn't tell if it was one or a dozen riders. All she knew was they came at breakneck speed through the brush, calling to her before they reached the cabin. Two men crossed into the yard, raising a storm of dust, but only one paused. The other disappeared into the woods on the path that led to Cozy Creek.

Lael took up the rifle and stepped onto the porch, feeling she might be sick. The rider removed his battered hat at the sight of her. "Name's Asa Forbes, miss. There's Indians comin' from the north, seeking revenge after two trappers ambushed a party of Shawnees near Tate's Creek. We're ridin' to warn ye." He crammed his hat back on his unruly brown head as if to hurry her, his solid frame taut with tension.

There was no choice but to fort up. Tears pricked her eyes— tears this man would take for fear but were instead a mortal dread. The prospect of meeting Simon was at hand, and she could do nothing to avoid it.

"My horse ran off," she said dully.

"I'll take you in," he volunteered, coming nearer the porch.

With a heavy step, Lael grabbed a basket of herbs, fastened the top shut with a leather thong, and got up behind the man who looked to be little older than she herself. With her gun tucked in the crook of her arm, its barrel pointing skyward, she took a last look at the cabin and wondered when or if she'd see it again.

As they crested Hackberry Ridge, the moon had never looked so big or so bright. It was during such a moon that travel by night would be simple and certain for their attackers. Lael shivered as they made haste to the fort's gates. Inside the common was a mob of anxious people and animals. Candles shone from every cabin window, including Ma Horn's.

Everywhere there was a queer feeling of chaos. She wondered who would step forward and take charge now that Pa was gone. Even Colonel Corey had moved on, though they had need of his marksmanship at such a tense time. Somewhere in the throng stood Simon, she felt sure. As soon as she was able she slipped off Asa Forbes's horse and disappeared into Ma Horn's cabin.

Inside, Ma Horn had a Bible open in her lap, the hearth's fire illuminating the Psalms. "The moon's ripe for trouble, child, and there's naught but a bunch of bootless rogues and ruffians to lead us. I'll be countin' on the women to bring us through. Jane McFee and Eliza Harold are dead shots—better'n most men."

Lael added several sticks of wood to the fire, the dread of a long siege coming back to her. "We'll have need of bullets come morning. Remember the time we had to melt your pewter plates? Now where's your lead kettle and molds?"

"Underneath the bed," Ma Horn sighed and stirred out of her rocker. "With bullets come wounds so we'd best be brewing some poultices as well."

They set to work, laying the filled molds to cool on the trestle table, cutting bandages from clean cloth, straining slippery elm and white oak for poultices. In time, Susanna and the children came seeking refuge, and Will, a member of the militia, left to join the men gathered on the common.

Lael stood by the shuttered window and watched the small company muster. At first her eyes passed blithely over the rows of men facing eastward and away from her, then they turned searching, almost beseeching, assessing height and girth. Even with a beaver hat covering his shock of red hair, Lael could have picked Simon out of a thousand such men, so engraved was his every manner on her heart.

He stood at the end of the second row, so near he could hear her if she called. He was head and shoulders above the other men, and this distinction made her feel a pride she couldn't own.

Turn away, her judgment warned.

Stay, her heart called.

Torn, she did both, turning a cold shoulder and then, succumbing to the desire to look at him after so long, she placed both hands along the sill and leaned forward and let the years melt away.

I never aimed to be your brother, Lael, he'd told her. Nay, once he'd wanted much more than that.

She didn't take her eyes off Simon until the report of a rifle made her stiffen. The men on the common scrambled, flying to their assigned posts. She watched as Eliza Harold and Jane McFee, dressed in breeches and hunting shirts, took up positions along the north wall. Simon and Will disappeared into the southeast blockhouse.

Within moments Susanna was beside her, face drawn. "So it's begun."

Lael closed the shutter. "One shot, is all. Will is—"

But her voice was drowned out by a volley of gunfire. A whimper on the loft ladder made them turn. Susanna went to the children, forcing a smile. "Come down for some breakfast, and Ma Horn'll tell you a story."

The three of them ran to Ma Horn's outstretched arms, while Susanna set about making mush. Heart tripping, Lael began filling a gunnysack with lead, ignoring the call to stay and eat. As she slipped outside, the smell of spent powder and the curl of smoke brought home the terror and uncertainty of the moment. But all she could think about was Simon. Simon was here, somewhere. And where Simon was, Piper surely followed.

She walked along the south wall, carrying her load, anxious to peer out a gun hole but all were taken. She found Asa Forbes in the process of reloading, and she boldly stepped into his position, her eyes sweeping Hackberry Ridge and then the river.

Asa swore under his breath as he uncapped his powder horn. "Beats all I ever seen—Wyandotte by water and Shawnee by land. Them rascals have joined forces against us. If you be any sort of a shot at all, miss, you best be joinin' us here at the wall."

She saw plainly the canoes that lined the beloved banks of the river, the painted, near-naked men who'd brought them there crouching low in the thick brush just out of rifle range. But the ridge? At first glance, the ridge looked peaceful and green as always. But the longer she looked the subtlety of movement there chilled her. The stirring of a bush when there was no wind. The flicker of the rising sun on a gun barrel. The sudden flush of a skittish bird.

Unsettled, she turned away. She'd not thought it would come to this. She'd counted on this being a false alarm like other times or, at worst, a short-lived skirmish. Fort Click was known for its guns and men like Pa who—

Another volley of rifle fire thundered as a large party of Shawnee came running down from the ridge, screaming like banshees and firing rifles of their own. Asa Forbes pushed her aside, shoving his gun through the hole, then sighting and firing.

Almost choking from the smoke, Lael turned away and saw someone fall from the pickets. With a cry she ran forward, forgetting the gunnysack. A man lay face down in the dirt, his hat several feet away. She turned him over, fear chewing a hole in her stomach, and saw that he was just a boy.

Dead? His wound was in the shoulder and though not a mortal

one, he was unconscious. She sighed with relief though blood was flowing into the ground. Ma Horn's cabin was only a few steps away. Soon she had him moved and lying on the corner bed in the cabin. As she cleaned the wound, Ma Horn came and looked him over.

"He's John Logan's boy, Sam. You'd best send for his ma when you're through. She can tend him while you see to another."

Another? Lael prayed there would be no others. But within an hour, two more men lay on straw pallets on the cabin floor.

Will returned, face grim. "They've begged off and want to parley. Captain Jack is calling for some of the militia to meet him outside the gate."

Captain Jack? Lael's hands stilled and she stared at Will.

One of the wounded men on the floor groaned. "It's a bloody trick, Bliss! They'll lift your scalp soon as you set foot outside. Them white trappers killed six of their warriors. You think they'll stop with any less of our men?"

"I ain't familiar with the new Shawnee chief," Will mused, passing an agitated hand over his beard. "I don't know whether his word is good or not, though he does speak English. With our powder gettin' low we have little choice but to parley."

"And if you refuse?" Lael asked, changing the bloodied dressing on the wounded boy.

Will looked directly at her, a nervous tic pulling at his left eye. "If we refuse, they'll likely set fire to the fort—and the cornfields."

He left them, and the ensuing silence was more terrifying than the gunfire. The cabin was overly warm and sickly smelling from the brewing herbs, but it was the sweat of the men, borne out of fear and pain, that made breathing a chore.

Breathless, she slipped outside. The moon was already rising above Hackberry Ridge, and a lull in the gunfire created a strained hush. Taking her gun, Lael went to a vacant gun hole

158

and peered out. A dozen or so redmen lay scattered between the fort's main gate and the river. In the moonlight their war paint and glossy hair and jewelry bore an eerie luster. Near the gate were two of their own. The white men lay as still as the fallen Indians, unmoving, their blood soaking the ground. This then was the result of the parley. In the gloom she couldn't determine who they were. Could one be Will?

Old Amos appeared at her elbow, gun in hand. "I been watchin' the dead men, and one don't seem dead at all. Have a look."

And so she did. One of the white men on the ground was indeed alive. As she stared she saw that his hand moved ever so perceptibly, not once, but twice.

"Best train your rifle," Amos said, stepping up to sight. "They's goin' to open the gate and bring 'im in."

She moved to the fort wall, taking up her rifle and thrusting it through the hole. She could hear the gate swing open just a crack, groaning as it did. It was Will who ran out to pull the man to safety. Just as he reached him, a half dozen fallen redmen leapt to their feet and stormed the gate, hacking at the air with tomahawks and firing wildly into the common.

"Lord have mercy! Them Injuns have risen from the dead!" old Amos shouted.

Feeling she might faint, Lael ran back to the cabin, bolting the door and the shutter behind her. Ma Horn and Susanna looked up from tending the wounded.

"What's happenin' out there?" Susanna asked, ashen.

"There's some trouble at the gate," she answered, willing her hands to stop shaking. Indeed, not only her hands but her whole body quivered like a leaf in the wind.

"It's Will, ain't it? I—"

"Get the children into the loft and draw up the ladder."

As the ladder disappeared through the dark hole, Lael wanted nothing so much as to run after it and hide as well. Outside, the screaming and gunfire mingled in a grotesque chorus as she stood by the hearth feeding sticks of wood to the flames. If the door was broken down, she might use the burning wood as a weapon. She'd given her gun to one of the wounded men who could still sit upright. At the door, Susanna had taken up an ax.

Oh, dear God, help us. Spare us.

She remembered Miss Mayella's parting words to her only weeks before. *May God watch between us when we are absent one from another.*

Was God watching over her now? Was Miss Mayella praying? For a fleeting, desperate moment she rued coming back to this fearsome place. She'd been away so long she'd gone soft. Images were ricocheting through her head like spent musket balls— thoughts of Simon and Captain Jack and Pa, even Piper—pushing aside all common sense. Where was God in all this confusion? Looking up, she saw Susanna studying her as if she sensed how upended she was. Not the old Lael Click she'd always known, her wary eyes seemed to say, but a weak and vulnerable woman.

Oh Lord, help us. Help me. I am not the girl I was.

27

A loud banging sounded on the door, but Ma Horn would only open it when she heard Will shout. He stood on the threshold, sweat streaming down his face, his arms filled with a large, blood-splattered figure. Behind him stood John Logan, and in his arms was Simon.

There was little room for either man in the crowded cabin. Ma Horn called for Susanna to pass down the loft mattress, and this she did gladly, her eyes drinking in the sight of Will.

At first glance Lael determined that Simon hadn't suffered a mortal injury, though he was unconscious. She motioned for Simon to be laid upon the mattress, while Will placed his burden on the trestle table before the hearth.

Looking on, Lael's first reaction was to weep. "His name?"

"Marcus Fowler," Will told her quietly.

A tomahawk had disfigured the left side of his face, and his scalp was so bloody and bare she had to swallow down the bile backing up in her throat at the sight. Numbly, she took a cloth and a bowl of water and began to clean him. His wounds were so grievous she couldn't tell if he was young or old, comely or plain. But he was no less brave. For a long time she stood over him until, finally, she was called away.

"My eyes fail me," Ma Horn said, showing her the gunshot wound in Simon's shoulder. "I ain't able to get the lead out, try as I might."

Simon had come to and was moaning now, moving his head

from side to side. His eyes, brown as coffee beans, were open but unseeing. Lael wiped her hands and took up the pincer-like tool. The lead ball had smashed a good deal of bone and was embedded deep within the shoulder. Blood seeped through his muslin shirt, dripping onto the corn-husk mattress, warning her to work quickly. She called for some whiskey, and Susanna brought forth a jug, holding her brother's head and forcing him to swallow.

Nearly nauseous, Lael probed the wound deeply as Susanna and Ma Horn held him fast. The light of the tallow candles was dim at best, and Simon, strong as a bull, would occasionally thrash about, unnerving them all. Sweat streamed down her face and neck in sticky rivulets as she worked.

"We need a doctor," she said aloud, her voice unsteady as the candle flame. A doctor—not like the ones at Briar Hill, befuddled by drink or their own self-importance, but a man with a steady hand and heart who earned his keep. A man who could extract a lead ball without mangling more of the shoulder.

At last she managed to remove the lead, dropping the ball in a cup and placing it on the mantle. Soon after, Piper came in, pushing past them and dropping to her knees by Simon's side. In all fairness, she'd never looked so lovely. Her dark glossy hair was knotted at the nape of her neck, and her dress, waistless to allow for a growing child, was a clean, pale blue.

Looking on, Lael saw that the rumors were true. With Piper pregnant, it had indeed been a hasty wedding. A stinging burst of resentment flared, and then her heart twisted at the sight. Once Piper had suffered the loss of her entire family. Now she was afraid of losing Simon as well.

Bone weary, blood covering her own dress and flecking her face, Lael looked at her and said, "He'll live."

But Piper cried as if her heart were broken. The three women looked on in dismay, then Susanna's voice rang out, sharp as steel in the cramped cabin. "You can take up your cryin' elsewheres, Piper Cane Hayes. You'll fracture the men's nerves with your wailin', and I'll not allow it."

In truth, it was their own nerves that were fractured, Lael thought. Most of the men were blessedly unconscious or, in Simon's case, medicinally drunk. She drew a sigh of relief when Piper fled the cabin.

Numb, she poured a fresh pitcher of water and tore strips of clean cloth to rewrap Marcus Fowler's head. His breathing was shallower now, scarcely breathing at all, and she knew he'd be dead by morning.

Near dawn she heard someone cry out. She stirred, stiff from sitting against the hearthstones, and came awake to a cold fire, her body trammeled by weariness. Susanna, who'd sat vigil with Simon, was nowhere to be seen.

She went first to Marcus Fowler and found he had died in the night. Taking a sheet, she covered him, feeling at a loss. She moved among the other men, examining their wounds and feeling for fever, wondering all the while if the dead man had kin.

"Lael."

Her hands stilled at the sound. The name was spoken like a caress, so soft she was certain only she had heard. When she turned, Simon grabbed her wrist. He was lucid now, looking up at her from his mattress on the floor.

"It *is* you. I heard—" He winced from the sudden movement, and his shoulder began to bleed afresh. "I heard—but I misdoubted you'd stay—but you come back—to me."

Frantic, she pulled free of his weak hold and turned toward the hearth, out of his reach. Taking up a poker, she scratched at the ashes for a live coal, hearing him call to her again, a lazy drawl in the suddenly still room. The tenderness in his voice threatened to undo her. Her hands were trembling again, and she feared her whole body would follow.

Would the pain in her heart never ease? Five years she'd been away, yet her feeling for him was fresh as yesterday. *Oh Simon! Simon! What have you done?* Coming home and hearing about him had been hard enough, but now—seeing him—seeing Piper carrying his child when it should have been her—

"Lael," he called again, his voice near breaking.

With a sob, she covered her face with her hands. The poker clattered to the hearth, awakening Ma Horn. As she stirred, Lael shucked off her soiled apron and hurried to the door just as Susanna entered. Lael nearly collided with her in her haste.

At once, Susanna's eyes widened. "Lael? What is it? What—?" She swung to Simon and saw the telling look on her brother's face.

Lael pushed past, wiping her eyes. "I've got to get shut of this place."

"Lael, you don't mean—?"

But Lael was already walking across the fort common, aware of the lull in gunfire. Susanna ran after her, pleading. They were making a spectacle of themselves, truly. Some of the men along the pickets turned to watch them in the pale morning light.

"Lael, you can't go. It's—it's—"

"Suicide?" Lael finished for her. "I'll need a good horse. I reckon Asa Forbes's bay will do."

"Lael—please—listen to reason . . ."

Susanna stopped, but Lael kept walking. Toward light and fresh air and freedom. Whatever the cost.

Will met her at the corral. The horses were restless, anticipating the next round of gunfire, the dust never settling. He put his hand out as if to soothe a fractious colt. *Whoa, Lael,* she half expected to hear him say. His voice was low but incredulous. "Ain't you even goin' to ask what's happenin' outside them walls?"

She reached for a bridle dangling from the fence. "I don't care, Will. I'm going out, plain and simple."

He grabbed her arm. "It ain't plain and simple, Lael. You'll lose your scalp if you go out them gates."

"It's my choice and no one else's," she said, pulling free. John Logan and another man approached warily, their eyes clouded with weariness. Would they try to stop her? She ignored them, finally securing Asa's prize bay.

As she led the horse out, Will threw down his hat. "Your pa did some rash things in his day, but this beats all I ever seen. What'll I tell your ma and Ransom?"

Her voice was hard, though her heart felt fractured. "Tell them it was more Simon than some Indian arrow that killed me, Will. That's the truth of it."

He turned his back to her as if unable to watch her destruction. Above the massive gates, she glanced skyward a final time and saw Pa's name chiseled in the rough wood. What would he think of her folly?

Father, forgive me.

Two sentries moved to open the postern gate just a crack, and drawing a ragged breath, she slipped through the narrow opening on foot, leading the borrowed horse behind her. The morning sun was cresting Hackberry Ridge, and a warm wind rippled the river's surface. Sometime in the night the Indians had gathered their dead. The grassy slope was picked clean of bodies, save the fallen white men.

Strange how she felt like a girl again, on the porch with Pa, facing the Shawnee. Only this time she was all alone and more afraid. Just as she had back then, she reached up and removed the combs from her hair. It tumbled down to her ankles, turning her into a golden target. She stood stone still and waited. Not a shot sounded.

Within moments an Indian came striding toward her from some brush along the river's edge. Though he was painted for war, one eye in a distinctive black circle, his tawny body bearing hideous markings, he moved with a familiar grace and authority. The years hadn't dulled her memory of him, and clearly he hadn't forgotten her. Time had only made him more striking, and his eyes, green as spring, sought her own as he stood before her.

She felt an old longing rekindle and her voice was soft. "Captain Jack."

His hard eyes seemed to soften. "Click's daughter."

For a long moment they just looked at one another, as if getting their bearings after years apart. "I'm sorry . . . about your loss," she finally said, thinking of the trappers who'd brought about this butchery.

He looked down at her with a startling intensity. Was he remembering their own meeting long ago, when he had surprised her in the woods with Pa? The memory settled her somehow and eased her traitorous trembling.

"I am sorry . . . about yours," he echoed.

At his poignant words, emotion spilled out of her. He'd obviously heard about Pa's passing and seemed nearly as grieved as she. Looking away, she wiped her face with her sleeve.

His voice was low, reflective. "You went away for many seasons."

"I've just come back."

His smile was almost imperceptible. "To the cabin of your father."

"Aye," she said without needing to. He knew she'd returned, perhaps to the very day, the very hour. The fact was strangely comforting. Did she dare question him further about the melee all around them? In truth, he looked as weary as she but for entirely different reasons. She swallowed hard and gathered her courage about her like a cloak. "Can you not call for a truce? Are you not a chief?"

He nodded and lifted his eyes to the white men lining the pickets. Truly, it was not safe for him to come so near the fort.

A trigger's breath from death, he was. She moved her horse to stand between him and the fort's guns.

"Though you are well within your rights to retaliate for the loss of your men," she ventured carefully, "why Fort Click?"

"The trapper who led the ambush is a member of the fort's militia."

Her expression turned grave. "Do you know his name?"

"McClary."

She nearly winced. "I know of him, but he is not within."

"We will find him then."

She did not doubt it. She wished he would. The grief McClary once caused her father was reason enough.

His eyes fell on her again, lingering on her hair. She remembered he'd once taken off the end of her braid with his scalping knife. Was he also thinking of the blue beads? Had Providence prompted her to bring them? Relieved, she drew them out, their blueness glossy and undimmed. Her girlhood seemed bound up with those beads. They had solaced her during the long years at Briar Hill, tethering her to her past, reminding her of just who she was. But she couldn't tell him such things. He wouldn't understand . . . would he?

She offered him the beads like a gift and he took them, only to give them back. "You want to go home," he said, more statement than question. She nodded slowly, and he turned toward the ridge and river and gave a signal.

"Go home," he told her. With that, he began to walk away, and a hundred Indians seemed to retreat with him.

She got up on the big bay and glanced back at the fort, relief making her woozy. She could well imagine the talk already abuzz inside those walls. Her tangle of emotions left her so tired she could barely sit astride her horse. But she was free, free of the stockade if not Simon.

One day, she vowed, she would be free of Simon as well.

28

Lael was cutting the last of the black-eyed Susans for a bouquet when she heard hoofbeats. It was always best to cut flowers in the morning, she could hear Ma say, when the dew was still on the petals. And it was such a lovely morning, the dew drenching her bare feet and the chickens clucking contentedly all around, scratching at the dirt.

Just three days before, she had been dead on her feet at the fort, smelling blood and burnt powder and molding lead, in the heart and heat of the trouble which now seemed like it never was. She'd not seen a soul but Asa Forbes, come to claim his bay horse and return her rifle. Her own horse had been waiting when she came home.

She moved to the porch to stand in the open door frame, the flowers forgotten in her arms. Her gun was just inside. She could hear the approaching horse plain now, just in back of the barn. When Simon rounded the corner, Lael took a small step backwards. He dismounted in the yard, not even bothering to tether his horse, and came to stand just beyond the porch stoop. His arm and shoulder were in a sling, but it seemed to hinder him not at all. He moved with the same easy grace as always, drawing her eyes and her heart effortlessly.

"I come to see if there's still a livin' soul here," he told her. "Or if you'd run off with the Shawnee."

"You can see I didn't," she said matter-of-factly. "Now get on your horse and go back to wherever it is you came from."

He stepped onto the porch stone and pulled off his hat. "That was a mighty daring stunt you pulled outside fort walls. You ain't been back two months, and you're the talk of the settlement again. Only this time the tattle's mostly good, considerin' you saved all our hides."

"You can thank Captain Jack," she told him, careful not to look at him overlong.

His expression turned almost wistful. "Captain Jack, is it? You never let your hair down for me, Lael."

Would he never stop saying her name? His words shamed and riled her all at once. "You never asked me."

"We need to talk."

She sighed. "The time for talking is past, Si—" She broke off, fearful of letting slip with something so intimate as *Simon Henry Hayes*. Looking past him, she fixed her eyes on the distant hills still purpled with early morning shadows. An uneasy silence hung between them, a silence she longed to remedy but had no right to.

"You were wrong to come here," she said dully.

"So were you. How do you aim to live here—a woman—alone? Everything I look at needs a man's hand. I see fences down in the pasture. The barn needs a new roof. Who's goin' to keep you in meat come winter?"

Pained to hear all that she had left undone, or had yet to do, she said, "I'm no longer your concern."

"You've been my concern ever since you were six years old, come to fort up with me. You're in my blood, Lael—a forever and endurin' part of me!" With his good hand he reached for her, and she spilled the flowers onto the porch. "Why'd you not tell me you'd come back before I—"

With a cry she tried to wrench her arm away from him. "Why didn't you ask Pa for my hand again? He might have believed you really loved me if you'd not turned tail and run the first time he refused you."

He held her fast, his face like stone, and said nothing.

"Why didn't you come after me these past five years? Why did you wait? Why, Simon Hayes? I'll tell you why!" She was crying now, so hard she could barely talk. All the pent-up hurt and longing came roiling out of her like an overfull kettle. "You made your choice long ago, that's why! My own pa told me you'd been dallying with the likes of Piper Cane before we'd ever left this place. But I held you to be true. All those years in Virginia I waited, hoping you'd come after me, dreaming of the life we'd make together . . ."

"Lael . . . Lael," he said over and over, encircling her with his good arm so that together they leaned against the door frame. "I made a terrible mistake marryin' Piper. It was you I said my vows to on my weddin' day—your face was in my mind. And that night 'twas you I—"

"Nay!" She covered his mouth with her hand, unable to hear it, but he only held her tighter.

She cried until the front of his linen shirt was damp with her tears, and when she pushed away from him he would not let her go. "There's never been another like you," he whispered. "And never will there be."

"There's no undoing what's been done," she cried, yet she could feel her ironclad defenses give way at the beloved nearness of him. This was the fabric of her dreams—the solid, familiar length of him supporting her, his hand weaving in and out of her hair, pulling it free of her braid.

All show and no stay.

But the lure of Simon Hayes was as warm and seductive as the swiftest river current, pulling her under and proving her undoing. Weak, she rested against him and heard the tinkle of bells. At first a far-off sound, the morning breeze carried it nearer and nearer. This time she pushed away from him and he let her go, a puzzled look upon his face. Lael raised her apron and dried her face.

Within moments a small covered wagon pulled into sight with a man driving. It was by far the most unusual contraption she had ever seen outside of Virginia, painted blue, the sides like chests of drawers, each little door opening, she guessed, to reveal wares to sell. The chapman called a greeting before climbing down from the seat.

Simon nodded tersely to the man before striding toward his horse, clearly irritated at the interruption. Lael turned and faced the stranger alone.

"The name's Gideon, miss," he said, removing a hat. "I hope I've not caused any trouble coming up so sudden on you and the gentleman."

"He's no gentleman," she admitted, wondering if her eyes were red from crying.

"Perhaps you'd be needing some wares. Some sea salt from Connecticut or some nutmeg from the East Indies."

She smiled despite her heaviness of heart. "Well, Mr. Gideon, I'd not thought to see the likes of a chapman in troubled times like these."

He smiled back, his eyes kind. "Indian trouble is never reason enough to keep me out of Kentucke, miss."

"That's what my pa used to say," she told him, surprised at her candor. "Please, water your horse. I've some beans and cornbread from last night's supper I'll warm for you if you're hungry."

"I'd be much obliged."

As he unhitched the horse and led it to a water trough, Lael picked up the scattered black-eyed Susans on the porch. They were a sad lot, the stems and petals crushed beneath Simon's feet. She felt like weeping afresh looking at them. They were a reminder of herself as she'd been back then—once lovely and fresh and new, but now sullied by broken dreams and empty promises.

"I'm sorry about your flowers, miss."

He was standing just beyond the porch stoop, his eyes so sympathetic it seemed he knew what had caused their brokenness—and her own. She straightened and gestured toward the end of the porch where the roses provided both scent and shade. "Please have a seat and rest while I see to your breakfast."

When she returned carrying a full plate and a cup of cold cider, she found him reading, an open book in his hands. A Bible, she noted, small and dog-eared like some of her own best-loved books. She left him to his reading but was not gone long, just out to pasture to fetch the mare. She returned to an empty plate and cup and a bouquet of flowers, just like the ones Simon had spilled out of her hands.

"Mr. Gideon," she called, but he and his wagon were gone. Not a bell tinkled. Not a wagon rut remained.

29

The despair Lael felt over Simon's coming permeated all that she did for days. Each time she crossed the threshold she remembered afresh the broken flowers and felt his hands in her hair and heard the words he should never have spoken. Nary a word she said to anyone, but Ma Horn had only to look at her to sense something was amiss.

"The best way to start anew is to shuck off the old," she said plainly, tying an herb bundle together. "Take this to Lovey Runion up the branch. She's fey, but don't let it bother you none. That's the way of it for some."

And so Lael mounted the mare with the herb bundle and traversed the bubbling branch in a sort of trance, hardly watching her way. Ma Horn's anecdote for heartache was neither tonic nor tea but busyness. She never chafed at the old woman's requests but carried and fetched whatever she asked. A sack of poke. A bunch of spicewood twigs. Baskets of salat and sang and other indispensables.

With a growing sense of sadness, Lael watched as Ma Horn's eyesight grew dimmer and her bent body a little more accustomed to her rocker. She hardly ever ventured beyond the fort's gates now. Those who wanted her services had to come to the settlement. Those who could not come because of illness or infirmity were given over to Lael's care.

Partway up the branch, Lael climbed down off the mare and sat upon a rock to soak her feet in the clear, cold water. Two days before she'd cut her left heel on some cane and it throbbed unmercifully. The moss she'd put in her moccasin helped some, but nothing relieved the soreness like the singing branch as it wended its way to the river below.

Truth be told, she was in no hurry to see Lovey Runion. Fey, Ma Horn called her. *Fey* was but a kindness, Lael thought. From the attic of childhood memory she searched for the sad tatters of Lovey Runion's life. Lael knew little except that Lovey once had a husband and child who mysteriously disappeared one spring, never to be heard from again. Some said they'd been taken by Indians; others swore they'd run off. Lael figured the truth would never be known.

By the time she arrived, the cool mist that had followed her up the branch departed, revealing a ramshackle cabin in the shadow of the mountain. Lael had never passed this way, nor had many others. Lovey Runion was fey, and folks stayed clear of her though she was a distant relation of the Hayes clan.

"Halloo," Lael called when she was just beyond shotgun range.

Hearing no answer, she reined in the mare beneath a towering chestnut and looked about. A garden, choked with weeds and thistles, occupied a sunny spot to the right of the small cabin, the branch singing merrily beside it. Three homemade bee gums sat on rocks out front, looking like small houses with their slanted roofs. Bees entered and exited the gums, humming as they went.

"Halloo," she called again.

"I heard ye the first time," came the answering call. "Light and tie."

There was no note of welcome in the words, but Lael went forward, making a wide circle around the humming hives. Hidden in the shadows of the porch sat a tiny woman in a straight-backed chair. In her lap lay some crumbled tobacco and a clay pipe. She was shaking badly, her hands fluttering like twin birds that refused to light.

Lael stepped onto the porch. "Mind if I fill your pipe for you, Lovey?"

Slowly she took the pipe, dumping the old ashes over the porch rail. "I'm Lael Click. Ma Horn sent me with an herb bundle."

The woman studied her, her faded gray eyes vacuous and searching. "Click, ye say? I never knowed Zeke Click to have a daughter. But ye do look some like him."

The pipe finally lit, Lael gave over the herbs. "I'll make some ginseng tea for you. Ma Horn tells me you're partial to it."

The woman nodded absently, drawing on her pipe, and the pungent tobacco drifted upward in spirals about her head.

Inside the cabin Lael kindled a fire and set a kettle of water to boil. Sparsely furnished, the cabin was nevertheless tidy, but Lael noticed a curious absence of food. There was no lingering smell of meat or grease, no beans set to soak, no strings of dried apples above the hearth, no telltale salt gourd on the table.

Lael went to the door and said quietly, "Lovey, when's the last time you ate?"

A slow, childlike smile spread over the woman's face. "I disremember exactly. Must have been when my Matthias come home with them squirrels. Fried squirrel we had that night with corncakes. And cress. I had a hankering for cress . . ."

"Would you like some cress now, Lovey? I saw some down along the branch a-ways."

But there was no answer. While the water warmed, Lael found a basket and went back outside, walking till she found the wild greens, then picking all the tender young leaves she could find. She came upon some wild onion for seasoning, hoping to make a nourishing broth, but without meat it was nigh impossible. As Lovey smoked, Lael cooked the greens and strained the tea. She did find some salt, damp with age, in a corner cupboard.

Lael set the simple fare on the table, but Lovey remained on the porch. "I believe I'll wait for Matthias and my boy. They'll be along directly." Her shaking had subsided, but the dull, vacant look remained.

Taking her arm, Lael led her to the table. "You know the cress is always better fresh, Lovey. Eat and I'll fill your pipe again."

Like a child, she did as she was told, sitting and taking slow bites as if she forgot what she did in between. As she ate, Lael talked, filling the silence with all the inane settlement news she could think of, hoping some spark of recognition would kindle. But Lovey Runion's isolation had been too long and too complete, and time had all but erased those nearest and dearest to her. That she remembered Pa was no small miracle, Lael thought.

But if rational thought was queer to Lovey, gratitude was not. Before Lael left the woman gave her a crock of amber-colored honey.

"Here's some long-sweetenin' for ye" was all she said.

"I'll be back with some meal and meat," Lael told her, but the strange woman had already turned her back and was heading for the porch.

All the way down the branch, the afternoon sun warm upon her back, Lael rode with a small stab of joy in her heart. A slow, satisfied smile spread over her face. Not once had she thought about her sore foot.

Or Simon.

30

At last her trunks arrived from Briar Hill, and Lael was over-joyed, opening the heavy lids and examining her schoolbooks one by one. In the first, wrapped in linen, was the rose gown she'd worn to a ball. With a sigh she drew it out, and its silken folds rustled and shone in the candlelight. She'd meant it to be her marrying dress. Despite being creased from travel, the gown was too grand for the likes of the rough cabin. She hung it from a peg nevertheless, for its beauty never failed to move her.

She'd worn it only once. Would she ever again? Not here, surely, for folks would say she was putting on airs. It would make a fine wedding gown, fit to be handed down to a daughter. Despite its grandeur, the color had always reminded her of pink dogwoods in spring. There were shoes also, narrow and long, of the same pale pink with small wooden heels. She remembered how they'd pinched her feet when she danced that long autumn's eve in Virginia and how she'd wished that her many partners had simply been Simon.

With a sigh she closed the trunks. Two stacks of books lay on the trestle table. One for keeping and one for sharing. She would give *Aesop's Fables* to Lovey Runion, for it had pictures as well as words. The rest she would take to Uncle Neddy.

She hadn't seen Ned Click since she left the settlement, when Pa had taken her away, and it was high time she visited him. Would he even recognize her? She misdoubted he would.

Before she had even alighted from the mare he came out of the cabin. "Why, Lael Click," he said slowly. "You're a sight for sore eyes."

"I'm a sight and I'm sore, is all," she said, removing her straw hat and fanning her warm face. "You live a far piece."

"That's how I like it." He grinned and helped her down and they stood face to face, studying the other.

Time, she determined, had been hard on her uncle. The sun had baked his face a tobacco brown, and he was even leaner than she remembered. A woman would have seen to that, adding pounds to his leanness, but he'd never married, nor did he come to the fort in times of trouble.

She followed him into the shade of a big oak where a blessed breeze blew. Gratefully, she sat down on a stump and looked out on steep fields of tobacco and cotton. Clearly, Uncle Neddy was a man of means. To come here she'd had to skirt Simon's land, for it bordered Ned Click's own. His proximity had kept her away this long, but it paled to what faced her now.

Did Ned know of Pa, his brother? Did he ever wonder about Ransom, or had he somehow seen him in her absence?

She smiled when he passed her a cup of cold cider.

"I reckon you come to tell me about your pa," he said, looking down at his boots. "No need, Lael. I already knowed."

She didn't ask him how. The loss was still so painful she dared not discuss it lest it bring on a fresh fit of weeping. Instead she spoke of the living, treading carefully, wondering if this was a sore subject for him as well. "Ransom's nearly grown now, but I haven't seen him since I went to Virginia. Ma says he looks some like you."

"More's the pity."

"He's never been one to shirk work either, so you can be proud."

"Reckon he'll ever come round here?"

The expectant question touched her, and she sensed his deep lonesomeness. "I reckon he would if we were to ask him."

He looked out on the nearly ripened fields, squinting into the sun. "Does he—was he ever told about me?"

"I don't know that he was. Maybe now that Pa's passed on he knows."

"And your ma?"

She sighed again without meaning to. Was her uncle once as sore about losing Ma as she herself was about Simon? "Ma's remarried now. To a barrister in Bardstown."

He grew quiet for a time. "Livin' in a town, she'll be safe from any Injun trouble. Sara never was one for the wilderness."

Lael felt at a loss then remembered the books. "I brought you some reading material." She went to the mare and retrieved the books from a saddlebag, gratified to see his eyes light up. Turning them over in his work-worn hands, he read the titles aloud. *The Navigator. Thomas's Hymns. The Order of Man in Ancient Times. John Donne's Poems.*

"They're yours to keep or to share," she told him.

He sat back down, clearly reluctant for her to go. "Tell me about that fancy school of yours."

And so she did, recalling the echoing rooms and ticking clocks and endless books. It pleasured her to picture again the sea, as blue as a raggedy robin in spring, then gray as a mourning dove in winter. They passed a pleasant hour, sipping sweet cider and reminiscing, and Lael felt sad to take her leave. Aside from Ma and Ransom and Ma Horn, Uncle Neddy was the only living relative she knew.

"I'll be back shortly," she promised, hooking arms with him. "And we'll talk books."

He walked with her a ways to the thin trail that led down off the ridge. Suddenly he called after her, "Will you—do you—forgive me for what I done . . . for runnin' off with your ma?"

179

Surprised, she turned around and looked at him from her perch in the saddle. "It takes two to run off, Uncle. And aye, I forgive you."

He nodded and again looked down at his boots. A wave of pity stirred her and she kicked her horse gently, the surrounding woods a blur of brown and green. She'd always had a soft spot for Uncle Neddy. But had she forgiven her mother? Nay, she decided. Never forgiven her or understood her, then or now. Nor for that matter had she forgiven Simon. The hurt they'd caused her still burned bitter and bright. The burden of it tired her so, but try as she might, she could not lay it down.

31

The small corn patch was Lael's pride. Tall enough now to whisper in the wind, the sound was as exquisite as the rustle of a silk skirt. In the cool of the morning she would hoe until the sun rose and touched her back, reminding her to go and eat. She could think of as little or as much as she liked, lost in the gentle monotony of hoeing and watering, and she could dress as she liked, barefoot and bonnetless, sometimes wearing nothing more than a shift, her long braid sashaying around her hips.

On one such morning she was thinking of nothing more than her new milk cow and the ball of butter she'd washed and salted and secured in a cold crock just that morning. She could hear a faint tinkling coming from the woods as the cow foraged in the brush. The fort's cooper had just finished her butter churn, and the dasher already seemed conformed to her hand.

She paused to catch her breath, staring at the cornplanter birds hopping from row to row. What a harvest she would have! The thought made her giddy. She thought of Ransom who loved to farm, like Neddy. She missed him with a fierceness she'd not thought possible.

That very night she penned him a letter and told him how tall the corn was, and about the gathering storm that growled outside her window behind a bank of blue-black clouds. But she omitted her fear about the prowling painter, whose large prints she'd found along the muddy banks of the creek. Nor did she tell him she had no firewood for winter. Or that the barn roof leaked and a beam in the springhouse was rotting.

With a sigh she began to sign her name, but it was no more than a scratch upon the page, for her ink had run out. Beyond the open door, rain began to fall, at first a whisper and then a pounding. All familiar, reassuring sounds. She wondered how it would be to hear another human voice break in upon her solitude. Would she, in time, grow fey as Lovey Runion?

She began to wonder where Captain Jack was and if he would come by her cabin. When she was out herbing in the woods or wandering the river bottoms, a strange yearning filled her heart to come upon him watching her, perhaps waiting to speak to her. Sometimes in her aloneness she sensed she was not really alone at all, that the very woods watched her, shielding him from view.

Nay, she wasn't lonesome . . . yet. But she was alone.

On a sultry afternoon in late August when the sourwood tree by the springhouse hummed from the thickness of the bees in its waxy white blossoms, Simon returned. Lael met him on the porch, gun in hand.

"You're a far piece from home, Simon Hayes," she said, and her tone put distance between them.

"I just come from Susanna's," he replied, leaning against a porch post and partaking of a plug of tobacco.

"I don't have time to talk."

"I reckon you don't with all the work that needs to be done around here. Still no wood for winter, I see."

The judgment in his tone riled her. She gripped the gun harder and found her hands were sweating.

"But I could remedy that," he said softly, the eyes that held hers a rich, inviting brown.

Her face turned crimson clear to the collar of her dress. "I'm sure you have plenty to do about your own place without worryin' about mine."

He stepped closer. "Seems like I can't turn my hand to nothin' when all I do is think about you."

Weak, she leaned against the wall of the cabin, the gun pointing down. "You've made your bed, and you'd best lie in it."

"Oh, I'm lying in it all right, but I'm alone when I'm doin' it," he said with heat. "I'm here to tell you Piper has my name but nothin' else, Lael. Our marriage is over."

His words forced her to look at him, to measure the truth of what he said. She ached to believe it, yet divorce was not to be reckoned with. Why, Pa would turn over in his grave. As if he took her silence for agreement, Simon stepped onto the porch and wrested the gun away from her.

Her fear doubled at his strength. "Simon—nay!"

But he pinned her against the cabin wall, the rough wood scraping her backside. His breath was hot on her face and held a hint of tobacco—and whiskey. There was no one to interrupt them now, no chapman with his wares in a wagon. He kissed her hard but missed her mouth when she turned her head away. Swearing, he tried again. Desperate, she ground her fist into his hurt shoulder, the very wound she'd plucked the lead ball from. With a fierce yell, he released her. Dodging him, she grabbed up her gun and faced him, sick at heart.

Looking into those eyes that in years past beheld her with warmth and affection but had since hardened into something chill and reviling, she felt violated. The Simon she knew was no more. She raised the gun until it was level with his chest. "You're trespassing, to my way of thinking."

His eyes never wavered. Nor did hers. For several eternal moments they stood, locked in a silent contest of wills. Then without a word he turned away.

She didn't lower the rifle until he'd ridden out of sight. When she did, she was trembling as violently as Lovey Runion. Shutting the door, she set the gun back over the mantle. A terrible, crushing grief took hold of her, and she sank down on a bench, put her head in her hands, and sobbed.

Thoughts of how different her homecoming might have been wove through her head, stinging her afresh. She should have returned to find Simon unwed and waiting, then moved up on his homestead. As it was, she was nothing but a workhorse, a woman alone, so soft she could hardly split wood or hoe her garden without sprouting blisters.

That night she took time to peel bark from a slippery elm sapling, scraping out the inner ooze to spread on a clean piece of linen. She bound her hands thus each evening, and by morning the blisters were less painful and turning callused. She'd grown weak, she knew, all those years at Briar Hill. But eventually her ladylike hands would become as hard and tough as the frontier itself.

Wearied by Simon's visit, only a bath in the river could revive her enough to make a simple supper. She overslept the next morning, coming awake to a bawling cow wanting to be milked. Not bothering to get dressed, she stumbled onto the porch and into the arms of a warm morning. The cow quieted at the sight of her, but in place of its bellowing came a piteous yelping near the churn.

A long-loved memory washed over her. There, just where the blue beads had once been years before, was a basket. An Indian basket.

Much like the willow ones woven by her ma, this was of a different pattern, its lid fastened with a leather thong. Inside was a wiggling, shivering pup. At her touch, he quieted and licked her chin. Laughing, she turned him loose, looking long at the woods.

She felt like a girl again, expectant, excited. But what a sight she made in her nightgown, her hair hanging down in a tangle, her feet bare and brown. Still, she stepped off the porch and scooped the pup up, her smile wide and satisfied.

"Why, you're all ears and paws," she exclaimed. *Just like Pa's dogs, Nip and Tuck.* Surely this was no accident. Had the gift giver thought so too? "I'll call you Tuck."

Reluctantly, she returned to the cabin, delighted when Tuck barked around noon, announcing company. From within the paling fence of her garden, she spied Susanna and little Lael emerging from the woods on a big mule, the boys and Will walking behind.

"How you keepin'?" he called.

"Right smart," she lied, thinking of Simon.

The boys ran toward the puppy, shrieking with delight. Will cast a long look at her and scratched his beard. "Looks like one of them Indian dogs to me." She said nothing, thinking she was becoming as much of a mystery as Pa with her long silences and short answers.

Susanna's face was alight, her hair a blinding copper in the noon sun. "Lael Click, I can hardly believe you're standin' before me hale and hearty after all that fuss at the fort." Lael only leaned on her hoe, squinting into the sun. She nearly sighed with relief when Susanna changed the subject. "This very night there's to be a corn huskin' at the Powells', and you're invited."

Listening, Lael attacked a clump of weeds vigorously with her hoe like she was killing snakes. Susanna stood just beyond the garden fence now, surveying the tidy rows of onions and potatoes and beans, and urged, "Say you'll go."

But Lael shook her head. "I've not been to a corn husking since I was twelve years old and danced half the night with your brother."

"Why, that was a hundred years ago!"

Lael paused and leaned on her hoe. "Maybe in another hundred I'll be willing."

"Willin' to what? Dance half the night? Eat somethin' beside meal and sallet greens? Be with folks you care about?"

"I'm sorry, Susanna," was all she could say.

Susanna looked as dashed as she'd ever seen her, but it was Will who looked straight at her. "You'd do right to remember that a man who has friends must himself be friendly, Lael Click."

Lael took the quoted Scripture as a rebuke but said not a word. That night, after another meal of sallet and cornbread, long after Will and Susanna and the children had gone, she stood on the porch. The roses were into their second blooming now, making her senses swim with their heady sweetness. A handful of petals had fallen onto the porch, dainty spent blossoms that looked more silver than pink in the moonlight.

Was it her imagination or could she hear the lilting call of a fiddle on the night wind? Tuck's ears were alert, his eyes fixed on the dark woods. For the briefest moment she was sorry she'd not gone with them. How she loved to dance! Her feet fairly tapped at the memory.

Turning abruptly, she went inside the cabin. Everything was in order. She'd swept the floor twice and returned the rag rug to its proper place before the hearth, washed and dried the supper dishes, and carried the rinse water to the garden. A bucket of fresh water sat near the door with a wooden lid, the drinking dipper hanging above it. She'd refilled the salt gourd and stored it alongside Lovey Runion's precious honey.

There was nothing to do but light a candle and read as was her habit. She'd written Miss Mayella to request a medical book, and she'd kindly sent one. *The Complete Herbal* lay before her, unopened and unread. Strange, but she'd never been able to resist the lure of a new book. Until now.

32

It was not a far piece to Dan and Avarilla Powell's place. Lael
literally followed the music. She imagined Susanna's surprise,
but there was no joy in her own heart. Every step of the mare
fueled fresh dread. Surely Simon and Piper would not be present, as their home place was so far away. It was this reassurance
that drew her.

She'd taken pains with her appearance, pinning her hair atop
her head beneath a lace cap the way Miss Mayella had done.
Her dress was an airy, cream-colored muslin sprigged with tiny
bluebells. Pa's cameo was pinned to her bodice, the blue beads
in her pocket.

As she rode toward the welcoming light of the fires she nearly
balked. But the fiddling wooed her ever nearer. Oh, to dance
again! She felt suddenly shy. Who did she know here? She'd been
away too long. She dismounted, surely the last to arrive. The
doors of the big barn were flung open and lanterns hung high,
illuminating a crowd of revelers. The bee had not yet begun. A
mountain of corn awaited as the last of the supper dishes were
cleared away. Lael spied Susanna talking with Jane McFee and
Eliza Harold, as yet unaware of her presence.

She hesitated in the shadows, and a group of children skit-
tered past her. "Lael, is that you?" Young Henry Bliss peered at
her, eyes bright as a coon's in the darkness. "We're so glad you
come!"

She laughed despite herself and made her way to the brightly lit barn. The tang of fresh cider and hay carried on a warm wind along with the hum of a hundred voices. Daniel Powell had already selected two captains for the corn husking race and teams were being chosen. Each team would be given an equal number of ears to husk, and the side finishing first won the race. Often, the race was settled by the two captains having a wrestling match or a fight. Lael grimaced. No doubt the corn liquor was in abundance too, making monsters of mild-mannered men.

Will Bliss was a captain and Susanna, delighted, sat on a hay bale watching him. Looking on, Lael envied them their happiness. If she'd had her way, she'd be an old married woman now with almost as many young 'uns instead of a spinster at twenty.

She started as a gun was fired to begin the race. Folks erupted in laughter at the antics of the teams as they began husking as fast as they could, making faces and gesturing at their opponents.

"Why, Lael! Lael Click!"

Jane McFee grabbed her elbow, propelling her to a circle where a group of women talked and shucked a pile of their own. Susanna followed, whispering a greeting and a compliment.

"Lael, I reckoned nothin' would change your mind, and here you are—in a purty dress, to boot!"

They sat down on some hay, spreading their skirts over their ankles. Lael was aware of all the feminine eyes on her, taking in her hair and dress and everything about her. This was her first social since being back, and she was face to face with the girls who'd been in pudding caps when she left the settlement.

She was, she knew, a spinster by settlement standards. *Not to worry*, she wanted to announce to them all, *I am forever and enduring an old maid.* No doubt they'd heard the tale of her and Simon and Piper. Their love triangle seemed nearly as old as the settlement itself.

Taking up some corn, she yanked at a husk, revealing a perfectly turned ear. "Reminds me of my new purchase," she said quietly to Susanna. "I bought a popcorn popper when I was last at the fort."

"A popcorn popper?"

"They're all the buzzel in the East. You put some dried kernels of corn in it like so and hold it over the fire. Before long you have a mess of popcorn."

"I never heard of the like," Susanna said slyly with an eye toward a knot of men. "Maybe you could pop some directly for Asa Forbes. He seems all but rabid at the sight of you."

Lael shot her a warning look. "None of that foolishness or I'll up and go as quick as I came."

"You'll stay for the dancin', I reckon. There's a sight of single men to choose from tonight. See any that tickles your fancy?"

But Lael kept her eyes down, intent on the shucking.

Susanna sighed. "Too bad my Will had all them sisters and nary a brother. You'd do right by a man like Will."

Picking up a handful of shuck, Lael tossed it at her, her flushed face tense. "I didn't come so you could marry me off, you hear?"

But Susanna merely laughed. "Why did you come?"

Lael gave no answer but gestured to her pile of shucked corn, which was larger than Susanna's own.

Susanna sobered and whispered, "No matter, Lael. Simon's not here. So you'd best smile and have some fun."

At these comforting words she did grow easier, smiling and laughing at the good-natured banter around the circle. Soon a shout went up as Will's team won and they pointed in proof to their pyramid of corn, leaving the losers to shuck the remainder.

"Looks like a late night," a man said, eyeing the pile of corn still waiting to be shucked. But no one cared as spirits were high and the cider was flowing freely.

As he passed, old Amos winked at Lael, bearing his worn fiddle. She smiled in return and before she looked back down to the corn in her lap she saw a curious sight indeed. To one side of the barn, in a pale circle of lantern light, stood a man. He was leaning against a beam, arms folded across his chest. Around him several settlement men were deep in conversation but he—he was not talking at all. Just looking. *At her.*

She took in his unusual clothing, finding him oddly reminiscent of Briar Hill. Was this why he looked her way? In a sea of buckskins and breeches and linsey-woolsey, he stood out as much as she.

Startled, she looked back down to the corn in her lap, but all she saw was *him*. And his fine linen shirt. Black breeches. Shiny leather boots. He was a newcomer, no doubt, or an outlander merely passing through. *A Yankee doodle dandy.* Lael wrinkled her nose in dismissal. He had the look of a gentleman, but there was no sign of the dandy about him. Or was there?

She dared herself to look up again and did. But he was no longer looking at her. He'd turned to take a cup of cider. His hair, black as iron, was worn in typical settlement fashion, longish and tied from behind with a simple leather whang. Though not as tall as Simon, he looked sturdy as oak, with thick shoulders and narrow hips.

Someone hooted and all eyes riveted to a young man brandishing a red ear of corn. Lael's lips parted in surprise. How had she forgotten this? Unmarried folks came from miles around in hopes of finding a red ear. The lucky fellow made a beeline to a red-faced young girl near Lael and, amid good-natured laughter, kissed her swiftly on the lips.

"Keep watch, ladies," Eliza Harold called. "There's likely half a dozen red ears awaitin', same as last time."

Several unmarried females grinned and blushed at this news—all but Lael. She had no one to blush about and certainly not to kiss. Why, she was safe as old Granny Henderson, who sat directly across from her in the circle.

The night grew deeper, and beyond the barn doors the fireflies winged about and the wind settled. Oddly, no other red ears had been found. Some of the girls looked a bit crestfallen as the pile of unshucked corn dwindled. In the back of the barn old Amos was tuning his fiddle.

Susanna sat beside Lael, holding her sleeping namesake, as Lael continued to work, amused at the children who played and hid in the mounds of shucks that lay in piles everywhere. The crowd was growing rowdier and more restless now. Some of the women were cutting pie and pouring coffee in anticipation of the dancing. She'd seen no more of the dark-headed stranger.

"I need a sip of cider. Can I bring you some?" she asked Susanna, feeling cramped from sitting so long. She stood as Susanna answered, but her reply was lost amid a series of deafening hoots and whistles.

A second red ear?

Lael turned to look behind her at all the commotion, then abruptly sat back down. It was the handsome stranger, turning a red ear over in his hands as if he were as surprised by it as she. Slowly, he made his way toward the large circle of women, grinning at the ribbing and back slapping of the men.

Some of the girls around her looked up expectantly, even brazenly, as he neared. She dropped her own eyes and—lo and behold—there was no more corn near enough to shuck. Her hands stilled in her lap.

Out of the corner of her eye she watched him walk ever so slowly around the circle of women as if judging the merits of each. Someone hooted as he came to a stop behind Lael.

She'd never felt so conspicuous, like a horsefly in new milk! Surely every eye in the barn was upon her. Heat began to creep up her neck and rose clear to her lace cap. Still as stone she sat, fighting the urge to flee.

Standing behind her now, he spoke, and his voice was rich and thick as molasses. "So mony bonny lasses, so hard tae choose."

A Scot! At his words, the barn erupted in laughter, easing the tension of the moment. Lael waited, certain of a kiss—but he walked on, stopping a second time behind Granny Henderson. With a devastating grin he bent and pecked the old woman's parchment-paper cheek as raucous laughter thundered a second time. Why, the old widow looked pleased as punch!

As he turned and walked away Lael felt a bit lost, wondering what it was about him that made her feel so odd.

Watching him go, Susanna finally said, "I don't know as I've ever seen that one before. More than likely he's just passin' through."

Passing through, never to be seen again. She felt a foolish urge to run after him and catch his arm and ask if he'd meant to kiss her. But that would never do.

"I believe—" she began, unable to finish. She watched him walk away, out of the barn, and disappear into the dark night.

I believe that's the finest man I've ever seen.

33

At the end of August a string of accidents around the settlement nearly brought Ma Horn out of confinement. Asa Forbes lost two of his toes to an ax, Sadie Harold's child's hands were scalded badly in a tub of lye, and Mourning Grubbs's son Titus broke his arm for the second time. Yet it was Hugh McClary's fall from his horse that most urgently required care, though Lael would not hear of it. Even Ma Horn's entreaties fell on deaf ears.

"I'll not set foot on McClary land," Lael announced, not caring that his son stood just inside the door frame. "Hugh McClary shot my pa inside this very fort and nearly killed him. As it was, Pa limped to his dying day." Winded, she paused for breath, mindful of the fracas he'd caused at the fort with Captain Jack. "Let Mister High-and-Mighty McClary heal himself. I'll see to the rest."

And so Lael rode off, bristling at the temerity of the McClary clan in seeking her out. She cared not a whit what became of the lot of them, nor did it matter what the settlement thought of her refusal.

Lael rode to the Harold cabin first, and the mare was in a lather by the time she got there. The burned girl was a pitiful sight, not yet two years old, her small hands blistered and drawn from the lye. She was still gripped by such convulsive sobs her whole frame shook. There was little to do but wrap the hands with a healing salve and linen. Lael produced a pouch of herbs to ease the pain, but her own lack of helpful knowledge made her heartsore. She left the cabin without accepting payment, for she felt she'd not earned any and promised to come again.

Titus Grubbs's broken arm was a simpler matter. As she pulled the arm into place to set it, albeit gently, the boy did not so much as wince. He stared at the cabin wall with faraway eyes, jaw slack. She spoke to him in low tones as she fashioned a splint. "Ma Horn tells me she set this same arm in the spring. It's a wonder you've lived to be ten years old." He said nothing, but a faint smile tugged at his mouth. She continued quietly, "Sometimes a bone is weakened by too many breaks. How'd it happen this time, Titus?"

He looked down at his arm and a single tear fell, wetting Lael's hand as she worked, surprising her with his sudden turn of emotion. His voice was so low she had to bend closer to hear him.

"I—fell—off the loft ladder."

Lael straightened, pausing to watch his mother through the open doorway as she tended a haunch of venison on a spit outside the cabin, and tried a different tack.

"Do you have any brothers or sisters?"

"Them's all dead."

"I'm sorry," she said quietly, thinking it an all too familiar answer. "I just lost my pa, as well."

A flicker of interest lit his eyes and he looked at her, then away. "I heard tell your pa was a real hero."

"I suppose he was. Want to hear a story of how he made an escape downriver from here?"

As she bound his arm she told him how Pa had jumped from the rocky bluff along the river into the towering maple. When she'd finished, he darted another look at her and whispered, "Tell another."

She smiled. "I'll tell about the time he tussled with a painter when I come back to tend your arm."

She gathered her bag and went out of the cabin to speak to

his mother. The woman wiped greasy hands on an apron but kept her eyes averted. "Thank you kindly. I'm always tellin' him he ought not to be so rambunctious, climbin' them trees and the like. But he don't never listen."

At the words Lael paused, her hands going limp on the saddlebag she'd just tied shut. Climbing trees and the like? What had Titus said? Something about a fall from the loft ladder?

There was no offer of payment. Had there been she wouldn't have taken it. She got on the mare and took a last look around. The woman had already disappeared inside. Everything Lael's eyes rested on spoke of neglect and decay. The barn, a poorly built affair, had a door off one hinge. The garden was choked with weeds and only half-planted in corn. Why, even the dogs looked half starved. She tried to recall what Ma Horn had told her about Mourning Grubbs and her son, but nothing came to mind. There was no man about, truly, nor it seemed had there ever been.

On the long trek up the mountain to Asa Forbes's place, Lael passed a group of wild hogs foraging on chestnut mast in the woods. They grunted as she passed, wild and almost comical in expression. The thought of fresh meat made her mouth water, as she'd not had any for some time, not since a settler had paid her with a haunch of venison in June.

She found Asa in a crude lean-to that seemed to cling to the rocky ridge. A bed of rock had been laid for the foundation of a small cabin, and a crop of corn was growing precipitously on a ledge, all that was necessary for proving up a settler's four hundred acres. His four horses, considered among the finest in all Kentucke, grazed near a creek.

Entering his humble dwelling, Lael felt awkward and tongue-tied. Women and children were one thing, but doctoring a man was quite another. She wondered if he was still sweet on her. He limped to a pile of blankets and removed the bloody bandages for

195

her to see. The ax had done its work, for the two smallest toes on his right foot were completely severed. The unmistakable smell of corn liquor threaded the stale air and, from Asa's manner, it had been employed, and perhaps enjoyed, liberally.

Working as quickly as she could, for the light was fading fast, Lael cleaned the wound and applied a mixture of walnut leaves and dock.

Wincing, Asa asked, "What's that?"

"A healing salve."

"I ain't used to such. Reckon they'll grow back?"

She looked up, amused. "Your toes?"

He nodded and winced.

"Asa Forbes, how much whiskey have you drunk?" He looked shamefaced as she wrapped his foot and said in her most bookish tone, "Man is incapable of regeneration, I'm sorry to say."

"I reckon that means no more toes."

"You reckon right," she answered, sitting back on her haunches. Though cleaned, the foot was still a sight, and the blackish skin, hidden now by bandages, troubled her. She would need to consult the medical book Miss Mayella had sent. Her own lack of knowledge continued to confound her. "Do you have enough liquor for your misery?" she asked.

Grinning, he gestured to a shed. "A right smart supply. I figure if it gets any worse I'll just chop the whole durn foot off—or see the doctor."

Standing, she brushed off her skirt. "You'll find no doctor in these parts, Asa Forbes. Well, maybe in Lexington, but that's a far piece."

He looked smug, as if he'd caught her in a lie. "There is too a doctor—least he claims to be. But I'm partial to you, Miss Lael."

Miss Lael. *At least,* she thought, *he minds his manners despite being rough as a cob. A doctor!* She shot him a last look. Perhaps delirium had set in already. She suspected he was courting blood poisoning but was hesitant to say so just yet.

Staggering to his feet, he hobbled out of the lean-to after her. "I ain't one to take up with a stranger, doctor or no. Him and his queer ways don't set right with me."

"So you've met this man."

"Aye, met him but can't say as I like him." He looked at her askance as she mounted the mare. "I ain't got nothin' to give you for your trouble."

"You loaned me your bay when I needed it. We'll consider that payment enough." She took her leave as quickly as she could, turning away with a wave of her hand.

All around her the forest light shifted and settled as she passed, shrouding her with black shadows. She found herself missing Tuck and her own warm hearth. Tired as she was, she rode on and took out a ginseng root to chew to keep up her spirits, but ere long the darkness overtook her and she could go no farther. Soon she found herself benighted in the woods.

There was nothing to do but wait out the night. The darkness was complete and heavy, pressing in on her like a humid black blanket. She was familiar with these woods, but on her way to Asa Forbes's she had noted that the sudden drops and ledges, precipitous enough by day, would be deadly by dark. So she sat on the ground, the mare breathing evenly beside her, and mulled her foolishness.

She'd failed to pay attention to the setting sun as she made her rounds. In truth, she was so troubled by her visit to the Grubbs cabin, all else had been forgotten. She thought of the boy Titus now. Something had been amiss, some word or action, but what?

She thought too of Asa Forbes. A doctor, indeed. She tried not to think of Simon, but here in the dark silence broken only by the hoot of an owl, what was to stop her? Unhindered, Lael came face to face with both Simon and her longings. Would she always love him? Perhaps some distant day . . . Nay, she shut her eyes against the flicker of hope that lay in the unknown future. It came unbidden nevertheless. Perhaps . . . one distant day . . . Simon would be free.

Twice her reverie was broken by the startling trill of a mockingbird. Her senses turned sharp, straining toward the coming dawn. She was not much afraid. Pa's blood pulsed too strongly in her veins for fear to have its way.

Tired as she was, she retraced her path to Mourning Grubbs's ramshackle cabin the next morning, tying the mare to a serviceberry bush well away from the cabin and walking the remainder. She crouched behind a thick curtain of mountain laurel rich with scarlet blooms and waited. Though it was early the chimney belched smoke, and Lael could smell salt pork and bread. Her mouth watered, and she remembered she had eaten nothing since yesterday noon.

In time the door opened and Titus himself came out, carrying a bucket in the direction of the spring. In and out of the cabin he moved, first with the water, then with a basket of eggs, and finally carrying some sticks of firewood with his good arm.

Lael waited, hoping to observe she knew not what. But it was an unremarkable morning filled with chores she herself should be doing. And so, backtracking, she untied the mare and returned home.

34

Each time she saw her, Lael felt Ma Horn slipping away. Her eyesight was now so poor she had trouble telling some herbs from others and knew this might someday cause a fatal mistake. Where she'd once been so tidy in person and surroundings, she was now unkempt and the tiny cabin cluttered. Some days it took all her strength to leave her chair. And she was more and more in need of her own remedies.

Yet she was gracious in relinquishing the wisdom of the years to Lael, committing others into her care. "Remember, boneset will nearly always break a fever," she would say. Or, "Mae Burl's youngest is hivey and in need of a tonic." And Lael would go, venturing out again and again, prodded by the weight of her growing responsibilities.

One day, fatigued after a feverish round of calls, she was in no mood to hear of fresh Indian trouble. "Seems like they always strike after fooling us with a false peace," Lael lamented.

"Your pa said there'd be no more trouble betwixt us or them one day," Ma Horn replied. "But now I wonder if he didn't mean one or the other of us would have to go."

Lael sighed and went to the door, fixing her eyes on the far panoply of purple hills above the fort's pickets. "Seems like we could all just abide together in peace."

She debated whether to ride home in the twilight or stay the night, picturing Tuck running to meet her as she rode in, hungry for some supper scraps. The cow needed to be milked and she'd left some wash out—

". . . come to the fort," Ma Horn's voice had risen as it always did with fresh news.

Lael turned, her color high. "What did you say?"

"I said a doctor has come to the fort."

"A doctor? But why?"

"I never asked him. Seems obvious to me. There's more people comin' into this country ever' day. Enough for the both of you."

"But we need a preacher—and a teacher—more than a doctor." Even as she said it, she recalled her frantic wish for a medical man as she'd dug the lead ball from Simon's shoulder during the siege. With a shrug she added, "Seems like you and I tend the settlement well enough."

"Well, the good Lord knows otherwise, for it's a doctor He's sent. He just moved into the old Hayes place. It's big as cabins go—says he plans to use it to keep real sick folks or ones who need surgery."

"Surgery!" Lael exclaimed, rankled that this man—a stranger— would occupy the blockhouse that held some of her dearest childhood memories. It had sat empty ever since her return, and its emptiness seemed fitting somehow, reflecting the emptiness in her heart.

"So you've met him."

"Aye, I've met him. And he wants to meet you. His name is Ian Justus."

She frowned. She hadn't wanted to know his name—or anything else. "So he's here—now?"

"Nay, gone to Lexington to pick up a fancy medicine chest. But he'll likely be back by dark, should ye stay."

That decided it. "I must go." Furiously, she began packing up her saddlebags and moving toward the door.

"Mind them fresh Shawnee tracks," Ma Horn warned. "And ride hard all the way home."

She rode hard, her thoughts centered on this man, Ian Justus.

Truly, it was a strong-sounding name. But what manner of man would journey into the wilderness to an obscure fort still in danger of Indian attack?

With all her heart she hoped he was old and infirm. But reason told her it was only a young man's fortitude and courage that would bring him to such a place. She considered that he was no doctor at all but a ne'er-do-well masquerading as such. The frontier was rife with these frauds, leaving their patients in worse shape than before. Her blood boiled just thinking of them.

At their first meeting, *if* there was a meeting, she'd ask to see his medical license. Whoever he was, he'd likely soon grow weary of the hardships and deprivations of fort life and return to wherever it was he'd come from. Though what person, when confronted with Kentucke and its blazing woods in autumn, or the redbud and dogwood's beauty in spring, could ever leave?

Nevertheless, he was an outlander. And he wanted to meet her. Well, she would simply not be met.

Lael was in a shady cove digging ginseng when she heard a horse approach. Hands stained with loamy soil, her dress now wrinkled and dirty, she stayed low. All around her grew maples and basswood and butternut and coffee, their leafy richness further shielding her from view. But she soon saw the horse and rider plain.

The mount was a chestnut bay and the rival of any owned by Asa Forbes. As for the man, she saw only his backside. His hair was dark and short by settlement standards. Only a small curl at the nape of his neck was tied back with a whang. Broad of shoulder but not overly tall, she judged, by the way he sat in the saddle. But it was his clothes that alerted her to his strangeness. He wore a linen shirt so white as to be a perfect target for an Indian arrow and—

The Scot!

She shot straight up, her sang hoe forgotten. She'd last seen him at the corn husking but had been too busy to give him a second thought since. Besides, she'd not thought to see him again. The path he took led straight to her cabin.

She wondered his reaction had she whooped and sprung out of the sang patch. She sank back down to the ground, out of sight. And then she knew—an inexplicable feeling told her the Scot and the doctor were the same. She let the reality of it trickle over her. Could it be? If so, she couldn't dodge him forever. Her refusal to go to the fort suddenly seemed childish. Perhaps . . . She wrinkled her nose at the peculiar thought before giving in. Perhaps all her questions could be put to rest by a single visit.

A windstorm had blown up the night before and the forest floor was deep in chestnuts and acorns and hickory nuts. Ma Horn had a hankering for butternuts, and in two days' time Lael had gathered several sackfuls for the both of them. Back at the cabin she began the tedious process of taking the hulls off before storing them for winter. She parched some of the acorns for coffee and ground the rest into flour. Every autumn Ma had done the same in case times were rough, which they invariably were. But she ate up her share of butternuts as soon as she dried them for they were sweet and uncommon and too few to store.

As she worked she waited, alert to Tuck's bark. No one called for her services, and the sudden lull made her wonder. Had word of the doctor's arrival spread so that folks were now taking their ailments to him? With a sinking sensation she pondered the possibility. He was easily accessible, being at the fort, the very heart of the settlement. Folks had reason to go there regularly for supplies. Why not see the doctor at the same time?

By the time all the nuts were in, her curiosity was at fever pitch. She could not sleep for thinking about him. When she sat down to her simple meals, they seemed tasteless. All the little tasks that had brought her pleasure and fulfillment lost their meaning. Why, she was acting lovestruck instead of vexed! Even sitting on the porch, bathed in the sun of Indian summer and the sweet breath of the fading roses, failed to move her.

As she loaded the nuts onto the mare she felt queer clear to the pit of her being, as if one of the butterflies Tuck loved to chase had somehow made it down her throat into her stomach. Taking up a small hand mirror, she took a good look at herself then rankled at the action. What did she care if her hair was disheveled or the hem of her dress soiled from work? But she remedied both, splashing cool water on her face for freshening and donning her favorite straw hat.

Not once did she think of Indian trouble as she rode. The sunlit woods seemed peaceable, and Hackberry Ridge was sun-burned and empty as it sloped toward the fort. Once inside, she found the common abuzz with activity. An unusual number of horses and pack animals were outside the sutler's. With a sinking feeling she turned her head away at the familiar sight of Simon's mare.

She'd not seen him since the day of his indecent proposal when she sent him packing. Pine for him she still did, but it was for the Simon of her youth—the boy with hair like fire and an unsullied spirit, not the uncouth man.

She rode on, the bags of nuts brushing against her legs. A young boy came from nowhere, his face earnest and eager. "I'll see to your horse for some of them nuts," he said, eyeing the bags.

Smiling, she turned over the mare and he was off, eager to earn his reward. The door to Ma Horn's cabin was ajar. As was her custom, she didn't knock. Clutching the bags of nuts, she pushed open the door. It swung forward with a familiar creak, and the sudden sunlight smote the cabin's dimness.

"Halloo," she called as she stood in the door frame.

"Halloo tae you," came a man's reply.

Pausing in the doorway, Lael was legitimately speechless. She stood as still and stoic as her father when facing a Shawnee war party. For a fleeting moment she thought she'd mistakenly entered the old Hayes place. She didn't mean to stare. After so long a ride in the sunlight, her eyes needed adjusting to the sudden gloom.

It seemed he knew who she was instantly. Had someone painted her likeness to him in words . . . said something particular to describe her?

"Miss Click," he said simply.

"Mr. Justus," she replied. She would not call him doctor, not yet.

He seemed to smile at the sound of her voice. It was a woman's voice with a girl's softness. A cultured voice, with all the underlying rawness of the Kentucke frontier.

"I'm here, child, if you're wonderin'," said Ma Horn.

"I've brought you some nuts," Lael told her, depositing the sacks at one end of the hearth.

"Much obliged." She came forward out of the shadows, leaning on a cane. "And nary the twain shall meet, someone said. But here ye both are."

"We've seen each other before," the Scot said.

"Aye, so we have," Lael said.

"At the corn husking," they both said at once.

Ma Horn laughed then, easy as a girl, and moved toward the door. "Well then, no need for me to stay and make howdy-dos twice. Since the doctor got me this here cane, I ain't so shut in. Reckon I'll go see to Airy Phelps."

And so she passed out the door, albeit slowly, leaving it open for decency's sake. Color high, Lael felt like running after her. How could Ma Horn leave them together—alone—at first meeting? To hide her befuddlement, she reached up and removed her straw hat, then chastised herself. *He will think I mean to stay.*

"So you're the settlement midwife."

Startled, she looked at him. His words, spoken with a strong Scottish brogue, put her on edge. To make sure she clearly understood him, she had to listen hard and weigh and measure his every word. Aye, his voice was rich and thick as molasses. A honeyed tongue, if ever there was one.

"Midwife? Nay," she replied. Truly, she had yet to birth a baby.

"Perhaps a modest one?" His slow smile was disarming.

"Not a midwife," she said at last, thinking it too smart a title. "Just a body with a knowledge of healing herbs, is all."

He studied her as she spoke, his eyes on her face. Furtively, she studied him. There was none of the fumbling of Asa Forbes or the brazen boldness of Simon Hayes about him. She was taken aback at his easy manner. He was taller than she, and his rugged features were handsome and tan as new leather.

"Have you lived here long, Miss Click?"

She felt a bit scattered standing so near him. His eyes . . . were they blue? Blue as berries. "All my life, nearly. I was the first white child born in these parts." With that, she took a step back, quickly replacing her hat. It caught on some pins and dislodged them, sending a portion of her hair tumbling about her shoulders in one sunshiny shock. *What a sight I must look!*

"Good day," she muttered as she turned away, intent on fleeing.

"Good day," he uttered after her, following her to the doorway and leaning against it. He watched her hurry across the crowded common, her hair spilling down nearly to her feet.

She turned back just once, nearly stumbling in her haste, impressing him upon the pages of her mind with that last look, all the while hoping she'd never see him again.

35

She'd hardly returned home and caught her breath before she was off to another frolic. Just ahead, Coy Miller's farm lay bright as a lantern. This time, she came with Susanna and Will when reason told her she should have been home with her hefty medical books, feet to the fire.

But she'd come anyway, in a fancy dress to boot, cheeks flushed and courting trouble. The cider making had begun at noon, and the dancing would commence at dusk. Old Amos needed little prompting to haul out his fiddle. As usual, the men outnumbered the women and the unmarried girls were the first to pair up, their colorful skirts swirling as they danced.

Lael surveyed the company of revelers and spotted Simon. Standing around one of the smaller fires away from the dancing, he was deep in conversation with some other men, a mug in his hand. Hard cider, she reckoned. A prickle of alarm coursed through her. Obviously, he had a fondness for it—in excess, some said. Rumor was he even had his own still, hidden high in the mountains.

How thankful she was that Will and Susanna were here! Will, once a notorious hothead himself but now somehow soothed and salved by religion, would be a calming influence if things were to get out of hand. And Susanna always had a steadying effect on Simon.

Try as she might, Lael could not help but study him. He stood out sorely, being the tallest man there. And tonight there seemed something odd about him—something in his gait and his exaggerated expressions that riveted her—but not pleasantly so. Where was Piper? Restlessly, her eyes scoured the crowd, searching, hoping for the first time for a sign of Piper's presence.

Her eyes fell—nay, feasted—on the Scot. He was in earnest conversation with Eliza Harold and Jane McFee. From the look of things, he certainly wouldn't lack for female patients. What, she wondered, did he think of these frontier frolics? She purposed to avoid him, wishing she had a bonnet to hide behind.

Beside her, Susanna's voice rose then faded against the music. Lael bent to listen.

"I said the doctor likes Sir Roger de Coverley, same as you," Susanna repeated as the familiar tune began. "Seems he can run a set with the best of them."

"You seem to know an uncommon amount about the doctor."

"He's come to our cabin a few times," Susanna said, obviously pleased by this. "Why, he and Will get on like a pair of bluetick hounds."

Lael said nothing in reply, wondering what Will Bliss could possibly have in common with a Scottish physician. She sat down on a hay bale beside Susanna, her own toes tapping beneath her skirt. Tonight, she would be content to do nothing more than sit and drink in the night air, letting the music be a salve to her sorry soul.

But it was not to be.

Perhaps it was her dress. The color of butter, the square neck and gathered sleeves trimmed with ivory ribbon. It was wrinkled from riding but fetching nonetheless. She'd not even admit to herself why she wore it, only that she'd chosen it in expectation, wanting to look her best. Already her hair was falling down her neck in wayward wisps below her lace cap.

But all her lofty expectations took flight when Simon swaggered out of the shadows, seeking her out for the next dance, a fire in his eyes that still kindled from their last meeting. She swallowed hard, knowing that if she denied him she could dance with no other man. Accept him and she could dance with them all. As liquored up as he was, she dared not refuse him. She didn't smile as he approached, just gave a curt nod and stood up, but she rued the gossip it was bound to cause.

Old Amos burst into a fiddling frenzy. She moved woodenly and haltingly. Simon, agile as always, was made more so by the hard cider, and he held her none too gently.

"Where's your wife?" she asked curtly, eyes averted.

"Where's your gun?" he shot back.

The curious onlookers seemed a blur to her. Would the dance never end? The steps were as familiar as the path to her cabin, but her feet felt leaden. Here she was, intent on a bit of fun, and she simply felt empty and terribly discontent—and near tears. When the set ended, she fled from the circle, past Susanna and a cluster of rowdies to the shadows.

At the cider press, now empty of apples, she got hold of herself. The tart tang of apple pulp still lingered in the air, and a large oak barrel beneath the press was half full of fresh cider. Beneath her hands, the rough wood of the mill was solid and reassuring. She leaned against it, wistful yet cautious. Would Simon follow?

"You look tae be flushed. Would you care for a wee bit of cider?"

She started at the Scot's voice and turned in its direction, dismayed at being discovered. Given his stance and demeanor, he had plainly been there all along, even before she. He stood on the opposite side of the press, leaning against a beam, a cup in his hands. From this vantage point he had a clear view of the dancing while remaining apart from the frolic itself. Fleetingly, she wondered why he'd not joined in.

"Nay . . . no cider. Thank you." Still breathless from the set, she stood where she was, planning her next move. Susanna would worry if she up and left. Besides, she'd promised she would stay. But neither could she stand here with the strange Scot, completely speechless.

"I'd ask you tae dance if I thought that was what you really wanted."

She swallowed, glad the darkness hid her face. "Nay, I . . . it's not quite as I remember. The dancing, I mean."

He said nothing to this, so she rushed on. "I—I last danced like this when I was a slip of a girl . . . just thirteen. Cider-makings were always a favorite of ours . . . my pa anyways."

The memory only made her melancholy, and she looked down at the solid lines of the press, a bit lost.

"I'm sorry aboot your faither," he said, and the gravity in his voice touched her and brought her round.

"Sorry?" she echoed.

"I used tae read aboot him in the eastern papers. He was a bit of a legend where I come from."

Her voice was rueful. "He never liked a fuss to be made about him. I recollect he said a newspaper was nothing but a pack of lies."

"I dinna doubt it." He took a sip of cider. "But 'tis true that Kentucke's first county is tae be named after him."

She looked up, surprised. "Did you read that in the newspapers, too?"

"Nae. I heard it firsthand from a judge in Lexington."

"Then you have friends in high places, sir, for even I have not heard that." Still, the news warmed her. *Click County.* It did sound fetching. She looked across the press and found that he was looking at her unabashedly just as he had the night of the corn husking.

"You're uncommon tall for a lass."

Surprised, she smiled. "Do you always speak your mind so?"

He nodded. "You'll find I do."

"Anything else?"

"Aye," he replied, coming around the press to close the distance between them. "Do you always court trouble, Miss Click, or does it just seem tae follow you where'er you go?"

Trouble?

Behind her, Simon was approaching and the hostility in his swagger chilled her to the bone. Did the Scot sense her unease? If he did, he gave no sign of it. Slowly, he set his cider down on the press and extended a hand.

"I was just asking Miss Click if she wanted tae dance," he announced to Simon with a quiet confidence.

Relief coursed through Lael. And gratitude. She took Ian Justus's outstretched hand and followed him into the firelight.

Before she returned home from the frolic her name had been linked with that of the Scot. But at least it was no longer tied with Simon's. It was only a single dance, her second and last of the night. Perhaps that is what set people's tongues a-wagging. Or perhaps it was the contrast they made—he so dark and she so fair. Whatever the reason, it made for good gossip.

All the way home and well into the next day, as she milked and churned and gathered eggs, she thought of the few words they'd spoken. Her hands slackened on the churn's dasher as she recalled the raw sympathy in his voice when he had spoken of Pa. In that moment something inside her had softened, then melted further when he'd asked her to dance.

And dance he could, holding her with just the right amount of gentleness and gentlemanly distance. Remembering, she nearly dropped her gathered eggs. He'd even escorted her back to Susanna and Will after the set, as if he knew tarrying would raise a ruckus with the drunken Simon.

Remembering every detail, she poured herself a cup of buttermilk and sat down behind the screen of roses. Fatigue pinched the back of her eyes. She'd not slept well after the frolic. All night long the questions she still hadn't asked pointed accusing fingers at her.

Why had the Scot come here? Where had he come from? How long would he stay? What was the breadth of his medical training? Did he believe in bloodletting? Did he look askance at the herbs she and Ma Horn used so extensively?

She finished the buttermilk and breathed in the perfume of the roses without truly savoring them. Though he had been gallant to her, she remained somewhat suspicious of him. Nor could she bring herself to call him Doctor. And it pained her greatly to admit that after a near kiss, two conversations, and one dance, he remained the finest man she'd ever laid eyes on.

36

Lael continued to make her way up the branch, her saddlebags full of herbs and other indispensables. Lovey Runion was always on the porch as if expecting her, her pipe in her trembling hands, some crumbled tobacco in her lap. After fixing the older woman a good meal with enough left over for the days to come, Lael would refill Lovey's pipe and sit down opposite her on the porch, a book in hand. She'd grown accustomed, even fond, of the pungent smoke as it spiraled above Lovey's head and sweetened the air. She'd even become used to her fey, almost endearing ways.

As for Titus Grubbs, his arm healed quickly. The day she removed the splints she accompanied him fishing. He was a ten-year-old child again, all soberness gone, fiercely determined to repay her for her treatment of him.

"I'll catch you the biggest fish you ever did see," he boasted, preparing his bait.

She stood with him in the sandy shoals of the river, just beyond the high banks where the wild grapes grew the thickest, and watched as he produced a sharp hook made of hawthorn and tied it to a horsehair line. She waded into the water after him, skirts held up at a modest level, and savored a few pawpaws she found hiding on shore. Within moments he'd jerked a fish from the water, proudly displaying it to her before placing it in a lidded basket.

By noon the basket was half full and they parted, Lael accepting the two biggest fish while Titus took the rest home to his mother.

"I can trap too," he told her. "I can bring you some squirrel or rabbit once you eat them fish. I reckon a woman on her own don't get much meat."

She thanked him warmly, touched by his thoughtfulness. She was already anticipating how she would prepare the fish for supper. Roll it in cornmeal and fry it in grease, Ma always said. And this she would do.

In the days that followed Lael would return home from foraging in the woods or from a call to a settler's cabin to find a wild turkey or a rabbit hanging out of Tuck's reach on the porch. Always, she took the meat down with a smile, filled with gratitude that one small boy could meet so pressing a need.

Now Lael was able to share meat with Lovey as well, and the added nourishment was good for them both. Lovey's hands seemed not to shake so badly these days, and the unhealthy pallor had begun to leave her face. She grew stronger and moved more steadily about the small cabin, sometimes venturing near her bees with Lael watching spellbound as she robbed them of their delicious honey.

Often Lael wondered what winter would bring; Lovey could not live on honey alone, nor could Lael brave the branch in deep snow. Her worries were not unfounded. Even Ma Horn turned dull eyes and ears to the signs, reporting what she'd observed or was told to her.

"The blackberry blooms were a mite heavy this year," she said. "And them hickory nuts you brung have a thick shell. Coy Howe tells me the fur on his sheep and cows is thicker than usual."

Lael pondered the signs herself. Everything she looked at seemed to call out a subtle warning. The dogwood berries were heavier than she ever remembered, and the leaves of the mountain laurel were rolled up. Even the beaver lodges that jammed the river had more logs.

Still, she had not a stick of firewood laid by. The thought dogged her for days, and to allay it she went in search of fallen timber in the woods bordering the cabin. What wood she found was green and would be hard to kindle and keep warm by. And she was no hand with an ax or saw. She returned home burdened, too proud to ask Will Bliss or anyone else for help.

Her garden was now overflowing, and she spent time drying beans and storing potatoes and onions. In the dog days of autumn there was a spate of sickness and the entries in her ledger grew. One deerskin. One and a half pounds of beeswax. Four bushels of oats. One venison ham. One coonskin. Two pounds of lard. Five pounds of tallow. One bushel of flax seed. Two candle molds. Three tin cups. One box of bone buttons. One saddle.

As she worked, she wondered how the doctor was doing. In rare idle moments, she looked to the woods or wandered onto the porch as if expecting some other gift would await her. Hoping. Almost praying. Was lonesomeness filling her with foolish romantic notions? Her nightly reading certainly was. Just yesterday she'd come across the story of an Indian princess and an Englishman. Long ago in Virginia, John Rolfe had written that Pocahontas captured his heart and he could think of no one else.

Entranced, Lael could hardly put the book down. The memory of Captain Jack standing steadfast near the gates of Fort Click held just as firmly in her mind. The pull of the savage and the civilized seemed at war within her once again. Only this time, the savage was gaining the upper hand.

37

Why, Lael wondered, did she recall each of the dark happenings in her life with chilling clarity whilst all the peaceful times were hazy and easily misplaced? Never would she forget the lonesome moment in childhood when she was told of Pa's capture. Or the precise shade of Ma's dress the night she ran off with Uncle Neddy. And then there was the black wax seal on the letter that bore the news of her father's fate. And now this. Years from now, what would she recall? That Simon had been the one to bring her the gruesome news?

She'd been standing in the cornfield, rejoicing in the harvest. Tuck was at her heels and they paced up and down the rows, ears filled with the whisper of the wind among the tall stalks. Neither of them heard Simon approach; he was simply there, savage-like, at the end of a long row facing them. Why hadn't she brought her gun? She was alone—defenseless. But strangely, it was the sober set of Simon's features that set her at ease.

Ever wary, she stopped a ways from him.

"Lael, it's Neddy."

"Neddy? Is he ailing?"

"Neddy's dead." He swallowed hard, as if digesting the news. "Killed by Cherokee. I found him towards evenin' yesterday in his cornfield."

A sickening dismay swept over her, and she thought she might empty her innards onto the grass.

"I put his body in his cabin. They didn't burn it down like usual." He did not look at her. "He—"

She put a hand up, afraid to hear more. Turning, she started to run, past Simon and the skeleton of fence that bordered the field all the way to the cabin. She didn't stop till she had stumbled onto the porch and caught up her gun.

Simon was right behind her, face flushed. "Put that gun down. I ain't goin' to hurt you."

"You already have," she cried. "And I'm not fool enough to be burned twice."

Would he not go and leave her alone with her grief? If he thought she'd fall weeping into his arms, he was sorely mistaken. Perhaps that was why he looked so shaken. Or was it because Neddy's death might well have been his own?

He went on slowly, "I had to come tell it to you. And Colonel Barr."

"Colonel Barr?"

"Philo Barr's the new colonel sent from Virginia with a couple dozen or so men to hold down the fort. You could say he's in charge of things like your pa was. He keeps count of all the trouble and any deaths and the like."

"I'm obliged to you for coming," she told him, fighting tears.

"Is that all?"

Her brows drew together in consternation. "Nay, 'tis not all. There should be a proper burial. I aim for Will Bliss to officiate. Now are you going to tell him, or am I?"

She was all business, belying the soreness in her heart. He took a step back and whistled for his horse.

"I'll tell him." He turned away only to look back again. "I'm sorry, Lael. I know how you felt about Neddy."

216

Why, oh why, had she waited so long to see Uncle Neddy again? The question dogged her clear to Neddy's to see him buried proper. Wearing a borrowed mourning dress stained a bitter black from the dye of walnut hulls, Lael set out on the mare.

Ma Horn had felt too poorly to travel and so the Scot had come in her stead, overseeing the task of preparing the body for burial. Lael had ridden alone up the mountain and found him inside the ransacked cabin.

'Twas a strange sight to see Neddy laid out on the narrow bed, the only upright piece of furniture about the place. Perhaps the Scot had righted it before beginning his work. She stepped over the threshold into the dim cabin, and he stood, his handsome face awash with warning.

"You dinna have tae come in, ye ken."

She understood only part of what he said, lost in the lilt of his speech. "Aye, I do," she replied quietly. But even as she said it, her senses turned skittish. The smell of death was strong, despite the open windows. She crossed to the closest one, drawing a deep breath.

In the distance, underneath a big elm beside the tobacco field, Will and Colonel Barr were digging a grave. 'Twas better than Pa's watery one, she thought, mindful of the hickory coffin just behind her. Blinking, she tried to hold back her tears. She cried not just for Neddy but for Pa. She'd said good-bye to neither.

Firm hands came and rested on her stooped shoulders from behind. She could feel their warmth through the ugly cloth of her dress. This only made her cry harder, as did the words he whispered between her weeping. Gentle words, words of depth and feeling. Was he praying? Was this his Highland tongue? He was so near, the lye-soaked scent of his linen shirt cut through her grief.

In time, she turned and took the clean cloth he handed her.

"I'm sorry aboot your uncle. I hear he was a kind mon . . . a learned mon."

Surprised, she dried her face. "Did you also hear my mother ran off with him when my father was a captive and they conceived my half brother?"

His composed features betrayed no surprise. "Aye, all of it."

She stole a glance at him. "Ned Click is a stranger to you, yet you came all the way up here today. Why?"

His blue gaze never wavered. "'Twas the right thing tae do."

The raw honesty in his face and voice stirred her. She moved away from him to sit on the bed and reached for Neddy's cold, heavy hand. He looked downright peaceful in his clean clothes, eyes closed. She wondered, but would not ask, just where he'd been wounded.

Ian Justus passed onto the porch, giving her privacy, but left the door open. Neddy's desk beckoned from the cabin corner. Books had been tomahawked and lay littered around it. She bent and began picking up scattered pages until her hands touched the intact leather of a small, black Bible. Neddy's own? She hadn't known him to be religious, though Ma Horn had implied otherwise. Wedged beneath the Bible's cover was a paper sealed with red wax. On the face of it, written in a heavy scrawl, was her name. Opening it, she devoured its contents and almost smiled.

Ned Click had deeded all that he had to the son he'd never seen. Ransom Dunbar Click. But he left his most treasured possession, so he wrote, to Lael: his old, dog-eared Bible. She hugged both the letter and the Bible to her heart, glad to be alone.

She stood beside the simple mound of earth where Neddy lay, flanked by Will, Colonel Barr, and the Scot. A lifelong loner, Neddy had had few friends. Lael lay an armful of wildflowers at the foot of the cross that Will had fashioned out of ash. While Will and the colonel went in to look about the cabin, she remained at the grave with Ian Justus. He stood a few feet from her, his hat in his hands.

She felt a bit skittish standing there without a gun, hovering over a fresh grave. In her grief she'd forgotten her rifle. Who knew when the dreaded Cherokee would strike again?

She'd heard that this outlander across from her didn't carry a weapon, which stunned her. She took another look at him around the brim of the borrowed black bonnet. "Are you a Quaker, sir?"

He almost smiled despite the gravity of the moment. "Nae, just a simple Scot, is all."

Nay, she almost shot back, *not simple at all*. What was it about him that so confounded her? His rugged good looks belied the easy grace of his speech and manner. He seemed to have come straight from the elegant drawing rooms of Briar Hill, and yet here he was holding his own on the Kentucke frontier. Was he a laird, like she had read of in her books, from one of those near-barbaric clans in the Scottish Highlands? A laird and a doctor? A hundred questions burned the tip of her tongue, but this was neither the time nor place for them.

Before heading back down the mountain, the men agreed upon a time to meet and harvest her uncle's cotton and tobacco. There was nothing left for her to do but to return to her cabin and write to Ransom.

38

In the days following Neddy's burial, Lael wandered the woods harvesting sumac and Indian peaches and serviceberries, filling honeysuckle baskets to the brim. Solitude was a potent tonic for her grief, and the silence of the woods solaced her like little else. Now that September had flowered, the river was at its warmest, and she took every opportunity to shuck off her shift and jump in. The water, like the woods, seemed to wash her worries away.

Tonight, Tuck swam right along with her, reminding her of Pa's old hounds. Had they died crossing the swollen river with him? She shut away the thought, took a deep breath, and went under, grabbing handfuls of sand to scrub her hair. Glory, but it was a wonderment to be free of her stays! She'd not worn them once since leaving Briar Hill.

Scrubbed clean, she sat upon a sun-warmed slab of limestone and wrung her hair out like a mop, then combed the tangles out with her fingers. Naked as a jaybird she was, her muslin dress dangling from a laurel bush. Men had all the luck, she reckoned, with only shirt, shoes, and breeches to fuss about. She sighed and stood, pulling on her dress.

"Come along, Tuck," she said, retracing her steps to the cabin. She had yet to do up the evening's work, fetching wood and packing water from the spring. The mare, which she'd finally named Pandora, needed to be watered and belled and turned loose in the meadow. But the obstinate animal was nowhere to be found. Lael called and whistled and waited. Truly, Pandora had earned her name; a prolific source of troubles, she was. Lately she'd been tempted to trade her for a mule.

The sun skimmed the western treetops as it bowed out in an orange ball to the west, and she headed that direction. Pandora had a fondness for the pawpaws growing along the far fork of the river. With Tuck at her heels, Lael moved quickly. Already fireflies were winging about, bearing tiny lanterns on their backs, and the evening air was sultry and still.

She'd nearly reached the river when Tuck whined and stopped. "Why, you're as stubborn as that old mare," she exclaimed, turning to scowl at him.

When she turned back around, she stepped straight into the path of Captain Jack. Amusement played across his handsome features as pleasure flushed hers. He was leading Pandora with an Indian bridle, and she whinnied as if chagrined at the sight of her mistress. Time seemed suspended as they faced each other once again. She almost sighed at the sight of him.

He seemed to have materialized out of nowhere, swept in with the evening shadows. Had she never noticed just how tall he was? Why, she hardly grazed his chin. His hair, black and shiny as a crow's wing, hung to his shoulders, and he wore no war paint, just a loincloth and leggins. A string of jade beads dangled across his bare chest. From the top of his head to the tip of his moccasins, he seemed all tendon and sinew.

"Captain Jack," she said, for lack of anything better.

"Click's daughter," he replied in the low, melodious voice she recognized.

With one fluid movement he reached out and caught a long strand of her loose hair and rubbed it between his fingers. Nearly dry now, it was bleached the color of cornsilk by the sun.

His eyes turned inquiring. "What is your name?"

His near-perfect English never failed to startle her. She stared back at him, tongue-tied. *Never look a gentleman directly in the eye.* But Captain Jack was no gentleman. And she, obviously, was no lady.

221

"My name is Lael," she said shyly, thinking how strange it was that he still didn't know and she'd never told him.

"Lael," he echoed, then smiled and shook his head no, murmuring something in Shawnee. "Yellow Bird."

Yellow Bird?

At her bewilderment, he said, "That is what your father called you."

Tears stung her eyes. Once she had thought this Shawnee was the key that would unlock Pa's past. Might he be proving it now?

Her voice was like a whisper. "Yellow Bird sounds . . . fine. What is your Indian name?"

"You know it well enough. Captain Jack," he said, then walked around her, leading the mare.

What does your Indian wife call you?

Quickly, she shut the blasphemous thought away. When she made no move to follow but stood studying the bow and quiver slung across his back, he paused.

With his free arm he reached behind and tugged her forward but did not release her. The hardness of his hand made her work-worn one seem almost soft. They walked out of the woods into a twilight meadow where heat lightning slashed the sky. Her heart felt overfull with his revelation about Pa. Suddenly, she was remembering the blanket he'd left for her on the paling fence all those years before, after the gift of blue beads . . .

"Are you alone?" she asked, glancing around. Never before had she seen him without a half dozen or so other Shawnee.

"No. With you," he said, eyes alight.

She smiled, warmed by his teasing. As they walked her tangled emotions ebbed and flowed and made her bold. "My father always thought well of you," she confided.

"Your father wanted me for a son," he said matter-of-factly.

Son? Or son-in-law? What had Pa seen in this man that had been missing in Simon? She studied his profile in the gathering shadows, as if she could find the answers in his face. Strange, but she felt as if Pa was shadowing them, giving his blessing. Did Captain Jack mean to woo her again as he had long ago? The thought seemed somewhat childish, and she felt heat bloom in her face. Never in her life had she heard of a white woman falling in love with an Indian man, though many a white trapper took an Indian bride. But then, Captain Jack was no Indian.

The possibility made her almost lightheaded. Quietly she asked, "Have you no wife in the Indian towns?"

He stopped walking and turned to her, so close the beads on his chest brushed her bodice. Could he hear her heart hammering? Her very breath seemed to stop at his nearness. Would he . . . kiss her? Did the Shawnee make love in that way?

A sudden noise in the woods gave them pause. Wordlessly, he moved her behind him and drew an arrow out of his quiver, readying his bow. Though they stood exposed in the open meadow, she felt completely safe, secure. The woods stilled again but not before they heard a horse nicker. Who watched them? Pressing the bridle into her hand, he motioned for her to go home, but she was loath to leave. He gave a reassuring half smile and nodded, so she did as he bade her.

Once on the cabin porch she waited, willing him to come to her, to give his answer. While she waited, she readied her own. Suppose she just slipped away with him? What then?

'Twould not be a bad life, Daughter.

Wistful, she lingered, watching the moon come up, wondering why he'd paid her a visit after so long. Pandora, she sensed, had merely been an excuse. At her heels, Tuck waited, tail thumping. Why, she'd not even thought to thank him for her dog.

Tired of standing, she sank to the porch step and wrapped her arms around her knees, a keen yearning filling her. He wasn't coming after all. Maybe he never would again. The thought wet her eyes, and she brushed them dry with the hem of her skirt. Sometimes, like tonight, she felt she'd simply dreamed him up.

39

Just as Simon's visits always left her with a sore, bruised feeling, her encounter with Captain Jack left a deep impression as well, though an altogether poignant one. The feeling followed her for days, infusing all that she did with a wistful uncertainty. She found herself almost wishing Pandora would again run off. Strangely, the mare stayed put as if the Shawnee had cast his spell on her as well.

One crisp morning, Tuck's howling fell to a low growl. "Hush now," Lael rebuked. "'Tis only the Scot."

The dog slunk out of sight beneath the cool porch as if he were as disappointed as she. Setting her gun inside the cabin, she took the straight-backed chair beside the churn. The screen of roses allowed her to take a long look without being seen, and her hands fell idly to her lap.

Slowly, Ian Justus rode into the yard, scattering windblown leaves of gold and crimson that lay like a carpet on the scorched earthen floor. He dismounted from his fine horse and approached the cabin.

"Miss Click."

So he had seen her. No hello. No greeting or awkward small talk. Just her name, spoken with a quiet confidence.

"Mr. Justus," she replied.

He came to stand by the cabin step and looked down the narrow expanse of porch to where she sat. For a moment the morning air was so still even the birdsong seemed to cease. His eyes moved to the tangle of blushing roses.

"My mother's roses," she said, sensing his admiration.

"'Tis a fine place you have here," he told her. "I'm on my way tae see Will and Susanna. Would you care tae come?"

She swallowed, surprised. "Why—I—my morning is chock full of chores." She felt a keen regret even as she refused him. Had she missed her chance to ask him all the questions that clambered for answers? "Do you—would you—like a drink of water?"

He nodded. "Later, perhaps. On my way home."

Home. Spoken with such ease! Was this how he felt about this newfound place—at home?

"Later on I'll have some supper. Some pie too . . . if you like," she managed.

His smile deepened, and she saw a flash of white teeth.

"I would."

She fairly flew through her chores, berating herself as she went. What had made her so bold to ask him outright to supper? And what had made him ask her to accompany him clear to Cozy Creek? Could it be he was as curious about her as she was about him?

As she boiled her clothes in lye water then hung them on a fence to dry, she feared someone would need a remedy and her invitation would be forgotten. At noon Tuck howled, but it was only a lone hunter passing through.

She stayed busy inside the hot cabin, making a meal to rival any spread she'd ever prepared. Leftover beans and cornbread seemed too paltry for the likes of the Scot, so with a stab of guilt she threw them off the side of the porch to Tuck. She'd heard Mr. Justus detested settlement food as well as the heat. Mouth wry, she was tempted to serve him bear bacon and greasy beans, but would fix her finest, if only to repay him for tending to Neddy.

With feverish activity, she shucked some corn and picked the last of the green beans. Her turnips were small but sweet, and the tops would be delicious seasoned with side meat. But suppose Ian Justus were invited to take his meal with the Blisses? Suppose he forgot to stop by after all? The prospect was so unsettling she dropped the pan of cornbread as she removed it from the hearth.

"Dog days!" she fumed, smelling scorched turnips. If she kept this up, she would have little to offer him but buttermilk. Her dress was splattered with grease, and a red welt glowered on one palm where she had burned it removing a kettle of potatoes from the fire.

With a sigh, she passed onto the cool shade of the porch and surveyed her clean laundry along the fence. The sun had already done its work, and even her yellow dress, the one she'd worn to the frolic, was sun-warmed and dry. But it wouldn't do for a simple supper.

She chose a plain dress, bereft of ribbon or buttons or lace, though an extraordinary green dyed from oak leaves. *The color of Captain Jack's eyes.* The thought gave her pause. What if he watched from the woods? She sighed and snatched up a cambric apron whose creases cried for ironing. Her only finery was a ribbon the hue of the roses on the porch which she wove through her hair as she braided and pinned it in place.

When at last Mr. Justus came, they sat on the porch where she'd spread a quilt over the freshly scrubbed planks. Its cheerful pattern of browns and reds was soon hidden by an assortment of dishes, plates, and cups. For a moment she lamented the fact that she hadn't a single saucer of Ma's chipped but fine old china. The sun kindly slipped to the west, casting them in a cool shadow as the food on her guest's full plate dwindled.

Lael ate little herself, so full of questions she had no appetite, but he seemed not to notice. Afterward there was warm apple pie and coffee laced with cream. As she poured she looked up

226

and saw that he was staring at her. The Scot's blue eyes bewildered her. She couldn't decide whether they were the color of a cloudless July sky or the hue of a raggedy robin blooming along the river bottom. His hair was as black as Captain Jack's own.

"Do you often make meals for outlanders, Miss Click?" There was teasing in his tone and in his astonishing eyes.

Scarlet, she looked down at her apron, now soiled by three spots of coffee, a bit lost in the richness of his speech.

"You've yet tae call me Doctor, which I dinna mind in the least. But it tells me you are questioning my credentials. And those eyes of yours demand I must somehow prove myself, pass a test. Like your faither did when he ran the Shawnee gauntlet."

"You read that in the papers, I reckon."

"Aye. Is it true?"

She nodded. "He carried the scars to his grave."

"So he passed the test. Will I?"

She smiled then without meaning to. Law, but she was nervous and ashamed of her pretense. The flock of questions that sat so heavily in her breast suddenly took flight, like a hundred startled birds. But she swallowed and pressed on. "I—I know so little about you. Like where you come from, for starters."

"Scotlain, first, and then Boston. My family is from the Highlands. I took my medical training at the Royal College of Surgeons in Edinburgh. The school is a fine one and specializes in medical surgery."

"Have you just come from there?"

He shook his head. "Nae, I am a Scot with a patriot's heart. I left Scotlain when war with the Crown broke out. There was a need for medical men with the Colonial army, and I signed on and stayed till the war was won. Then I went to Boston and practiced with an older established physician. Until now."

Boston. From her geography lessons at Briar Hill she knew Boston to be large and civilized and cultured. And dirty and

227

plague-ridden and crowded. Everything Kentucke was not and might never be.

"You longed to leave the city, then?"

He shook his head. "No' particularly. I was tae busy. Though I admit tae a certain wanderlust, I had no' thought tae come here."

"Then why did you come?"

He took his eyes off the river and turned to look at her. "When the Almighty puts a thing in a mon's mind it willna be moved. Kentucke became like that for me."

She looked hard at him, taking the strange words to heart. Never in her life had she heard such talk. She finally found her voice and said, "Sounds like you should have been a preacher."

He smiled and the lines about his eyes deepened. "Perhaps. But the Lord saw fit tae make me a surgeon."

"You've led an interesting life."

"No' so interesting as yours, truly," he said with a strange intensity.

She began gathering up the supper plates where she sat, as if signaling him to go, though she sensed he had more to say. Beside him, she felt like she was back at Briar Hill again, making polite conversation, pretending to be a lady. With Captain Jack she was simply Lael Click, Pa's daughter, which required no effort at all.

His eyes were on her, unnerving her so much she dropped a pewter plate. It clunked to the porch stone, sparking her temper. Her voice was soft but a tad sharp. "You call yourself a gentleman, yet you stare at me."

"I never called myself a gentleman."

"You *are* a gentleman and you *still* stare."

"If I do, the fault is your own. You are a complicated lass, Lael Click."

She set the dishes down with a clatter. *Complicated?* She wouldn't ask him to explain himself. She didn't have to.

He leaned back against a porch post, stretched his legs, and crossed his shiny black boots. "You went tae one of the finest finishing schools in the colonies, yet I find you barefoot and bonnetless and making social calls tae Indians, wi' your hair down tae boot. And unchaperoned, as weel."

Her eyes widened. So it had been *him* in the woods watching her! She turned as pink as the porch roses but managed to say, "You'd best watch your backside. You outlanders are always gettin' killed wanderin' where you don't belong."

"And you, Miss Click? Are you immune tae Indian arrows?"

Their eyes locked. She could tell he had a temper as his speech was threaded with heat and becoming more Highland by the minute. As for herself, she was nearly choking on settlement vernacular in her dander.

He reached down and retrieved the pewter plate. "I ken you want me off your porch and out of the settlement as weel. But I'll no' oblige you till you answer a few questions of my own."

Her voice was cold as creek ice in January. "I don't have to."

His blue eyes flashed a warning. "If you want tae be rid of me, you'll answer. Or I'll still be here come morning."

She didn't doubt it. "You Scots are a stubborn lot."

He grinned and rolled his eyes. "And you colonials are no'?"

She sighed and folded her arms across her chest. "Very well. What do you want to know?"

"I'm curious about where you took your training in midwifery."

Her color deepened. "As I told you, I'm not the settlement midwife. I've not birthed one baby."

"But you are an herbalist."

"I suppose I am. The woods and Ma Horn have been my teachers since I was a girl." She looked away from him, embarrassed. Here she was, considering him a quack, and he was unraveling her own lack of expertise fast as a spool of thread.

"I'm finding the settlers here a superstitious lot. I dinna doubt you are much the same."

She sat up straighter. "What do you mean?"

"Axes under the bed tae cut the pain of childbirth. Garlic charms and spells. Boiling beaver tails tae cure snakebite. No' tae mention the misuse of useful herbs."

Her own face clouded. "I do none of those things."

He looked doubtful. "Prove it."

"How do you expect me to do that?"

His steely eyes held a challenge. "Work alongside me."

Her lips parted in astonishment. She shook her head warily. "I have no desire to become an indentured servant, thank you kindly."

Though he kept a straight face, his eyes were smiling. Would he never leave? She had dishes to wash and the night chores to see about . . .

He stood up suddenly, casting a long shadow. "If you've nae more questions, Miss Click, I'd best be going. Thank you for the fine supper. It's the best I've had since leaving Boston."

Night was falling fast. The only sound was the plaintive call of a dove looking for its mate. She stood up but laced her fingers behind her back so he couldn't kiss her hand or do whatever a Scotsman did when parting company with a lady. *Only I'm no lady.*

"Good night, Doctor," she said.

He turned and went to untie his horse without another word. She stood and watched him go until the purple twilight had completely swallowed him up. Would he be safe in these woods? 'Twas a far piece to the fort.

She felt unsettled as a river current, wending this way and that in his wake. She sighed and went into the cabin, drawing in the latchstring and barring the door. Like herbs and conventional medicine, they obviously did not mix well. In the future, she must avoid him.

40

The next morning she went to the fort to see if a letter from Ransom was waiting and was greatly relieved to find Ian Justus absent. The doctor had gone to Lexington, Ma Horn told her, and would not be back until the morrow. There was no letter either, and so she returned home.

She performed her chores by rote, her mind on her recent encounters. But the treasured memory of her meadow meeting with Captain Jack was muddied by that of her visit from the doctor.

Often she thought of Uncle Neddy. In the evenings when she sat on the porch, stripping sassafras leaves or bundling spicewood twigs, she tried not to think of how it had been that fateful day. Tragedy seemed far from her fragrant, sun-rimmed porch, though trouble had never needed an invitation.

For days now she had seen no sign of Titus Grubbs. No telltale meat hung on her porch, not even one fish in a willow basket. So she set out to find him, concern marking her every step. The Grubbs cabin was not far but nearly hidden in a shady cove. How many people had passed by and not even known it was there?

She tethered her horse to a fading laurel and began a slow walk to the cabin. Mourning Grubbs was on the porch in a rocker that creaked with each movement. Once again the half-starved hounds did not so much as bark. She couldn't see her clearly—was she rocking and crying?

Mourning had risen and now stood inside the door frame. For the first time the shifty-eyed woman looked directly at her and Lael read the fear in her eyes.

"I ain't set for no company," she muttered.

Lael put a foot on the porch step. "I thought I heard crying."

The woman coughed and made a move to go inside, muttering something unintelligible.

"I do hear crying." Lael stepped to the door just as the tiny woman tried to shut it. But Lael, easily the stronger of the two, pushed it open.

One sweep of the cabin told her the pitiful sounds came from the loft. She climbed the rough ladder, dread filling her heart. Titus lay on a dirty pallet, his face so bloody and bruised she hardly knew him. His torn shirt was a brilliant ruby red, seeping into the pallet. Whatever the trouble, it was fresh— and brutal.

"Titus." Lael spoke the name through a throat so tight with tears she feared she would choke. A cold fury filled her as she backed down the ladder to find his mother gone.

Clutching some rags and a bowl of water, she returned to the loft. The boy's eyes were closed now—was he unconscious? She whispered his name over and over as if this would somehow soothe him. Were there internal injuries? She prayed not. The loft was dim as a cave. How could she possibly move him? But move him she must.

If only the doctor were here.

Dear Lord in heaven . . . help me . . . help me move him. Past feeling now, she carried him precariously down the ladder and out onto the empty porch and across the yard. His silent, shame-faced mother was nowhere to be seen. A cart she'd not noticed before rested by a trickle of creek. She hitched the mare to the cart then lay the boy in it as gently as she could. It was not until morning that Titus opened his eyes to find a sleepless Lael hovering over him as he lay in her corner bed. And, bless him, through cracked lips he smiled.

"I—knowed—you'd—come," he whispered as she gave him a sip of water. "I prayed—you'd come." His face was bruised and swollen, but all traces of blood had been sponged away during the long night.

She longed to fetch the doctor but was afraid to leave the boy. Afraid that whoever had done this terrible thing would somehow find him and take him away from her forever.

"Titus, who has done this ugly thing?"

But he would have none of it. The light in his eyes faded as she asked it, and he turned away from her, his face to the wall.

In the morning, when she returned from milking, he was gone.

All the next day Lael combed the woods and hillsides. She came upon the abandoned Grubbs cabin, but the shiftless hounds did not so much as raise their heads. Where was Mourning? Hollow-hearted, she returned home, where she took a bit of cold cornbread that crumbled dryly in her mouth and chased it with cider that tasted oversweet. Taking up her gun, she passed onto the porch to wait for the deepening darkness.

In time she heard the rustle of brush and a sob. Out of the shadows came Mourning Grubbs, bent and weeping. Setting aside her gun, Lael went out to meet her. In truth, she'd never cared much for the woman. But the sight of her cut lip and blackened eye filled her with compassion.

"Mourning, what's become of you?"

But she merely repeated, "I got to see Titus."

Lael stood firm, arms crossed. "I'll not take you in—nor let you near Titus—till you speak your mind to me." She kept her eyes on the woman's battered face. "Did you take a hand to your boy?"

Mourning shook her head vehemently, trembling now. As if wounded himself, Tuck let out a mournful wail by the door and would not stop till Lael took off one of her moccasins and hurled it in his direction.

She was unnerved herself but tried not to show it. "I'll say it again. Did you take a hand to Titus?"

"Nay!"

"Who, then?"

It took time but the whole sordid story spilled out, not ending till moonlight had edged the porch in silver. Mourning's husband had died some months past, leaving her and her young son alone. Pining for her family in North Carolina, she met a man who promised to take her back over the mountains. Soon he was visiting her cabin and demanding her favors, never telling her where he lived, only that he made a little moonshine for a living up on high. Desperate to return home, she endured his visits, only to find that the promised trip never materialized. Now when he came he was drunk—and violent. When a meal or a word did not suit him, he struck her—or her boy.

"Twice he broke Titus's arm," she confessed.

Lael was sickened. From somewhere deep within, Mourning Grubbs had summoned the courage to tell him he was no longer welcome. When he attempted to beat her, Titus stepped in and took the licking in her stead.

"I—I thought he would kill him he was so drunk—and so riled. I'm a-feared he'll come back."

"You must tell me the name of this man." She remembered Pa once said that a man who struck a woman was no man at all, not even a beast, for almost always an animal took care of its own. Would Mourning tell her? Or was her fear too great? Lael nearly held her breath in the ensuing silence.

234

"The man who like to have killed Titus is one of them Mc-Clarys," she said at last, turning flinty eyes on Lael. "Hero Mc-Clary. Brother to Hugh."

The name came out a whisper. Hugh McClary. Hero McClary. Two brothers cut from the same cloth, if there ever was, Lael thought in revulsion. Years before he'd shot her father, Hugh McClary led his clan over Cumberland Gap for no other reason than to escape the trouble they'd made in Pennsylvania. But there was one telling difference between the two brothers. If possible, Hero was worse.

Mourning stood up and looked beseechingly at Lael.

"Your boy's not here," Lael said. "He ran off early this morning."

And with that, the woman fainted.

With Mourning settled in the Click cabin, Lael set out alone. It took two days of tramping through stinging nettles and briar patches to find Hero McClary. She finally came across him on a tangled slope of ridge made nearly impassable by large rocks. A stingy wisp of gray smoke gave him away. He was crouched, back to her, feeding a small fire. All the makings for a fresh batch of corn liquor were at hand. Though she'd never before seen a still, she knew it to be a crude operation but a profitable one. This particular contraption looked to have taken some time, finely wrought by a cooper and reinforced with metal bands.

She paused behind a stand of mountain laurel. All her exertion from crawling over rocks and wading streams and unfamiliar woods had not assuaged her anger. She felt fairly white hot with it, fueled by Mourning's sad tale and the disappearance of Titus.

Her own anxiety over the missing boy had left her sleepless and surly. Her dander rose higher when she realized that Hero must have been party to the recent ambush of the Shawnee, and she rued the future trouble their misdeeds were bound to cause the settlement.

She stepped out from behind the laurel, deliberately brushing against the heavy leaves. At the sound, Hero McClary whirled around, face strained. She knew what he feared. Shawnee. Or Wyandotte. Or Cherokee.

Would that it had been him rather than Neddy.

Seeing her, a mere woman, his face relaxed. Worse yet was the look on his shabby, bearded face—the smile that curled but held no warmth, only contempt and lust and arrogance.

She raised her gun slowly and her hands did not shake.

"Hero McClary, if you ever lay a hand on the woman or the boy again, I'll bring every man in the settlement down on you." She paused, surprised to find her voice as strong and steady as a man's. "And if the men don't come fast enough to suit me, I'll shoot you myself."

And with that, she blasted a hole in his still.

41

"You did what?" Susanna's face was pale in the early morning light. "Why, no one messes with the likes of Hero McClary. Word is he never stays anywhere very long 'cause he always kills a body and has to move on."

"I'm only concerned about finding Titus," Lael told her, not bothering to dismount from the mare.

"There's been nothin' queer up here. The dogs ain't so much as barked at a coon these past few days. I disremember if I ever saw the Grubbs boy before. You say he's smallish and dark-headed?"

Lael nodded.

"You figure he's hurt bad?"

"I hope not, but it's likely. Mourning's at my cabin. That's why I can't stay." She spoke woodenly in a voice that was not her own. Her head thudded miserably from lack of sleep, and a fire burned behind her eyes.

"I'll send Will down to see after you when he gets home from huntin' this evenin', and don't try to talk me out of it." Susanna stepped out of her path. "Were you ribbin' me when you said you shot his still to bits?"

"It's true."

"Law, Lael—and you a lady!"

"I don't know what I am, Susanna, except mad—and awful tired."

Susanna sighed. "I reckon so. You sound as if you'd take pleasure in killin' him."

"I believe I would," she replied slowly, as shocked as Susanna.

Indeed, that was the worst of it, Lael thought as she sat awake
and soul-sore in her rocker that night with her gun across her
knees. In confronting Hero McClary's evil she'd come face to
face with her own. Perhaps she should have aimed at him and
not his still and left Hugh to Captain Jack.

The next morning Lael packed a small kettle of victuals, an
empty honey crock, and a book and started up the branch. It
had been well over a week since she had last seen Lovey Runion,
and the gap chafed at her.

She should have come sooner, she knew. She didn't like to
leave Lovey alone for this long, but now she had Mourning to
see to as well, though the latter was well fed and resting at the
cabin, Tuck at her side.

"Don't you worry none about me," Mourning told her. "If Hero
comes, he comes. And if he don't, he don't. I ain't handy with a
gun no-ways. But I'll keep an eye out for my boy."

And so with time and trouble suspended between her cabin
and the branch, Lael set off on the mare. The morning was
breathless with not so much as a sigh of wind, only the honest
damp of early autumn where the sun had yet to filter through
the turning trees.

Overnight it seemed the whole forest had been set ablaze.
Green leaves had turned a brilliant gold and crimson and ochre.
Indian colors, Pa used to say. The stately maples were always
the last to give up their leaves, but the generous oaks led her
down a golden path. As the ramshackle cabin came into view,
Lael thought that truly there were few places on earth as lovely
as the branch come Indian summer.

This time, before Lael could holler a familiar greeting, Lovey called out to her from the cabin. "My boy—my boy's come home!"

Lael drew up, thinking she'd misheard, but Lovey echoed the words again. Puzzled, Lael recalled what she knew. Lovey's son, along with her husband, had disappeared long ago. If indeed he lived, the boy Lovey so fondly remembered had by now become a man.

Slowly, she carried the basket past the bee gums and up the steps. The cabin door creaked open a crack, but it was not Lovey's face she beheld there. It was the wide-eyed countenance of Titus Grubbs.

Colonel Philo Barr fell into step beside Lael as she crossed the fort common. She'd just come from the sutler's and was headed to Ma Horn's cabin, a small keg of gunpowder in her arms.

"Miss Click," he said in formal tones. "You have just saved me a trip out to see you. A rumor has reached me that concerns you—and me as well."

She said nothing but continued walking.

"'Tis the matter of the old Click-McClary feud, renewed as of late."

She nearly smiled at his gentlemanly phrasing. "'Tis a simple matter, sir. And one that's been settled."

"Hardly settled, Miss Click, but rather ignited. The McClary clan is shouting what you've done all over the settlement."

"And what have I done? Defended a helpless woman and child? Shamed a drunken, abusive scoundrel?"

"You should have come to me and left the matter to the law."

She stopped and looked square at him. "And what would you have done, colonel?"

"I doubt I would have shot up his still."

"I doubt you would have done anything at all."

His left eye twitched suddenly, and he looked a trifle exasperated. "I fear for your safety, Miss Click. I am within my rights to demand that you move to the fort this very day."

She looked hard at him, weighing the truth of what he said. Will Bliss had already come down from Cozy Creek and begged the same that very morning. Only he had given her a choice: move to the fort or take up with them. She had refused both.

"'Tis a free country," she challenged. "And the answer is nay. If you need to be forting anyone up, sir, let it be Hero McClary."

She left him then and hurried on to Ma Horn's. Would the doctor be there? It was nearly noon and she recalled that the two of them sometimes shared a meal. She found the old woman stirring a pot of turnips, a spoon in one hand and her cane in the other.

"Stay and sup with me, child. The doctor's gone out to see to Hugh McClary. He ain't long for this world, looks to me, ever since that horse throwed him good and hard."

"Well, let the devil take him," Lael muttered, sitting down at the trestle table. She was only too glad to stay and eat a bite. The turnips were sweet and, cooked with the greens, made a fine meal taken with cornbread. As she poured herself a second cup of cider, the door swung open following a sharp rap.

It was hard to keep her dismay down at the sight of the doctor. Their last meeting made her so uncomfortable that she'd hoped to avoid him and wondered if he felt the same. But he'd clearly made himself at home here and was in Ma Horn's good graces anyway.

His eyes fell on her straightaway. "Good day, Miss Click. I saw your horse outside the sutler's and wanted tae speak tae you."

He deposited a leather satchel by the door and took a bench opposite her. Ma Horn placed a steaming bowl in front of him, and he murmured his thanks but made no move to eat. And then, just as she had done once before, Ma Horn started toward the door with her cane. Turning in her seat, Lael started to protest, but he quickly intervened.

"Let her go. We need tae talk."

The intensity in his tone shook her. She turned her eyes to him, wondering what it was about him that so unnerved her. His abruptness? Or the way his astonishing eyes seemed to look right through her?

He smiled slightly as if to ease her. "I asked once before, do you always court trouble, Miss Click, or does it just seem tae follow you where'er you go?"

She flushed. So word of her run-in with Hero McClary had reached the doctor as well. Her face grew pinker, not from his mention of the feud but from his intense scrutiny. She managed as calmly as she could, "As I told Colonel Barr, the matter is settled."

His eyes sparked. "Nae, no' settled. Nothing is ever settled with a clan like the McClarys. It matters no' that you're a woman. It matters greatly that you live alone."

She swallowed, not taking her eyes from his, and saw the warning and concern in their blueness. Wearily, elbows on the table, she rested her face in her hands.

Gently but firmly his fingers encircled her wrists like iron bands and brought them back down. "Look at me, Lael, and say that you'll come tae the fort, just for the winter."

Lael. Lay-elle. In his Highland brogue, it sounded like no name she had ever heard, yet she bristled at his familiarity. Her resistance to the notion of forting up doubled.

"Nay," was all she said as she looked away.

Releasing her, he looked down at the bowl of food Ma Horn had set before him. Did he find turnips and greens disagreeable fare? Or was he regretting saying her given name? In a few days' time, "Miss Click" had changed to "Lael."

"I'd best be going," she said but made no move to do so.

"Nae . . . stay."

He took up his spoon then, but not before she saw out of the corner of her eye that he bowed his head for a moment of silence. A prayer? Undoubtedly. For the doctor, she recollected, should have been a preacher.

After a few quiet moments she said, "You are keeping busy, I reckon, for you are seldom here when I come."

His blue eyes held a denial. "Busy? Nae. It isna work, truly. I see a few people passing through the fort. And your cast-offs."

"My cast-offs?"

"Aye. Hugh McClary."

Her eyes sparked. "He shot my father."

"So?"

"He might have killed him!"

"But he dinna do so." He pushed aside his half-empty bowl. "Besides, that isna why you shun the mon. 'Tis your grudge that prevents you from doing him a kindness."

"I owe him no kindness."

"'Tis reason enough tae see tae his injury," he challenged. "'Twould be a fine thing tae mend both body and spirit, would it no'?"

Her voice turned indignant. "You make no sense."

"And you do? Taking a grudge tae the grave? Nursing another?" His eyes held hers in challenge. "Pardon me, Miss Click, but I see no sense in that."

Stung, she could only stare at him.

"Good tae forgive, best tae forget, aye?"

"You forget yourself, doctor."

He shook his head as if scolding. "Dinna be so wranglesome, Lael Click. It doesna become you."

She shot back, "I'm not the only wranglesome one here!"

For one befuddled moment longer she sat, anger swirling

inside her. Who was he to take her to task? Their every meeting seemed a blatant contest of wills. With as much dignity as she could muster she found her feet and left the cabin. As she walked briskly across the common she fumed.

He was wrong, pure and simple. He knew nothing of the feud between Hugh McClary and her father and how its ill effects clung to her like a burr. She was justified in holding her grudge, holding it tight and letting its hardness fester and foment inside her, and she had no qualms about extending that grudge to include Hero as well.

Until moments ago. Until Ian Justus exposed it all for what it truly was.

Foolish. Dangerous. Perhaps deadly.

Suddenly she felt afraid—and ashamed. The disappointment she'd read in his eyes was like a bucket of cold water in her face, dousing her anew each time she thought of it. He'd thought well of her, perhaps even admired her. Though he'd never said so, she had sensed it. Until today, when he'd glimpsed the meanness hiding deep inside her soul.

She shut her eyes tight, but the look he had given her still haunted. Why? What did it matter what he thought?

Why did it matter to her at all?

42

The steadiness of her hands belied her skittishness as she poured frothy milk into the churn, then clamped on the lid and dasher. Lael half expected Hero McClary to emerge from the woods at any moment and fan the feud she had fueled. But it was early morning and she knew him to be the kind to slink about at night, like a polecat or a coon.

One thought consoled her: If there was to be trouble, at least she was alone. Mourning and Titus were now settled up the branch with Lovey Runion, out of sight and danger. The arrangement was a mite amusing. Titus had suffered no lasting injuries from his beating, and the two women doted on him.

"How I come to be here is this," he had told Lael when she found him at Lovey's. "One day I follered you up here just to see where you was headed. And you know what? Lovey's the beatenest granny I ever met."

Truly, he seemed a tonic for the old woman. He answered when she called him Henry and helped her with a multitude of tasks about the cabin, even sharing her fascination with the bees. As for Mourning, she cooked and tidied the cabin and seemed more content than Lael had ever seen her. There was no more talk of their returning to North Carolina, at least none now that winter was coming on.

At noon Will Bliss rode down to fetch her as little Lael had come down with a fever. All through the night and into the next day she worked to bring the fever under control, finally breaking it with boneset. She arrived home hungry, thirsty, and fell bone weary into bed.

Strangely, it was not the smoke or the eerie glow seeping through the shutter cracks that woke her. It was Tuck pacing the length of the porch with a low whine the likes of which she had never heard. At once she shucked off sleep and threw back the bedcovers, reaching for her gun.

Through the largest shutter crack she stared out at a wall of fire.

The barn!

Stunned, she stood rooted, her eyes moving to the springhouse not far beyond. It seemed only a matter of time till it caught, and then the cabin. But not a breath of wind stirred. The flames shot straight up, red arrows leaping at the night sky, devouring the precious corn stored so carefully within.

The shock of it chilled her. There was no use trying to put it out, not with Hero McClary likely waiting for her in the shadows. The barn was gone. She could not even fight her despair by running for a ladder and pouring buckets of water on the springhouse and cabin roofs. Instead she could only wait and watch—and pray.

By dawn's first light, a group of men had gathered, drawn by all the smoke, among them Colonel Barr, Simon, and Will. The doctor was noticeably absent.

With a flicker of uneasiness she noticed the surprise in Simon's eyes when he saw her. "Last week a party of Mingo burned out a place on Tate's Creek," he said tersely, surveying the smoking rubble that had burned so thoroughly it had charred the earth. "I thought you got the same."

"Any livestock lost?" someone asked.

She shook her head. Thankfully, she had been too tired the

night before to see to the animals and had left them free to roam. Lael spotted the cow at the edge of the woods, staring dumbly as the last of the flames licked a charred beam. Pandora was likely at the river.

"We can rebuild the barn for ye," Will Hendry said, and the other men nodded in agreement. "Will take but a few days iffen we all pitch in."

She was glad for their generosity but would have none of it. "Maybe come spring" was all she said.

Truly, she was so busy tending sick folks that she hardly had time to tend to her animals. Now, with both feed and shelter destroyed, she had no recourse but to part with her horse and cow and the few sheep she'd begun to acquire.

"I'll take the cow," offered Dick Harold.

Will Bliss stepped forward. "I'll see to the sheep. You can fetch 'em back come spring."

She nodded. That left her with a horse, a bunch of chickens, and a stubborn, mangy old mule she'd recently been given for tending a broken leg. A mule wouldn't care much about shelter, just feed, though it might need a lean-to out of the wind. At least she had a mule, ornery or no.

One by one the men left until only Simon and Will tarried. She looked on as Will circled what was left of the barn as if looking for some sign or footprint. Simon approached her with eyes unclouded by drink or animosity, and she felt she had taken a step back into her childhood. Inside her chest her heart thawed a bit, and tears stung her eyes.

Turning toward the flickering ashes, he asked, "Who done this, Lael?"

She shrugged, one of the most unladylike gestures she knew.

He shook his head. "You always was a terrible liar."

Suddenly, in her weakness, she wanted to fall headlong into his arms and blurt out what she knew. Had he not heard? *Hero*

McClary has gone and done it, she wanted to cry, *all becau* *I shot a hole in his still*. Mercifully, Simon did not take a step toward her.

"I reckon you'll be fortin' up come winter," he said, keeping his eyes trained on the rubble of barn. "It's gonna be a hard one—the signs are right."

She wondered if he'd seen the logs at the far side of the cabin she had dragged in using the mule. It was a far cry from stacked firewood, but it was a start.

"When the snow flies, who's gonna keep you in meat?"

She continued to stand and watch Will, outwardly stoic. "Powell Cummings gave me a whole raft of bear bacon for treating his snakebite. It's hanging in the springhouse. And I've got a good store of meal and dried vegetables. I'll keep."

"There's painter tracks along the creek. You know how ornery a painter gets come winter."

She nearly smiled at his persistence to expose her folly. "Oh, I know all about painters. But I don't believe half the stories I hear, like them coming down the chimney and such. Pa skinned a couple, remember? But Ma said they stunk, so he sold them."

He nodded and looked sour for a moment as if any mention of the past aggravated him like a burr. She looked up to see Will approaching the porch. "I'll bring you some corn for feed," he told her.

When they'd left, she went inside and bolted the door, but her thoughts were not on the barn. Where, she wondered, was the doctor?

43

At twilight, Lael ran to the river to wash away her troubles, Tuck at her heels. She wanted to forget this day and leave the smoke and ashes far behind. Standing on the sandy bank she paused for a moment, testing the water with her toes. Not nearly as warm as Briar Hill bathwater. Still, a smile not even a McClary could dim softened her face. Soon her work dress lay puddled at her feet. Best not shuck off all her clothes, she decided. Her thin muslin shift remained though it hardly covered her from shoulder to knee, its once fine embroidery frayed.

Nay, it wouldn't do to be caught completely uncovered. Lately, settlers had been coming downriver in flatboats, and one had run aground on this very bank two nights before. The sight of so many people, their belongings piled like beaver dams atop their rafts, sorrowed her somewhat. Despite the Indian threat, people were still pouring into Kentucke. No wonder Pa had left the settlement and headed for the Missouri territory.

She waded in to her waist, her shift floating like a lily pad atop the water. Here and there the fading sun turned the waters green, then golden. She held her breath and went under, then broke the still surface and heard doves cooing on both sides of the river. This was utter bliss, utter peace.

To anchor herself, she glanced back at her favorite perch, a slab of limestone that jutted out over the water. It looked different in the shadows—perhaps a play of light upon the shore? She swam nearer and her breath caught. Lying atop the rock

248

was a bow and quiver full of arrows beside a pair of beade
moccasins.

She spun around in the water, joy bubbling up inside her. But
before she could take a breath, firm hands caught her ankles
and tugged her under. She came up sputtering and laughing, but
he'd still not surfaced. *So he swims like a fish.* She remembered
he could also run like a deer, overtaking her in the woods all
those years before.

"Yellow Bird." The voice behind her seemed almost to drown
her with its depth. She turned to Captain Jack, hard pressed to
keep her pleasure down. How many days since they had walked
in the meadow? Too many, from the feeling inside her.

In one glance she took in the doused eagle feathers of his
headdress and the fine silver bands encircling his solid upper
arms. Shimmering with water, Captain Jack's hair was blue black.
The beads about his neck were the same startling jade as his eyes
and made him even more appealing. Suddenly shy, she ducked
beneath the water, then swam away. Would he follow?

They did a dance of sorts in the warm current, circling, gliding, swaying. Each time he caught her she pulled free and swam
farther downriver than she'd ever been before. But he continued
to woo her, pursuing her until she was so breathless she could
only lie upon her back and float, the river like a watery bed. He
swam beside her, his eyes roaming both banks.

He turned his head to watch her. "Did your father teach you
to swim?"

She nodded, gladness filling her each time he mentioned Pa.
"Aye, and you?"

A furrow creased his brow as if the memory was denied him.
"I must have learned as a boy from my white father. I came to
the Shawnee knowing how to swim."

She heard the waterfalls before she felt their mist. Catching
hands, they tumbled together over a gentle falls, coming to rest

neath a rock overhang out of the way of the rushing water. She looked around in wonderment, the thunderous spray hemming them in on all sides, making speech impossible. But truly, words were unnecessary.

Gently, he framed her face with his hands. Her lips parted as she looked up at him, expectant, drinking in every line and shadow of his striking face. She was trembling now, not from the chill of the water but from his nearness. The sweet ache he created inside her drew her against him, and she flung her arms around his neck.

He began covering her with kisses, on her open mouth, her neck, her hair. She kissed him back, stunned by her need of him, her hands tangled in his wet hair. Gone were the careful kisses of her girlhood, given her by Simon. This was a wild, possessive declaration of a passion too long denied, sparked years before when he called her out of her cabin, then lay banked and smoldering while at Briar Hill, only to blaze up here and now.

His raw strength took her breath away as he held her, but it was his restraint that won her heart. He drew back slowly and removed a silver bracelet from his arm and put it around her own, then took her hand and led her over rocks and rushing water to the bank.

Silently, they walked hand in hand back to the great slab of rock that held his weapons and moccasins, and he helped her with her discarded dress. She was shivering now in her sodden shift, and the dry dress had to be tugged into place over it. But before she could tie her bodice strings, she was in his arms again, touching him and trading his kisses and being touched and tasted in return.

It was only when they drew apart that she saw that he was wounded. His left side had been grazed—by a bullet?—and he was bleeding afresh. Blood streaked his thigh and dripped onto his moccasin.

"You're hurt." Concern darkened her features, and she reached down and tore a length of cloth from the hem of her dress.

He raised his arms slightly as she bound his waist and tried to stop the bleeding.

"I have some herbs in my cabin . . . I'll make a poultice."

"I am not much hurt," he protested, turning with her up the trail. "Just lucky some settler cannot shoot straight."

Her sudden smile turned pensive. "What is happening beyond the Falls of the Ohio?"

He hesitated, as if weighing how much to tell her. "The white officers have built two forts along the river—to turn settlers away from Shawnee lands, they say."

"Did your chiefs sign a treaty guaranteeing this?"

He nodded. "The treaty was signed at Fort Pitt with many paleface chiefs, but while our braves were there, several of our villages were burned and many of our crops destroyed. Some of our people were killed or taken prisoner."

She felt ashamed and looked away from him. Hadn't Pa said such treaties were carefully couched lies written in English by greedy men? In this case, it had become a cover for murder and mayhem as well. "I've not heard of such trouble, just reports of white men's boats being raided as they come downriver, or so the militia tells us."

"We take back from the whites what they took from us when our towns were burned—salt, gunpowder, lead, furs. And we work to rebuild before the coming winter."

Her steps slowed. "Is that how you were wounded?"

He nodded but said no more. The throaty lilt of a whip-poorwill sounded as they came into the clearing. Immediately her eyes went to the remains of the barn. She said nothing, not wanting to spoil their time together talking of such things. Did he know of her trouble with the McClarys? No surprise lit his features as they walked past the still-smoking rubble.

He merely turned to her and said with a slight smile, "You are in need of a husband."

Hiding her surprise, she ducked into the cabin. "And you are in need of a gunpowder poultice."

As she moved among her baskets, mixing what she needed, he stood by the hearth, touching and dismissing each item inside the cabin with his eyes. She took care to pour him some cold cider from the springhouse and set out what was meant to be her supper. While he sat and ate, she cleaned his wound and applied the poultice.

Soon he pushed his empty plate aside. "So you are a medicine woman." When she did not reply, he added, "You do many things well."

She flushed and began wrapping him with clean linen, but he caught her hands and she went still. *Oh, best not kiss me again . . .*

But he did, straddling the bench and bringing her against him, making her forget where she was. 'Twas almost dark out, the cabin even darker.

"I must go—" he finally said.

"Nay," she protested, shaking her head. "I have so many questions . . . about you—my father."

His mouth was warm against her ear. "I still have not answered your first one."

She remembered all too well what she'd asked him in the meadow. *Have you no wife?* Dare she ask again? Swallowing hard, she said softly, "You are not married?"

He held her tighter. "I have been waiting for you."

Gently, he brushed back a strand of her hair. "Soon, I will come again and we will talk of such things."

"Promise me . . ." she whispered, "promise me one thing."

He bent nearer and she worked to keep her voice from fraying.

"Don't stay away too long. Sometimes it seems you're not r... ... that I only dream of you."

He took her hands and gestured to the bracelet he'd given her, his voice like a caress, and his heartfelt words only deepened her feelings for him. "This is real. When you doubt, you have only to look and remember."

"But I have nothing to give you."

He smiled slowly. "I have your heart. A long time I have waited." He took her face between his hands in the tender, almost awed way that she loved and kissed her again.

To think that she had once feared this very thing. Was it just six years ago she'd been terrified of her own capture by the very man who now held her? She'd simply been too young. Pa had known this and wisely sent her away. Now she'd returned, with a woman's heart and mind and needs. She was attracted to him in ways she couldn't fathom, and her heart was already twisting at his leaving.

"Soon," he told her.

He left her then, but she could not even pass onto the porch to say good-bye. A trace of foreboding seemed to shadow him, and she felt it—and feared it. Remaining at the table, she lay her head down on Neddy's Bible, beside the empty plate and cup, and wept.

44

Truly, she had never felt so tired. From where she sat she could smell the sour ashes of the barn. Trouble made one tired, she reckoned. That was why she sat on the porch with Tuck and her gun when she should have been inside fixing supper. She was too tired to eat. Or perhaps it was her bewildering longing for Captain Jack that made her so, acute as any illness.

From the porch the river looked like yellow satin in the sunset, and upon its brightness was a canoe, small as one of Ransom's toys carved by Pa long ago. She'd last ridden the river with Simon when she was a girl and he'd asked her to run off with him. They'd rowed upriver back then, against the current under a full moon. Downriver was best, she decided. Full of winsome twists and turns, its banks thick with wild grapes and juicy pawpaws in season, and crowned with the beautiful falls that had wooed her just yesterday.

The canoe was turning now, heading toward shore. *Her shore.* Forgetting her gun, she took the river path, her steps light on the leafy trail. She'd heard Ian Justus sometimes rowed the river, but she'd not thought to see him this far. When she reached the bank, he was waiting in the shallows, paddles stuck in the soft river mud.

His grin was a trifle roguish. "Get in and I'll promise no' tae drown you." He sobered suddenly and said, "I have some settlement news."

News? As she waded the few steps to the boat, holding up her skirts modestly so as not to get them wet, he stood up and helped her in. The canoe rocked then settled as she sat.

The Scot turned slightly to maneuver the canoe back into t?
current. Sweat glazed the back of his neck and turned his dark
hair riotous along the collar of his linen shirt. She stifled the urge
to reach out and brush the waves with her fingertips.

I'd do well to mind my own hair.

The thick braid dangled to her knees and had dragged in the
water as she'd gotten into the boat. It hung over one shoulder,
its wet end curled in her lap, white as straw. She wished now
she had put it up in a more genteel way. What must he think of
her flyaway braid and callused hands and sunburned skin?

What did she care?

When they were drifting in the middle of the river, he turned
back to her. "There's been some trouble with the McClarys."

"Trouble?" A deep dread knotted her stomach. Had Hero
found Mourning and Titus at Lovey's?

His eyes studied her, slipping from her tense face to the silver
bracelet circling her wrist. "The McClarys—both brothers—are
dead."

Her lips parted, but she made no sound.

"They were found lying among their traps at Drowning Creek
yesterday, shot through with Shawnee arrows."

The image of Captain Jack's full quiver flashed to mind. She felt
breathless and a bit ill. Had he avenged not only his ambushed
warriors but she and Pa as well? Truly, not a soul in the settlement
would be sorry to see the McClarys go, least of all herself.

Ian Justus's eyes returned to her bracelet. "'Tis a dangerous
game you play, Lael Click."

Alarm filled her. "I—I did not kill them."

His face was grave. "I ken you know who did."

"What if I do?" The sharpness in her voice forbade him to
press further. "The McClarys deserved what they got, and I dare
anyone to argue otherwise." That said, a sweeping relief settled
over her. Mourning and Titus would no longer live in fear, and

either would she. The evil the brothers had wrought had come
to a just, if not merciful, end.

The paddle continued to part the dark water, neither of them
speaking. After a time, he said, "Have you considered coming
tae the fort?"

But her mind and her heart were wandering and she hardly
heard him. Would Captain Jack be hunted down by the militia
if they learned he'd killed the McClarys? Her dread deepened
and she had a hard time drawing an easy breath.

"Do I have tae beg you?"

"What?" She turned back to him then, forbidding any dark
thoughts.

"Do I have tae beg you tae come fort up with the rest of us
miserable wretches?"

She almost smiled at the absurdity of his begging for anything.

His brows knit together in contemplation. "I guarantee you
would no' be bored. I am in need of a good nurse."

"I've had my fill of forting up," she said. "Seems like I spent
half my childhood behind those walls."

"You dinna ken, do you?"

"Dinna . . . ken?" She stumbled over the strange words.

"You're a stubborn lass. I do think you want tae be begged."

"Begged to do what?"

"Tae work alongside me. Tae teach me what you know."

"Me teach *you*?"

"Aye. And I teach you as well."

"Teach what?"

In mild exasperation he waved the paddle, blue eyes flashing. "I'm no' askin' you tae marry me, Lael Click, but I do need
your help."

She managed a half smile, suddenly understanding. A strange
warmth filled her with the knowledge that he needed her. He,
who seemed to need nothing at all. Yet here he was in need of
her knowledge of pokeweed and sassafras and shepherd's purse

256

and dozens of other things. The harsh words they'd last spoken at Ma Horn's seemed like they never were. He was quick to forget, she thought with a twinge of conscience, and, unlike herself, forgive. She said innocently, "Why don't you ask Ma Horn?"

He began paddling again, suddenly sober. "Because she canna always remember."

They fell silent for a time, the only sound the splash of the water. Without meaning to, she sighed.

"Is my offer so painful tae you, then?" he asked.

She shook her head.

"Yet you hold back. Why?"

She gave a small shrug and said impishly, "I dinna ken why."

He smiled and began rowing her back to shore. Her spirits sagged at the thought of returning to her empty cabin, and she stood on the bank watching him slip away from her. But Tuck was there to meet her, nuzzling her hand, reminding her it was time for supper.

September 23, 1783. Lael dipped her quill in ink and wrote slowly and deliberately in her journal. *A man has won my heart and now he has gone away again.* Unable to continue, she set the quill down, eyes on Neddy's open Bible next to her.

Since the barn burning, she had begun to study the Scriptures. When she was sad or lonesome or perplexed, she felt drawn to its worn pages, often reading till one tallow candle had to be replaced with another. Before bed each evening she would drop to her knees and try to pray. For Captain Jack and herself. For Lovey and her guests. For her mother and Ransom. Even Ian Justus. Often she would cry herself to sleep.

Once the Click cabin had been full of secrets; now it seemed full of ghosts. Outside, the nip and tang of autumn filled the air.

Soon, she thought, just as he had promised.

Soon, but not soon enough.

45

Susanna Bliss filled the leach barrel with several buckets of wood ashes and water, while Lael tended a large kettle of lard over an open fire. From the barn Will rolled out a fresh wood barrel that would, at day's end, be filled with the soft soap the two women were making. It was a monotonous chore made lighter by shared talk and laughter. There was no hurry to be home before the evening shadows as Lael had agreed to spend the night at Cozy Creek.

As the children and dogs played outside around them, filling the air with happy chatter, Lael felt glad she'd come. Soap-making was a handy excuse to spend time with Susanna and bury the matters hanging heavily on her heart. She wiped her hands on her apron and went in search of small sticks and dry leaves for the fire. The children followed after her, intent on finding the prettiest autumn leaf to show their mother. The maples and oaks were ablaze now, full of showy splendor.

Could it truly be nigh on October? She had left Virginia in April to come home again. Just six months had passed, and yet it seemed she'd lived a lifetime within their days. She tossed an armful of sticks onto the fire as Susanna called for more water. The boys ran to do her bidding, taking little Lael with them.

"I have a hankerin' for some of them fancy hard cakes of soap from back east." Susanna looked askance at the lye seeping out of the leach tub.

"Bayberry soap," Lael said wistfully, recalling the pleasant-smelling fragrance. "I picked a bushel of bayberries at Briar Hill. They grow right along the sea and are the queerest silver gray."

Susanna studied her a moment. "Do you miss it, Lael? Virginia, I mean?"

"It was tolerable enough, but I never liked it. Sometimes though I miss the sight of the sea on a summer's day. But there's a heap of things I don't miss."

Susanna took the bucket of water from the children and poured it into the ash tub. "I was a-feared you'd go back."

"To Virginia? Not hardly. Right here is where I'll always be." But even as she said it, she felt a twinge of conscience. If Captain Jack were to ask, would she not go with him?

They worked till dusk, finally filling the barrel to the top with the jelly-like soap. To Lael's delight, Will brought in an oak tub and set it in front of the hearth after supper so she and Susanna could take a true soaking. Gleeful, the boys took turns pouring buckets of heated water into it and then disappeared with Will to wait their turn while Lael and Susanna and little Lael bathed first.

"Why, I ain't been wet all over at once these twenty-five years past," Susanna exclaimed in delight, rubbing some of the soft soap into her hair. "But I guess that's a sight better than old Granny Henderson who last had a bath on her weddin' day."

After the six of them had bathed and dried off by the fire, Will took the children to bed, leaving Lael and Susanna alone. As Susanna poured sweet cider into pewter cups, Lael popped corn in the contraption she had purchased at the fort mercantile.

"Why, it's the strangest stuff I ever et," Susanna exclaimed, seemingly torn between swallowing and spitting it out. She examined the puffed kernels with a wondering eye as Lael sprinkled it with salt.

"Popped corn is all the buzzel in the east," Lael said. "If you don't like it, save it for your least 'uns to try."

Susanna sampled another piece and looked up at the herbs hanging in festive bunches from the rafters. "I'm awful thankful for the herbs you brung me. I can't abide meat hangin' and spittin' at you as you pass underneath."

"Sweet fern and sassafras always sweeten things a bit. My own place is full of it."

Sitting back, Susanna folded her hands across her lap in a rare moment of idleness. "I'm so glad you come, Lael. Seems like I hardly ever see you. I've been wonderin' if you don't get awful lonesome, livin' like you do. I think I'd go plumb crazy without the sound of children scrappin' and Will snorin'."

Lael took a sip of cider. "I'm not home much lately. And when I am the silence isn't lonesome. It's . . . lovely." She felt an odd pleasure in the revelation. "If I feel the need for company, I head to the fort."

"So I hear."

Their eyes met and held. Something—what could it be?—was suddenly grave in Susanna's face, and the shadow there alarmed Lael.

Susanna's voice dropped to a whisper. "Are you . . . sweet . . . on Doc Justus, Lael?"

Lael set down her cider. "Why, Susanna Bliss! You don't have a spoonful of sense thinking such things as that."

Susanna gave the rocker an agitated push. "I was hopin', after Simon, there'd be somebody else to settle on. But the doctor won't do at all. Will says he's spoken for."

Spoken for? For a few moments Lael just sat.

Susanna went on quietly. "Her name is Olivia. Ain't that pretty? She's from Boston. A doctor's daughter. He's known her for a long while."

Olivia. From up east. Was this the daughter of the older, established physician he'd worked with after the war? Though not surprised, she felt a queer pang hearing it. "I misdoubt he'd settle for the likes of us settlement folk. We're all rough as cobs."

"Not you!" Susanna exclaimed, a trifle loud. With a quick glance at the loft she whispered, "You're educated and the like. Why, you're a lady yourself."

Olivia. The name conjured images of satin skirts, violet-scented handkerchiefs, and snow-white hands. *Aye,* she thought brutally, *such a man deserves an Olivia—or some highborn genteel sort.* The sight of her own bare feet, still stained with dirt after her bath, made her tuck them out of sight under her worn nightgown. No doubt Miss Olivia had never known a barefoot day in her life.

Susanna poked at the fire with a tong. "Of course, the doctor don't say much about her, only what Will asks him. Just bits and pieces. He's invited her here for a visit. That's about all I know."

Olivia? At Fort Click? The idea seemed impossible, like snow in summer. The last lady at the fort had been Miss Mayella. She'd stayed on less than two years, but in that short span had brought refinement to roughness and knowledge to ignorance. Perhaps that is what Ian Justus hoped to accomplish with Olivia as well.

"Ladies never stay long in Kentucke," Lael said. "They just pass through, like Miss Mayella."

Susanna's face brightened. "I recollect Miss Mayella's fine lace caps . . . and her small gloved hands. Remember when we took her to that flowery meadow Simon always called Possum Kingdom? It was your birthday and Simon give you that little carved bird—"

"Don't, Susanna." Lael looked into the fire, her face hard. Truly, it seemed a better time, a happier time, with their lives yet uncharted before them, unstained with the angst of regret and longing. "I don't want to remember. I prefer to forget."

"Forgivin' comes before forgettin', Lael."

"Meaning?"

"You need to let go. Forgive Simon for what he's done. Lord knows he's paid the price for his foolishness with Piper. Don't make his foolishness your own." She took a deep breath and forged ahead, heedless. "Maybe it weren't meant to be noways, you and Simon. There's somethin' different about you, Lael—somethin' fine and free that don't set well with Simon's ways." Susanna smoothed her nightgown with knotty hands. "Someday there'll be someone else for you. I've been prayin' about that too."

Lael looked away, wishing she could share her heart, feeling nearly torn in two by the secrets she withheld. Was Captain Jack the answer to her prayers? What would Susanna say if Lael told her about their time together in the meadow and then the river? What would Susanna think if she knew how much Lael longed for their next meeting? There was a time for everything, Scripture said. She reckoned this was one time to stay silent.

46

The tallow candle flickered as Lael lay down the quill. Her second letter to Ransom lay unfinished before her. What, she wondered, might have happened to the first? She'd written to him of Neddy's death but had yet to receive a reply. Guilt nudged her, making her consider the lengthy distance from here to Bardstown. Perhaps she should have delivered the news in person, but her resentment still simmered over Ma's remarrying in such haste. And she was so busy here she'd gotten by thus far simply by sending letters. She'd written so much of late, to her mother, her brother, and Miss Mayella. A small callus had even formed on the third finger of her writing hand. But that was not the reason she paused.

She lay cool hands against her closed eyes. The burning lessened briefly, but when she took up her quill again the words on the page danced and dipped like insects running for cover, and nothing she did would bring them into focus.

"I'm plumb give out, is all," she said aloud, lapsing into settlement vernacular.

Hadn't there been two broken bones and a drowning this week, as well as a second trip to the branch to deliver meal and a tonic to Lovey and Mourning, just as her mare and mule were acting queer and refusing to eat or be ridden? She'd had to hoof it herself until the soles of her moccasins were thin as paper.

And yet the sweet sleep she sought would not come. Instead, there were dreams—vivid dreams of river water and Captain

Jack calling her Yellow Bird, only she could not answer. Was he all right? Did he think of her?

She sighed as she looked at the unfinished letter. She had gotten into a bad habit of sighing of late, and it annoyed her no end. Aye, she was simply worn out and needed a rest. With a second sigh she snuffed out the candle with her fingers. The darkness was profound, almost unfriendly. If she'd ever been inclined to believe in haints, now was the time.

She crawled between cold bedding, shivering despite her nightclothes and heavy woolen stockings, and let her hair down so that it covered her like an extra blanket. When she awoke she found herself in a room filled with light and silence. Beyond the shutters, snow was falling steadily, outlining the roses like frozen lace and lying in gentle swells along the porch. It was deep and sharp and cold.

It was not yet mid-October.

Shivering, she broke the skim of ice on the bucket of water and came suddenly awake. Never had she been so glad to see a live coal in the ashes of the hearth waiting to be kindled. Soon the curl of smoke and snap of dry wood was like a familiar song as she heated water and mixed meal and water for bread. She set out beans to soak for supper and wished that the bear bacon she needed was hanging from the cabin rafters and not in the springhouse.

Outside, the mule was braying and Tuck lay shivering beneath the porch. She went about her chores beneath the weight of a buffalo robe. The snow pelted her face and bare hands so fiercely she was nigh frozen, and her coat sagged with the weight of wetness. Surely the early snow would make him come sooner. She was confident he knew the signs pointed to a hard winter.

Colonel Philo Barr had issued an order that all area settlers report to the fort. Asa Forbes brought the confounding news, lingering a bit too long as if in hopes he could bring her in like before. Reluctantly, Lael prepared the mule for travel and then herself, donning two dresses, the buffalo robe, and a bonnet instead of her favored straw hat. The silver bracelet was hidden beneath her sleeve, while the blue beads stayed in her pocket. She packed Tuck in her biggest basket and a few of her beloved books in a saddlebag, all the while fighting the feeling that she was running away from home.

As she rode she spotted fresh buffalo tracks, now nearly covered by the fast falling snow. The brilliance and beauty of the day was nearly blinding. All the familiar landmarks along the way now appeared strange to her, wrapped as they were in a coat of white. The twin oaks atop Hackberry Ridge, so fiercely twined, huddled together as if for warmth, and the creek she traversed sang a muted song beneath its icy skin.

She had no strong liking for Colonel Barr and his two dogs, Judas and Jezebel. Biting and acrimonious in speech and manner, he put her on her guard. Nevertheless, he was an educated man who, it was rumored, had once studied to be a doctor. But the loss of a wife and a son in the Indian wars made him abandon his studies and turned him bitter.

"Enter!" he barked at the rap on his cabin door. At Lael's appearance, Judas and Jezebel elicited fierce growls from beneath a massive desk situated in the center of the room.

She entered, unperturbed, removing her bonnet and shaking snow on the smooth dirt floor. The growling didn't cease nor did the colonel make an effort to silence the odious creatures. Lael had a strong desire to hiss back and silence them herself but instead came straight to the point, her voice quiet but respectful. "How long must I stay at the fort?"

"Long enough for me to conduct a census."

"It seems a bit odd to call for such in the middle of a storm. Your numbers may be a mite skewed."

He licked dry lips and shifted his eyes to his watch. "Orders are orders, Miss Click. Mine come from Virginia where they don't give a whit about settlement weather. The edict was issued long ago. Besides, who could predict snow in October?"

"Any settler worth his salt could have foretold it," she answered, so nettled by being here she was downright cantankerous. "All right, mark me down and I'll go back to my cabin."

He laughed, but there was no mirth in it. "How like your father you sound. A pity you weren't born a man, Miss Click."

"If I had been, sir," she retorted, struggling to hide her dislike of him, "that might well be my desk you occupy so grandly."

He laughed again and, oddly, the dogs commenced growling once more. She snuck a peek at them, lank black beasts with sunken yellow eyes and deep red jowls. Good thing she'd left Tuck outside.

Barr got up and went to a small table where he poured himself some cider and offered her a cup, which she declined. "Why are you so anxious to leave the fort, Miss Click?" At her silence, he grew pensive. "Are you still fraternizing with Indians?"

She looked down, if only to escape his stare. The bonnet she held in her cold, stiff hands was dripping onto the toes of her boots. Did her face betray her fears? Did he know anything about Captain Jack that might put him in danger?

"Miss Click, I am keeping you here till I conduct my census," he told her, finishing the cider. Seeing she was about to protest, he added quickly, "If you attempt to defy my orders I shall confine you to the blockhouse, just as I would any other offender."

She let herself out. Walking across the common, she glanced at the gates where settlers were slowly trickling in. The snow was spitting rather than pouring now and would likely melt in the face of an Indian summer sun.

As she entered Ma Horn's cabin, leaving Tuck outside to wrestle with the fort dogs, the smell of fried apples, jowl, and biscuits welcomed her with open arms. Ma Horn straightened but expressed no surprise at the sight of her.

"Set a third place," she said. "Doc Justus nearly always takes the noon meal with me."

They were a strange trio, Lael, the doctor, and the wizened, shrunken woman older than Kentucke itself. Lael wondered how long they would be thrown together before the census was complete.

Distracted, she pushed her supper around her plate, sipped her cider, and simply listened. Listened to the rich lilt of the doctor's voice with its rolling r's and sonorous inflections. Smiled as if lighthearted at the sound of Ma Horn's girlish laugh. Absently digested the scraps of settlement news that peppered their conversation. But she said not one word.

Eventually the doctor pushed back his chair and stood. "'Tis always a pleasure tae see, if no' talk tae you, Miss Click."

Miss Click. Once he had called her Lael.

But here, now, in his simple greeting and good-bye, a certain formality had returned, or so it seemed. How must he speak to Olivia, the one he loved?

She made herself smile at him and acknowledge his greeting. He was putting on his coat, the finest she'd ever seen. Wool, she guessed. A deep, dusky blue, a shade darker than his eyes. Beside it, her buffalo robe looked barbaric. Outside the snow continued to swirl, creating a cocoon of the fort.

"Reminds me of the snow in Scotlain," he said, looking out the shutter. "It comes early and is deep . . . knee high tae a horse's back some winters."

"You talk of the Scottish mountains then," said Ma Horn. "Is that where your people hail from?"

"Aye. From the Grampian Highlands. Castle Roslyn. On the North Sea."

There was a touch of wistfulness in his voice, and Lael's own heart thawed a bit. She knew all about missing hearth and home and all things familiar; the ache was palpable as any illness. She wondered if he pined for Olivia as she pined for Captain Jack.

"Good day tae you, ladies," he said and was gone, lost in a blinding squall of snow that obliterated the common and the cabins beyond.

47

Two days passed and the colonel was still tallying his census. The fort was near bursting. A family heading to the Green River in western Kentucke had been forced into the confines of the fort along with a handful of surveyors and trappers. No sooner had the family occupied an empty cabin than the news came that one of the children had a fever.

Lael was standing by the window, peering through a crack in the shutter, when help was sent for. She watched as Colonel Barr headed across the common in her direction. He moved slowly, the snow reaching to the middle of his boots, fine as flour and twice as white. But the colonel did not come for her or Ma Horn. He passed instead to the old Hayes blockhouse that now housed Ian Justus. Lael's anticipation melted into surprised irritation.

Within moments the doctor was crossing the common with the colonel, carrying a black leather satchel. The tools of his trade, she reckoned. How she longed to be a fly on the wall and watch him at work! The desire gnawed a deep curious place inside her and kept her rooted to the shutter despite an icy draft that chilled her to the bone.

That noon he did not come to dinner. His place sat oddly empty, and Lael was surprised at the missing force of his presence. She and Ma Horn chatted easily enough, but the meal seemed incomplete, like bread without sweetening or meat without salt.

The day stretched taut, then at dusk there came a knock on

the door. Lael moved to open it and came face to face with Ian Justus.

"You come to get your supper, I reckon," Ma Horn called from the hearth where she began dishing up a bowl full of beans and corncakes. Lael poured a mug of cider and set out a salt gourd along with a leftover dab of fried apples and wondered, with a slight smile, how he was adjusting to frontier fare.

As he ate there ensued a silence so profound Lael could hear the snow spitting against the shutter. Ma Horn took up some raw cotton and began picking out the burrs and dirt, while Lael sat with a book in her lap and pretended to read. She scarcely knew which one she had selected—*The Poor Planter's Physician* or *The Complete Herbal*. Her eyes were playing tricks on her again, the words dancing this way and that in the shadowy gloom.

She was far too aware of Ian Justus. Out of the corner of her eye she saw him put down his fork and rake a hand through the dark hair at the nape of his neck, hair that curled and moped along his collar and had come free of its usual leather tie. It was a gesture she had observed half a dozen times now, indicating, she guessed, that he was distracted—or wished to be. He had hardly touched his meal.

With a slight twinge of alarm, she asked before she thought, "Are you unwell?"

He looked up at her, his eyes tired but still a merry blue. "Nae, Dr. Click."

She blushed then in a way she'd not blushed since girlhood, and Ma Horn let out a chuckle.

"I'm fit as a fiddle," he said.

"Speakin' of fiddles," Ma Horn said, at work on her cotton, "I've a hankerin' for some of that music you've been promisin'.'"

"I suggest you send for old Amos then," he told her, finishing his cider.

"It ain't old Amos I'm after. I been listenin' to him ever since we come over the Gap together in '70. It's new music I need."

270

The doctor nodded slightly and moved to the door where he shrugged into the wool coat, eyes on Lael. Nearly indigo, she decided, like the sea on a stormy day.

"Are you fond of fiddle music, Miss Click?"

She shut her book. "I like old Amos's just fine."

Ma Horn snorted. "If you ain't careful, she'll be dancin' with the fire tongs. As for me, I ain't set for a full frolic but would cotton to a little music."

He left then, and after a time, when the damp logs sizzled in the hearth and the coals gleamed a brilliant crimson and gold, he reappeared. Sitting at one end of the trestle table, he took the promised instrument from its case. For once Lael had good reason to study him, hands idle in her lap while Ma Horn continued to pick at her cotton and rock.

So he can fiddle. Why, he is full of surprises.

Within moments the quiet cabin was turned on its ear with his rendering of Sir Roger de Coverley. Lael listened, both mortified and transfixed, as a tickled smile pulled at Ma Horn's face. The doctor's squeaks grew more pronounced—and painful— till they could stand it no longer. Ma Horn covered her ears as Lael wrapped her arms around her middle and choked down her laughter.

Finally, all at once, the bow slid violently off the strings and there was only the sound of women's laughter—Ma Horn's high as a girl's, and Lael's own, as clear and pure and bubbling as the branch.

"So what do you make of it?" he demanded from the shadows.

Ma Horn gasped, "I think—you—should stick—with doctorin'!"

Lael looked on, mouth wry. Something told her that this was a man who would not do anything he could not do well, fiddling or otherwise. "I think," she followed quietly, "that you are just having a wee bit of fun."

He laughed and moved closer to them, into the firelight, and the gleam on the burnished maple instrument nearly made her gasp. Here was something fine and rare, held in a surgeon's hands like a woman would cradle a newborn child.

Without a word he began playing again, and this time the notes were clear and sweet as birdsong. Lael sat spellbound, cast back in time to Briar Hill, where she once sat in the still, warm conservatory amid a fluttering of painted fans in the heat of summer. And his music blended perfectly with the notes she remembered.

When he had finished, she said quietly, "Haydn."

"Hy-who?" Ma Horn asked.

"Haydn," Lael whispered, as if it was a secret she and the doctor shared.

He began again, playing a melody so sweet she wanted to weep. Never in all her life had she heard such music.

"What was that?"

"A slow air," he said simply. "'Tis Scottish." He played one more, this tune more lively, like a reel. "A strathspey," he told her, but before he'd finished Ma Horn had nodded off in her chair.

"You play very well."

"Tolerably well. I learned during the war, tae take my mind off battle."

She remembered he had been a field surgeon in the war. How old could he be? Older than she, truly, but it was nigh impossible to tell. Ian Justus possessed high-handed good looks untouched by time. Only his eyes seemed aged, with fine lines etched about them from too much sun. Or sorrow.

He put the violin away in its case, and Lael felt a keen disappointment. She had sensed a restlessness in him ever since he'd come to take the evening meal. His thoughts, she gathered, were not on his music or anything else in the cramped cabin.

He said very quietly, "Across the way there lies a wee lass, no' yet five years old, suffering from a fever. Her name is Sadie Floyd. I want you tae go with me tae see her."

272

48

They walked across the fort common, shoulder to shoulder in the bite of a bitter wind. The snow was deep, but paths had been worn to the various cabins, though none was so trammeled as the approach to Sadie Floyd's.

Inside, a candlelight vigil had begun as the girl's parents took turns sitting by the bed. Three boys played quietly by the hearth and all looked up with wide, solemn eyes as they entered. The smell of boiled potatoes and turnips lingered, and despite their odor Lael recognized something else—the smell of death.

Introductions were quietly made by the doctor. Lael looked into the faces of John and Isabel Floyd, and she wondered if they knew what was to become of their daughter, if they too felt what she felt. The presence of death was so palpable it seemed to stand with them in the shadows, a hideous, hidden figure emanating a fearful smell. Once it had come she had never known it to leave without finishing its ugly work.

She started as the doctor removed the buffalo robe from her shoulders and hung it from a peg alongside his own. Feeling empty-handed without her herb bundle, she followed him to a corner bed. The tired rope springs that supported the thin mattress sagged nearly to the floor, they were so worn, and the girl he had spoken of seemed lost in the middle of the bed. Sadie Floyd was a tiny thing with an otherworldly flush staining her features and dampening her dark, unkempt hair.

"She ain't no better," her mother said wearily. "And no worse."

Lael reached out and touched the girl's small hand. It was cool and still, belying the fever that ravaged the rest of her.

"She was real fitful till the doctor give her that powder," said Isabel. "That seemed to ease her a mite."

"Calomel powder," Ian Justus explained to Lael, taking a tin cup from his bag and asking for water. Carefully, he lowered the thin blanket and drew the child's shift up, revealing a swollen, bloated stomach. Lael struggled to remain stoic at the shocking sight.

"The infection is spreading," the doctor said, speaking so quietly she had to bend to hear him. "At first the swelling was confined tae the bowel . . . now it has reached the upper abdomen. 'Tis likely the organs are slowly shutting down and the blood is being poisoned as weel."

"Can you not operate?" Lael asked.

"Nae, surgery would be deadly on a child so small."

"Perhaps a poultice then to draw out the poison. There's snakeroot and boneset—"

"I done both." Isabel came behind them with some water. "We even packed her in snow," she told them, eyes wet.

"You must rest," Lael told her, touching her arm. "If the doctor allows, I'll set up with Sadie tonight and spell you—"

"It ain't me that's set up with Sadie but the doctor here."

"Then I'll stay with her tonight."

But Ian Justus was not listening. He studied the tin of powders in his hand as if looking for answers. The gleam of candlelight cast a dull glow on the open bag at his feet, reflecting off an assortment of surgical tools. "There's nothing more tae be done for Sadie," he said. "Nothing outside of prayer."

There was resignation in his voice—and raw sorrow. All at once long shadows were cast over the girl on the bed as the other children came forward and gathered around them. Save their combined breaths, there was no other sound in the room.

Ian Justus turned and looked at them squarely. "Scripture says the prayer of faith will save the sick and the Lord will raise them up. If Jesus Christ is Lord over both body and spirit—and I believe He is—then prayer is all that can save your daughter."

Lael simply stared at him. How could he preach to them at such a time?

The ensuing silence was excruciating, but Isabel Floyd finally spoke out. "I believe, Doctor. My husband here, he ain't a believer, but I am."

Bewildered, Lael looked from the gaunt woman to the doctor. It was John Floyd who spoke next, a trifle shame-faced, eyes on the dirt floor. "I ain't one to stand in the way of a prayin' man, Doctor, not when it comes to my Sadie."

My Sadie.

All eyes were fastened on the tiny girl, their faces blank as slates. The doctor ran an agitated hand through his hair and took a chair by the bed. From behind him, Lael could see the cords in his neck tense taut as rope. He seemed to be struggling for words . . . for sound.

She hardly heard his prayer. Her mind was still fixed on Isabel Floyd's strong, convicting words. *I believe, Doctor.*

The prayer soon ended, and Lael mumbled an amen. Sadie Floyd lay on the bed, visibly unchanged, still lost in the shadows of suffering.

But the shadow of death had left the room.

49

Sadie continued to improve in the days to come, impressing Lael with her progress. Though she disliked the fort's confines, the evenings were blessedly full. Twice Susanna and Will came over from their cabin, two doors down, and brought the children. They roasted chestnuts with Lael and Ma Horn, then cracked them and washed them down with sweet cider.

Often the doctor would bring his violin or a book or newspaper to help pass the time. They talked of many things—of the war's end and newfound independence; the sea and Scotland and the purple heather on the moors; the price of cotton and the changing currency; and medicines, wild and patented, debating the merits of each.

But Ma Horn was not fit company these days. Soon after supper, she was fast asleep in her chair, head lolling above her bosom. Yet she was there in body, and though the fort's wags might gossip, there would be no salaciousness with Ma Horn present.

And so it was just Lael and Ian Justus truly, evening after evening, a trestle table apart, talking quietly or not talking at all. The flicker of the fire, the candle flame a-dance in the icy draft, the sight of his dark head bent over a book, or his hands, square and clean and callused, making music on his violin, worked to keep her there. She both willed and hated for their strange intimacy to end. He was becoming a friend to her, and she sorely

276

needed one. Not once did he raise the subject of the McClarys or Captain Jack.

By week's end, Sadie Floyd was playing on the snowy common with Tuck and throwing snowballs with her brothers. There was a sense of the miraculous in those first days of November. Lael liked to stand at the shutter and watch her at play and recall how she'd escaped the shadow of death.

Slowly the snow began to melt. Lael had been at the fort nearly a week when on a whim she crossed the common and rapped sharply on Colonel Barr's cabin door. He scarcely looked up from penning a letter, his quill pushing furiously across the paper before him. The room reeked of stale tobacco and damp dogs. She could feel the error of her timing. The captain was in a foul mood, and she was immediately sorry she'd come.

She got straight to the point. "I am in danger of wearing out my welcome here."

Philo Barr paused, gray eyes flashing in irritation. "The census is nearly done. Tomorrow, Miss Click, you may leave at sunrise."

She nodded solemnly and let herself out. But on the doorstep, in the harsh early light, she smiled.

"I saw you leave Colonel Barr's cabin," said the doctor. "I dinna think tae keep you here this long."

Lael smiled and ladled stew into a wooden bowl. "Colonel Barr is nearly done with his counting and has finally agreed to open the gates."

Her voice was so light, so airy, both he and Ma Horn looked at her. Truly, the cares of the world seemed far away when she would be free of the fort at first light.

Tonight, their last together, she looked about with new appreciation. The light in the cabin was fetchingly dim and the hearth smells beckoning. At home, her lonely supper was little more than a chore. Here it had come to be a small celebration. Was this why he came? Ma Horn said they often shared the noon meal together but hadn't mentioned the evening meal as well. Yet here he was, day after day, at both.

Earlier that morning she'd ventured to the river and picked a handful of cattails and a bouquet of bittersweet, untouched by the snow. Ma Horn had cackled as she arranged them and set them in a cracked pitcher on the table, admiring their winter beauty.

Ian Justus noticed as well, saying nothing but picking out a cattail and examining it with a surgeon's eye. And now as they took their places, she and Ma Horn side by side and the doctor across from them at the table, they readied to say grace.

But she couldn't close her eyes. Her eyes lingered on him instead, touched by his bowed head and humble tone. Truly, his prayers were the most heartfelt she'd ever heard. He prayed as if God were there at their very table. Her own prayers were rote, like reciting one's sums or letters; his varied with the day's needs though the ending was always the same: "May the words of my mouth and the meditation of my heart be acceptable in Thy sight, O Lord, my Rock and my Redeemer."

Before Lael had washed and put away the supper dishes a final time, Ma Horn was asleep in her chair, her discarded pipe still smoking on the hearth. Lael drew in a deep breath, remembering that Pa once said it was nearly identical to the Shawnee's *kinnikkinnik*—shredded dried leaves of tobacco, sumac, willow, and dogwood. She'd sometimes wondered if Captain Jack liked a pipe.

She dried her hands on her apron and glanced the doctor's way. He was at work with quill and paper—perhaps a letter to

Olivia? He looked a bit weary, she thought, and lost in thought. But the moment she sat down in the rocker nearest the fire, he pushed his papers aside.

"Why are you so anxious tae leave here, Lael?"

Lael. Miss Click. The way he alternated between the two was plumb unnerving. She didn't know who she was from one minute to the next. Surprised by his question, she met his eyes and answered as carefully and truthfully as she dared. "I miss the wide open spaces outside these walls. And my own cozy cabin."

"I've never seen you so heartsome as you are tonight," he said thoughtfully. "You are downright douce."

Heartsome? Douce? "I dinna ken Scottish," she reminded him with a smile.

He rolled his eyes. "Merry. Happy. Tonight you are both."

She looked down at her apron. "And that nettles you?"

He nearly grinned. "Nae, but you are usually so quiet . . . so reserved."

Unnerved by his scrutiny, she got up and stepped onto a bench to fetch a sack of chestnuts. She must do something—anything—to occupy her hands and still her hammering heart. Sometimes his candor almost cut her. The silence in the room deepened. She began to shell the nuts, aware that he was still studying her from where he sat. Did he think she didn't notice? If Ma Horn were awake, he wouldn't stare so. If Miss Olivia were here . . .

"You're in love with him, aren't you?"

The bold question left her breathless. Slowly she looked up at him. His eyes, such a startling, intense blue even by candlelight, held hers and dared her to deny it. Before she could steel herself, her own eyes flooded with tears.

"So that is your answer, then," he said quietly.

She couldn't speak. She didn't need to.

He looked away. "Why do I get the feeling you're aboot tae do something rash?"

She wiped her eyes with the back of her hand. He knew too much. He'd seen her walk hand in hand with Captain Jack across the meadow. By now he'd surely heard about their meeting during the siege, outside these very walls. And he suspected Captain Jack of killing the McClarys. Did he guess she was willing to run away with him as well?

Her voice was nearly a whisper. "Am I such an open book?"

He ran a hand through the hair at the nape of his neck as if agitated. "It stands tae reason that, feeling as you do, you may marry."

"We've never spoken of it."

Still, he did not look at her. "Does he no' love you in return?"

Her hands rifled through the chestnut hulls in her lap. Not once had they spoken of love. Perhaps voicing such things wasn't the Shawnee way. "I think he does," she finally said.

His expression was incredulous. "You dinna ken if he loves you or no'?"

She lifted her shoulders in a slight shrug.

"You play a dangerous game, Lael Click."

"So?" she retorted.

"*So?* If this goes forward and you wed this mon, you wed his whole way of life."

"I would welcome it. Perhaps our union would help smooth relations between the Shawnee and the settlers."

His eyes flashed. "You canna be naive enough tae think your marriage tae a minor chief will bring aboot peace."

"It has been done," she told him. "Chief Powhatan's daughter married an Englishman in Virginia, and relations between the colonists and Indians improved—"

"Their marriage lasted but three years until her death, and then the fighting began all over again." Intensity lit his every feature. "I'm no' talking aboot John Rolfe's antics but your own. Do you no' ken what you do? The Shawnee practice polygamy like many other tribes. Will you share your husband? Are you willing tae worship their gods? Your children will be half-breeds—"

She glanced at Ma Horn. Would they wake her? Her whisper fell flat and held a warning. "Captain Jack's as white as you are. He was taken captive as a boy in North Carolina. But even if he was pure Shawnee, that wouldn't matter to me."

His answering glance told her he believed none of it. Truly, he was as riled as she'd ever seen him.

"Why do you care what becomes of me?" she asked in bewilderment. "What does it matter to you?"

He looked like he wanted to shake her. "Your faither is gone. Your uncle is dead. There is nae one tae speak reason tae you, tae save you from yourself."

Anger stiffened her spine. "You forget my father lived with the Shawnee and was well versed in their ways. He cared for Captain Jack like a son. I doubt he'd take offense if I were to run off with him."

"I canna argue with a dead mon. But if he were here, your faither would surely tell you the invasion of Shawnee territory has begun. There will be nae peace between them and the whites— no' now, no' ever. A hundred years of history has proven it. If you marry this mon, you will be caught in the growing conflict and likely killed, or removed far from here. If you dinna care aboot yourself, at least think of your children."

She stood up and tossed the chestnut hulls into the fire, shaking out her apron as if to shoo him away as well. "A pretty speech, truly, but a bit belated. I misdoubt the Almighty sent you all the way from Scotland to straighten out my future affairs. You'd best stick with your fancy doctorin.'"

She nearly wilted from the answering heat of his gaze. Without another word, he got up and walked out, slamming the door behind him.

She went up the loft ladder, leaving Ma Horn asleep in her chair. The once gay quilt spread upon the corn-husk tick had faded to a dull blood red over the years and now looked uninviting. She didn't bother to undress or turn the covers down but simply lay upon the bed and stared up at the rafters just inches from her face. The cold seeped in and settled over her, but she no longer cared. She doubted she would sleep at all. The doctor's words were bitter, and she tasted them again and again as she recounted each one.

He'd raised more questions than she had answers. The thought of sharing a husband made her shudder. She'd heard polygamy was no longer practiced except by the oldest members of the tribe and was now dying out. Why had she not thought to argue that very thing? As for religion, wasn't the Shawnee god the same as the white man's?

She pressed cold fingers to her aching head. She couldn't deny the growing conflict between the settlers and the Indians. Captain Jack had told her of the danger. Strange how, when she was with him, all the things she meant to ask him flew right out of her head like a flock of frightened birds. Would her questions ever find answers?

Promise me, she'd almost begged the last time she'd seen him. *Don't stay away too long. Sometimes it seems you're not real . . . that I only dream of you.*

50

Did all Shawnee men attend their children's births? Or could he, because he was a chief with a white wife, buck whatever custom he chose? All day she had labored with only an Indian midwife present and then, as if he could stand it no longer, Captain Jack entered the wigwam at dusk. His eyes took in everything at once before he came and sat behind her, acting as a headboard upon which she leaned, his fingers entwined with her own. She wore her usual buckskin dress, but a length of trade calico modestly covered her to the waist, and beneath her was a huge buffalo hide. Oddly enough, the Shawnee woman attending her reminded her of Ma Horn.

It was already the blackberry moon—July—but she'd stopped keeping track of time months ago. Outside their shelter, a concerto of fiddling crickets and the latent perfume of honeysuckle ushered in the summer twilight. Despite her pain, she could hear the rushing of the cold Scioto River, a sharp contrast to the oppressive heat that had hardly dimmed at day's end.

Sweat beaded her upper lip and turned her loose hair riotous about her flushed face. Determined not to shame him or herself by crying out, she bit her lips till they were bruised and bleeding. What had begun hours ago at dawn as a mild twinge had become a torrent of terrible pain rivaling the Falls of the Ohio itself. Once she forgot herself and nearly screamed. How could such pain both sap her yet give her unusual strength? Her fingers dug into her husband's hands, but he was like a wall, unflinching and unmoving as he held her.

His face showed little expression, but the English endearments he whispered in her ear told her he was nearly as anguished as she. As she labored, he wiped her face with a cold cloth as she leaned against him. Was there no end to this? Was this the way of it for all women?

At the end, when she felt she was being torn in two, she sobbed in Shawnee, "Dear God . . . help me . . . save me . . . spare my baby . . . let me live . . ." The baby's head was crowning, capped with such a wealth of blue-black hair the Indian midwife chuckled with glee. Looking up, she assured them only a son could have such hair.

Lael tried hard to smile, to show her relief. She did not want their son to have her cornsilk hair, to stand out like she did among the people . . .

Lael came awake at once. Her heart seemed to swell her throat shut with its rapid rhythm, and she opened her mouth to breathe.

The dream was slow in leaving, but her muddled feelings remained. Love for her husband, tenderness toward their child, yet both framed with fear. In the dream she was one of several wives, and each had many children. She was looked down upon because, as the favorite of her husband, she was not made to work like the other women. She was Ezekial Click's daughter—a kind of coup, a prize. And she was white. That Captain Jack was white had long been forgotten.

She sat up, bumped her head on the rough ceiling, then fell back onto the quilt instead of Captain Jack's waiting arms. What had the doctor done to her? Sleeping on harsh words begat bad dreams, truly. Peeking through a loophole told her it was indeed daylight. She tiptoed past Ma Horn, still asleep in her chair. Outside on the common, she whistled for Tuck and went in search of the mule. She did not want to see Ian Justus.

When she left the fort, she made her way straight up the branch where the snow lay untouched. As she rode she exhaled an icy breath and shook off the effects of the lingering dream.

Lovey Runion and her two guests were snug as snug could be, and it seemed to Lael that they had always been that way, their lives entwined like knotted thread, and her bruised feeling from the night before mended a bit. With Hero McClary dead, Mourning and Titus were safe and could stay with Lovey until Lael figured out a way to send them back to North Carolina, if they still wanted to go. So much for Colonel Barr's census. She doubted he even knew of these three tucked away in the bosom of the branch.

With the feud ended, she too was free to return home. When she came around the charred ruins of the barn, she gave a little gasp. To the left of the cabin, under a crumbling eave, was a small mountain of firewood, deftly chopped and neatly stacked.

Just like Pa would have done.

51

Since her return from the fort she lay awake nights, unsettled by her dreams. Thoughts of her harsh words to the doctor were interspersed with images of a laughing, living Sadie Floyd, brought back from the brink of the grave.

Try as she might, she couldn't get the Scot's mealtime prayers out of her mind. She'd heard them so often the week of the census she had unwittingly memorized parts of them, particularly the benediction he always said at the last: *May the words of my mouth and the meditation of my heart be acceptable in Thy sight, O Lord.* These were no mere words. They had somehow become living things, probing and questioning and penetrating her thoughts day and night. They simply would not let her forget them, nor would they let her be.

Were the words of her mouth and the meditation of her heart acceptable in His sight? In answer, she thought of her violent anger at the McClarys and their whole wretched clan. Her jealousy of Piper. Her past fury and longing for Simon. Her tenuous relationship with Ian Justus. And a hundred other things she would never want brought to light. She was, she concluded, sorely lacking in God's sight.

In her disquiet she roamed the river bottoms where the melting snow sluiced through her moccasins and turned them black. Always she watched for Captain Jack. But there was only the eternal stillness of the woods marred by a passing animal or a moody wind promising a bitter winter. When her days were spent, she returned home to a cold cabin, where the mountain of firewood resting within arm's reach of the porch was welcome indeed. Whom, she wondered for the hundredth time, did she have to thank for that?

In the evenings she read or wrote letters. Often she paused to consider what the doctor called her rashness with Captain Jack. She looked down at the half-finished letters to Ma and Miss Mayella, imagining the stir she would cause if she told them about her Shawnee courtship. With a sigh, she took up a book but couldn't read, at least at night. Even by the light of two candles, the words seemed to melt together like wax on the page.

She consulted the few medical books she had, studying the swimming words, and came away wretchedly disquieted. She could no longer plead weariness as the cause since she had just had a week's rest at the fort. There was nothing else to do but face the thing she feared: She must see Ian Justus.

She sighed just thinking about it. What if he dismissed her as rudely as she'd dismissed him in her fury over Captain Jack? She realized now he'd just meant to caution her, as any true friend would. Although she'd shunned his personal advice, she did need his medical expertise.

Against her better judgment she took out her second-best work dress, heated a hand iron at the fire, and pressed out the fiercest wrinkles. It was cold in the cabin, but she bathed anyway, pulling a wooden barrel to the hearth and washing herself with a cake of bayberry soap saved for a special occasion. Instead of the usual girlish plait hanging to her knees, she wrapped her long braid like a crown about her head then peered skeptically in the fragment of mirror.

The girl who peered back at her was not a girl at all but a

woman—a woman who didn't dare admit why she took such pains with herself on a wintry morning when her buffalo robe and worn boots would spoil the entire effect.

Will had taken Pandora to Cozy Creek, for the mare was lame and Lael had had little luck tending her. She glared fiercely at the mule as she mounted, daring him to give her a moment's trouble. He took off down the path as if glad to move his cold bones and was at a near run when the fort came into view. Smoke from a dozen chimneys wrapped the river valley in a hazy scarf. To her left the river itself was no longer a summer sapphire but a pearly winter opal.

As always, she went first to Ma Horn. The old woman sat huddled by the fire, sewing new soles on a pair of old moccasins. There were two places set at the table, Lael noticed, well in advance of the noon meal, and a pot of beans and side-meat simmered at the fire.

"I've come to see the doctor," Lael told her.

Ma Horn didn't pause from her sewing. "You ailin'?"

"Just my eyes."

"Too much readin' and writin'," she surmised. She set aside her work and gave a sigh which, coming from her, was an unusual utterance. Immediately, Lael sensed trouble. Olivia . . . had she already come? Or had the doctor gone?

Ma Horn reached for her pipe, which was still smoking on the hearth. "I got some sorry news to tell you about the doctor. He's taken a lickin'."

Lael simply stared.

"He rode out of here pretty as you please and come back lookin' like painter bait."

Slowly, Lael sat. "When?"

"Yesterday mornin'."

"Who?"

"He ain't sayin'."

288

Ma Horn took a draw on her pipe, her mouth pinched with sorrow. "All I know is he was going to see to that trapper and his Indian wife over on the gulch. I reckon somebody ambushed him on the trail—somebody who don't take kindly to his strange speech and ways."

They sat for a time in uneasy silence. Lael felt queer and lightheaded at the news, and her heart hammered so hard she had trouble drawing an easy breath.

"I made him up some healin' salve just this mornin'," she said, handing her a small bowl. "Give it to him when you go."

With some trepidation, Lael approached the blockhouse and knocked lightly. At the sound of muffled voices, she let herself in. The large room had been divided by a sheet and two chairs sat facing the fire. She took one, noting everything was clean if spare. The voices behind the screen told her the doctor was with a patient who, from the pained howl he let out, was not taking kindly to his treatment. The delay gave her time to compose herself and study the objects on the long mantle.

There was a small clock with bold Roman numerals that, she was soon to discover, chimed the hour. Some books and a pouch of tobacco sat beside it. Lastly, in a small silver frame, was a portrait of a man and woman bearing a remarkable resemblance to the doctor himself. Near her on a table lay a book—a Bible—open to the Psalms.

In a few moments old Amos appeared from behind the curtain, nursing his mouth with a blood-stained rag. He flashed her a winsome grin nonetheless, holding up the extracted, once-troublesome tooth before he ambled out the door.

Ian Justus appeared soon after, wiping his hands on a cloth, unaware of her presence. She cleared her throat, and he turned toward her. Wary, she sat stoic under his scrutiny. Was he remembering their harsh words at last meeting, before he'd gone out and slammed the door? She certainly was. But the sight of his battered, swollen face, one eye nearly shut and his lower lip split at the corner, made her nearly forget why she'd come in the first place.

"Miss Click."

Ian crossed the room, not in his usual agile way, but slowly and deliberately and obviously in pain, taking the chair opposite her. How it hurt her simply to look at him! She struggled to maintain her composure, but a tear fell anyway, making a trail to her chin.

"So you've come tae see me," he said slowly, giving her a crooked smile. "Well, I'm sure 'tis nothing tae cry aboot. You look well enough tae me."

Finally she stammered, "W-who has done this terrible . . . thing?"

He stood up and moved to the table where he poured steaming water into a basin. "You might say I met up with one of your Kentucke panthers in the woods."

A fierce protective passion rose up inside her, swelling her voice. "You must tell Colonel Barr, so the person who did this may be brought in—and punished."

"Nae."

He was so firm—so calm—she nearly faltered. She watched as he methodically cleaned a few surgical tools, laying them out on a clean cloth to dry.

She swallowed back her scalding emotions. "Someone attacks you and you do nothing but say nay? You might have been killed! Suppose it happens again—"

"Suppose it does? My standards remain the same. And they are no' settlement standards, Miss Click. They're scriptural." The conviction in his voice nearly left her speechless.

"But the Bible says an eye for an eye, a wound for a wound."

"Dinna you also read 'love your enemies and pray for those who persecute you'?"

She shook her head vehemently. "You make no sense."

He arched an eyebrow. "Need I remind you tae tend tae your own business? You often advise me tae do the same." There was teasing in his tone, bringing back the heat of their last meeting, but it only left her shame-faced.

She sat mute, suddenly so tired she didn't think she could rise from her chair. But worse than his strange words—worse even than the beating—was the feeling that she didn't understand him. He was, after all, an outlander, a stranger to their ways.

Getting up, she set the healing salve on the table and turned to go.

"Lael—wait." He caught her elbow and his voice was far gentler than his grip. "You dinna come here tae argue with me. Why did you come?"

She started to cry again at the tenderness in his voice. "Something's the matter with my sight. At times I cannot see."

Who, she wondered, was most in need of soothing words and healing hands?

"'Tis a scratch, is all," he said when she protested over his injuries. "If you'd ever seen a mon near death from battle and disease, you'd no' be making such a fuss."

And so she fell silent, letting him shine the light of a candle into her eyes and instruct her to read aloud some letters and numerals from a chart hanging on the opposite wall.

"Your eyes are a wee bit weak," he told her. "But I have just the remedy. You must wait, tho', till I next go tae Lexington."

The quiet confidence in his voice reassured her. She continued to sit as if hoping his nearness would somehow take away the sting of his earlier rebuke and they could be friends again.

291

He said gently, "You can go, if you like. But no' tae your own cabin. Night is falling fast."

"To Ma Horn's, then."

"Aye," he said, adding, "I would have you stay here in hospital quarters, but you're hardly sick enough tae do that."

Just lovesick, she thought miserably.

He came and sat opposite her. His face was so battered she nearly winced. She worked to make her voice strong and sure. "You must let me help you with the healing salve. Then I will go."

He smiled despite his cracked lip, and she fervently hoped he'd not broken his fine nose or the cheekbones that made his handsome face so noble. Would the cuts heal or scar? The one over his eye was deep, while the rest were more like scratches.

Ma Horn's salve was pleasant-smelling, made from crushed rosemary and comfrey and mixed with the ooze of white oak. Lael applied it with a clean cloth as gently as she could. He did not so much as wince, but she sensed some inner struggle within him. Anger? Fear? Exhaustion? He looked as though he'd just come from battle though he bore no musket wounds.

She left the salve on the table then started to go, but he blocked her exit. His eyes were as earnest as she'd ever seen them. "Will you forgive me for the things I said tae you when we last met? Before I went oot and slammed the door?"

She looked up at him. "I came here to ask you that very thing."

Only when I saw you, I forgot.

"Forgiven, then?"

She softened. "You were only trying to warn me, as a friend."

"Aye, as a friend."

"I shouldn't have sassed you so."

He smiled, or tried to. "But you are so good at it."

She almost smiled as well, then looked again at his face and went solemn. "Is there nothing more I can do for you?"

"Aye," he answered. "You can pray."

Her eyes filled again. "I'm not very good at that."

"You dinna have tae be. Just honest before the Almighty."

She was suddenly struck by a curious thought. "Do you ever . . . pray for me?"

His eyes fastened on her face. "Aye, I do."

Her heart turned over. If he prayed for her . . . what did he pray about? She quickly shut away the question lest her heart grow too soft toward him.

"I still think you should have been a preacher," she said softly, then turned her back and departed.

52

Two days later, on a raw November morning, one of Simon's nearest neighbors arrived on a mule even more ornery than Lael's own. It stopped just short of the cabin, nearly sending the boy sailing off its bare back and onto the slippery porch.

"Lael Click! Piper Hayes is bad sick, and Simon wants you sent for!"

She finished adding wood to the fire and poked at her cornmeal mush with a spoon, scarcely believing her ears. But when the call came again she opened the door a crack. "Come in and thaw out."

She poured mush into two bowls and passed him some sweetening. He said gleefully, "I reckon she ain't so sick I can't eat a bite."

Having lost her appetite, Lael began packing her bags, speculating on what might await her. Piper had recently given birth to a stillborn girl. Was this the trouble?

All the way to the Hayes' homestead she chafed at the wind and the slow plodding of the mule. Her stomach gnawed in empty complaint, and her feet began to ache in her worn stockings and boots. Mile after bitter mile fueled her fury that Simon Hayes had the gall to call upon her after all that had transpired between them, when the doctor could have been had for half the trouble at half the distance.

As Simon's land unfolded around her, signs of prosperity and abundance were everywhere—in the numerous fences and grazing livestock, in the fallow fields that lay like a drab quilt, in the solid cabin, twice as big as her own, with real glass windows that bubbled and streaked in the noon light. Like salt in a wound, it was, coming here like this for the very first time.

A pack of dogs rushed to meet her, then Simon's aging mother appeared on the porch to call them off. Lael had last seen Matilda Hayes at Pa's court-martial years ago. Before that, through the years of forting up in her childhood, Mrs. Hayes had treated her like a daughter. Today though, with hardly a greeting, Lael was ushered into the spacious cabin.

"She ain't been well since the birth," Mrs. Hayes said. "But here lately she seems different somehow. She's got a misery in her stomach and is all a-tremble."

"How long?"

"Oh, a good week or more. She's weak as water and can't do her chores, so I come over from McAfee's to pitch in."

Shirking her chores? Complaining of weakness? Prejudice rose up in Lael hard and strong. Piper had ever been one to slack, to her memory, even in the schoolroom with Miss Mayella.

At the back of the cabin, hidden away in the luxury of a second room, lay Piper, prostrate on the bed she shared with Simon. At the sight of her Lael felt a queer revulsion. She wanted nothing so much as to run out of the cabin and flee on her mule. But sheer stubbornness of spirit won out.

"Hello, Piper."

The closed eyes fluttered open. Somehow, Piper Cane Hayes managed to look sullen even in sickness. She'd changed little over the years, and her hazel eyes narrowed at the sight and sound of Lael.

"Lael . . . Lael Click? You get on away from here! I ain't lettin' no Indian lover lay a hand on me!"

Lael looked down at her. *I am just what you say I am, in more ways than you know.* Still, the slur stung, though she'd been saying such things since settlement school.

Strangely, Piper's eyes closed again and her face resumed its gray pallor. Lael spent the rest of the afternoon blending tea and tincture and asking questions of Simon's mother. Nay, she did not think it was a mortal illness, she told Matilda Hayes. A weakness of the blood, perhaps. *Nothing that a little backbone and a day's work wouldn't cure,* she wanted to add. Pausing, she took in Piper for the last time—in the bed that should have been hers.

A stray thought, black as smoke, curled through her brain. What if . . .

She swallowed, stunned at such evil. What if she were to leave not willow bark and feverfew but mayapple? Simon's mother could give her the fatal dose and still her hateful words forever. None would be the wiser. None but God. She bit her lip and packed her bags, wondering if she could make it home before dark.

There was no offer of payment, though Mrs. Hayes fixed her a cup of coffee with cream. The cream was payment enough, Lael decided, its sweet richness lingering on her tongue. She'd sorely missed her milk cow since the barn burning.

Simon was curiously absent, but she'd given it little thought. As she crossed the hard ground in search of the mule, she saw a flicker of movement. The barn door that had been ajar moments before was now closed. She paused, awash with a queer sensation.

Without reason or understanding she bypassed the smokehouse and walked uphill to the barn, dodging frozen puddles and muddy ruts, her saddlebag heavy in her arms. A bitter breath of wind pressed against her skirts.

She pushed at the heavy door, and it opened noisily. Inside, Simon stood, his back to her, working on a harness. He did not turn. Did he not hear?

"Piper's weak but she'll live," she announced across the hay-strewn expanse of barn.

He did not turn around but said, "I reckon you'll be wantin' payment."

"Nay, seeing to Neddy like you did is payment enough. We'll call it even."

He worked the harness in his hands as if she'd never come in at all and said nothing in response. No turning around. No mumbled good-bye. The shadows in the barn were lengthening and the winter darkness would soon overtake her. She should have been well on her way home by now. But something held her fast.

Slowly—did he think she'd gone?—Simon turned.

When she saw him face to face, a shocking fury filled her. Something new and queer twisted his features. Fear? Shame? His face was badly battered, even more so than the doctor's own. If not for his shock of red hair and powerful height, she would have been hard pressed to recognize him.

Her voice, when it finally came, was as harsh as the winter wind. "Is that why you didn't send for the doctor, Simon? Were you afraid he'd refuse to come after you ambushed him in the woods?"

Silence.

In that moment something broke within her—some hard and binding chain—freeing her from him forever. She saw him as he truly was: hardly a man at all, but someone weak and enfeebled by his own passions.

Without another word she turned and fled down the hill.

53

She arrived at the fort at dusk. Snow had begun to fall, and the bitter cold and darkness forbade her to go farther. Dispirited, she got off the mule just inside the gate. She had a passing fear that the doctor, given this recent trouble, might leave. Was this what Simon hoped? She had a terrible suspicion that Simon might have killed him had he not fought back . . . and fought back well.

There again was a puzzle. Simon, a veritable bull of a man, had clearly taken the brunt of the beating. There was clearly more to Ian Justus than met the eye. Surgeon . . . fiddler . . . fighter?

But would he stay on? The settlement could no longer do without him. She was hearing reports of his treating all kinds of ailments, most of them successfully. Numbly, her near-frozen legs walked the length of the common. If God had called him here, would God not also call him away at the appointed time? And when might that time be?

There were no lights on in the doctor's cabin. By the time she reached the sanctuary of Ma Horn's, her soul felt as numb as her feet.

Ma Horn sat alone at the table. No second place was set. No fiddle case or wool coat was in sight. A wild, irrational fear seized her. "Oh, please—tell me—where is he?"

"He went away, child. To Lexington. He'll likely not be back before mornin.'"

But just as Lael had removed her wet coat and boots, there came a commotion outside. She reached the cabin door first and opened it wide. In the swirling snow, she saw him, boots frozen to the stirrups of his saddle, his blue coat layered with a mantle of white. He looked as surprised to see her as she was to see him. Inside, door shut to the wind, Ma Horn set about warming the doctor's supper, while Lael moved their coats and boots nearer the fire. But she couldn't eat. The knowledge of Simon lay too heavy on her heart. The green-eyed monster, Shakespeare had called it. Jealousy. Was this why Simon had attacked him in the woods?

As was her custom, Ma Horn soon fell asleep in her chair. The doctor got up and moved closer to the fire, leaning against the hearth. His face was healing nicely, she noted. He looked down at her, his eyes the same merry blue as always, despite everything.

"I've been tae Lexington and back and brought you this." He passed her a leather pouch. Curious, she untied the closure and carefully emptied the contents into her lap.

A ring spilled out, glittering and golden, and she saw a flash of diamonds as well. Before she could right the bag a string of pearls followed, filling her open hand like so many drops of cream. But what came next truly astonished her. It was a miniature, its gold casing bearing the face of a lovely russet-haired woman with emerald eyes. Stunned, Lael could think of but one thing. *Olivia.*

There was an awkward silence as he realized his mistake. She'd never before seen him flustered. A sudden flush turned his rugged features swarthy, and he looked confused and apologetic. She felt deeply wounded herself, and all thumbs, as she tried to return the lovely jewels to the bag. Mortified, she felt the ring slip from her fingers and fall to the floor, rolling beneath the trestle table.

All at once they were kneeling, hands touching as they searched.

"Lael, I—"

"Please," she whispered. "There's no need to explain. Perhaps . . . is there another bag?"

There was. An identical leather pouch was produced, but its contents weren't nearly so magnificent or thought-provoking. They were her spectacles, wire-rimmed and small and round, the glass clear and thin as creek ice.

"Thank you, truly," she said though it fell a trifle flat after all the excitement. Though he still looked vexed, the bag of jewels was nowhere to be seen. Safe in his pocket once again, she guessed.

"Try them on before you thank me. And read this, tae be sure." He handed her Ma Horn's Bible. She opened it at random to the Song of Solomon. *Hardly the book to be reading aloud to the doctor.* Deuteronomy, the book of laws, was far safer, she decided.

She began a bit hesitantly, unsure of the strange device perched on the end of her nose. But the longer she read, the greater her confidence grew. The words no longer blurred but stayed in their proper place.

She looked up, elated. "I must pay you."

He smiled. "'Tis payment enough tae hear your voice. Keep reading."

She finished one chapter, then two. It dawned on her that she was no longer reading to ascertain the veracity of her new spectacles. She was so often quiet in his presence . . . could it be he truly liked to hear the sound of her voice?

She stopped abruptly and removed the spectacles. "I must look a sight—"

"You look . . . lovely."

In the still room his words, though softly spoken, had tremendous force.

Lovely.

No one had ever called her that. He was looking at her again—she could feel it—though she dared not look at him. The flush that stained her neck and face made her feel feverish.

He moved to put another log on the fire.

She kept her eyes on the book in her lap. "I am truly grateful, Doctor."

"Doctor?" He turned back to her and leaned against the hearth. "I meant tae talk tae you aboot that some time ago."

"Talk about what?"

"My Christian name. You canna say it?"

She swallowed, nervous as a schoolgirl. "But of course . . ."

"Then say it."

"Ian . . . Justus. But I should call you Doctor Justus."

"Why?"

"'Tis only proper."

He grinned and rolled his eyes. "I dinna notice you Kentuckians observe such social niceties."

She fingered her spectacles. "What does everyone else here call you?"

"Doc Justus."

"And you want me to call you . . . Ian."

"Only if you want tae."

He was teasing her again. She couldn't help but wonder what Olivia called him. All at once she was overcome with a dreadful certainty that she shouldn't be sitting here at all. This was Olivia's place, not hers. And yet she was struck by the fact that, unlike Olivia, she would never have remained in Boston. She would have followed Ian Justus clear to Kentucke, come what may.

Simply put, she, Lael Catherine Click, knew a good catch when she saw one.

But he was as forbidden as Captain Jack.

She stood up. "You must be tired from your long ride. I don't mean to keep you."

He studied her for a long moment, and then he put on his boots and coat. When he was almost to the door, she said very quietly, "Ian . . . I know . . . about Simon."

He turned and his blue eyes seemed to bore a hole in her. She rushed on, "He fetched me to see Piper, who's been ill. He never meant for me to see him, but I did." She continued, fresh anguish filling her at the possibilities. "He might have killed you. It's a wonder he did not."

His face was grave. "Perhaps he would have, but for one thing. I was a boxer in college—in Scotlain. Like my faither before me."

In college, in Scotland, years before. Before he'd dreamed of or possibly even heard of Kentucke. Before God called him here. Even then he was being prepared . . . for this.

Whom God calls, He equips. Where had she heard that?

They stood an arm's length apart, and the silence was expectant, filled with heartfelt things they could not say. Feeling near tears again, Lael stuttered out the question that seemed ready to rend her in two. "Are you going b-back to Boston?"

His expression softened, so poignant she felt breathless. What could he possibly be thinking? Feeling?

His voice was low, measured. "Nae . . . no' now. No' yet."

Without another word, he let himself out. She sagged against the door frame, suddenly weary. The blast of icy air that struck her in his wake was nothing like the blow to her heart. Truly, Ian Justus was forbidden, and not because of Olivia or Captain Jack. Ian Justus belonged to God.

And Lael Click did not.

54

Christmas was approaching, and the land lay frozen in the grip of winter. How long had it been since she'd last been at the fort? Fourteen . . . fifteen days?

And how long had it been since she'd last seen Captain Jack? The memory of their encounter at the river had faded somewhat. How tall had he stood? How green were his eyes? Just what had he said before leaving her at the last? Her forbidden feelings for him lay tucked within her heart, but they no longer warmed her as they once had.

Her days were relentlessly the same. She woke up, trading her warm bed for a frigid cabin. From the ashes she made a fire, boiled tea and mush for breakfast, and watched her store of honey dwindle even though she meted it out in miserly fashion. She washed dishes and swept out the cabin, needed or not, then set out dried beans or apples to soak, ground meal for bread, and cut a small hank of meat for seasoning from the ham hanging in the springhouse. There were Tuck and the mule to tend to and, on kinder days, a walk to the river.

To her dismay, some days she did not so much as wash her face or comb her hair. Besides, who was there to see—or care? Soon she lost all track of time. She was too much alone, she reasoned, forever fighting the urge to ride to the fort. The solitude was making her strange. Was this how it had been for Lovey Runion? Fine at first . . . and then fey?

At least she had her spectacles and her books. But the medical volumes rested at one end of the table, coated white with a sprinkling of dust. Shakespeare and *The Pilgrim's Progress* were no different, sitting idly on the mantle where she had left them a month before. Only the Bible was in use, lying open and waiting for first one reading then another. How was it that she could read the same passage twice and come away with a different understanding each time?

"'Tis a rude book," she pronounced one day in irritation. The words demanded her full concentration, prodding and provoking her, assailing her with questions even when closed. Lately, in the stillness, it seemed to speak to her, calling her back after she had shut it.

Like Ian's prayers, the Bible would not let her be. It demanded something of her, though she knew not what. The more she read, the deeper she looked into its truths, the more she felt herself being looked into, laid bare and open.

Not one soul had sent for her in weeks, not one request made. Visiting Lovey and Mourning and Titus up the branch had been her only call, and even there she had felt like an intruder. Though they were glad to see her, they needed nothing from her except a little tobacco. Why, Lovey had even given up her tonic.

She returned home, dreading the cold cabin, then remembered the firewood that had been mysteriously split and stacked. This time, however, the change was more subtle: Just beyond the rick of firewood the fence in the pasture had been mended. And there were new shingles on the shed.

Tuck barked furiously in welcome and circled the mule in a frenzy. Laughing, she got down, wondering who'd done these needed repairs. Will Bliss? Simon? It was Will's way to do good deeds in secret, but not Simon's. Her rush of gratitude was soon overshadowed by a nagging sense of failure. Who'd been here? And why? She was a woman alone, hard pressed to do the repairs herself, and that was her answer.

Hadn't Will had to plow for her in spring? Hadn't he brought her feed corn when the barn burned and taken care of her mare? Wasn't she a thorn in Colonel Barr's side? As it was, she'd already spent too much time at the fort, living off Ma Horn's meager supplies and replenishing little.

And then there was the matter of Doc Justus, who cared as much about doctoring people's souls as their bodies. Nay, he didn't know much about walnut poultices or the properties of ginseng, but with his medical training and prayer, what need did she herself serve? The time was ripe for running away.

The folly of living alone and courting danger went against her own good judgment. What had Ma Horn once told her? *There's only one thing worse than a broken heart. It comes of getting what you want and finding out it ain't what you thought it would be.* Lael had come home and found that to be true.

As Christmas drew nearer, her thoughts turned to gift giving. She wanted Susanna and Ma Horn to have something memorable, even sentimental, something that couldn't be had at the fort store or even Lexington. It was best, she decided, to give the gift of oneself or the work of one's hands. And so she set to work, cutting pieces from the skirt of her second-best Briar Hill gown and a bit of the lace besides. Susanna dearly loved fancy things and an apron and pincushion would be both pretty and practical, embroidered with some words of friendship.

For little Lael she dug into her trunk and brought out the fashion doll the Rose Hill seamstress had given her. Its small wooden frame bore an exact replica of her rose gown, complete with lace sleeves and tiny glass buttons. For the boys, Will and Henry, she had Ransom's toy tomahawk and a few flint arrowheads she'd found. Perhaps Pa's remaining farm tools would go to Will, for all the trouble he had taken with her, and maybe Pa's budget as well, if she could part with it.

At the bottom of her trunk was a new pair of ivory stockings held up with garter ribbons. On each she embroidered Ma Horn's initials in scarlet thread. As she sewed, she dreamt of Christmases past. From the simplicity of a corn-husk doll in her childhood to the grand, candlelit firs of Briar Hill, the day was magic, wherever she happened to be. Should it be any less here without so much as a pine bough for decoration or a cup of mulled cider?

A gift for Ian required much thought . . . and prayer. A practical gift it must be, yet she couldn't give it without a touch of sentiment besides. Night after night, her new spectacles perched on her nose, she sat at the trestle table, quill in hand, composing a book in gothic hand to make her former writing master proud.

In alphabetical order she painstakingly transcribed all the herbs and plants and roots known as healers, giving a detailed description of each, their benefits and dangers, and a sketch as well. From basswood to red clover to sassafras, she wrote down all she knew. For the cover she applied some rose petals she'd pressed in late summer, then signed her name in one corner.

Next she sharpened some scissors and cut her hair. Just a small piece, about the width of her little finger, taken from the nape of her neck after it had been brushed and braided. The long golden strand, tied at each end with a bit of moss green ribbon, would make a fine bookmark.

She sat back and examined her work with a smile. She'd not felt so satisfied in a very long time.

55

Toward dusk on Christmas Eve, a light snow began to fall. She put her head down on Neddy's Bible, spectacles in hand, and went to sleep. She awoke to fading firelight and the tinkling of a bell. But the snow spitting against the shutter and a rising wind soon drowned out the sound.

Her imagination, she decided. Or had she simply dreamed of Christmas bells? A dream, she reckoned, for Tuck did not bark. She got up to add wood to the fire and heard it again. *Bells.* Not one but several, ringing out a blissful melody in the growing darkness.

Still Tuck did not bark. Without a thought for the cold she flung open the cabin door and stepped onto the frozen planks of the porch. In the yard Tuck was like a dog possessed, running in crazy circles, ears flying and eyes bright.

Around the burned barn came a figure in a blue coat on a beautiful bay horse. An unfamiliar hat was pulled low, hiding his features, yet she knew him instantly. A warm, lilting feeling clutched her heart. Ian Justus rode up to the porch, smiling at her through a snow suddenly gone wild. The bells about the bay's neck quieted, and Tuck began to lick his boots.

Speechless, she stood, hands clasped behind her back.

"Since you're no' going tae ask, I'll just tell you tae come," he called. "Come as you are. But if you dinna hurry, we'll miss Christmas."

Christmas. She felt the delight of it clear to her toes. He leaned forward in the saddle, looking frozen. "Are you coming, Lael lass, or are you no'?"

"I—well . . ." She turned and flew into the cabin, smoothing her hair, banking the fire, and disposing of her uneaten supper all at once. Suddenly she reappeared at the door. "I don't even know where we're going!"

"Tae Cozy Creek. Till the new year."

The prospect threw her into action and sent her rummaging through her trunk, stuffing her rose silk gown into a saddlebag along with a nightgown and the gifts she'd made. On a whim she grabbed the popcorn popper before she flew out the door again.

He was tying her mule behind the bay. She noticed his violin case hanging from his saddle, and her heart sang a note all its own. Before she could even step off the porch he was picking her up.

"Light as thistledown," he teased. "'Tis what I suspected."

She laughed at this for she had never been scrawny. With a bark, Tuck brought up the rear.

As they climbed the gentle mountain path the snow both blinded them with its brightness and lit their way. The solid warmth of his back and his wide-brimmed hat kept the wind from devouring her as she leaned against him.

And then, out of habit, came a dire, dreadful reminder. She had forgotten her gun. Despite this trespass she'd never felt safer or more serene. Truly, she felt she'd passed from darkness into light.

At the top of Cozy Creek the lights of the Bliss cabin shone like stars. The baying of Will's hounds shattered the stillness, then the cabin door was flung open wide in welcome. Lael was at once relieved and rueful. Oh, but she hated for the night to end, with the magic of every snowflake shaken down from heaven all around them and the ride, not cold and long, but sheer bliss. Ian's arms were snug around her, helping her down from the bay, bringing their time alone to an end.

"Come in!" shouted Susanna in her merry way. "You must be near froze and starved half to death. Supper's waitin.'"

Behind her, filling the door frame, was Will, puffing contentedly on a pipe, two of the children entwined about his legs. Inside, a roaring fire sent their shadows dancing about the room. Susanna and the children had draped laurel leaves on strings and they gleamed waxy and bright, while the scent of candles competed with the smoky smell of roasting goose. Susanna hugged her hard in welcome, and Lael realized just how long it had been.

"Lael Click's become a stranger," Will said with a grin. "Cavortin' about with her remedies and forsakin' her friends. We'd hoped the competition with Doc Justus would change all that."

"It might yet," she answered, shedding her buffalo robe.

Ian was removing his coat as well and stood looking at her so intently she knew something was wrong. Her dress? This was one of her two work dresses, and the plainest of the two, with grease spots that refused to budge despite repeated scourings with lye. Or maybe it was her hair—damp and bedraggled and completely free of its pins so that it hung in wild waves down her back. Or her shoes! *Oh, law!* She stared at her stocking feet in mortification. A double layer of stockings . . . but no shoes!

Deep down, from somewhere in his belly, Will Bliss began to laugh. Susanna followed, clutching her sides, then Ian as well. "You could say we were in a wee bit of a hurry tae get here," he admitted as Lael finally broke into laughter herself.

"Wet feet never hurt a body," Will said with a wink. "Besides, the doctor here will take care of you."

Susanna skirted the table, so heavily laden it seemed to list, and motioned for them to sit. "Lael, set out the bread. Will, you can pour the cider. Doctor, you'll have to fend off the least 'uns for a place."

Little Lael, pink-cheeked from the novelty of company, was in a fit of giggles brought on by Ian's carrying her like a keg of powder under his arm. She insisted on sitting at his knee until Susanna intervened and she squirmed into place between him and Lael.

Surveying the table before her and the people all around her, Lael felt such a rush of gratitude she wanted to weep. What had become of her? Soft as mush, she rebuked herself, bowing her head to hear Will's prayer.

But what of Ma Horn? Lael asked after her as the dishes were passed.

"Ma Horn," Ian said, "is making merry with Colonel Barr and Airy Phelps."

Susanna chuckled at this. "Making merry with the likes of Philo Barr? Now that I would like to see. Though Airy Phelps is a merry old widow woman if ever there was one."

"Perhaps the colonel will be a changed mon come the New Year," said Ian with a grin, lifting his mug of cider in a toast. "Keep good company and ye will be counted one of them, so the Scots say."

They laughed, and talk turned to more banal matters. There was no fresh settlement news and the hope was that everyone in Kentucke could rest easy for Christmas. Indians weren't known to be winter raiders, though reports of trouble still trickled through the settlements despite the intermittent snows.

Will scratched his beard. "I heard there's been some ruckus upriver with the Shawnee raidin' flatboats and the like. I was goin' to ask the doctor if Colonel Barr—"

Lael felt a woozy rush of alarm and kept her eyes on her plate as Susanna scolded, "Oh, hush about trouble. Tonight we're together, safe and sound, and trouble seems far off. Let's talk of better things to come."

Will winked at her. "Like spring and calvin' time?"

She gave an unusual blush and Lael stole a glance at her friend knowingly. Even Ian smiled as he reached for more cider.

"And what of you, Lael?" Susanna asked. "What are your plans come the new year?"

Lael paused and took up her knife to butter a biscuit. Did she look as scattered as she felt? "I don't rightly know . . . not yet." *True enough.* "I thought I might leave for a spell. Finally visit my mother and Ransom." She kept her eyes down and was relieved when Will asked Ian the same.

"Forting up," he said simply.

Susanna looked pensive as if keeping some secret. "Spring'll bring about some changes in the settlement, I reckon. Don't you agree, Doctor?"

They exchanged a glance, though he said nothing. But hearing it, Lael knew.

Olivia. In the spring when the dogwood was flowering and the sarvis berries were ruby red, Olivia was to come to Kentucke. Contemplating it, Lael felt like all the breath had been knocked out of her. Knowing made her own uncertain future that much harder to bear.

That first night they stayed up till midnight, sampling Will's blackberry wine and talking among themselves. Susanna was expecting her fourth child in spring and wanted both the doctor and Lael to attend her. The new year, Ian told them, would indeed bring a new county to Kentucke in honor of Lael's father. Colonel Barr had only lately received official word of this and had asked that the news be passed on to Lael. Hearing it by the fire, among friends, Lael felt a deep glow of pride. The tide of conversation shifted to Pa as Will and Susanna recounted stories of his exploits, with Lael adding or detracting as they went, her lingering grief softened by their friendship.

And yet the evening soon came to an end, with Will and Susanna joining their sleeping children in the loft and Ian disappearing behind a makeshift partition of coverlets hiding a corner bed. As for Lael, a pallet beneath a window suited her fine, stuffed full of clean straw and graced with a feather pillow and Susanna's best quilt.

At half past midnight the only sound was the wind blowing an icy breath against the shutter and the logs settling in the fire. It was plumb unnerving, Lael thought, to have Ian Justus lying so close. She lay fully clothed atop the pallet, baiting sleep, but sleep wouldn't come. Perhaps neglecting her nightly ritual was the trouble. Silently, on stocking feet, she left her bed.

A fire always drew her, and this one was especially enticing, warming the plank floor directly in front, glowing golden on the smooth hearthstones till they looked polished, even wet. Hoping the heat would lull her to sleep, she sat as close as she dared. Fragments of the evening's conversation echoed in her head . . .

Click, show us your pretty daughter . . . let down your hair.

To Lael's dismay, Will had recounted this tale over blackberry wine. But how had he known? She'd never spoken of it to anyone, not Susanna nor Simon. But there it was, out in the open, the stuff of legend. Hearing it afresh, she wanted to slip under the table. Ian said not a word during the telling, and she dared not look at him.

Law, but she could add a few more tales of her own, but they would hardly believe her.

She let down her hair now as she'd done then, pulling the pins loose and letting the heavy locks fall. Her horsehair brush was old and missing some bristles, but the mother-of-pearl handle conformed to her hand, smooth and worn. Absently, she began to brush. One stroke . . . two . . . ten . . .

From the shadows came the slightest sound. Startled, she looked up and the brush fell to the floor. Ian sat in the shadows, in the same chair he'd occupied all evening. Had he never left? She had seen him go herself, but perhaps he found sleep as impossible as she. With a trembling hand she retrieved the brush and hurriedly braided her hair, gathering up the pins in her lap.

He said quietly, "Lael, what is happening between you and the Shawnee?"

She nearly flinched at the sound of her name, so softly spoken. It was just like him to come straight to the heart of the matter. Slowly, she sat back down and glanced anxiously at the loft. Could they be heard? But Ian kept his voice so low even she had to lean forward to make out his words.

"Why . . ." she began, uncertain. "Why do you want to know?"

"You are nae longer so lighthearted—so blithesome. Have you no' seen him?"

She smoothed the wrinkled ruche of her skirt. "Not since fall." The admission grieved her, but she wouldn't give quarter to tears. Not this time.

He tread gently yet persistently. "Is there nae understanding between you?"

"Aye . . . nay." Must she unlock her heart for this man? The silver bracelet lay hidden beneath her sleeve, warm against her skin. Not once had she been without it since he'd given it to her three months before.

The fire shifted and popped, and he leaned forward. For a fleeting moment she felt as if she was face to face with Captain Jack. Ian's black hair, free of its usual tie, had grown longer since she'd last seen him and hung about his shoulders, framing his handsome, intense face. Her breath caught. What was happening here? She looked away, confused.

"He's not come again for some time now, though he promised to return. But truly, what does it matter?"

"It matters more than you know." The poignancy in his voice hurt her, and she felt the urge to stem his words with her fingertips, but he kept on. "I ken one day he'll come for you and you'll simply disappear. Withoot a word tae anyone. Withoot a trace."

Put this way, it sounded so selfish, so unfeeling, if it ever did happen. "I—he—" she began, then stopped, contemplating all the uncertainties before her.

His voice dropped lower, yet more a whisper. "You're needed here, Lael. The settlement needs you. I need you."

She'd misheard him, surely. In the darkness, their eyes met. His face was partially hidden by shadows, but hers, framed by firelight, felt vulnerable and exposed. He got up and took a seat beside her at the hearth, shoulder to shoulder. "Colonel Barr asked me tae deliver this. A courier brought it just yesterday, but I forgot tae give it tae you till now."

In his hands was a letter—addressed to her. The heavy seal had not yet been broken, and she recognized the bold but elegant scrawl of Briar Hill's headmistress. She took it, searching in her pocket for her spectacles.

She felt a bit breathless. "You'll have to read it to me. Please. I've forgotten my glasses."

He took it back and broke the seal. Listening to the lilt of his voice, she became lost in the richness of his speech. Distracted as she was, she hardly heard the invitation in the letter, then sat slightly open-mouthed when it came. The school was offering her a position, he read. One of her instructors had recently passed away, and they were in need of a replacement. She could come to Briar Hill and begin at once, if she so desired.

Did surprise and relief show on her face? Surely it did, for he folded the letter and said a bit heatedly, "What can you be thinking?"

She looked up at him. "I did not write them asking for a situation."

"Nae? Yet you are considering it. I see it in your face."

"And what if I am?"

"A place for you—as a spinster teacher? Do you no' ken what you do when you shut yourself away from life at some fancy school?"

"You make no sense."

"The Master made you a Click, and a Click you'll always be. You belong tae this place and these people."

"I don't belong here—you belong here," she nearly hissed, as quietly as she dared. "I—I'm not the healer I thought I was. I don't truly have the gift, but you do. You heal body. And spirit."

"Nae. No' I." His eyes, so alive, so intensely blue, were lit by a fire that was not his own. "There is but one soul mender, Lael, and He is no mere man."

"You speak of God."

"Aye."

"You know Him well."

"He wants tae be known." His eyes seemed to challenge her, and she faltered under his scrutiny. "Are you no' a believer?"

"I know about religion."

"That's no' what I am asking."

"What are you asking?"

"Do you know of God's forgiveness?"

"I—I have read about it in Scripture," she murmured.

"But do you know of it—for yourself?"

"I—nay." The admission pained her in a way she couldn't fathom. She looked down at her hands and thought of how often they had held Neddy's Bible, her heart and head full of questions.

"You must make a choice tae believe, Lael. His way or your way—you canna have both. Ask Him tae show you the truth."

The truth. Though she had no name for it, that was what she longed for. The truth about God. The truth about herself. The truth about sin and forgiveness, prayer and eternity. Beside her, he said no more, but it seemed he was loath to leave her. Yet how could she possibly tell him all that was in her heart? Things she didn't rightly understand herself?

Surely the Almighty had heard her feeble prayers of late and was giving her a way of escape. Although once she'd literally fled from Virginia, she was now willing to walk—nay, run—there once again. That was the simple truth.

But it was not the complete truth. What *was* her motivation to return to a place that seemed to seep the very life from her with its strict, staid ways, tight as corset strings? To answer, she needed only to look at the man beside her. Her feelings for him could no longer be swept aside like so much settlement dust.

As astute as he was, he would soon look at her and know. She, Lael Click, was fickle as the weathervane that sat atop the Bliss barn. She was falling in love with Ian Justus.

Aye, that was the whole truth.

56

Dawn's first light lay pink as a rose petal on the new snow as Lael and Susanna began preparing for Christmas dinner. The men had long since left to go hunting, taking the boys with them, and only little Lael remained behind, playing at one end of the warm hearth.

"Cat got your tongue?" Susanna teased, passing Lael a rolling pin. "I thought I heard you and the doctor up late."

Lael said nothing and continued rolling dough.

Susanna arched an eyebrow. "Why, you look worn to a frazzle. Ain't you slept?"

"Some." But truly, she hadn't. Her muddled emotions wouldn't let her.

Susanna began paring apples. "Sounded like some spirited talkin' to me."

"Well, we're not done talking yet," Lael told her, hearing the men and dogs return to the yard. Excusing herself, she put on her coat and Susanna's shoes and went outside onto the porch. Will and the boys were skinning rabbits in the side yard, and she bypassed them, finding Ian chopping wood behind the barn.

She said without preamble, "I'm considering leaving for Briar Hill in the spring."

He did not lay aside the ax but kept working. "Wheest! You canna expect me tae congratulate you for that."

She folded her arms. "And why not? It will make things all the easier for you as the settlement doctor."

"I'll no' repeat my argument tae you, Lael Click, for you are tae mule-headed a lass tae listen the first time."

"What argument?"

"The one aboot my need of you."

"You only fancy you need me. Any settlement woman can tell you about herbs and the like."

"Nae, 'tis you I need. The people here know and respect you. I am an outlander. And that's all I'll ever be—withoot you."

"But you've had patients—"

"Old Amos and Colonel Barr. Some people passing through the fort, like Sadie Floyd. But few settlement folk."

"What about Granny Sykes?"

He sent the ax into a stump. "'Twas simple enough. You were gone and she settled for me."

Settled? She sighed. He was the finest doctor—nay, man— she'd ever known, yet he spoke the truth. He was an outsider. Settlement folk had ever been leery of strangers. Hadn't she once been suspicious of him herself?

She said quietly, "If I went away, for good, the settlement would have to accept you."

"What choice would they have then? The settlement needs us both."

She could not dispute this. If only she had the gumption to tell him the truth. *I've fallen in love with you, and I must go away before Olivia comes, because I can't bear to see you with another.*

He had always been uncompromisingly honest with her, but he didn't even know she knew about Olivia. Oh, how she wished she'd never set eyes on the miniature, or that Susanna hadn't mentioned her name!

She watched him at work, his handsome face intense and almost brooding, and felt herself give way. He said he needed her. Well, she needed him for entirely different reasons, reasons she didn't rightly understand. She would stay till spring, and they would work together. It sounded so simple. But it was utterly, irrevocably complicated, like stealing honey from a bee gum. The prospect of working alongside him loomed sweet as honey. She would be stung severely, yet she was willing to do this very thing.

She went and lay her hand on his arm. The gesture seemed to catch him off guard. He looked down at her, and there was a poignancy in his face she'd not seen before.

Very carefully she schooled her emotions and said, "I'll work with you, I promise. Till spring."

The answering smile he gave her hurt, and she turned away.

"Till spring," he said. Strangely, it sounded like a vow.

That night, when the candelabra was lit and boughs of mountain laurel gleamed waxy on the mantle with a bit of mistletoe and holly, Lael swept up her hair with ivory combs and put on the gown she'd brought. But she left the silver bracelet behind, rolled up in her work dress. When she came down from the loft, Susanna gave an appreciative gasp.

At once, Lael's confidence fled. "It's too fancy, then. And too wrinkled." She sighed and looked down at her shoeless but stocking feet.

"Law, Lael, you look so lovely . . . even Doc Justus will fancy himself back in Boston," Susanna exclaimed as little Lael came forward to stroke the shiny fabric in awe.

"I have no corset or hoops," she lamented, and without them her skirts did not look fashionably full.

"The color . . ." Susanna said in wonder, wiping her hands on her apron and coming closer. "Why, it's like pink dogwood. And the lace!"

White lace lay pale and fragile as fallen snowflakes about the rounded neck and sleeves. Cut from pale rose silk, the gown's bodice was embroidered with tiny flowers and leaves sewn with silk thread imported from France. It was Lael's favorite gown, more beloved even than the regal purple from which she'd fashioned Susanna's gifts. She'd worn the rose gown only once, when she had danced the minuet at her first Briar Hill ball. She'd not thought to wear it again.

"'Tis called a sack dress," Lael told her. "On account of the back pleat." She turned around to show Susanna the way the pleated fabric hung from her shoulders to the floor like a train. "If you think it's too fancy, I'll—"

But Susanna would have none of it. She disappeared up the loft steps and soon came down in her wedding dress, giddy as a girl, and they laughed at how it strained the seams about her growing waist. They stood at arm's length, sharing each other's delight, just as the men and boys came in from outside.

Little Will and Henry entered first, noisy as wolf cubs, their cold, chapped faces sobering quickly at the sight of the women in their finery. Will had eyes only for Susanna, truly. And Ian? Lael had thought to look away. It wouldn't be fitting to stare at him as if fishing for compliments. But look she did—just for a moment—and found he wasn't looking at her at all.

Her face, already flushed from the heat of the hearth, turned a deeper crimson. Suppose he believed she had worn the dress just to please him! The thought, accompanied by the little notice he had just given her, stung like a bee. She felt ridiculously snubbed—and near tears. She, Ezekial Click's daughter!

Suddenly, little Lael was there, looking up at her with such tender concern Lael knew the hurt she felt must be mirrored on her face. She shut her eyes quickly and prayed a silent, passionate prayer to master her emotions.

In that moment she felt a strange peace pour over her like a pitcher of water. All her hurt over Ian and what he must think of her, all her muddled feelings about Captain Jack, even her grief about Pa and her fears about the future, seemed to wash away. She reached out and touched little Lael's cheek and smiled.

⟋⟍⟋⟍⟋

Christmas dinner was filled with laughter, and they all lingered long at the table, warmed from the mulled cider and sated from the abundance of food. Sitting but an arm's length from Ian, Lael wondered if he was missing Boston and the company of family and friends. As for herself, she felt curiously light in spirit despite his snub. This Christmas rivaled the holidays of her childhood, when a taste of hard candy or a corn-husk doll brought lasting delight.

When the dishes were cleared, Will opened his Bible and read the story of Jesus's birth, and the children listened as attentively as the adults. Beyond the steady cadence of Will's words came the spattering of snow and a draft that blew the candle flame about in a merry dance. Lael wished, childlike, that the seven of them could be snowed in like this forever.

"All right, children, to bed—all of you!" boomed Will, adding another log to the fire.

"But Pa!" the children chorused, rushing him all at once in a frenzied protest.

But there was still corn to be popped, cider to be drunk, and a tale or two of Scotland's fairies and castles to be told by the doctor, followed by his fiddling. And then there were the gifts, exchanged when the candles had nearly smoked out and the wind had driven a deep drift against the cabin steps.

Lael took deep pleasure in the family's appreciation of her presents. She hadn't yet taken out Ian's. It remained hidden in a saddlebag beside her though it would be easy enough to pass to him discreetly as he sat beside her on a bench, one knee brushing the folds of her silk skirts. They faced the fire while Susanna and Will occupied the two chairs, surrounded by the children.

Not once had he spoken to her directly all evening. He hadn't ignored her, truly, but neither did he seek her out as he usually did, and she missed the attention. She stole a look at him as he said something to Will. The firelight illuminated his face, calling out all its rugged lines and making him all the more striking. His face was nearly healed, but he would have a scar above the one eye, she thought ruefully. It seemed odd to her that across from them sat Susanna, unaware of her brother's dark deed. As far as Lael knew, the secret smoldered between the three of them—just she, Simon, and Ian.

He turned to her then and caught her studying him. Flushing, she bent down and took what she'd made from her bags and gave it to him. For a few moments he sat studying the homemade book in his hands before turning the pages. His face was inscrutable, and she couldn't tell what he thought, until he found the braided lock of hair pressed between the pages. For the first time all evening he truly looked at her, lingering on her upswept hair as he held the cut braid across his open palm. And his blueberry eyes were like a mirror then, reflecting his soul's surprise. And she couldn't look away.

Susanna called to her right then to help cut the pies. She got up abruptly, glad to have something to do. The children were clamoring for a bite before bed, and so she served them small pieces, pouring cream and grating a sprinkling of nutmeg on top.

When she returned to the bench, Ian got up to fetch a second cup of cider. When he sat back down beside her, he placed a small oblong pouch in her lap and it sank into the folds of her rose gown. Her hand covered it wonderingly, her fingers stroking the soft buckskin, and it struck a familiar chord.

But she was not the only recipient. He had gifts for them

all—a pocket watch for Will, some fine cloth and a packet of buttons for Susanna, hard candy and a wooden toy for each of the children. She sat watching their enjoyment, and soon all eyes turned to her. Glancing down at the pouch, she had the uncanny feeling that he'd again given her the wrong one.

Turning it upside down, she let the contents spill out into her open hand. *Pearls.* But not the ivory ones she'd mistakenly opened before. These were—could it be?—a very pale pink. They glowed warm and smooth in her palm, their astonishing rosiness unbroken except for a delicate golden clasp. Rarely had she seen anything so lovely.

"'Tis a token of my affection for you," he was saying in her ear, his shoulder pressing against her own. "For your friendship."

Tears sprang to her eyes, not at his gentle words, nor the priceless pearls, but for what he could not say.

'Tis a token of my love for you.

Susanna saved her. She came from behind and took the necklace, attempting to undo the clasp. But after a few moments of fumbling she looked to the doctor. "The clasp is so small!" she exclaimed. "'Tis a task for a surgeon's hands."

And so he obliged, coming to stand behind her. Without a trace of awkwardness he opened the clasp and circled her neck with the strand of pearls. They lay cool and heavy against her warm skin, complementing her gown and catching the candle-light.

"Your gift—" she stammered in a near whisper. "It is so . . . kind."

He swallowed and she could see his throat tighten. Was he as moved as she? But his voice, when it came, was rock solid. "I dinna mean it as a kindness, Lael."

"Are these . . . from Boston?"

"Nae, Scotlain."

"Scotland," she echoed, reaching up to touch them.

323

"From Castle Roslyn, tae be exact."

She looked at him, her face full of questions. "Are these family pearls?"

"They were my maither's. My faither wasna but a poor preacher, ye ken, until he married my maither."

A poor preacher! Hearing him speak of his past, her eyes widened. She remembered the small portraits on the mantle of his cabin. His parents? And these were his mother's pearls? Priceless, indeed.

She looked up then and found Susanna and Will readying for bed. The children were making a fuss and taking their gifts with them, little Lael amusing them all by blowing kisses to Ian before she disappeared up the loft ladder. Watching them go, Lael felt a keen disappointment. It was late, nearly midnight, she guessed. But she suddenly felt far from weary. Was he?

She looked at him openly, wanting him to linger, not wanting the night to end. "You've rarely spoken of your family."

"What do you want tae know?"

She grew thoughtful. "Tell me about your mother."

He looked into the fire and crossed his arms. "Her name was Brenna Roslyn and she was an earl's daughter."

"And your father?"

"Alexander Justus. He was preaching at a revival in Edinburgh when my mother first saw him. She had a heart for spiritual matters. They married soon after."

She could well imagine how it had been. The handsome Scottish preacher, so much like the son, and the lady Brenna, probably smitten at first sight. "And her family? Were they happy with the match?"

"No' at first. But my faither, God be thanked, soon saw them all converted."

She smiled at this, full of wonder at the tale. "And did they live at Castle Roslyn?"

"Aye, and spent half her inheritance printing Bibles." He paused and looked more solemn than she had ever seen him. "They died in a smallpox epidemic when I was twenty."

"Oh, Ian, I'm sorry," she said in a rush, hardly knowing she'd spoken his name. But it was not lost on him. His eyes were full of light and mischief when they met hers again, as if daring her to take it back.

She studied him carefully. "Were you not . . . angry at the Almighty when it happened?"

"Nae, just full of sorrow. The rain falls on the just and the unjust, ye ken."

"You have no other family?"

"I'm an only child."

"And what," she asked, "has become of Castle Roslyn?"

"It waits for me. Or my son. Though it might be a heap of rubble and old roses by now. I've no' been back in five years."

The poignancy in his face turned her heart over. But he spoke with such assurance, full of faith that it was there for him and always would be, and for his son after him. How she would love to see it, she thought, looking into the fire. The same wistful longing she tried so hard to put down returned. She imagined his future son. Handsome. Strong. A man of steadfast convictions. A man of faith. The kind of son she would be proud to call her own.

Her hand went to the pearls again, not cold any longer but warmed by her skin. How she longed to keep them! If she did, she would always have something to remember him by. A token of affection, he had called it. But hearing the story of Brenna and Alexander Justus, she knew she could not hold onto them. They were fine for a wife or a daughter, truly. But too priceless to be given in mere friendship.

"I—they are so lovely—but I—I cannot keep them."

Because of Olivia, she could not say.

325

She spoke slowly, afraid to look at him. "But if I return them, I'll need your help."

He hesitated but she'd already turned her back to him, waiting for him to unfasten the clasp. He took them off as effortlessly as he had put them on, and the sudden spareness of her neck was no match for the barrenness in her heart.

Had she hurt him? She feared she had and was hurt in kind. But his silence was in no way nettlesome or brooding or dejected. Clutching the pearls in one hand, his voice, when it finally came, was near her ear and held only warmth and understanding and tenderness.

"Till spring," he told her.

57

"I'm so housebound I feel fretful," Susanna exclaimed to Lael, shucking off her apron. "Let's walk out to the knob."

It was the last day of the year, the day before Lael would depart the Bliss cabin. She felt fretful herself but for entirely different reasons. There was to be but one more night of shared supper and conversation and Ian's fiddling and the children's funning, and Lael was already feeling the loss.

Leaving the children behind with the men, Lael and Susanna started out. Soon they were carrying their coats as the sun winked at them, melting the frost and warming the woods to almost spring-like temperatures.

"I never did see any Indian sign up here atop the knob," Susanna told her. "But it would make a fine lookout, be it redman or white."

"Seems like you can see clear to Virginia," Lael said as the knob came into view. "Can't you just picture a cabin right here, with a wide porch taking in this pretty place?"

"This land's here for the takin'," Susanna told her. "Though up so high and on so much rock it'd be awful hard to farm. But say you were to marry somebody other than a farmer. I reckon the doctor could give a string of them pretty pearls for this piece."

Lael looked at her friend, about to hush her teasing, but there was no mirth in Susanna's eyes.

"Lael, we need to speak plain to one another."

"All right."

They continued on side by side until they stood atop the rocky knob, a dizzying drop just steps away. The sun shone unhindered here as the trees had fallen away, leaving only a mass of jagged dark rock overlooking the river valley below.

Susanna spoke slowly, as if weighing her words. "I never saw you and Doc Justus together in one place until here lately. Always before, you come alone or he did. I knew you'd met, is all. But I never figured on him falling in love with you."

Lael turned, suddenly feeling as though she were falling. "What?"

"Over Christmas it was made plain to me. To Will too."

"But he hardly looked at me!"

"I know. And that was what give him away."

Lael said nothing, only shook her head.

But Susanna kept on, as gently as she could. "Seems like you were a terrible temptation to him, lookin' as you did. He's a different sort than Simon, Lael. The doctor's got a lot of self-control. Maybe it comes from tryin' to live a godly life. But you nearly got the better of him."

"Susanna!" Hearing such talk, so private and unspeakable, made her face burn like never before. Oh, it was one thing to think such things, but never to speak them. Never to—

"Now I know you meant no harm by it, Lael. You merely wanted to look sightly and wear your fancy dress, same as me. It was Christmas, after all. But it seemed at times like it was more than he could bear."

"You make it sound so . . . *wicked.*"

Susanna cracked a knowing smile. "I think he wanted to kiss you good and hard, is all."

Lael turned away and looked out on the gentle swell of mountains without truly seeing them. In her most private thoughts, she'd stopped short of having Ian hold her . . . kiss her. Nay, that was not altogether true. Lately, on cold nights, she'd wondered how it would be to lay alongside him, to be warmed by him.

"I don't know as a man can be in love—for sure and for certain in love—with more than one woman at a time. Will says it's nigh impossible," Susanna confided. "So I don't know where that puts poor Olivia."

Poor Olivia? Ian Justus in love with Lael Click? Even the joining of those words, the very idea, seemed laughable. Susanna came and placed an arm around Lael's shoulders. "You don't have to say anything at all, Lael. I can just look at you and tell you love him right back. You might as well try hidin' a light underneath a bushel basket."

Lael sighed. There was no use pretending she didn't, perplexed as she was. "So you think he knows too?"

"Nay, that's the bewilderment of it. I don't think he knows at all. I think he believes you're still pinin' for Simon."

Or Captain Jack.

Dismayed, Lael looked down at her borrowed boots. Was this what he'd thought when she'd given him back the pearls? But there was still the matter of Olivia. They were more Olivia's pearls than hers.

"Oh, Susanna." Her voice was almost pleading in its sorrow. "I don't know what to do."

"I don't know as you can do anything. Except pray."

On New Year's Day, Lael felt a despondency she'd never known. She rode back down the ridge behind Ian, with the mule and Tuck in tow. Neither of them spoke a word, but the silence between them was not burdensome.

All about them the snow lay melting under a January sun. Her breath came in ragged clouds on the crisp air, and although it was not bitter, she leaned into him as she'd done on Christmas Eve. Her arms were anchored firmly about his waist, and the big bay beneath them moved with an easy grace.

At the south fork of Cozy Creek, the trees thinned and provided them with a view of the river bottom below. In the distance, not far from the meandering Kentucke, was her cabin, crowning the rise and bordered by a bleak winter tracing of trees.

They halted, taking in the expansive sight, and his voice cut into the stillness. "Are you expecting company, Miss Click?"

The smile on her face, brought about by his teasing tone, faded as she caught sight of the cabin. Thick gray smoke plumed from its rock chimney and rolled toward the river, buffeted by a west wind. A tremor of alarm shot through her and she felt a fierce, protective rush toward her homeplace. In that moment she wondered how she could leave it, now or ever.

"Expecting trouble is more like it," she replied, wondering at the gall of someone who would set up in her cabin while she was away, building such a fire as to burn the place down. And her rifle! She'd left it behind in its rightful place over the mantle, thinking it undisturbed. If anything should happen to her gun . . .

If it were a traveler put out by the storm, in want of a dry spot, she could understand. But travelers were few in winter, and by now, with the thaw, any such trespasser should have been well on his way.

By the time they reached the cabin, her dander was high. Without waiting for him to help her down, she slipped off the bay and made for the porch in her stocking feet, taking notice of the large, muddy footprints of someone who had gone before.

With Ian at her heels, she pushed open the cabin door. And there at the table, cleaning his rifle, sat Ransom.

Ransom Dunbar Click had come home. That first night he lay a considerable sum of money on the table from Neddy's savings and divided it equally with her. When she protested, he said slowly and thoughtfully, "I reckon you earned it, seein' Uncle Neddy like you did when nobody else would. Besides, he'd want you to have it."

And so she tucked her portion away in her trunk, thinking of how it might carry her to Briar Hill come spring. But the money mattered little and by the second day was forgotten. What mattered was that Ransom was home—Ransom, who had grown so tall he had to stoop to enter the door frame, whose big boots now dwarfed her moccasins as they dried together by the fire, and whose appetite promised to keep her elbow deep in flour and meal as he ate his fill of bread and pudding and pie. And he was only fourteen.

That first night they sat up and talked long past midnight.

"When I got your letter about Uncle Neddy, I knew I'd best shuck off. But I had to study on things a while first," he told her, depositing a small plug of tobacco in his jaw. "Turned out to be what I'd been waitin' for, hatin' Bardstown like I did."

"I hardly recognized you, it's been so long."

"Too long. I ain't no town-lover, that's for sure. Bardstown was makin' a hard man out of me. Ever spring I dreamed of settin' out corn and tobacco and havin' my own homeplace. But I couldn't leave Ma, not till she was settled. When I got your letter and learned the facts about Neddy, I just had to come."

Her smile was bright despite Ian's simple good-bye on the doorstep and the hollowness she felt without him. "I'm glad you've come back, Ransom. You'll be good company, truly."

He looked about the tidy cabin, noting its clean spareness and the herbs that crowded the rafters. It might have been a man's cabin, save the colorful quilt atop the corner bed and the rag rug at the washstand. A bunch of bittersweet graced the table.

"I misdoubted you could keep on here, being so lonesome and the like. But I done took a look around and things ain't unsightly. You sure got a heap of firewood."

"The wood's not my doing," she admitted, and told him of coming home and finding it split and stacked, as well as the fence mended and new shingles on the shed. She told him too about the burning of the barn and Hero McClary and how not a cinder had touched the cabin or the springhouse on that windless night. But she didn't mention how the McClarys met their demise.

Despite his fatigue from travel, his eyes shone. "I been prayin' the Lord would give you your daily provision and keep you from harm. I reckon He has."

His words gave her a slight start, and she felt the boy before her was more stranger than brother. But the warmth of his manner and the openness of his speech drew her in. She studied him, trying to tease out what had changed about him, despite his being much the same. He was lean like Neddy and taller than she herself, and the winning smile that had been his in childhood was warm and unaltered, as was his shock of dark hair.

"You ain't my baby brother no more, for sure and for certain," Lael teased, lapsing into settlement speech.

With a grin, he leaned forward and spit into the fire, a gesture she had always disliked but one that oddly did not mar his charm. All at once he sobered and discarded the tobacco.

"I ain't the same, Sister," he said. "I died back there in Bardstown. Died to my trespasses and sins. You see, like it or not, I'm a believer."

A believer. What did it all mean? Lael recounted the number of believers she knew. Ian Justus. Will and Susanna. The mother of Sadie Floyd. And, in her quiet way, Ma Horn. And now, her own brother.

Truly, they needed a preacher in the settlement.

58

Blessedly, there was a break in the weather. The sun deigned to shine on their first medical call together, banishing the rain yet leaving behind mud as thick and black as chicory coffee. Will had returned Pandora hale and hearty, and Lael now rode beside Ian, saddlebags full of herbs, just as his own were full of his medicines. Curiously, the call had not come from Fort Click or even the settlement itself but from Cobb's Station, many miles north, a recent hub of military activity.

"I never thought to see you packing a gun," she said as they rode out.

"Neither did I," he confessed, eyeing hers. "But 'twas either that or have half the militia accompany us, including Colonel Barr."

"Well, if you can shoot as well as you fiddle, I might have left mine at home," she teased.

He grinned, then sobered. "I'm sorry we have tae spend the night. With all the soldiers aboot, you'll likely have half a dozen marriage proposals by morning."

She squinted up at the sun beneath her straw hat and smiled. "What a bother."

He tipped his hat forward. "Of course, I could simply tell them you're my wife."

"And what would you do with me come nightfall?" she said. "Best say I'm your sister, like Abram of old." She'd just read the

Old Testament account and was amazed that a man of God could be so deceitful.

"The lie earned him nae favors with Pharaoh or the Almighty," he reminded, reaching for his canteen and offering her a drink.

"Or Sarai," Lael added, taking out her own water. "Scripture says she was very beautiful."

"Bonny women drive men tae desperate measures," he murmured, eyeing the woods.

She leaned forward and patted Pandora's sleek neck. All her carefully ordered emotions, reviewed and subdued in the eight days since New Year's, began fraying. What if Susanna was right? What if he *was* in love with her?

Mercifully, the pickets of the station finally came into view. It was dusk when they rode in, bone weary and famished. An aura of tension penetrated the gloom, and when the gates swung open to reveal a dozen armed men, Lael knew there had been trouble.

An officer approached and took their horses with a terse command. "Major Bristow needs you in the northeast blockhouse." There they found several men on pallets, while one, the most gravely wounded, lay on top of a table near the fire. But this was not why they'd been summoned to the fort in the first place.

The major greeted them, his news of the attack followed by a coughing fit. The fort's commanding officer was sorely in need of a doctor, as was his wife, who awaited Lael in a nearby cabin. *Consumption*, she thought, and glanced at Ian who was removing her cape and then his own coat. But the prostrate soldiers demanded their immediate attention.

There had been a small skirmish shortly after dawn when the livestock was driven down to the river to drink. A small party of Indians had been hiding in the dense brush along the bank and fired upon the unsuspecting soldiers.

Lael could see straightaway their bandages needed changing, and she set about doing this, fetching warm water and a pile of clean cloths, while Ian tended to the man on the table, talking in low tones with the major.

The clock on the mantle ticked sure and steady as a heartbeat and proclaimed it nearly midnight when she finally sat down, dog tired, to watch him work. Many miles they'd ridden this day, and he had yet to rest. Would he stay up all night?

Soon a soldier entered carrying a tray of venison broth and bread. From where she sat, the aroma smelled like the richest of foods, and even the stale bread was a delight. Ian said a brief blessing, his voice quiet and steady, and they sat side by side, crumbling the bread into the broth and sharing a jug of sweet cider.

"You're an answer tae my prayers, ye ken."

"I've not done much," she said, ashamed she'd held out on working with him so long. "You seem to manage fine all by yourself."

"'Tis a strange thing tae finish one war and begin another," he uttered, finishing his food.

"George Washington's war, you mean? And now this?"

"Aye." He took the empty bowl from her hands. "You need tae rest. Take the loft. I canna sleep tonight."

Without protest she climbed the steps to the simple pallet, guided by the light of a single candle. Before dawn she was on her feet again, as much to check on him as the wounded men.

"I dinna ken," he said from the shadows. "Tho' the wounds are clean, they still fester."

She came to stand beside him and looked down at the unconscious soldier. "All the lead is out?"

"Every ball."

The man's pallor beneath his bushy beard was ghostlike and his breathing uneasy. Some dim memory pulled at her from the past. "I remember Pa saying the Indians used some sort of poison to taint their lead and arrowheads for battle."

"Poison?"

"Some herb or plant extract that could taint a man's flesh."

"And the remedy?"

"I don't recollect exactly," she said wearily. "But a walnut poultice gives the best draw."

He ran one hand through his hair in agitation, though he managed a wry grin. "I'm afraid I dinna have any walnuts in my medical bag."

She looked up at him and smiled. "You don't, but I do. I picked a good bushel for Ma Horn in the fall and kept a few in my saddlebags. But we'll have to borrow some salt and flour to make the poultice."

Together they began the tedious process of cracking the tough hulls, then beating them with salt and flour to make a paste. He watched closely as she smeared the mixture on clean cloths and placed them over the man's chest and leg wounds.

"If walnuts are scarce, sometimes honey will do. We'll know by morning anyhow." She turned and began washing up, aware that he watched her. "I suppose they don't teach you such things in medical school."

He shook his head, and the lines of weariness deepened about his eyes. "Walnut poultices? Nae. I'm beginning tae find my training sorely lacking."

The other men began to stir, and Lael moved about spooning them broth and water until Major Bristow appeared, calling her away to see his wife. She was glad to go, breathing in the fresh air outside the stale blockhouse, taking in the gunmetal-gray sky and the persisting feeling of gloom all around her.

She was ushered into a spacious cabin where a woman lay in a corner bed. Lael started at the sight of her, so different than what she'd expected. This was a mere girl, a fading flower next to the much older major. Lael sensed the harshness and deprivations of frontier life did not suit her. Indeed, she hardly smiled and returned no greeting as Lael came near.

"Your husband tells me you feel poorly," Lael said. "Perhaps I can help, if you tell me what the trouble is."

The girl colored, then rested thin hands atop her stomach. "I think I might be expecting but hope to heaven I'm not."

Lael was relieved, for this was a simple matter next to consumption. "I'll just ask you some questions, and that should tell us if a baby's on the way and when. Dr. Justus is more skilled than I in these matters, but he's busy treating the wounded men. He can follow up with you when I'm finished."

Tiny and narrow-hipped, she hardly seemed fit physically to be a mother. Lael blended some raspberry tea to help with any nausea and calculated the baby would come before the heat of July. The girl looked sour as buttermilk at the news, though lately the thought of babies turned Lael herself to mush. As she packed up her saddlebags, she remembered her own vivid dream. Of childbirth and Captain Jack. Even in her dream the desire to hold her baby had been sure and strong. Would the major's wife not feel the same in time?

As she shut the cabin door and walked across the busy common, the feeling of being hemmed in grew stronger. Surely they could get away soon. She missed hearth and home in this forbidding place, though at least Ransom was home to tend to matters in her absence. She chafed at the thought of the long ride ahead. Emptying herself of all feeling when with Ian was proving harder than she'd ever imagined.

The blockhouse was empty save two soldiers moving among the wounded. "Where's Dr. Justus?" she asked.

One shrugged. "He wanted to see the prisoners, though I ain't sure why. They're to be executed on the morrow."

Prisoners? She turned to go, but one soldier came forward and caught her arm. "Major Bristow don't want any womenfolk around them Cherokee."

She pulled her arm free. "I don't take orders from the major. Now tell me where Dr. Justus is, or I'll hunt him down myself."

His expression turned surly. "You ain't no Indian lover, are ye?"

She opened the door and went out, saddlebags heavy in her arms. Truly, she didn't need their help. It was obvious enough where Ian was. In the middle of the common stood a crude building, heavily guarded, with metal bars at the lone window. Why hadn't she noticed it before?

The soldier dogged her every step. She walked with confidence, like she'd been ordered to the stockade instead of away from it, and shifted the saddlebags in her arms. Her purposeful stride paid off and a guard moved to open the thick door. But the man behind her whined, "Major Bristow said she ain't supposed to mingle with them Cherokee."

But she was already inside despite the angry murmur of the soldiers looking on. Her breath caught as she took in the Indians, their familiar dress and bearing. Ian looked up, warning in his gaze. Whirling, she pinned the soldier to the wall with one look. "Cherokee? Don't you even know the difference? These men are Shawnee."

Overcome, she kicked the door shut with her boot, blocking out the sight of his loathsome face. Three Shawnee warriors were being held in the cold, smelly room. Not a blanket was in sight, nor a scrap of food or water. The smell of urine assaulted her. Legs weak, she dropped her load by the door. The Shawnee were staring at her. At least one of them looked familiar.

She uttered the only Shawnee words she knew, "*Oui-shi-cat-tu-oui.*" *Be strong.* Long ago when he'd returned from captivity, Pa had taught her this, and she'd never forgotten. It seemed to sum up his life among the Indians and admonish her as well.

One Indian, who looked to be a chief, echoed the words back to her. She took in the eagle feathers affixed to his hair with a silver disk, his buckskin leggins and frock shirt, the fine beadwork on his moccasins, so like Captain Jack's. Looking at him brought back a swift, intense longing, further muddying her feelings. He sat proudly on the dirt floor beside another warrior, his face impassive.

At the back of the dim room lay a third man, mortally wounded. She smelled decay and saw clearly the devastating injury Ian worked to treat. Gut shot, she knew. When he drew back, she looked away from the bloody rags that bound him. She could do but one thing to help.

She pushed open the door. "I need hot broth and fresh water," she ordered, but the men only stared, some glaring with contempt, others simply stoic.

One soldier said, "We'd sooner scalp 'em than feed 'em. And since we cain't scalp 'em, we ain't gonna feed 'em either."

"They're dead men tomorrow, anyhow," said another. "Best not waste good grub."

The hate in their voices nearly made her falter. Looking on, Ian rose from tending the men and went to speak to the nearest officer, and in time he returned with what she requested. She took it gratefully, though she felt it mattered little to men who had hours to live. Working together, they did what they could to make the men comfortable, easing the dying man with a blend of her strongest herbs and Ian's most able medicines.

Finally she sat back, spent and unable to ignore the forlorn feeling that permeated the fetid room. If only she'd known what the day had in store, she wouldn't have come. Ian might handle it dispassionately, outwardly stoic at least, but she could not. As long minutes ticked by, memories of Pa and Captain Jack and the past were being resurrected, and she felt herself unraveling.

"We canna do any more this day," Ian finally said, and she breathed a silent prayer of thanks, scooping up her saddlebags and following him to the corral.

Her melancholy deepened as they rode out. At the gate, Ian was detained by Major Bristow, but Lael kept riding, pushing

Pandora ahead, thinking they might not make it home before nightfall, if they ever did.

Were more Shawnee waiting outside the walls? She looked around at the naked winter woods and ridges with a growing unease. The cold bit into her, and she lowered her head in the rising wind, a light snow stinging her damp face.

She was crying now without really knowing why, and she couldn't stop shaking. Within minutes she heard the drum of hoofbeats behind her, and the sound only made her ride faster. She wanted to be alone, to put distance between her and the past. But Pandora was no match for the big bay. All at once they were neck and neck and Ian was reaching for her reins, slowing her. He stopped her completely beneath an enormous elm, out of the way of the falling snow. She dismounted and turned her back on him, leaning against the rough trunk.

Without a word he draped his wool coat around her shaking shoulders, though it was his arms she wanted. She saw his hair had come loose of its tie and hung like a black curtain against the white muslin of his shirt. She'd not stood so near him before. Why, she barely grazed his chin. It had been the same with Captain Jack.

She shut her eyes tight, aching to shut out the angst in her heart as well. His voice was laced with misery, and that hurt her too. "Lael, I never meant for this tae happen. If I'd known aboot the Shawnee, I'd no' have taken you there."

She nodded, understanding.

"I'm glad it wasna *him*, ye ken." His breath hung like a cloud in the bitter air. He looked every bit as grieved as she felt. If it had been Captain Jack, what would she have done? Something rash, surely. But the silver bracelet beneath her sleeve now seemed cold and tarnished and empty of meaning. She didn't know how he was or where he was or even *if* he was. Would she ever?

Her voice was brittle. "Did you ask to see the Shawnee?"

His mouth tightened. "Ask is a wee bit weak for what I did. The major finally gave in, but I couldna save the worst of the three. And he wouldna listen when I argued tae let them go free."

"Holding them—mistreating them—will only make matters worse. The Shawnee will retaliate one way or another."

"And the conflict will continue," he agreed. "But both sides will answer for their evil in the end, ye ken."

She looked down. "I'm beginning to see the way of things, how there will be no peace, just like you said. Sometimes I think I can't stay here another day to see Kentucke overrun with settlers and soldiers and the destruction it will bring."

The snow was swirling now, the lovely flakes like lace upon his blue coat. Though her expression grew firm, almost resigned, tears continued to make their way to her chin. She kept her eyes on his muddy boots and wondered what he thought of her silence and tears and confusion. Practicality prodded her to pull herself together and consider matters at hand. Ian needed his coat back, and if they didn't start soon, they'd both be benighted in the woods. But before she turned away to go, he stepped nearer.

Gently, ever so carefully, as if she was spun glass and he might break her, he framed her damp face with cold, callused hands and brought her head up. At his touch she trembled and saw a flash of concern darken his eyes. Was he thinking of Olivia?

His hands fell away and he stepped back. Looking at him, she felt bewildered. He was the doctor again, his expression carefully schooled, betraying nothing.

With great effort she emptied her voice of all emotion. "We'd best make haste or we'll find ourselves frozen by dusk." With a nod he helped her into the saddle, taking care, she thought, not to look at her again. They rode side by side for miles without speaking, but strangely, the silence was full of solace, and she felt that he understood her, even as she struggled to understand herself.

59

One dreary January eve there came a knock, and even before she answered, Lael knew who it was. Ransom stood behind her as Ian emerged from the rain into the cozy cabin.

"I've been tae the Blisses," he said, eyeing Lael. "And I couldna pass by withoot stopping tae see my favorite patient."

Since the fiasco at Cobb's Station, Lael had been housebound with a severe cold, unable to make any calls. He'd stopped to see her more than once and dosed her with some of his own remedies, but none, she informed him, had been as effective as her herbs.

As he hung up his coat on the peg by the door, she felt a queer, near speechless joy. "Come in and thaw out, and I'll fix you something warm."

As he sat down by the fire, she set about grating her best brick of tea and adding a generous amount of ginseng. Soon the voices of the men were as steady as the rain on the roof. Ransom had taken up his pipe again, but just as abruptly put it out as she approached with the steaming cups.

To her surprise, he stood up. "Pardon me, Doc Justus. But I'm off to hunt."

Lael stared at him. "Hunting? In this weather? You'll soon be as sick as I was."

Shamelessly he winked at her. "I hunt rain or shine, just like Pa."

She felt her dander rise, but across from her Ian seemed nonplussed. She passed him a cup and kept one for herself. He'd taken Ransom's chair, and she sat down in her own across from him, facing the fire. An awkwardness crept in and she hated that it came between them. Did he feel it too? Yet she dared not look at him. "I—I'm sorry about Ransom leaving so all-fired fast."

"I'm no! How are you?"

She looked up then. How was it possible, she wondered, that his eyes, even in the shadows, were such a startling, soul-arresting blue? "Much better," she answered, stifling a sneeze.

His eyes turned intense. "So how are you, *truly*?"

Truly? Still sore from Cobb's Station. Still thinking of Captain Jack. And Olivia. Still wondering about the man who now sits staring at me. "I'm better now, in body and spirit," she said simply but sensed her answer didn't satisfy him.

He took a drink. "English tea, Miss Click?"

She smiled faintly at his formality. "Nay, Dr. Justus. Mostly ginseng."

He raised an eyebrow. "Ginseng. 'Tis in my book, the one you made for me."

"Aye." She nodded and prattled on, color high, despising herself. "Ginseng is a medicinal herb that flowers in July. 'It cheers the heart even of a man that has a bad wife, and makes him look down with great composure on the crosses of the world.' And its leaves make a pleasant tea."

He smiled and a bit of her nervousness passed. But with him so near, she could never be at her ease. Even if his company was the most pleasant thing she knew.

"So," she said, "you've been to see Will and Susanna. Are they well?"

"Aye. They asked the same aboot you."

"Oh? And what did you tell them?"

"I told them I would come tae see."

They were making polite conversation, and she found it maddening. She was past all pretense now. Each time she saw him his nearness gnawed at her, and it seemed nothing between

343

them would ever be right . . . until he'd taken her in his arms. She thought it now as she sat across from him and tried not to notice the way the wind and rain had whipped his hair into damp waves. Or that his linen shirt, no longer white but more a dingy gray, still fit his sturdy shoulders so snug despite the slight tear in the sleeve that she longed to mend.

She sensed he had something on his mind, and she feared it was Olivia. Not since Susanna had spoken her mind at the knob had Lael given serious thought to her belief that he loved her and not Olivia. He didn't—couldn't—love her. He was always so careful with her, rarely touched her, never let his eyes linger on her overlong. She was his friend and fellow helper. Nothing more. But oh, how she wanted more . . .

She never had to wait long before he spoke his mind. She almost smiled when he looked straight at her and said, "There's tae be a revival in Lexington, and I came tae ask if you care tae go."

"A revival? When?"

"In a fortnight. The tenth of February, tae be exact."

She knew she must look surprised. A revival in Lexington, and they didn't even have a preacher in the settlement. His question, spoken innocently enough, seemed to ask something more of her besides, and she sensed it was far more than a mere invitation, after all. It seemed strangely like . . . a test.

When she didn't answer, he said, "A fellow Scot will be preaching there. His name is Duncan Leith. He was a friend of my faither's."

Her face brightened then faded. "Can't both of us be gone at once. I—"

"I've asked a fellow physician from Lexington tae come in our stead, tae stay on at the fort until we return."

"I guess I'll go, then."

"I wanted tae ask Ransom besides. 'Tis a wee bit of a journey. We'd have tae stay the night in a tavern and take our meals there."

She sat back in her chair and cupped the warm mug in her hands. "I've not been to Lexington in years." Not since Pa's court-martial. She took a sip of tea, the excitement of something new and unexpected dawning on her face. "And it's been a long while since I've heard a true preacher."

"All right then. Ask Ransom tae come. If he canna, Colonel Barr may go in his stead."

"Colonel Barr!"

He smiled. "God's ways are a wee bit mysterious, tae be sure."

Like yours, she felt like answering. He finished his tea and now stood looking down at her.

"Why, you've hardly dried out," she protested.

"It doesna matter, truly. I'll be wet all over again by the time I reach the fort."

"Oh, please stay . . ." It was the closest she'd ever come to asking something of him, and she teetered on the brink of taking his arm.

He hesitated. "If I stay till Ransom returns, that might be a verra long time. Besides, we have nae proper chaperone . . . and no' a single courting candle tae be had." His eyes went to the mantle as if in search of a candlestick and then fell on her again, full of fun.

Her lips parted, then closed again. *But I miss you*, she could not say. Their time together over Christmas, bittersweet though it was, begged repeating. She followed him to the door and, on impulse, helped him on with his coat. If the gesture surprised him, he gave no sign of it. He stood a pace apart, hat in his hands.

"You havena changed your mind aboot Briar Hill?"

Oddly, the simple question hurt her. "Nay," she said softly. "I'm still thinking on it."

When he'd gone, she stood, hands on the latch, hating to shut the door on his presence. Soft as sap she was becoming! Ransom found her by the fire, sitting very still and staring into the flames.

"Why, you're wet and then some," she said.

He took a chair and made a move to dry off. "I just had to set my traps."

She shook her head in wonderment. "Maybe you *are* like Pa."

"Actually, I have to confess—it ain't no traps I've set. Well, maybe a small one. For that purty little gal over on Drowning Crick."

"What? You've not been here three weeks. You sure haven't wasted any time finding her."

He grinned. "A man's not meant to be alone."

"You're hardly a man yet," she chided.

"I'll be old enough come spring."

She sighed. "Well, I'll be glad when you're settled up at Neddy's, like you plan. Living alone was hard on him. When I last saw Neddy, he had the look of a man in need of a good woman. Maybe it isn't good for a man to be alone, like Scripture says."

He crumbled some tobacco and lit his pipe. "You could take a lick of your own medicine." She looked at him, and he continued matter-of-factly, "Ain't you ever gonna get married?"

She stopped rocking suddenly but said nothing. Her eyes were on her hands now, and she pretended to make a fuss over the cut she had taken skinning a deer he'd shot that morning.

He went on, guileless. "I never cared for Simon much. But I like the doctor a heap."

So do I, she mused.

He puffed on his pipe in silence for a time before saying, "I wish you wouldn't try so dadgum hard not to like the doc, Sister. It's plain to see you're sweet as sorghum over him."

Her chin came up. "Sweet as sorghum!"

He pulled his chair closer to her own, his expression conspiratorial. "How'd you figure it'd settle if you just told him?"

"Told him what?"

"That you're plumb crazy about him."

She gave an agitated push to her rocker, face hot, thinking she should just go on to bed. But she couldn't resist setting him down a tad. "It's the man who does the telling, you'd best remember, Ransom Click. I'm no Jezebel."

"So you *do* love him."

She sighed. "I'm fond of him, I reckon."

He hooted and she jumped a bit, annoyed.

His grin growing wider, he asked, "And is he *fond* of you besides?"

"Nay," she said flatly with a firm shake of her head. "His heart lies in Boston. With a lady named Olivia."

He fell quiet, puffing on his pipe. "Olivia. That's a mighty fancy name."

"Word is, she'll be here come spring."

He quieted again, taking in all the facts.

She stirred from her rocker, her heart so overfull and sensitive she feared it might burst. "And since we're setting things straight, you might as well know that Ian came over to ask if we'd go to Lexington with him—to a revival. And you also need to know I'm not a—a believer."

He looked straight at her. "I bet Miss Olivia is."

She looked hard at him, too tired for a drawn-out discussion but too curious to quit. "How so?"

He set his pipe on his knee. "Doc Justus ain't one to tie to no unbeliever. Scripture is dead set against it."

She stood stone still on the loft ladder, tempted to question him further, but she was too weary. Best to puzzle it out herself in the morning, she decided, with Neddy's Bible.

His voice came again just as she collapsed on the bed, and it almost seemed he spoke to himself. "I know you ain't a believer, Sister. But that don't stop me from wishing it was so. Or praying that it comes to pass."

347

60

Ransom's voice, when it came, drowned out the pounding of the rain on the roof. "Where's Doc Justus?"

Lael shrugged, then sneezed, further ruffled by the disappointment in his voice. "Gone home, I reckon."

Rarely did Ian bid her good-bye at the door after they'd made a call together somewhere in the settlement. Lately his habit had been to stay on, taking supper with them or at least talking some with Ransom. But today he had departed immediately, seeming preoccupied and a bit distant. She felt a bit wounded, too quick to catch his every mood.

"That's a cryin' shame," he said, going to the hearth and removing a skillet from the spider. "I made a heap of supper."

She smiled despite herself and peeked into the pan. "Smells good enough to eat. I'm glad the doctor passed on lest he find out you're the better cook."

He grinned back at her and began ladling generous helpings into bowls. It was just one of the things she'd noticed about him since his homecoming. He didn't shirk women's work, as Pa would have called it. And he took notice when she was tired or unable to cook and did his part, and sometimes, when she came in tuckered from a call, he did her part too.

"Tastes like Ma's cooking," she told him appreciatively after he'd said the blessing.

He grinned. "Sometimes Ma needed a hand, so I learned a

few tricks. But just so you don't get too set on my victuals, the cookin' stops when the plowin' starts."

She smiled again, her sour mood sweetening a bit. He took her attention for the next hour by drawing a crude map of their farm, outlining for her the timberland he hoped to turn into tobacco and cotton. There was a plow for sale at the fort, the kind that was all the buzzel in the east, and he was thinking of buying it. "Now's the time to do it, iffen we're ever, now that we got the cash."

It pleasured her to listen to him but she offered a word of caution. "Just take care and leave some trees."

"You sound just like Pa." He pushed the map aside and took out a pipe he'd been whittling.

She wondered that he still called him Pa after he knew all the facts, but she supposed it was a hard habit to break. Neddy would simply be uncle to him, and no more. She took up some knitting by the fire, absently working on some socks.

"You ever stop to think," he said quietly, "that Pa's not really dead . . . just somewheres else?"

Her knitting stilled. "What do you mean?"

"What if he's not drowned, Lael? That old trapper he was with saw him go under, but they never found his body."

"Oh?" she said.

"I thought it was queer myself. Pa's well known. Word spread along the river. Sooner or later a body's bound to wash up."

She sighed. "I disbelieved he was drowned myself when I first heard. I like to think he's gone off somewhere real peaceful-like."

"Back to his Indian life?"

She couldn't hide her surprise. This was exactly what she had thought, but she'd always dismissed it as fancy imaginings. She wondered if she should tell Ransom about Captain Jack. "We may never know."

He whittled faster now, dropping shavings onto the floor. "Sometimes I have a hankerin' to go find out. Take the Warrior's Trace up to them Shawnee towns and—"

"They'd have your scalp!"

He stared at her. "Don't you want to know for sure?"

"Nay, not enough to put you in danger. Besides, what would Ma do with a second husband if her first came back?"

He grinned, speculating. "Sure would be interesting. The barrister's not a bad sort. But he ain't Pa."

They fell silent for a time, and she thought how nice it was to have him beside her after so long, taking away some of the sting of her lonesomeness. *Till spring*, she thought. She would enjoy his company till then, though she hadn't told him she might be leaving. Only Ian knew.

He held the pipe up to the light. "Why do you reckon the doctor took off so sudden-like today?" She shrugged, but he persisted. "You two have a spat?"

"Nay, he just received a letter—some unsettling news from Scotland, though he didn't say just what it was."

He lit his other pipe and smoke soon wreathed his head, making him look like a fallen angel. "This here's mighty fine tobacco the doctor give me. Scotland, you say? That's a far piece. Reckon he's thinkin' of goin' back there?"

"I have no idea," she said, miserable at the thought.

"I hear he's got some high and mighty title. And yet here he is, dallying with the likes of us Clicks."

His expression grew reflective, but before he could say more she switched to a safer subject. "So when am I going to meet your girl?"

"Annie?" He took another draw on his pipe. "At the barn raisin.'"

"What barn raising?"

"Ours," he told her. "On Saturday next. It's got to be done

before spring plowin' and summer's heat. I've asked Annie's pa and brothers. The doctor too."

"Well, now's a fine time to tell me!" she exclaimed, gladness filling her. At last she would not have to look at the heap of blackened rubble any longer. And it was a handy excuse to be near Ian again, and meet Annie besides.

"I figure we'll roast us a pig. There's some fine ones runnin' wild over on Hackberry Ridge. Nothin' sweeter than a hog fattened on chestnuts. Besides, we got to have somethin' to feed all them people."

"Who all did you invite?"

"Nearly everybody but the McClarys," he said. "No sense invitin' that clan to rebuild a barn they burned down."

61

With the approach of the barn raising, Lael's thoughts of leaving the settlement in spring weren't as consuming as they once had been. Now that she was working with Ian, and Ransom had come home, her life seemed more settled. Yet the upheaval in her heart continued as she thought of Olivia and her impending visit in spring. Though Ian never spoke of her, Susanna's words lingered in Lael's mind, overshadowing all she did.

The coming revival in Lexington was also on her mind. Though she'd told no one, she anticipated it in a way she didn't understand. She hoped to speak to Preacher Leith in private. She had composed some heartfelt questions she reckoned only a preacher could answer. They would be staying at the Blue Coat Inn, and it seemed both Ransom and Colonel Barr were to go.

On the day of the barn raising, Will and Susanna and the children rode over from Cozy Creek in a clear, cool dawn. Will was soon helping Ransom yard logs to the site, while Susanna set about helping Lael in the cabin. For the past few days, Ransom had been hard at work chasing pigs on Hackberry Ridge, and now it was Lael's turn to prepare the two he had taken. A spit in the side yard was already smoking and browning the meat, while inside the cabin a collection of fruit and game pies were baking.

About midmorning, a fresh cambric apron about her waist, Lael greeted a crowd of settlers arriving on horseback, many driving dry sleds laden with sundry tools. Watching them in the cool February air, she felt a bit lighthearted. Susanna, heavy with her coming child, kept to the cabin and tended the food, while Lael roamed the yard, minding the roasting meat and making small talk with the other women. Try as she might, despite her freshly washed hair and pressed dress, she couldn't stay clear of the smoking spit.

"Smoke follers beauty, so I hear," Hallie Ledford said.

"And that ain't no lie," Eliza Harold drawled as the breeze shifted and drove the smoke westward toward a line of trees from which the doctor was just emerging.

The women laughed good-naturedly, the younger ones flushing beneath their bonnets. But it was Lael who looked the longest as he rode into the yard. She'd not seen him for nigh on a week, and she'd missed him sorely. Missed his easy grin. Missed the familiar, deliberate way he ran his hand through his dark hair when he was pensive. Missed the charming, direct way he had whenever he spoke to her.

Her reverie ended when Jane McFee's voice came sharply from behind. "Ain't you the one, Sophie Lambert, who's been complainin' about that queer pain in your heart?"

Another titter from the women erupted that carried far on the cool morning air. Lael straightened from stirring the fire and turned around. The widow Lambert? What had she to do with Ian? Looking at her pretty, flushed face across the way, she knew. Sophie Lambert, not yet thirty and recently bereaved, was as smitten as she.

"Might be the good doctor could remedy that heart trouble iffen he was a mind to," joked another. But Lael paid no mind to the chatter. She was suddenly seeing the widow in a new light, and what she saw vexed her sorely.

Had it only been last fall that Sophie's husband died after a fall from his horse? She'd been set to return to her family in North Carolina soon after but had suddenly changed her mind. Since then she'd been living with another family at the fort, occupying the cabin between Colonel Barr and Jane McFee. Could it be that the delicate constitution Sophie claimed to have brought her in close proximity to the doctor?

"Ladies," he called as he rode past, lifting his hat.

Lael started. Since when had he taken to wearing a new hat? She hated to acknowledge that it looked good on him, pulled down low on his brow, the dun-colored felt a striking contrast to his charcoal hair. A titter of female voices greeted him in return, and when he was well out of earshot, Lael turned and addressed them all, her voice as level as she could manage. "The doctor's been spoken for, I'll have you know. By a lady in Boston. So don't any of you go settin' your bonnets for him."

The heated scolding brought no immediate comment. Instead, Sophie and the others regarded her seriously, for who should know best about his comings and goings but Lael, working closely with him as she did?

"Boston's a mite far off for courtin'," Eliza Harold said at last.

"I don't reckon a lady in Boston could prevent me from dancin' with the doctor in Kentucke," challenged Sophie, as if anticipating the evening's frolic.

Lael turned away, walking in a huff toward the cabin. What had come over her? She was not half as put out with the women as with herself, standing her ground and defending the unknown Olivia! But in her heart she knew Olivia was merely an excuse. It was herself she defended, in a pathetic attempt to keep these women apace from him.

She plunged into the shadows of the cabin and found Susanna stirring a pot of beans. With one look Susanna said, "Your feathers are as ruffled as I've ever seen them."

Lael waved an exasperated hand toward the yard. "It's those women—wed and unwed alike—circling the doctor like a bunch of buzzards!"

Susanna suppressed a smile and bent to take a pie from the

hearth. "Well, I reckon they can circle all they want. They just can't light."

The rest of the day passed swiftly enough. The barn was built, beam upon beam, until it stood nearly finished by sunset. A cartload of cider pulled into the yard to commence the evening's frolic. Bonfires were laid and the leftovers from the noon meal were consumed with relish by the host of workmen and their families.

Lael surveyed it all with forced gaiety, hiding the hollow feeling in her heart. What good was a barn if she herself would not be here to use it? But it would be of use to Ransom. And Annie. She'd met her that afternoon and greeted her warmly, masking her surprise. Annie was plain and small, with light brown hair and hazel eyes, and given to plumpness beside the strapping Ransom.

Soon the moon rose, shining cold light on the dancers who felt only the heat of the bonfires and the exertion of the sets. Ian and old Amos riveted them all with one lively tune after another, spelling each other by turns, with nary a lull in the music.

Lael hung back in the shadows with Susanna, the one not of a mood to dance and the other not of a condition. "The doctor ain't had one dance," mused Susanna, eyeing Lael. "There's no reason for both them men to fiddle themselves to pieces."

"They look happy enough," replied Lael, unwilling for him to stop. When he played she was able to soak in the sight of him unawares, thrilling to the intensity of his fiddling and the slow, easy grins he shot at them by turns when he began and ended a piece.

By and by he lay down his instrument and disappeared into the shadows while old Amos played on. When he touched her arm, Lael started. The familiar notes of Sir Roger de Coverley sang out, and she knew what he wanted. Smiling slightly, she followed him out onto the grass. In and out of his arms by turns, her heart was warmed by the fact she'd shared his first dance, though the fiddling stopped woefully soon.

Lael watched him spell old Amos and partner Sophie Lambert twice. Two reels, to her one! They danced well together, Lael thought. How fetching the young widow looked with her red tresses caught up in horn combs and her supple figure wrapped in blue linsey-woolsey. She'd seen that shade of red before on the miniature of Olivia. Same fiery hair. Same milky complexion. Same heart-shaped face. And Sophie claimed to be a believer. Did he have a penchant for red hair? Ian said something and Sophie laughed, throwing back her head and revealing a long, slender neck adorned with a green ribbon.

Riveted, Lael stood in the shadows. The longer she watched them, the more intense grew the stranglehold on her heart. It had overtaken her subtly at first, when the women had fawned and cackled as he rode in, and now its ugly tentacles tightened as she watched him partner Sophie not once but twice.

Unable to watch a moment longer, she turned and fled to the empty cabin where a mountain of dirty dishes hid the trestle table. Tears stung her eyes as she thought of Simon for the first time and realized he was absent from the frolic. And the memory of his ugly, battered face brought a sickening revelation to her soul. For tonight she understood him . . . and what had led him to do what he'd done to the doctor in the woods.

She worked feverishly, as if keeping time with the music, body weary but soul alert. So intent was she on washing and scrubbing that she failed to hear the cabin door open and shut.

"I couldna find you. Why are you no' dancing?" Ian stood at one end of the hearth, hat in his hands.

"I have no heart for it tonight," she replied brusquely. "There's work to be done." He said nothing for a moment and the silence rankled.

"I came tae ask if you'd call on Loy Tucker with me in the morning."

She suppressed a sigh. Loy Tucker was ever complaining about a misery in his chest, and everything they'd tried had fallen short of a remedy. In the morning she wanted nothing but to go up alone into the mountains, rain or shine, and sort out her tangled thoughts. But they had an understanding. When they were needed, they were of a mind to go, no matter the personal inconvenience or sacrifice.

She nodded and added another log to the fire. In the background old Amos ground out a final tune. She wondered dully if Ian would be escorting Sophie back to the fort.

"I'll meet you here at first light," he said.

She took up the ash bucket. "No need. I'll meet you there."

"I'd rather we ride together."

He was being as mule-headed as she tonight, and it sparked her temper. She nodded and turned away, willing him to go. But the next sound she heard was the scraping of a chair against the rough floorboards.

"Oot with it, Lael Click. Or do I have tae stay the night?"

She perched at the far end of the hearth, a dusting of ashes on her face. "I'm tired, is all."

His eyes were sharp. "More than a wee bit tired, I ken."

He was looking at her in that straightforward manner that demanded she respond in kind. She couldn't bring herself to look at him for fear he would see in her eyes the ugliness reflected in her soul. The jealousy. The self-revulsion. The unworthiness. Not to mention her fickle, unbridled heart, swinging first from Simon to Captain Jack and now to him.

Beside this believer she felt unclean, soiled in soul and spirit. Dead in her trespasses and sins, the Bible called it. She could hear wagons rumbling out of the yard. Would he never leave?

"You're no' ill, are you?" The sudden gentleness of his question caught her off guard. Hot tears stung her eyes, and she blinked them back with sheer stubborn will. She didn't want his pity.

She wanted his love. And if she couldn't have that, she wasn't sure she wanted anything at all.

She set the ash bucket down with a thump and made her voice hard and cold. "Just tend to your own business, Doctor, and I'll tend to mine."

Soon the clearing in front of the cabin was bare, gently lit by the dying bonfire and a full moon. The revelers had all departed. Even Ransom had gone to see Annie home. The dishes were done and put away and the floor swept clean.

Try as she might, Lael couldn't stop crying. The neckline of her sprigged muslin dress, softened with a bit of embroidery, was damp from her tears, her apron soiled, her hair falling free of its pins. No one remained to see her misery and so she let anguish have its way, her whole being suffused with angst and longing and lonesomeness.

She hadn't heard the cabin door open and was startled to see Ian standing there. It was nearly midnight. Had he not gone long before?

She stood, a bit lightheaded from hunger. Oh, that he should see her thus, weeping and dirty and disheveled! She wiped a hand across her face, unable to find her hankie.

He came closer, his expression inscrutable, and tossed his hat onto the table. Before she could fathom it he was facing her and taking her chapped, soap-scented hands in his own. Turning each one over, palms up, he smoothed her callused skin with his thumbs, his touch feather light, almost ticklish, the gesture oddly intimate. He'd rarely touched her, and the feeling it wrought made her weak. Though his head was bent, his eyes on her hands, hers remained fixed on his handsome features.

He was intoxicatingly close. She could smell the masculine scent of him brought on by the exertion of the fiddling and dancing. It drew her inexplicably, flooding her senses and turning her insides to jelly. What must he be thinking? Feeling?

If he looked up even slightly, he could kiss her. Their lips were but a breath apart. Oh, would he not kiss her? If he loved her, he would. All her composure began to crumble. For once she wished he wasn't so careful with her . . . so self-controlled . . . so *godly*.

Slowly he lifted his head. His features remained inscrutable, but his eyes were like deep water, reflecting love and longing and all things inexpressible. They held hers, much as his hands did, and she couldn't look away. Looking into his eyes, her head told her what her heart could not believe: he did care for her— deeply.

"Lael."

It was only one word yet spoken with such yearning she longed for more.

She sensed some terrible inner turmoil within him as her nearness gained the upper hand. Above them, the two candles on the mantle smoked furiously, then the one went out, casting the cabin in further darkness. Here and now there was no chaperone, no Olivia, no impediment. No one need know. What did Scripture say about the way of a man with a maid, that it was beyond understanding?

She shut her eyes, unable to look at him any longer. His hands moved up her bare arms, then lay warm against her shoulders and neck, his fingers entwined in her tumbled hair. She leaned into him, breathless with longing, her palms flat against his chest.

His own voice was ragged with desire, his mouth warm against her ear. "Lael lass, if I kiss you . . . just once . . . I fear I canna stop."

Then don't stop.

Oh, Lord in heaven, help us.

Was it her plea or his own? Only heaven could help them now. With a cry she pulled away from him just as he removed his hands from her hair. Backing away, he caught up his hat and was gone, leaving her alone with her weary, wounded heart and all its brokenness.

Long before dawn, with but an hour's fitful sleep, Lael left her cabin. Loy Tucker hardly needed to complain to both of them, she reasoned, imagining Ian's surprise when he came to the cabin and found her gone. If he came.

Shame stained her face and soul as she thought of what she could possibly say to him next time they met. Why in heaven's name had he left the barn raising only to return? Did he mean to tell her something only to find that he could not?

Lael lass, if I kiss you . . . just once . . . I fear I canna stop.

Ever honest he was, yet she was even more shocked by her unspoken response. *Then don't stop.* Strangely, there was no pleasure in knowing he desired her. 'Twas wrong what they'd nearly done, what they'd wanted to do. A simple near kiss it was *not.* Their mutual wanting had pushed them past propriety's neatly hedged borders to a wild, seductive wilderness beyond. 'Twas wrong before God . . . before Olivia . . . before themselves. Yet, mercifully, some restraining hand had kept them apart.

There was naught to do but leave for Briar Hill. Now. She could follow the fort courier out at week's end, telling Ransom and Ma Horn but no one else. The thought of escape was like a balm to a gaping wound. *Aye,* she thought, crying afresh, *'tis the prudent thing to do.* Olivia would come soon, but she would leave sooner.

Fumbling with the drawstring on her saddlebag, she reached in as she rode and withdrew a ginseng root. Would that it could cure heartache and dispel desire. Or turn back the clock and erase her folly. What must he think of her now? She was chaste but acted wanton, leaning against him, begging to be kissed. The memory shamed her to her boots. Hadn't Ma tread the same path and lost the battle? Thinking on it, she felt sudden sympathy for her fickle mother. Were her mother's sins not her own?

62

Nothing had changed at Lovey Runion's ramshackle cabin. Patches of snow still lingered in places, and the bee gums sat silent. Smoke curled from the chimney, and the shutters were closed against the cold. A leather hinge had torn on the cabin door and it hung crooked.

Titus appeared and held open the door for her. "Ma's poorly," he whispered.

Lovey rocked by the hearth, eyes vacant, puffing on her pipe. But Mourning lay abed, face to the wall as if asleep. Quietly, Lael drew up a chair and sat beside her for a time without speaking.

When Titus quit hovering and disappeared outside, Mourning turned over. "I hoped it was you," she said feebly. "You need to know what I cain't keep secret no longer."

Lael waited, alert. There was a burden about Mourning, in her face and voice, and it bespoke bad news. Just when they'd been faring so well up the branch, Lael thought in dismay, the three of them, safe and sound as they'd ever been.

"I—I'm weak as water, and everythin' I eat I vomit up . . . It was the same with Titus, only this 'un here's worse."

This 'un here? Lael tried to keep her dismay down. It was a skill she'd learned, first from Pa and then Ian, practiced after watching him countless times. No matter the illness or wound or his own conflicting feelings, his countenance remained as smooth and untroubled as a summer sky.

"I know what you must think of me, you bein' a lady and all—"

"Hush now," Lael told her. "You're not the first woman to have a child out of wedlock."

"Well—he—Hero—" She broke off and looked away, mouth trembling. "Just before he was killed—"

"Don't you be ashamed. I can just imagine Hero McClary's tricks, bullying you in all sorts of ways. It's a wonder you didn't kill him yourself."

"Well, I did ponder it a time or two . . ."

Lael sat back, thinking of another McClary with revulsion. She'd brought none of the proper herbs this trip. The thought came—wicked though it was—of what she did carry. Ma Horn had told her the root of black cohosh must be used with care, for it would kill an unborn babe.

"You'll be needing a bundle to take away your sick stomach and shore you up," Lael told her. "I don't have it here, so I'll need to fetch it from home. I'll be back before nightfall."

As she prepared to go, Mourning grasped her arm. "Don't tell it to no one, Miss Lael. I'm ashamed to be tied to Hero, dead or alive."

Lael felt a softening, sorry Mourning was so sick. "Don't fret so, Mourning. I aim to see you and Titus and the baby safely settled in North Carolina with your kin one day."

Mourning's tenseness eased, and Lael let herself out, riding down the branch the same way she'd come, backtracking across the same muddy hoofprints, her gun in the crook of her arm. The gloom of the woods was less threatening now. She had Captain Jack to thank for ending the Click-McClary feud. She just wished she could see him and tell him what it meant to her.

A misting rain was falling by the time she reached her cabin. She'd have to hurry and gather the herbs she needed from the rafters, bundling them together and returning to the branch quickly or be benighted in the woods. Spending the night in a balmy summer forest was a far cry from bedding down in the cold damp of late winter. She wondered how Pa had done it.

She was in such a rush that she burst through the door in one long stride. Ransom had gone to the fort to dicker over a plow, and the hearth's fire had nearly gone out, leaving the cabin cold. She didn't remove her buffalo robe, just stood studying the bunches of herbs hanging above her head, puzzling over what she needed. As she set one foot on a bench to reach for them, she heard a voice behind her.

"You look tae be in a hurry."

Startled, her foot came down from its perch and she turned. In her haste she had overlooked Ian's horse—or perhaps he'd hobbled the bay in back of the cabin. He did not smile. Was he thinking of their parting last night? Or her absence this morning? No matter. He was the good doctor once again, cordial, self-controlled, even commanding, though he looked to have spent a sleepless night and was sorely in need of a razor.

She said all in one breath, "There's some trouble up the branch. I have to ride back up with an herb bundle."

"There's trouble at McClary's. And I came tae ask you tae go."

His voice was deep and thoughtful and he looked right at her. She nearly faltered under his scrutiny but for that one word. *McClary*. If it were anyone else, she would gladly go and see to Mourning as soon as she was able. But not a McClary! Not even a widow, an orphan, or otherwise.

"I must see to Mourning."

"It canna wait?"

"Nay, it cannot."

"What is the trouble?"

"One of Hero's own making," she replied hotly, and as soon as she uttered it the light of understanding dawned in his eyes.

"I dinna ken such trouble takes precedent over the fever I speak of," he insisted.

Fever? He was right, truly. No woman had ever died of the birthing sickness to her knowledge, miserable though it was. But she stood her ground. "I cannot go."

He walked to where she stood, but he didn't touch her. "You canna? Or you willna?"

Aye, it was her will that prevented her and well he knew it. She said nothing, only looked away.

"I have reason tae believe this is no ordinary fever, Lael. I rode over here because I need your help. If you willna do this for the McClarys, then do it for me."

At this, she almost buckled. His eyes, so gentle yet firm, nearly proved her undoing. There was a humbleness about him that puzzled her, for it was equal to his strength. He stood tall before her, telling her in no uncertain terms that he needed her. He'd ridden miles to fetch her. What was she to do?

Torn, her eyes filled with tears. "Nay—I can't."

He took her by the shoulders, and she was cast back to the night before when he'd done the same, only his touch had been far gentler then. "Lael, I beg you tae consider what it is you do!"

She pulled away. "Please—don't ask me again! I—it's impossible!"

He was angry now, angrier than she'd ever seen him, and it startled her into speechlessness. The sudden cold fire in his eyes and the rigid set of his jaw made him somewhat fearsome, and oddly, even more handsome.

She took a step away, unable to face him any longer. But she didn't have to. He was not one to waste time arguing when he was needed elsewhere. The door thudded shut behind him, and he rode away at full gallop.

She looked down at her hands and saw they were trembling.

His face remained in her mind—stern yet full of compassion. And deep down inside she felt a faint flutter of fear . . . and the certainty that her simple nay was not simple at all but hurtful to them both in ways she could not fathom.

At dusk Ransom found her in the barn. She'd unsaddled Pandora and watered her but not much else. She sat crying on a pile of hay, face in her hands. He'd never before seen her like this, and when she realized how it rattled him, her own sorrow deepened. He just stood at the barn door, letting the wind and rain soak him. Finally, gathering his wits, he dropped down next to her, though facing away as if to give her some privacy.

After a time she said quietly, "How, Brother, do you become a believer?"

He took a breath. "Well, you got to be sorry for your sins. It helps a heap if you recollect all the mean, low-down, ornery things you ever done."

"And then?"

"Then you take 'em to the foot of the cross—right to the feet of Jesus—and you leave 'em there."

"That's all?"

"Once you ask the Almighty's forgiveness, you ask for His help besides and aim to be better'n you are."

She sighed and wiped a sleeve across her wet face. "I am so unworthy."

He nodded. "That's why He came, Sister. That's why He came."

63

At dawn Lael saddled Pandora and rode to the fort. She knocked directly on Ian's door, but there was no answer. Dismayed, she crossed the common to Ma Horn's and let herself in. Things here were the same as they'd ever been. Ma Horn sat by the fire, finishing her breakfast, and smiled when Lael entered.

Lael's own smile, in return, was hollow. "I've come to see the doctor," she said, sitting down on the hearth and removing her wet bonnet. "I behaved badly. I refused to go to the McClarys' with him."

"And now you're lookin' to tell him you're sorry," Ma Horn surmised. "Well, the doctor's made of good dirt. He'll forgive you, once he comes back."

"He's still away?"

"Aye, for nigh on two days now. One of them widows is mighty sick. But he should ride in directly."

But Lael knew she couldn't wait. As she rode out of the fort's gates and headed west a great dread nearly turned her back. In her befuddlement, she'd forgotten her gun. Suppose one of the McClary clan shot at her? The mere sight of her would surely raise a ruckus, gun or no gun, though perhaps the lack of a weapon was best. Years before she'd been to the McClary homestead with Ma Horn. Just a child then, she recollected someone having a fever and their breaking it with boneset. Ian had spoken of a fever as well. But this was no ordinary fever, he'd said.

When she reached the north fork of the river, the rain had

367

eased and she paused to let the mare drink. The water was brown and churlish, the current swift. Should she cross? Nay, she thought, but she was wet to the skin anyway so it hardly mattered. Steeling herself, she urged Pandora forward into the water.

She ended up far downriver, and the mare had a hard time getting her footing on the slippery bank. Above the roar of the water she thought she heard hoofbeats. There, coming through the trees, was Colonel Barr on a big chestnut mare. At the sight of her he reined in his horse, no welcome warming his face.

"You're too late," he said tersely. "One of the widows is dead."

She stared at him, speechless. Dead? Of a fever?

"I didn't go into the McClary cabin, understand, and neither will you. We'll return to the fort together and sound the alarm." His face showed his revulsion. "'Tis the pox, Miss Click. The smallpox."

There was nothing to do but wait. While Colonel Barr gathered men to ride and warn the settlement, Lael sat in Ma Horn's cabin. When Ian didn't return by nightfall, she rode out in the heavy twilight toward home and Ransom. Once there, she scoured her medical texts but found little to allay her fears. She rode back to the fort the next morning, increasingly anxious to see Ian.

All around her, birds sang in the still dawn and she marveled that such sweetness could exist alongside the horror of the pox. She was weary, oh so weary, but how much more so must Ian be, working alone as she'd left him to do, facing the dreaded disease. His own parents had died of the same. What memories of that terrible time were being resurrected by all this? Her refusal to accompany him was unforgivable, and guilt dogged her every step, haranguing her till she could make things right between them—if they could ever be right again.

By day's end he'd returned to the fort to find both blacksmith and sutler in his quarters. Lael was soon at his door, saddlebags in hand, prepared to do what she should have done from the first.

He met her at the door but wouldn't let her enter. "Go away, Lael. I'll no' have you exposed tae the sickness. I have tae shut myself away for a time, tae be sure of the inoculation."

Inoculation? The strange word might have been spoken in Gaelic.

She returned to Ma Horn, heartsore and bone weary, but her idleness was not to last. By week's end, five more of the fort's inhabitants lay ill, and the gates of the fort were closed in quarantine, imprisoning all within.

Those who still stood hale and hearty eyed each other with grim sympathy and wondered who would be the next to fall. It was a tense, desperate time, made all the worse by waiting. Unable to stand it any longer, Lael positioned herself by the shutter, her eye on the far blockhouse.

"Pray that the Indians make no trouble," Ma Horn told her. "Can ye imagine it? Any unrest would drive the settlement to our gates and what would be the worst—slaughtered by Indians without or the pox within?"

Lael looked up, unable to eat her soup. "Didn't you hear? Colonel Barr says the Shawnee are sick with the same. Some traders gave them infected blankets upriver."

The news had only deepened her grief. Her thoughts were suspended between Ian and Captain Jack. She prayed as she watched and waited but felt her petitions were small and hypocritical, yet she continued feebly.

On the eighth day of their confinement, when darkness enfolded the fort like a shroud, the door to the quarantined blockhouse cracked open, casting a triangle of light onto the muddy, empty common beyond. Amazed, she watched as Ian himself slipped out, silent as a shadow, and crossed over to the cabin of Colonel Barr.

With a quick kiss on Ma Horn's wrinkled cheek, she let herself out and nearly ran to the blockhouse. She cast a quick look behind her but found herself alone in the gloom. She pushed at the heavy door, and the wave of sickness—and death—was suffocating. Nauseous, she wondered if she could even enter without a handkerchief to cover her face.

Before her, in the flickering candlelight, lay four men and one woman. Bland Ballinger. Flowner Beel. Jemima Tate. Nathaniel Hart. Galen Wood. She willed herself forward, hand pressed to her nose and mouth. All were lying on pallets, with enough room to walk between them, and all eyes were closed in the fever's grip or, she guessed, a drug-induced slumber. A fifth man lay apart from the rest, against one wall, and his eyes were open. She stood over him for just a moment before she realized that he—the fort sutler—was dead. And so covered with the great oozing boils she hardly recognized him.

"Lael!"

She spun around at the sound of Ian's voice. He stood in the doorway, Colonel Barr behind him. The anguish in his face was so plain she felt stricken. But it was too late to turn back, and they both knew it.

"You shouldn't be here, Miss Click," the colonel said at once.

"I should have been here from the first," she replied quietly.

Even Philo Barr was loath to enter. Though he shut the door he stood against it, his eyes roaming the room in apparent horror. But Ian was beside her, looking down at her, his hands on her shoulders.

Oh, those eyes! They seemed to look right through her, past all the turmoil and meanness, and regard her with affection anyway. But then their welcome light faded and a harshness crept in. "You canna be here, Lael. I'll walk you back tae Ma Horn's cabin."

Her own eyes were pleading. "I won't leave you. Not now. Not ever. You do need me. I—I can see that you do." Oh, but she wanted to go! Could he sense that? Yet her love for him made her stay. Did he know that too?

He released her and turned back to Colonel Barr who barked, "Where is the dead man?"

Ian moved to the body of the sutler and began wrapping him in a sheet. "You'll have tae help me move him tae the travois tae bury him."

Still, Colonel Barr did not move. A bit gruffly, Ian said over his shoulder, "Have you no' had the pox, mon? Your scars tell me you have."

"Well, I—as a lad—many years ago."

"Then you canna take the pox again, Colonel. Once a mon has had it, and lives tae tell the tale, he is safe."

Truly? Lael stared at the door and then at Philo Barr. The relief on his face was almost laughable. He came forward then, and the two men lifted the body off the pallet and carried it to the horse and travois waiting outside.

Ian turned to her and said, "I'll soon be back. Tend tae the sick as best you can."

Near midnight he returned, having buried the body well beyond the fort's gates. Lael had built up the fire and made some broth and cornbread, and in the small circle of firelight they sat and ate together in silence.

When they had finished, he took one of her hands in both his own. The gesture startled her so much she looked down at her hand, slender and pale and nearly lost in his. At his touch a delightful warmth spread through her. Had he forgiven her, after all?

"Lael, I need tae speak tae you plain."

She looked up at him, suddenly wary. A sudden groan from Nathaniel Hart took their eyes off each other. But Ian turned back, face firm. "I'll speak plain—and fast. Tae be here is tae put your very life in jeopardy. There is but one hope. You must take the pox by inoculation."

"What?"

"'Tis a simple procedure, one that I have already done on myself. I pass a needle and thread through an infected pock and then underneath your own skin. Here." He touched her upper arm. "You will still get the pox, tae be sure, but it will likely be a mild case."

"Likely," she repeated, though she heard the warning in his voice.

"Likely but not certain. It could kill you," he confessed.

He had done this very thing, and because he had, she would also.

"So be it," she said, a growing dread in her heart.

"You are sure?"

She nodded and he took up a needle and thread and talked quietly to her. The inoculation for pox had begun in Boston. A clergyman had vaccinated himself and his own children during an epidemic there. Though it was still opposed, several Boston doctors had become convinced of the soundness of the practice, including the physician Ian had once worked with.

She nearly balked when he ran the needle through a pox on Bland Ballinger's arm. Ballinger looked about to die, so grotesque were his sores. When the incision was made on her own arm, she shut her eyes tight, then opened them when the prick was over.

For a moment he sat staring at the needle, and she wondered what he was thinking. Or was he praying? She looked past him to the human misery that lay about them in the flickering light, and her heart was so heavy she burst out, "Oh Ian—how do you stand this?"

He said simply, "I pray and think of Scotlain. And you."

64

That same night Colonel Barr joined them, and Jane McFee was soon to follow. "I saw you come over," she told Lael. "And I said, 'What's good enough for Lael Click is good enough for me.' Now that my Matthew has passed on, I don't have nobody to tend but myself."

Ian's smile was warm if weary. "Well, Jane, if you're as good a nurse as you are a crack shot, we're in good hands, tae be sure."

And so Jane took the pox by inoculation, but Colonel Barr had not fared so well with the others. "I've informed everyone of the practice and find all opposed but one."

"Ma Horn?" Lael asked hopefully.

"Nay. Hamish Todd. And there's word the sickness is spreading beyond our walls. The McClarys' neighbors—the Simmons, I believe—have two children ill. And the oldest Tucker boy, the one who was helping out at the McClarys' since Hugh and Hero died, he's sick as well."

Ian looked up from where he sat examining Jemima Tate. "Any word on the rest of the McClarys? They took the inoculation before I left, every one of them."

"All sick," the colonel reported. "But mildly so."

"Any word on my brother or the Blisses?" Lael asked.

"They're keeping to their cabins, as instructed. I know little else."

The four of them decided that the women would go upstairs

373

and rest while the men remained below, then later they would trade places. The medication Ian had used to ease the suffering began to wear thin, and the patients grew fitful, tossing on their pallets and murmuring or crying aloud outright.

"'Tis the nature of the illness," he explained. "The fever brings aboot delirium and an aching of the joints. Next a rash develops and gives way tae the pox themselves. There's little tae be done tae ease their suffering except opium, and I've precious little left."

"Perhaps I can ride to Lexington on the morrow," Colonel Barr volunteered.

Slowly, Lael and Jane climbed the stairs, holding a single candle aloft. They were to share the doctor's bed, but would sleep ever come? The simple pallet had been made grand by a lovely blue-and-tan coverlet, the likes of which she'd never seen.

And there on the nightstand, momentarily forgotten by him, perhaps, lay the exquisite pink pearls and her own sunny braid. She sank down onto the bed, the shucks rustling beneath her weight, and blew out the candle. As she lay down, the soft weight of the blankets that enveloped her, warm as a man's arms, was the essence of Ian himself.

Was there ever, Lael wondered, more tender care? The sick lay unresponsive, beyond all hope or reason, and yet Ian's thorough administrations never ceased. As she and Jane worked alongside him, she watched him at work, marveling at his composure. The days seemed endless, blending into one everlasting series of chores. There were feverish bodies to wash with cold rags, soiled bedding and clothes to change and boil in lye water, meals to cook, and water to draw and force past parched lips.

The thought that she herself would soon fall ill was dreadful. But at least he would be there to care for her. And gentle

Jane. Jane, who could stand up to a gun hole as well as any man. Lael developed a new fondness for the older woman overnight, impressed by her self-sacrifice and the tireless way she took up any task.

Lael's own motives were tainted—she was here out of guilt and duty and a desperate love—but Jane and Ian shared the same spirit of self-sacrifice. Several times she caught Jane's lips moving in silent prayer as she worked, and Lael found herself praying as well, asking for mercy so that when Jane fell ill it would be only mildly so, and that she would not bear the hideous marks.

Two children were soon brought to their door, then Colonel Barr returned carrying Sophie Lambert in his arms. Flushed with fever, the young widow still managed to look lovely, and Lael prepared a pallet for her against one wall. She was beginning to see why Ian had moved into the big blockhouse after all, as the smaller cabins could not possibly hold such a number. As it was, they were now hard pressed for room, leaving little space to walk between the pallets.

All her ill will for Sophie dissolved as she ministered to the widow, holding a pan for her when she was sick and sponging her hot face with a cold cloth. The sight of her once flawless complexion now dotted with the red rash filled her with compassion. But it was the children—Sophie's own niece and nephew—that made her heart nearly break. So sick and so small they were.

Lael found Ian gently undressing them. She moved to help him, and the youngest, a boy of about two, began crying for his mother.

"'Tis always hardest on children," Ian told her. "The pox weakens them so, and withoot a maither's care it seems tae break their spirit."

He took out a small tin, which she saw was nearly empty. "I'm loath tae use opium, but 'tis the only way tae ease their pain. Only a small amount is needed, ye ken, but you'll need tae hold their heads up."

Afterwards, she took the crying boy, still a baby really, and wrapped him in a blanket and sat rocking him before the fire. The room was cold for Ian had opened the shutters to let in the morning air, but the sun shone in with beguiling light. Lael kept rocking, long after the baby had cried himself to sleep and the opium had done its work.

Behind her she heard the exasperated if hushed voice of Philo Barr. "For God's sake, Doctor, when will this misery come to an end?"

"Only God knows, Colonel."

"Don't you have any idea?"

"What I can tell you, you dinna want tae hear. The last epidemic in Boston lasted a year and killed half the populace."

"Were you there?"

"Aye. But I dinna take the pox."

"A miracle, wouldn't you say?"

"I consider it so."

"And to what do you contribute your remarkable health?"

"The Almighty, ye ken."

"Oh yes, of course." The colonel wiped his brow with a rag. "Do you recall today is the day we had planned to go to Lexington?"

Lexington? Lael slowed her rocking, her arms aching from the weight of the child. As she recollected their planned trip, a great tide of disappointment swept over her. The revival. This was the day they were to travel to the revival to hear Duncan Leith. Was his disappointment as great as hers? When she had a spare moment she said to him, "Ian, I'm sorry about the revival."

He paused from mixing a powder. "It doesna truly matter, Lael."

Surprised, she stared at him.

He said simply, "It only matters that you cared tae go."

Later, lying on the upstairs bed beside a sleeping Jane, she pondered his words. What had he meant? *It only matters that you cared tae go.* And what of his other words, ones that left little room for doubt? *How can you stand this?* she had asked.

I pray and think of Scotlain. And you.

She turned on her side and reached for the pearls on the bedside table. Their unusual beauty solaced her as did the memory that he'd meant her to have them. Their color still stole her breath. Pink, like a dogwood, she mused, somewhat solaced by the thought of spring. But where, she wondered, were the other pearls, the pale ivory ones . . . and the miniature of Olivia?

65

By the tenth day, Sophie Lambert and Flowner Beel had been buried, and four more lay dying. Lael leaned over the little boy, no longer crying now for lack of strength, the long-lashed eyes closed, the tiny body a mass of pocks.

"Just rock him, Lael," Ian told her. "Just rock him oot of this world and in tae the next."

Gently, she lifted the child and her tears fell on the little face that had once been soft and white. Not far from them, on a shared pallet, lay both the boy's parents in the grip of fever, oblivious to their wee son. And so Lael rocked and rocked. For hours she rocked, until her arms and legs grew numb and Ian knelt beside her chair, making her stop.

"It's over, Lael," he was saying as gently as he could, taking the small, still body from her. When they went to bury him, she put her face in her apron and sobbed. Try as she might, even Jane, now crying as well, couldn't comfort her. When Ian returned, he picked her up as if she was light as a corn-husk doll and carried her up the steps.

His voice was stern as he placed her on the bed. "Your strength is gone, Lael. I canna have you downstairs any longer. Jane has made you a cup of tea. Drink it and rest."

He walked away from her then, going over to where a handsome medicine chest stood against one wall. She took a sip of tea and found it strong, almost bitter, and wondered if he'd added something to it. He was mixing medicines now, adding water, and rummaging through a drawer in the chest. She marveled at his endurance, and yet she knew his strength was not his own.

God's strength was in him. How many times had she seen him at prayer, lips moving silently as he leaned over first one patient and then another, taxed to his physical and mental limits? There had often been an unmistakable sheen in his eyes, and the sight made her own composure crumble.

It seemed odd as she lay there and watched him, how he stood so tall one minute but now leaned a bit. She saw his right hand reach out and grasp the top of the chest as if to steady himself. Then he swayed and fell, and the glass vials he had been holding shattered to pieces on the hardwood floor.

She bolted upright, the hot tea spilling on her as she dropped it in horror. By the time she reached him Colonel Barr was beside her, his own face a mask of fear.

"Dear God in heaven," he nearly shouted, "what shall we do now?" And it seemed to Lael more anguished words had never been spoken.

Together, they dragged him to the bed. Weeping once more, Lael removed Ian's boots while the colonel removed his linen shirt, stained with the medicines he had been mixing.

In that short time he'd already passed into unconsciousness. She lay a hand against his flushed cheek. He was burning with fever, and she knew the pox had him. Why hadn't she seen it sooner?

"I must send for Ma Horn," Colonel Barr said and then left them alone.

Sitting on the edge of the bed, Lael took one of Ian's hands in her own, much as he had done that first night. She looked down at his long, strong fingers, lacing them through her own. "Ian, if you can hear me, know that I will take fine care of you." But to her own ears the pledge seemed woefully inadequate. Leaning over, she pressed her ear to his chest and listened to his heartbeat, sure and strong. He had a mild case, is all, she reasoned. Soon he would be up and they would all go on as before.

Ma Horn arrived, and though Lael was heartened to see her, she worried that at her advanced age she wouldn't last long. In all her years, Ma Horn had never known smallpox, had only heard of it. Having lived most of her life in the wilderness, she'd never been exposed to the disease until now.

At Lael's request, Colonel Barr rode out to see how Ransom and the Blisses fared and came back with a good report. They were likely to be fine as long as they stayed put. Lael was thankful, though it seemed a wonder that only a few miles away life went on as peaceful as before, while in this room they seemed trapped at the very gates of hell.

Just as Ian said, it helped to think of things other than the misery around them. While he'd confessed to praying and thinking of Scotland and her, she thought of him and her own homeplace, now more dear than ever before.

She was loath to leave his side. Always someone was with him, providing him the same care he'd given others, but she stayed near. Through the first days of fever she waited, for now she knew what to expect. Always the fever first and then the rash, which gave way to the unsightly pocks—with a great deal of suffering in between.

When she could no longer keep her eyes open, she lay down beside him atop the coverlet. What would have shamed her before now seemed of no consequence. When the fever climbed and he grew restless, she pulled a chair close and read aloud from his Bible. Which passages were his favorites? She wished she'd asked him sooner.

There were so many things about him she didn't know. His middle name. His birthday. The story of his conversion. She found that he'd marked Psalm 23 with black ink and scribbled a date in the margin as well, and this she read aloud again and again until he quieted.

"He sure ain't restin' easy," Ma Horn said, bringing rags and a fresh pail of water with which to cool him.

"I have some brandy in my cabin. Some rum as well," the colonel told them. "Perhaps a good dose of that would help."

But Lael shook her head. "I think he would oppose it. I once heard him say liquor is good for amputations and little else."

"He ain't got no more of that opium, does he?" Ma Horn asked, wringing out a rag. "That poppy powder is powerful stuff."

"I believe he used the last of it on the children," Lael said. But she rose and went to the medicine chest anyway. Lifting the lid, she read the inscription there. *Medicine Chests. Put up or Refitted at Marshall's Drug and Chemical Store, No. 56, Beacon Street, Boston.* An assortment of vials and bottles were arranged within, bearing such bewildering titles as Scot's Pills, Rochelle Salts, Daffy's Elixir, Goddard's Drops, and Seignette's Salts. Plus a number of herbs, both benefits and simples, as they were called, stood alongside the mysterious nostrums. Only a few names were familiar: foxglove, garlic, lavender, rose hips.

The second drawer contained a collection of lancets and surgical tools, and beneath these were mortars and pestles. At the bottom was more mixing and bandaging equipment and . . . the pearls. She stopped rummaging when she saw them. They lay curled in the corner, and beneath their milky whiteness lay a letter.

For several moments she stood, transfixed. Why were her pearls on the nightstand while these—Olivia's pearls, as she'd come to know them—lay hidden in a drawer? She should not . . . dare not . . .

With one finger she pushed the necklace gently aside and saw the face of the letter.

In an ornate feminine hand the address read, *To Doctor Ian Alexander Justus, Fort Click, Kentucke Territory.* The return address bore but three words: *Olivia Lowe, Boston.*

At once she shut the drawer.

"There is nothing—nothing but a supply of medicines unknown to me," she told them slowly.

And an exquisite string of pearls and one mysterious, lonely letter.

66

Soon Jane lay sick and three more were buried. With Ian so ill, the task of loading the dead onto the waiting travois and digging the graves fell to Lael and Colonel Barr. Riding out in the open air was bracing, even invigorating, but pulling a dead body was another matter. By the time she'd helped dig just one grave, she was spent.

"I believe," Colonel Barr told her, "that your father would be rather proud."

Would he? She looked at the man she'd never truly liked, the hard-won compliment warming her. Perhaps Pa would, at that. Eyes wet, she leaned against her shovel, letting the late-winter wind lick her cape. One buried. Two more to follow. She no longer looked at the faces of the dead, for at night they'd begun to appear in her dreams.

Riding back to the blockhouse, the movement of her horse lulled her to sleep. She swayed but the colonel caught her before she fell. Her body felt strangely detached, so weary as to be beyond feeling, and her head throbbed.

"You must eat," Colonel Barr reminded her, but she couldn't, and she wouldn't, till Ian and Jane were well.

That night, Ma Horn cried out from the loft. She'd been tending the doctor, wiping him down and forcing water past his cracked lips, while Lael and Colonel Barr saw to Jane and the others. At the sound of her cry they rushed up the steps, and Lael felt she would never reach the top.

Ma Horn was as shaken as Lael had ever seen her. "He stopped drawin' breath not once but twice now. I had to work his chest hard—both times—to make it start up again."

Lael faltered, but the colonel's hand gripped her arm, keeping her steady. "Twice, you say?"

"Aye. And his color's changed a mite."

Pulling free of the colonel's hold, Lael went to the bed. Ian's head lay heavy on the pillow, his disheveled hair a melee of damp black strands. Ma Horn turned the coverlet back to reveal a well-muscled chest covered with the telltale red spots. Reaching out, Lael placed one hand over his heart and waited. The beat that had been so strong and sure just yesterday was barely there. Dropping down on the bed, she pressed her ear close and listened. Weak, truly.

Ma Horn was looking at her, but Lael was afraid of those old, knowledgeable eyes, afraid they would tell her what the old woman could not bring herself to say. Numb, Lael sat up but did not withdraw her hand from his chest, afraid to let go.

"He's awful weak," Ma Horn said. "Goin' out to the McClarys' plumb sapped his strength, and then he come here to all this. He ain't stopped yet, neither to sleep nor eat, to my way of thinkin.'"

"There's nothing you can give him? No herb or remedy of your own making?" the colonel asked.

"All I know of is foxglove, to shore up the heart. I could make a tea and we could try and ease it down."

"Then do it," he advised.

Lael was hardly aware of their leaving. How long was it before Ma Horn came back up and the two of them were trickling the tea, spoonful by spoonful, down his throat? This, Lael thought, was her own doing. He had given out because she'd refused him the day he'd come nearly begging her to help him. All of her pent-up hate and bitterness and stubbornness had not only killed the McClary widow but was killing Ian as well, right before her eyes. She'd felt the weight of her sin then, and she felt it now, along with a great and crushing grief.

Oh God . . . help me!

Dropping down beside the bed onto her knees, she put her face in her hands. But she couldn't pray. Not one word passed from her heart to her lips. "Oh God . . ." she tried again, but the simple words seemed to choke her.

Ian was mumbling now, and her head came up. She reached for his hand and squeezed it as if that alone could stop the torrent of jumbled words. He was hot—so hot—was there no help for it? Even his hand seemed to singe her own. She heard him mumble snatches of Scripture and then her own name.

"Lael . . . Lael . . ." But it was not said in joy. She'd never heard him in such anguish, and it hurt her deep down, where she'd never hurt before.

"Ian—Ian! I'm here, right here beside you. You mustn't fret so." She lay cool hands on his perspiring face and called for more rags and cold water. Crying now, her tears fell onto his face and chest as she tried to cool him. *Oh Ian. I love you, love you, love you . . .* Her heart kept repeating the words, though her lips stayed silent. She had no right to love him at all. Why then did she feel the need to tell him?

She thought of Pa and the loving words she'd often thought but never voiced to him. Had he sensed her love? Could love be felt—or did it have to be spoken? Since Ian had returned to her cabin that one night, she'd dared to think he loved her. She'd felt it, hadn't she? It was in his eyes when he looked at her . . . in his voice when he spoke to her . . .

Olivia? Did he just call out her name? Nay, it was her own name she heard, uttered again and again with the same intensity and sadness.

"I'm here, Ian. Right here."

She could not stop crying. Was this love? Wishing his pain was her own? Wanting to take his place? The love she felt for him was unlike any she'd ever known. Didn't Scripture say that God is love? Had He given her this love? Would He now take it away?

She lay her head on his bare chest, and the next thing she knew urgent hands were shaking her awake. Sitting up, she rubbed her eyes and saw that Colonel Barr and Ma Horn were cooling him down with snow. Like a sleepwalker, she got up and walked to the small loft window. Unlatching it, she propped it open with a stick. Great, white flakes swirled in a lovely winter's dance. She left the window ajar and returned to the bed to help them.

It was late when Ma Horn sat back, resigned. Lael knew the look, and it set her heart to pounding. "I'll set up with him a spell," she said dully, looking more worn than Lael had ever seen her.

But Lael would not leave him.

"All right, but if there's any change, you fetch me quick, you hear?" Ma Horn cautioned.

She was alone with him again, but there was nothing she could do for him. Nothing at all.

The shadow of death had come into the room.

67

How had it come to this?

They were all gathered by the bedside—Lael, Colonel Barr, Ma Horn, and Jane. Jane had risen from her sickbed and had to be helped up the stairs, but she insisted on seeing the doctor a final time.

Ma Horn had fretted over him some. He now wore a fresh linen shirt, and she'd combed his tangled hair. Lying so quiet atop the coverlet, he looked like a sleeping giant. Lael had never thought to see him so still. Gone was the quicksilver grin that marked his teasing. His mouth was now drawn in a solemn line, and his eyes—had they really been so blue?—were shut, the circles beneath them sullen. She couldn't bear to look, nor could she bear to turn away.

At the top of the stairs stood a familiar figure. Will Bliss? His hat was in his hands, but he made no move toward them. He just stood and Lael stared at him, too sore and too worn to be amazed. But there he was, the flesh-and-blood Will, his eyes fixed on Ian. Did he love him too? Was that why he'd come? Didn't he know he risked his very life by walking into the sickroom? The shadow of death was all around them. Did he not feel it?

In time Will's gaze turned to Lael. She stood at the foot of the bed. The others began to move away, and it was Will who came to stand beside her. He put a hand on her shoulder, and she crumbled. She had cried herself dry, she reckoned, so how could she possibly cry again?

Behind her she heard a chair scrape against the floor as he sat. Dropping to her knees beside the bed, she took one of Ian's hands and brought it close to rest beneath her cheek. There was no one else now, just she and Will. The others had gone below to wait. She wondered dully if Colonel Barr was preparing the travois for burial.

His hand lay heavy in her own, still warm but growing colder as if the life was slowly ebbing out of him. He was no longer there, she knew. He was moving away from her to a place she could not follow. As she sat holding onto him as if to anchor him to her forever, she felt a strange release—a slight but unmistakable pulling away that both frightened and bewildered.

She began praying and weeping again. Must she lose everyone she held dear? Pa, Neddy, Simon, Captain Jack, and now Ian? The weight of her sorrow was too much to hold.

Will's lips seemed to move without ceasing while she felt her own prayers went no higher than the blockhouse ceiling. What had come over Will? She'd grown up knowing Will and, truth be told, never liked him much back then. He was a bullying boy, hotheaded and unkind, striking out with words or fists. But Will the man had somehow become gentle and kind—and meek.

His hand was on her shoulder again. She felt its weight and he said, "Let him go, Lael."

The shadows on the wall deepened, and only one candle was left burning. She brushed her lips against Ian's, much as she had longed to do that night in her cabin after the barn raising.

Oh God, please. Help my unbelief. Forgive me all the times I've hurt You . . . and others . . . and myself. I'm a sinner, for sure. I deserve to die but for Your mercy. I believe You are love, that You loved me enough to die for me. You gave me a love for this man . . . a gift . . . undeserved. I wish You'd take me instead . . . in Ian's place . . . my life for his . . . like Your Son did for me.

Thinking gave way to speaking, then praying to pleading. "Ian, do you hear? I want you to forgive me . . . to come back to me from wherever you are. It is I, Lael. Ian, I love you. *I love you.* Do you hear? I can't hide it any longer. Deep down you must know God has given me a love for you too sweet to bear."

With a trembling hand, she reached toward the bedside table. The pink pearls were cold and almost heavy, but somehow— unsteadily, miraculously—she opened the tiny clasp and placed them about her neck. The simple act seemed to confirm her love and commitment but brought no comfort. She wished she'd done so sooner, when he could have seen her, when he might have done it for her. At Christmas.

Before it was too late.

68

The throbbing in her head was steady, like the beat of a drum. Could they hear it too? There were people around her—moving, talking shadows. She could hear voices . . . she knew Ma Horn's first; she'd been hearing it so long it was a part of her. She tried to sit up, but the shadows deepened and the pain in her head made her moan. Why did her hair feel so heavy? It hurt clear to her scalp.

She felt cool hands on her. They were pressing her down and removing her clothes. Without them she felt light as thistledown. She was beside the river, but she'd forgotten her bonnet. The sun's reflection off the water burned her, yet when she moved into the shade beneath the sycamores, she was covered in a tide of goose bumps. Light and dark. Hot and cold. Voices without name.

She was beside the river and there, standing on the far shore, was Pa. A great joy swelled her soul. She called out to him. Did he hear? Her breath caught as he turned. He was looking at her now, and the love in his face hurt her. She'd forgotten how tall he stood. And his eyes! Nearly as blue as Ian's own. He was smiling and motioning for her to come over. Between them, the water looked still and deep and inviting. But she held back, torn. How she wanted to cross . . . to hear his voice again!

Lael . . . Lael!

Somebody was calling her name, but who? Not her pa, though it was a man's voice, sure and strong. She was being lifted and a warm liquid poured down her throat. She thought she might drown. She tried to fight it but couldn't lift her hands. Why couldn't she see? The taste in her mouth was bitter . . . the darkness complete . . . like someone had pulled a sheet over her head.

She was on the river now, in a canoe. Ian was holding the paddles, and she sat across from him. He was smiling at her. *Let's stay here like this,* she was telling him, *just the two of us, forever.*

But there was Olivia . . . always Olivia . . .

And then there was blackness.

Like a sleepwalker, Lael got up from the bed. She was at Ma Horn's, she knew. But where was Ma Horn? The shadows of the cabin shifted and grew longer, and she swayed with them. She smelled the peculiar odor of camphor, and it sharpened her senses somewhat. She'd never liked the smell, had always preferred her herbs by far. At the end of the bed she stumbled over her own two feet. She was half-floating, half-walking. She was alone . . . was she not?

Her eyes struggled to focus on something—anything. The room tilted and spun. Nay, she was not alone. Yellow flames licked and hissed at hearth logs. A figure sat before the fire—bent and, she sensed, weary. Reaching out her hand, she tried to touch whoever it was, but they were too far off. She stumbled again, but, blessedly, there was a table, breaking her fall and lending her strength. Looking down, she saw she wore a nightgown, but whose? The pink pearls were about her neck. And her hair . . . the hair that felt so heavy of late, still hung to her knees, swaying like a windblown curtain as she walked.

She put out her hand . . . the darkness was rushing in again threatening to take her with it. With a cry she grasped for some support but there was nothing—nothing—

And then there was.

Strong, hard arms encircled her. *Simon?* Sheer terror overtook her and she began to push them away, but they were like iron bands about her.

"Lael . . . Lael."

At her name so tenderly spoken she melted soft as candle wax in those arms. And then she felt nearly smothered by a man's closeness. He was kissing her, truly. Kissing her face . . . her neck . . . her hair . . . saying her name again and again. Despite her weak and ravaged state, those words and kisses filled her with the most wondrous, exquisite feeling.

In time he carried her back to the bed. The darkness was again overtaking her, and she was sliding back into blackness and emptiness and confusion and crying, "Oh Ian—Ian, I'm so afraid!"

Picking her up, he carried her nearer the fire, where he sat and rocked her in Ma Horn's old chair for a very long time.

When she awoke it was to Jane McFee spooning her some broth. Without a word, she weakly swallowed it. So she'd dreamt it, then. Those kisses and whispered endearments were naught but the queer imaginings of her strange illness. Ian wasn't even here, she realized with a start. Just gentle Jane, determined that she finish the strengthening broth. Ma Horn would come in any minute and take up her pipe by the hearth, like always.

When the bowl was empty, she whispered, "Where is . . . Ma Horn?"

Jane's face puckered slightly and she said nothing.

Frantic, Lael clutched at her sleeve. "Jane, tell me, please. About Ma Horn. And the doctor." Yet even as she spoke, she feared hearing. Her whole world was upended and queer. She would never be right again without them. They must be here— they must be near . . .

"Ma Horn's done crossed over, Lael."

Hearing it, she felt like she would break into a thousand pieces. Ma Horn gone, and not one good-bye. Just like it had been with Pa, then Neddy . . . "Oh Jane, nay!"

Jane began crying herself, and Lael stuttered a desperate plea, "A-And Ian?"

"Simon Hayes took sick, and he was sent for."

Simon? Jane continued, "Piper's nearly dead with the pox. Now Simon's sick as well."

It was too much to take in. "But Ian is . . . all right?"

Jane passed her a handkerchief. "Weak yet, the doctor is, for he nearly died hisself. Don't you remember, Lael? It was you who nursed him."

Did she remember? She remembered nothing, nothing at all but those fleeting kisses. Yet a river of relief flooded her soul, nigh to drowning her, at hearing he remained. Surely heaven had heard her pitiful prayers.

Jane looked away, thoughtful. "You were right sick yourself. It was queer how when you went down the doctor rose up. We'd give him up for dead. But the very day you dropped he came round. And he wouldn't let nobody tend you but hisself. Why, he just give you over to me today before he rode out."

"Thank you, Jane, for taking good care of me. I can see you were sick yourself." At the sight of the pocks on Jane's face, Lael's hands went to her own, feeling the upraised sores.

"You got just a few, like me. Them who died got 'em the worst."

Slowly, like awakening from a dream, their trial in the block-house came back to her. Sophie Lambert. The sutler. Flowner Beel. The children and the others. Even Ma Horn. She swallowed down the hurt of not saying good-bye to the woman who had taught her so much.

"The fever took Ma Horn right off," Jane reassured her, rising. "Fourteen dead and twenty living. I ain't been to my cabin yet, and

I aim to go if you can make out all right for a spell. The doctor'll be back directly to see you. And he told me to give you this."

Jane handed her a piece of paper—a letter. She took it and turned it over. *Olivia's letter. But why?* She remembered her surprise at finding it in the medicine chest. She stared at the seal on the back, dark blue and broken, and then Jane's shutting of the door jarred her to action. She was alone, free to read it and let the emotion pulsing through her show on her face. She opened it and breathed in the faint scent of lavender.

October 12, 1783
My dearest Ian,

How peculiar it seems that on the very day I take pen in hand your own letter has come to me. I did not doubt that you would find the wilds of Kentucke to your liking and that it would someday woo you away from me. Always in my heartfelt prayers for you, I sensed God Himself was calling you apart for His own special purpose, though I had not imagined He was preparing a helpmate there to love you and help you as I cannot. That she is the famed frontiersman's daughter surprises me not at all. I hope, one day, to meet her as your wife.

Since your leaving I have come to understand that my mission remains here in Boston, making the rounds of calls with my dear father. There is so much suffering in the world! And such a need for our gentle Savior! My parents were rather dejected about our parting. But I trust that one day they will understand and accept what was more man-made than God-ordained. The truth remains that I could never be reconciled to the hardships of frontier life—or even Scotland—and thereby am unable to be by your side and love you wholeheartedly as you deserve. Therefore, I release you with open arms.

Yours truly,
Olivia Lowe

Lael read the letter a second and a third time, hardly believing the words before her. She was still befuddled, is all, reading meaning and emotion into the message where there was none. Back before Christmas the letter had come. Before Cozy Creek and the pearls and the Christmas merriment in the Bliss cabin.

Ian had not seemed a spurned man then or now . . . *because he was not*. There had been another letter, she surmised, before Olivia's, written by Ian himself. And in that letter he had made mention of the famed frontiersman's daughter. She . . . herself.

Could it be?

The door opened and the letter fluttered to the floor from her fingertips. Ian stood on the threshold, sunlight peeking over his shoulder. The sight of him, standing so hale and hearty, when she thought she'd lost him forever, proved her undoing. She dropped her face into her hands and sobbed. His own eyes were wet when he sat down on the edge of the bed, the letter at his feet. His strong arms encircled her, and her head rested against his shoulder.

"'Twas tae soon tae give you the letter," he murmured against her hair. "But I wanted tae reassure you. When you were sick you kept saying my name—and Olivia's. I dinna ken you even knew aboot her."

"Susanna told me."

"She told you but there was really nothing tae tell."

"Just that you cared for her and asked her here for a visit."

"Aye, but Olivia would have none of it. And it didna truly matter. God had willed otherwise. So I gave you the letter tae read. If there is tae be anything between us, Lael, you should know Olivia doesna stand between us."

Nay, Lael thought, *not even God.* Was this His will? That she be well and in Ian's arms? Was this all a part of His purpose?

"Lael, I canna speak of these things now. You are tae weak.

You must promise me tae rest and be well. For until that day I canna court you—or kiss you—good and proper like a true Scotsman."

Despite her great weariness, she smiled and drew back a bit. "I hear kissing is the best sort of medicine."

He grinned and it was so roguish her heart turned over. "Och, if I kiss you now like I want tae kiss you, you'd faint dead away. Nae, when I kiss you, I want you tae be strong enough tae kiss me back."

To listen to him talk filled her with a deep, abiding joy such as she'd never known! And then her face clouded. "Oh Ian, I have so many questions. How long have I been sick? And when did Ma Horn pass?"

He hesitated, his face almost haunted. "You took the fever ten days ago, the very day I came tae my senses. Ma Horn died three days after. We buried her apart from the rest, partway up Hackberry Ridge, beneath a sycamore. Colonel Barr has marked it with a cross."

She pictured this and thought she knew the very spot. But her sadness was pushed aside by a rush of other pressing questions. "And Susanna and Will? Will came to see you when you lay dying—"

"They're all well and anxious tae see you. Susanna wanted me tae bring you tae her so she could nurse you herself."

"And Ransom?"

"The pox passed him by, but took Annie."

Annie. She felt another stab of sorrow and leaned back against the pillow. Why had God let Annie die and she herself live? She could only imagine her brother's heartache, yet there was nothing to be done for it except pray. Wasn't that the only thing that truly mattered in those dark days in the blockhouse? Prayer had comforted the living and the dying when all else failed.

He gently pushed her back onto the pillow. "Jane will be here soon tae bring you supper. But first you must rest."

How she hated for him to let her go! Fighting sleep, she watched as he built up the fire and brought her some cider. But no sooner had he shut the door than she closed her eyes and slept straight through Jane's fine supper, not awakening till morning's light.

69

Fort Click was but a shell now, with so many of its inhabitants buried on the hillside behind the high north wall. Without Ma Horn, the tiny cabin seemed inhospitable and hollow as a gourd. Lael couldn't wait to leave it. Jane tended her without complaint, wondering aloud, as Lael had done silently, why so many had been taken while they themselves had been spared. The fort store eventually reopened with a new sutler, and the blacksmith's anvil rang out again, restoring routine and order to the settlement.

With Ian still tending the remaining sick, Lael grew restless. The rain kept her cooped up, sitting by the fire and sewing or reading. Ransom brought her spectacles, and at the sight of him she fought to keep her composure, for he looked ready to fall to pieces himself.

She spoke her feelings outright as he sat down across from her. "Ransom, I'm so sorry about Annie."

He swallowed hard, his eyes on the hat in his hands. "I would have took her sufferin' if I could."

"I know," she said quietly. "I felt the same about Ian."

He studied her a long moment. "I come to get you today and take you home, but the doc won't allow it. Says he aims to do a little courtin' first."

She flushed despite her pleasure. "And what did you say to that?"

"I asked what in blazes took him so long."

397

"You didn't!"

He grinned. "Yessir. I also told him to just go ahead and marry you if he was of a mind to."

She knotted her hands in her lap. "Tell me you didn't."

He laughed, then sobered. "We've done enough buryin', Sister. Some marryin' would be a mighty fine thing for a change. Lately I've been thinkin' how Pa never cared for the likes of Simon. But I think the doctor would please him a heap."

After that she worked twice as hard to get better, eating every morsel that Jane brought her, resting by the fire in Ma Horn's old rocker, hardly leaving the cabin. Still, her recovery was slow. *Why, I'm weak as water,* she thought, taking up the hand mirror Jane brought her. She stared at her pale reflection and felt ashamed of her revulsion at the slowly healing pocks on her face. Would they scar? She supposed it didn't matter. A changed heart rendered a poor complexion of little consequence. And she *was* changed. This was not a mere feeling but a certainty that the God who'd brought her through the pox could bring her through anything at all.

Ian came in the evenings but could not stay away for long from his patients in the blockhouse, who were recovering as slowly as she. As of yet, there were no more of the whispered endearments or feverish kisses she recalled from her sickbed just days before. But she thought of them and longed for them more than she yearned for sunlight and fresh air.

"You need tae be beyond these walls," he told her. "When this infernal rain ends we'll go oot, just the two of us."

He kept his promise on a raw windy day in March when the sun reflected in a hundred puddles across the fort common. "'Tis tae wet tae ride," he told her, putting a shawl about her head and shoulders. "So we'll row."

Before she could protest, he picked her up and carried her over the muddy common and beyond the fort's gates, down the gentle sloping bank to the river. Catching sight of the water again, she felt as gleeful as a young girl. Sunlight was everywhere, warm on her face and hair and glistening off the wet leaves that whispered in the trees above their heads. They pushed off from shore and within moments the current carried them away. Smiling with delight, she pushed the shawl from her head and let it rest about her shoulders.

As Ian paddled she took in all the beautiful, beloved surroundings she'd nearly forgotten, her eyes lingering on the far bank and the first raggedy robins pushing up like blue fringe along the muddy shore. They seemed bluer and lovelier than ever before. Or was she simply seeing with new eyes?

"Why, I don't even know what day it is," she said in wonder. "But it's spring, at last."

"'Tis the third of March," he replied. "My nameday."

She looked at him in surprise, wondering that she hadn't known till now. "How old are you, Ian?"

"One and thirty."

She smiled and let her fingers trail in the cold water. "I'll be one and twenty come April."

Past marrying age, both of them. In the stillness, she grew shy. "You must know, I've been made new. God has shown Himself to me. The old Lael Click is gone, with all her sorry ways."

He maneuvered the oars easily, his eyes never leaving her face. "I ken, Lael. As I lay sick I heard your prayers."

Her face turned beseeching. "I'm asking you to forgive me, Ian. For treating you badly when you first came to Kentucke. For refusing to help you make your calls—"

"Only if you forgive me for my arrogance and door-slamming and all the rest."

She nodded, then drew a deep breath, a bit lost in the depths of his eyes. "Once you told me you prayed for me. Would you mind telling me . . . what you asked?"

He hesitated, and for a moment she thought he might not say.

"That you'd come tae know Him, nae matter the cost."

His honesty took her breath away. The cost had nearly been his life—and her own. Her eyes filled, as did his. Awed, she looked away. God had answered his prayer, there could be no doubt. Her heart and her head couldn't hold it all, and she fell silent.

The river's blue path unfolded around them. Deep thatches of pea vine and clover smothered the banks. Spring had come and she'd nearly missed its coming. Everything pulsed with life. Even the wind smelled fresh and newborn.

"Where are you taking me?" she finally asked, as the stretch of shore grew familiar.

"Home."

Home? "But there's nobody there, with Ransom up at Neddy's now. And I'll be so far from you . . ." Already she was missing him and not ashamed to show it.

"You need tae be home, Lael."

Her face eased. "I reckon you're right."

He got out of the boat, pulling it ashore, then helped her out. When her feet were firmly planted on the path to her cabin, he reached back into the boat. "We had tae burn your dress and underthings when you fell ill," he told her. "But I kept these, in case you'd be wanting them."

The blue beads and silver bracelet passed from his warm hand to hers and seemed to build a wall between them. They looked strange to her, a part of her past, the old Lael not made new. She couldn't even say thank you. With one hand she clutched the jewelry, and with the other touched the pearls at her throat. Their beauty jarred sourly with the borrowed butternut dress of Ma Horn's.

He got back into the boat without so much as a fare-thee-well. Had she only dreamt he'd kissed her when she'd risen from her sickbed? Bewildered, she watched him return to the river.

"I'll be back tomorrow, ye ken." His voice carried over the muddy water—yet another barrier between them.

She turned slowly and started up the trail toward home. All was quiet in the cabin clearing. Tuck was not there to meet her, for Will had long since taken him to Cozy Creek when she'd fallen ill. The new barn stood green and unfinished. To the side of the cabin, the mountain of firewood remained, warming her with its mystery. Lovingly, she looked at everything she'd missed and said a silent greeting. Everything was unchanged.

Everything but she herself.

"You're a poor patient, Lael Click," Ian growled, holding up an untouched bottle of Daffy's Elixir to the fading light.

She crossed her arms, glad for the soft, clean feel of her moss-green dress and crisp cambric apron. He studied her then tossed the bottle back into his leather satchel. She tucked her bare feet under the hem of her skirt, out of sight, and looked down demurely at the planks of the cabin porch.

"I think I'm well enough to go calling with you again," she said softly. "That way you wouldn't have to come all the way out here every day."

He looked tired tonight, and a trifle irritated, though he'd stayed for supper. She'd fixed his favorite things—cornbread with honey, a mess of fried fish Ransom had caught, some fresh poke salat. Even a dried apple tart and tea. But he'd hardly eaten.

"You look in need of that elixir yourself, Ian. Or a bundle of herbs." She longed to touch him, to lay a hand on his sleeve. But distance sat squarely between them, like the pile of supper dishes dividing them on the porch.

He ran a hand through his hair, dislodging the leather tie. It fell to his feet, and a bit absently he ground it into the dust with the heel of his boot. Loose now, his hair hung well below his shoulders. Coal black hair. She doubted it had been cut since he'd first come to the settlement. Memories of Captain Jack pulled at her, erecting yet another wall.

She fingered the pearls at her neck, her voice sounding strained and far off. "Any more smallpox in the settlement?"

His eyes remained on the distant river. "Some. Simon Hayes is recovering. But Piper was buried yesterday."

She went completely still. Piper dead. Would the sickness never leave them alone? Would it continue to change and rearrange the whole settlement? Was this why he seemed so distant—so preoccupied? Did he think that if Simon was free, she might . . . ?

Suddenly he turned toward her. "I canna keep quiet any longer, Lael."

The silence loomed large and lonesome. She leaned toward him slightly, her eyes studying every detail of his handsome, slightly scarred face. Had he changed his mind about her? Was that why he hadn't so much as touched her? Her supper sat uneasily in her stomach, and she feared she'd have to dash to the edge of the porch if he said what she dreaded.

"I'm soon tae sail for Scotlain."

Scotland? "When—why?" She could barely say the words.

"In April. I've estate matters tae settle there. But after a time, I'll return tae Kentucke."

"Estate matters?"

"I've been away five years now. In my absence, a factor has handled things in my stead. But I've just learned he's no' an honest man and has mismanaged some of what I've given over tae him. I have tae go and set things right. Scotlain is my home, ye ken, just like Kentucke is yours. I've been gone a wee bit tae long."

She knew Scotland was weeks, perhaps months away. She'd studied navigational charts at Briar Hill and well remembered sailing times and distances. It held a peculiar fascination for her, hemmed in as she'd been in Virginia. Dreaming of distant lands had solaced her somewhat while there.

Crushed, she fought for composure. As he stood on the porch step, his eyes were on the river, seemingly unaware of her struggle. Utterly deflated, she sat, hands in her lap. *He's changed his mind about me. And he's telling me as gently as he can.*

He called for his horse. "At dawn I leave for Lexington. I willna be back till Friday."

The finality in his tone shook her further. Four days he'd be away. How much longer would he be in Scotland? What if he never came back? He stepped off the porch and was gone. Without one look back. She watched him ride away with an ache in her heart too big to hold. She wanted to run after him, but pride pinned her to the porch.

What now, Lord?

70

To everything there is a season, and a time to every purpose under the heaven . . . a time to keep, and a time to cast away. Time to do a bit of both, she decided.

On either side of the fading fire were her twin trunks from Briar Hill, their lids open, the leather straps that bound them loosened. The first trunk she designated for keeping, the second for casting away. Her fancy Briar Hill dresses went into the one, along with an assortment of fans, shoes, stockings, a neat stack of embroidered undergarments, and the cameo Pa had given her.

The tiny carved bird Simon had made so long ago went into the second trunk, along with Pa's budget and a pile of old linens. A small, sun-bleached bonnet of her own was discarded along with some too-short, too-tight dresses. But she nearly balked when she came to the beads and bracelet. Holding them in her hands, she wanted to weep. Were they all that remained of Captain Jack?

She passed through the open door onto the porch. The early spring air bit into her, but the twilight was clear and tinted pink and there hardly seemed a shadow. She stood still, listening to the sighing wind, her eyes willing the shivering woods to bring forth the figure she'd not forgotten. Had he lost his life in the growing conflict? Had he succumbed to the dreaded pox? Was it just September when she'd swam the river with him and he'd held her face and her heart in his hands beneath the waterfall?

Turning, she put the jewelry in her pocket and went to light a single tallow candle. The trunks seemed a reproach to her now, open and waiting, demanding her decision. She stood between them and felt the pull of the savage and the civilized once more. A final time she took out the beads and studied their color, desperate to remember. *Blue as robin's eggs.* Is that what he'd thought when he'd given them to her? Alongside them the fine bracelet shone silver in the candlelight.

Bending over, she cast them away and closed the second trunk. There were some hurts, she reckoned, too deep for tears. When she turned back around, a shadow filled the open door frame. She sucked in her breath and stepped back. Ian? Captain Jack?

The commanding height and fine physique were nearly the same. Tonight, he looked more Scottish laird than frontier doctor. His buckskin breeches, all the rage in Paris, so she'd read, tapered to highly blacked boots. The fine linen of his pressed shirt was startling white against his dark hair, now freshly cut and tied back in a neat queue. And the clean, close-shaven lines of his jaw gave him an intense, almost brooding look. He was as handsome as she'd ever seen him. *Oh, the looking at him is too easy . . .*

She finally found her voice. "I didn't hear you ride in."

He stepped over the threshold. "I didna ride. I rowed."

She looked past him through the open door. A full moon was rising, near perfect to ride the river, if it wasn't too breezy. "You're back early from Lexington."

He nodded and surveyed the trunks, one open and one shut, with all its secrets.

"Where are you going?" he asked.

Did he think she was returning to Briar Hill? She smoothed the clean cambric of her apron with unsteady hands. *To everything there is a season . . . a time to keep silence . . . a time to speak.* The Scripture echoed in her head like a song. 'Twas time to speak. Past time, truly.

His voice was hard, almost unfriendly. "Tae Briar Hill?"

"Not Briar Hill, Ian. *Scotland.*"

He stood before her, eyes intense. "And what will you be doing in Scotlain?"

Her chin came up. "Living with the laird."

Still, he didn't move. His face revealed nothing. Did he doubt her feelings for him? Her face grew hot, and she was glad of the gathering darkness. She sat down atop the closed trunk, her hands turned up entreatingly.

"'Tis you, Ian . . . and only you whom I love . . . and no other." When the heartfelt words left her lips, she realized what she'd done. Not once had he ever said he loved her. Her voice fell to a whisper. "I've never before spoken such things." *Not to Simon. Nor Captain Jack.* "But I mean them—every word—and I will not take them back."

Before she'd even finished, he was pulling her into his hard embrace. The sudden movement snuffed out the candle, but the darkness couldn't hide the sheen in his eyes, or her own. For long minutes she stood locked in his arms, unable to speak, her heart hammering wildly.

"Lael, I want you tae be sure of me. I dinna want you tae ever think I took you away from this place, or these people, or coerced you tae marry me—"

She shook her head, stilling his words with her fingers. "Nay—don't."

He framed her face with his callused hands, concern shadowing his features. But she only pressed his fingers more firmly in place, her voice almost pleading, "Oh Ian—please—just love me."

He began kissing her just like she remembered, his mouth soft yet insistent against her own. He smelled of fresh linen and tasted like raw honey. Wild. Pungent. Tantalizing.

When they drew apart, he took her hand and moved to the open door, snatching up her shawl as they exited. At the river's edge beneath a full moon, the water was black and silver. He tied her shawl in place, then picked her up and waded into the water. The boat rocked and settled as she sat. Across from her, he took up the oars.

She was glad for the chance to catch her breath. She still felt the tick of her pulse in her wrist and was glad to be shed of the closed cabin. Out here she was free to breathe, to think. Surely he felt the same.

He moved into the gentle current, the oars splashing water. "I wanted tae talk tae you aboot that piece of land atop the knob by Will and Susanna's."

Her heart fairly stopped at the question. "Pa used to say there'll never be any more land made so buy a piece and hold on to it," she replied evenly. "It's a pretty piece, if ever there was one."

He let the oars rest. "I want tae buy it, Lael, and give it tae you as a wedding gift."

Her mouth formed a perfect *O* in surprise.

He smiled. "But you'll have tae marry me first."

Leaning forward a bit, her voice came out a whisper. "Are you asking me, then?"

His eyes were as earnest as she'd ever seen them. "Och, that I am, but if I get on bended knee I'll turn the boat over."

She grew hushed. There was teasing in his tone, but it in no way brooked the seriousness of the moment. He got on one knee anyway, his arms encircling her waist and pulling her against him. Before he even touched her she felt woozy at his very nearness. His hands were in her hair pulling it free of its pins. She could hear them fall like pebbles to the boat's bottom. He kissed her again, and she almost melted into him.

"Lael, I've loved you and wanted tae marry you almost since I first saw you."

"Almost?" she whispered.

"Since our picnic on the porch."

"Truly?" Even though she'd sassed him and he'd stared at her in a most ungentlemanly fashion? She grew quiet, her mouth near the curve of his ear. "There's something I need to know—why you came back to my cabin the night of the barn raising."

He smiled and wrapped a strand of her hair around his finger. "You were so wranglesome when we parted, I had tae come back. I returned with a ring in my pocket tae ask you tae be my bride."

She well remembered how he'd taken her hands and turned them over, caressing them by the hearth. Had he meant to slip a ring on her finger then? She said softly, "Why didn't you ask?"

"I didna have tae. Your answer was already in your eyes, telling me you'd gladly give your heart and soul and body as my bride—"

"Oh Ian, I—" she began, the memory still shameful. "I behaved badly but I—I've never before been with a m—"

He placed his fingers lightly on her lips, stilling speech. "I ken, Lael. I've only tae look at you. I was wrong tae return to your cabin. 'Twas a lover's moon that led me. We needed the Almighty's blessing on our union, and that we did no' have."

"Marriage, you mean."

"Aye." Relaxing his arms from around her, he withdrew something from his coat pocket. So fine a ring she'd never seen. Small and elegant, the Scottish gold gleamed in the dark, the engraving of a swan reflecting the light of the full moon.

He took her hand again, whispering words both foreign and familiar. "With this ring I thee wed . . . with my body I thee worship . . . with all my worldly goods I thee endow. Soon, Lael, soon."

What might have been a perfect fit was not perfect any longer. The ring was loose upon her finger. Indeed, all her lissome curves were gone, taken by the pox. She felt as though a puff of wind would scatter her like so many dandelion seeds.

As if reading her thoughts he said, "You are still a very loosome lass, Lael Click."

"Loosome?"

"Lovely. But you need tae regain your strength. I canna wed and bed so wee a fairy."

She flushed crimson, his roguish tone reminding her of unknown intimacies to come.

Taking her left hand, he kissed her palm and then her ring finger. "So you promise tae make me a fine wife?"

"With God's help, I will, though we'll be hard pressed to find a preacher to marry us."

"Colonel Barr will suffice for now as justice of the peace. Later, we can be married in Scotlain by a true preacher."

They'd drifted far downriver to a small cove overhung with rambling vines and branches. His voice was low against her loosened hair. "So we'll row back and be married. Tonight."

"Tonight? Nay. Day after tomorrow," she decided, thinking of all she must do.

"Then the day after that we leave for Scotlain."

In confirmation, she wrapped her arms around his neck and kissed him.

He groaned. "'Twill be a very long two days, tae be sure."

Laughing, she kissed him again.

Epilogue

Lael held the piece of paper in her hands, studying the deed to the knob, granted by the newly formed Kentucke Land Company. Ian had given it to her the day before, the promised wedding present, and it was then she'd seen his signature for the very first time, her eyes lingering on the heavy elegant hand.

Ian Alexander Justus, Fifth Earl Roslyn.

She'd never really thought of his title. What then would that make her?

Just yesterday he'd taken her by the shoulders, his eyes a dazzling azure blue. "Are you timorsome aboot anything, Lael? Anything at all?"

She was, but only in regards to his happiness, not her own. "I'm just plain and simple, Ian. But you . . . you're fancy in a way I'll never be. You're a nobleman, Ian. A Scottish earl."

"Nae, Lael. I'm just a mon, a simple Scot, graced with a title. It means but little, truly."

Taking out Neddy's Bible, she wrote inside its cover, *Today, 29 March 1784, is the day I am to wed.* At three o'clock she was to be a bride. She placed the deed to the knob within its pages and packed it in her trunk. Whatever she might forget to take to Scotland, it must not be her Bible.

Her eyes made a clean sweep of the tidy cabin, almost ready for her leaving. Ma's Sunday-best quilt lay across the bed. On a whim she'd scattered dried rose petals upon the faded, clean coverlet. Their sweetness was faint but still telling. A bridal bed, truly, if only for one night. After that their courtship could continue on the trail to Virginia, beneath the same blanket and a million stars.

Oh Pa, I wish you were here today to see me wed. I think you'd be proud.

She'd wanted a quiet wedding with little fuss. The settlement was still too sore for any festivities, their grief compounded by two dozen lonesome graves. Before they departed, they would announce what they'd done in the stillness of this spring afternoon with no witnesses save Colonel Barr.

She hardly knew who stared back at her in the looking glass. Pink and white dogwood blossoms held in place a whisper-thin veil of lace. Around her neck was the strand of pink pearls. She felt weighted down in the heavy silk of her dress despite its beauty.

She passed onto the porch and stood, the lushness of spring snatching speech, and tried to impress all of the wilderness sights and sounds upon her heart. Everything was just as it had been all those years before when the Shawnee came. The dogwood was blooming in the side yard and the porch still sagged, weighted down by time and roses.

A sudden movement—a bird?—caught her eye. The wind shifted the shadows in the clearing, but she saw past them nevertheless. There, against the lush woods, stood a man. A flicker of familiarity coursed through her. For just a moment she fell back in time. It seemed she was a girl again, standing on the porch, her hair falling to her feet. Could it be?

Bewildered, she stepped into the sunlight, her silk skirts rustling. She was afraid . . . afraid if she didn't run to him he'd disappear. Across the clearing she could hear a horse and rider coming—and Ian calling her name. Torn, she paused and looked over her shoulder, then back to the woods.

Behind her, Ian had dismounted in the clearing and stood watching.

411

She made it to the dogwood tree, her breath coming in short bursts. Aye, she had seen more than a shadow . . . sensed she wasn't alone. Her heart hurt. But there was nothing there, after all. The wind in the trees—the shifting shadows—were merely playing a wild game.

She turned around slowly, keeping her eyes fixed on the Scotsman before her. Arms open wide, she began to run toward him, away from the dark woods. There was no need to look back now . . . perhaps never again. For as long as she lived, Lord willing, she could look forward. The past no longer had a hold on her.

No more secrets.

No more shadows.

Acknowledgments

I am deeply grateful to the people God has placed in my path. To my very gracious editor, Andrea Doering, for opening the door. To the editorial staff and the entire team at Revell. What a joy!

I am blessed with a wonderful brother, Chris Irwin, who gave me all manner of support—technical and otherwise—and parents who prayed for me.

To my dear friends and mentors Grace Huckleberry, Cindy Reynolds, and Kathy Vogel. Only heaven knows what your prayers and godly examples have meant to me.

To Darlene Putnam, my first reader and fellow artist. Bless you.

To Nicia, my sister-in-love and second reader. Your encouragement kept me going.

To my husband, Randy, and my sons Wyatt and Paul, for riding the writing roller coaster with me. You give me daily inspiration.

To the Kentucky Historical Society and Fort Boonesborough, for untold treasures.

My story is about history, which I love, but more importantly, my story is "His story." It began many years ago when God planted a dream to write books in the heart of a little Kentucky girl, and when she'd grown up and almost given up, He began fulfilling that dream. He really is the Father who never fails. "The LORD will accomplish what concerns me; Your lovingkindness, O LORD, is everlasting; do not forsake the works of Your hands" (Ps. 138:8).

Laura Frantz credits her one-hundred-year-old grandmother, who passed away during the publication of this book, as being the catalyst for her fascination with Kentucky history. Frantz's ancestors followed Daniel Boone into Kentucky in 1792 and settled in Madison County, where her family still resides. Frantz is a former schoolteacher and social worker who currently lives in the misty woods of Port Angeles, Washington, with her husband and two sons, whom she homeschools. Contact her at www .laurafrantz.blogspot.com or LauraFrantz.net.